...ptability, compassion
...ourage'

BIBLIOSANCTUM

'A solid continuation of *The Detainee*. Peter Liney doesn't
let his story falter at any given moment'

THE BOOK PLANK

'An impressively dark, dystopian piece with much to say'

FINANCIAL TIMES

'Fascinating'

THINKING ABOUT BOOKS

'*The Detainee* is definitely a book that should be read by all'

FRESH FICTION

'Equal parts exciting, terrifying and thought-provoking . . .
if this debut is a well planned bonfire then I'm thinking the
sequel will be fireworks'

J FOR JETPACK

'In 30 or 40 years time, *The Detainee* could become a work of
genius . . . Totally recommended'

Also by Peter Liney

The Detainee

INTO
THE
FIRE

PETER LINEY

Jo Fletcher
BOOKS

First published in Great Britain in 2014 by Jo Fletcher Books
This edition published in 2015 by

Jo Fletcher Books
an imprint of
Quercus Publishing Ltd
Carmelite House
50 Victoria Embankment
London EC4Y 0DZ

An Hachette UK company

PB ISBN 978 1 78206 039 0
EBOOK ISBN 978 1 78206 038 3

10 9 8 7 6 5 4 3 2 1

Typeset by Jouve (UK), Milton Keynes
Printed and bound in Great Britain by Clays Ltd, St Ives plc

To my mother

CHAPTER ONE

I've said it once and I'll say it again: it's not the bars that break you, it's the patches of sky in between. When you think you're finally free of your particular prison, only to discover that, actually, you're in an even worse place than you were before.

When we escaped from the Island, when Lena and me were bobbing away over to the Mainland on that barely buoyant wooden door – with Jimmy, Delilah and the kids a little ways up ahead, lost in that great rag-tag flotilla of Detainees and floating junk – I swear, I never been happier in my life. Why wouldn't I be? After all those years of being stuck out on that pile of crap, at last I was free. I had the woman I waited all my life for beside me (who, and you probably ain't gonna believe me, reckons she loves me every bit as much as I love her) and now we could go wherever we wanted. In fact, all around us there was this huge tidal wave of joy and optimism as thousands of Detainees paddled, sailed or merely swam that mile or so back over to the Mainland.

Time and time again defiant cries echoed out into the starry night, skipping across the water, letting those in the City know we were on our way back. Occasionally there'd even be some singing, laughter – dammit, if it hadn't been for the fact that we were in water, I reckon we might've formed a conga line and danced our way across. Old folks and kids, away from that terrible place – the stench, the filth, the casual and constant violence, the Wastelords – off to find a better life. But it didn't last for long. In fact, it was over almost before it'd begun.

I keep thinking about that expression: 'out of the frying pan and into the fire', though that don't exactly do the situation justice. Even before we got ashore, I knew something was terribly wrong.

The thing is, I wasn't just escaping, I was going home. The city where I lived for over fifty years, the city that, though I never cared to admit it, I used to look longingly at from the Island almost every day. But the closer we got, the less familiar it seemed. Nor was my unease helped by the fact that I could see several of the satellites Jimmy had reprogrammed to destroy each other looked to have started fires that seemed to be – not just *bursting* into flames, but more *erupting*.

Opposite me, holding on to the other side of the door, her hair hanging in wet tresses, Lena listened for a moment, her sightless hazel eyes reflecting the City's unnatural glow. 'What's going on?' she asked.

'Satellites,' I replied, keeping my voice as nonchalant as I could. 'Started a couple of fires.'

A quizzical frown formed on her face. 'Sounds loud.'

I leant over. As I gave her a supportive hug, the door momentarily slipped below the water under my weight. She was doing her best, but I knew what a challenge it had to be. To leave somewhere she'd been so familiar with, where she could 'see' almost as well as a sighted person, to go to a place where she didn't know one solitary step. I mean, I haven't said anything to her, 'course I

2

haven't, but if she can't cope, then screw a new life, screw freedom, screw everything. I'll go back and live on that damn island with her. We'll fix it up somehow.

'Just echoing amongst the buildings, I guess,' I reassured her.

And yet there was something about the way those fires were burning, the flames leaping into the night, that felt almost appropriate: as if they were issuing a warning, telling us to keep away, and again I cursed myself for not having found us a proper boat, big enough for all seven of us – four adults and three kids. We could've gone round the headland and landed somewhere up the coast, away from all this.

There was a large swell, the sea bucked and broke and for a few moments I lost sight of the land. As it came back into view, another fire glimmered into life further round the bay, in one of the residential areas up in the hills. Was this really all down to satellites, or was it something else?

'What's wrong, Clancy?' Lena asked.

'Nothing,' I told her, doing my best to keep up the enthusiasm that had propelled us away from the Island.

She ignored my reassurances, also levering herself up on the door, sniffing the air as if it could give her a better idea of what we were approaching.

'There's a smell,' she said, slipping back into the water.

'What sort of smell?'

'I don't know. Not nice.'

I didn't say any more, just concentrated on kicking my feet, maintaining the same steady, slow progress as everyone else around us.

The subject I was doing my best to avoid, but in truth had been nagging at me ever since I saw those burning satellites plummeting down from the sky, was how people were going to respond. Without satellites to punish us, there was nothing: no cops, no judicial system, no rules or regulations – no judgement of right or wrong. All we ever had – all we ever needed as far as the authorities were concerned – was satellite policing. In the matter of a few spectacular minutes all law and order had disappeared and I didn't know how people were gonna react. In fact, tell the truth, I wasn't even sure how I was gonna react.

I tried to speed up our progress, kicking a little harder, but we immediately collided with this old couple rolling back and forth on a water barrel. I apologised, gave them a shove, my legs starting to protest at this unfamiliar exercise. I ain't any kind of swimmer, not with this bulk, all my energy goes into keeping me afloat, but I needed to get ashore and find out what was going on.

I don't know how you can tell if buildings are friendly or not, but as the long, jagged bottom jaw of the City began to loom over us, I got the distinct impression that these weren't – just an endless row of preformed concrete, each gravestone slab a statement for a different commercial concern, and dominating them all, like some huge black mausoleum, was the new Infinity building.

That is one helluvan intimidating construction. Even from the Island we were aware of its day-to-day progress, how it grew and grew, but up close it's something else. It looks more like a fort or prison. There's no access on the ocean side, just rows and rows of windows on the upper floors, whilst on the very top sits its golden crown: that squinting two-eyed symbol of theirs. Talk about appropriate. I know they're supposed to be media, but that don't mean we want them spying on us all the time. And anyways, 'supposed to be' is right. Those Infinity Specials who came over to help the Wastelords search for us on the Island didn't look like security personnel to me, more like something closer to military.

We reached that point where the ocean's swell flipped over into waves and our wooden crates and boxes, the sealed drums and even the occasional small boat started to bump into each other. Fortunately, at that same moment, my feet touched the bottom.

I took Lena's hand, warned her about the rapidly growing chaos in front of us and began to splash through young and old celebrating at having made it across. They were all whooping it up, hugging each other, congratulating everyone within earshot, high-fiving and shaking hands. Up ahead, dotted around the beach, I could see several small groups of seated Mainlanders, probably wondering what the hell was going on, where this endless line of flotsam and jetsam was coming from. Though there didn't seem to be much in the way of a reaction: as the first dripping Detainees waded ashore, collapsing onto the sand, they just stayed where they were, in anonymous huddles, barely even glancing our way.

Finally Lena and me managed to weave our way through everyone and everything, splashing up onto the litter-strewn urban beach, the only injury a bruised shin I collected from a plank tossed at me by a wave.

'Big Guy!' shouted a familiar voice, and I turned to see Jimmy pegging his way over; Delilah and the kids – Gordie, Arturo and Hanna – following on behind. 'You okay?'

'Fine,' I said, turning to Lena, who promptly gave an encouraging smile.

'Wow! Can you believe it?' Jimmy marvelled, gaping round at the City, shaking his head, his straggly old scrap of a ponytail, the only hair on an otherwise bald head, flapping from side to side. 'How cool is this?'

I nodded, doing my best to shelve my concerns, more surprised than reassured by how quiet it was. 'What d'ya think, kids?'

All three of them stared at the towering buildings in front of us. Hanna, as ever, wordless, Gordie shrugging his usual indifference, whilst Arturo was plainly more impressed.

'Can we live up there?' he asked, pointing to the very top of a tower.

I shook my head. 'Nope. We're getting out of this place as fast as our legs can carry us.'

I turned to Lena to fill her in on where Arturo wanted to live, but she was more interested in getting her own view of things by repeatedly sniffing the air, maybe still trying to identify that bad odour. A fire flared up – somewhere on the other side of the block, crackling away like the multiple breaking of branches, an orange glow bouncing off the walls – and she gave this little nod, as if she'd been expecting it.

'Where is everyone?' Gordie asked, as surprised as I was that our welcome committee consisted only of a few disinterested stragglers sitting on the beach.

'Good question.'

It was eerie. Apart from the occasional passing automatic bus, most of which seemed to be empty, the bay road was practically free of traffic. It didn't strike me so much as a ghost city, more a heavily preoccupied one – as if somewhere something big was going on.

'Thought we might have to fight our way up the beach,' Delilah commented, putting her arm round little Arturo in case he needed her protection.

Neither the little guy nor Hanna had ever known any life but the Island. Gordie lived on the Mainland for a while, but it was probably too long ago for him to clearly remember. As for Lena, she lived here 'til her early teens, but without sight now that probably wasn't a lot of use to her. Again I gave her a squeeze, our wet clothes so impregnated with the grime of the Island that they felt all cold and slippery, like fish. I was a little concerned I might be overdoing it, being too attentive, but I couldn't help but worry about her, especially with that confused little frown that kept tangling her brow.

'They say anything?' I asked Jimmy, indicating the nearest group of Mainlanders, five or six of them sitting in a circle.

'Nah. Barely seemed to notice us.'

Delilah grunted. 'Addicts or alcoholics,' she muttered, as if she knew such people all too well. 'They wouldn't know if we beamed down from Mars.'

Just at that moment, the fire on the other side of the block must've found a new source of fuel 'cuz there was a sudden loud explosion and flames shot high enough in the air to appear over the rooftops.

Several of the Detainees screamed and crouched down on their haunches, as if expecting the world to fall in on them, but as the flames subsided, they laughed nervously at their own behaviour and got to their feet. I gave Lena another squeeze, told her it was all right, and just as I knew she would at some stage, she pulled away, going to talk the kids, as if she'd had enough of me and my fussing.

I turned to Jimmy, at last having the opportunity to voice my concerns. 'What the hell's going on here?' I muttered. 'Where is everybody?'

He shook his head, plainly every bit as worried as I was. 'Beats me.'

And it wasn't just us either. A lot of the Detainees had been determined to celebrate being back – to kiss the ground, do a little dance, whatever – but slowly they were falling silent, as if no longer sure it was a cause for celebration. Most of them just stood there, gaping at the City as if expecting to see something terrible come out of it at any moment. Nor did it help when an automatic bus came into view engulfed by flames, still following its programmed route, still making its usual stops, but passing by like some disintegrating mobile beacon, with sparks and embers flying off into the night.

'Shit,' Jimmy muttered.

By now there was quite a crowd huddled all along that narrow strip of sand. The slower ones were still arriving, wading through the lazily somersaulting water, their eager smiles fading as they caught the general mood.

'Let's go,' I said to the others.

Again I caught that frown on Lena's face, but I insisted on leading her away, making sure Jimmy, Delilah and the kids were right behind, deliberately taking a route past the nearest group of Mainlanders, just to see what they'd do, if they'd give any indication of their attitude towards us.

At first they didn't so much as glance our way, and I thought Delilah must be right, that they were so far out of it, nothing mattered. There was this woman sitting there with her outstretched partner's head in her lap – it kinda spooked me – she suddenly locked onto us, giving out with this squeal, pointing over. Immediately the others turned our way, also getting het up, starting this chorus of plaintive wailing. In that moment, the flames of the nearby fire exploded into the sky once more and I caught a glimpse of their faces. They looked like ghouls, pale and lifeless, their eyes so dark and recessed you could barely make out a pupil.

I just kept on walking, pretending I hadn't noticed. Out of the corner of my eye I saw one guy trying to struggle up, apparently about to give chase, but he simply didn't have the strength. We left them howling away behind us, stretching out their arms, begging us to come back.

8

'What was that all about?' Lena asked.

I hesitated, still mindful of not adding to her concerns. 'Nothing.'

She paused for a moment, then gave this long irritated sigh. 'Clancy, if you don't stop this, I'm heading off on my own.'

I didn't know what to do. No matter how concerned I was about her, I also knew she was more than capable of carrying out such a threat. 'Just a bunch of addicts with crap in their heads, that's all,' I muttered. 'Like Delilah said.'

At that point, Jimmy came sidling over to me, positioning himself on the other side to Lena, making this face, gesturing back at the group. Behind us, I could hear Gordie and Arturo teasing Hanna, making these wailing sounds, circling around her, baring their teeth as if they were about to attack. 'Zombies!' they kept chanting, though she just ignored them, walking on with this superior air, like you just got to expect that kind of crap from boys.

I nodded at Jimmy, all the while mad at myself for communicating with him in a way Lena couldn't see. I also gave a slight sigh of relief that he, along with everyone else, hadn't spotted what I had – leastways, what I *thought* I had. That guy lying on the beach with his head on the woman's lap, the only one who didn't react – there was a good reason for that. He was dead. Those people'd had a corpse amongst them. And yet, the oddest thing of all was, the way they behaved, it was almost as if they thought we could've saved him.

Behind us, the other Detainees were starting to follow our example: splitting into groups, going only with those they trusted, dithering over which direction to take.

We'd just about made it to the road and started to cross when I heard a chopper. I looked up, and there, wouldn't you know it, rising off the top of that massive dark edifice, was an Infinity Dragonfly.

'Shit!' I groaned.

I tugged Lena, and shouting to the others to follow, ran towards the far side of the road. Delilah was grumbling away somewhere at the back, asking why I was making such a fuss, until the chopper swooped down, lights blazing, buzzing over the heads of the Detainees.

'Stay where you are! Do *not* leave the beach!' a female voice commanded. 'Do *not* leave the beach!'

'Keep going!' I told the others, scrambling over a low wall and ducking down behind.

'Leaving the Island is a Crime Against the State,' the voice boomed. 'Do *not* leave the beach!'

There was a momentary stand-off, the Dragonfly hovering menacingly, the Detainees looking at one another, wondering what to do. I mean, strictly speaking, it *was* a Crime Against the State, and 'til only a couple of hours ago, punishable by death from a satellite. But what the hell did that have to do with Infinity? They were supposed to *report* the news, not make it.

Maybe the same thought struck the other Detainees – or maybe the prospect of freedom, so tantalisingly near, was just too much. Whatever, one group suddenly made a dash towards the road and the shelter of the buildings on the far side and immediately others followed. The Dragonfly wheeled in their direction, about to issue another warning, I thought, maybe intimidate them further by flying lower over their heads, but in fact, it opened up with its lasers.

'*Noooo!*' Delilah screamed, and Hanna buried her face in her hands.

I swear, if there was one moment when all our optimism, our hopes for a new life, came tumbling down, that was it. What the hell were they doing? What gave them the *right*? And they weren't just stunning people either. They were blasting them to pieces. Everywhere you looked, Detainees young and old were getting cut down. People were screaming, running this way and that, some managing to escape into the City, others so panicked they just ran blindly back into the sea.

The Dragonfly ceased firing and the woman again warned everyone not to leave the beach, this time mentioning something about 'emergency powers'.

'Let's go,' I told the others.

'Big Guy!' Jimmy protested, fearing we'd be spotted.

'Come on!' I urged, glancing up, seeing another chopper leaving the Infinity roof.

That was all the persuasion anyone needed. I took Lena's hand and began to run as fast as this hulking old frame was able, calling at the others to keep up. Where we went exactly, I don't know. It just became this mad headlong dash down alleyways and through back streets, clinging to cover and shadows, desperate to get as far away as we could.

At one point we turned a corner and came face to face with this huge blaze. I never seen anything like it, roaring and crackling away, not only sending flames several blocks into the air, but occasionally shooting them out horizontally, so they ignited other buildings. The heat was that intense, even from a hundred or more yards away, we had to back off and find another route. Nor was anyone doing anything about it. It had just been left to burn, to consume whatever it wanted. For sure there were no emergency vehicles around. I guess there were just too many fires and not enough resources.

A couple of times, no matter how much we tried to avoid it, we literally ran into Mainlanders. The first group were like those on the beach – pale, ghostly; we were gone before they could even react – whilst the others more or less ignored us. Amongst everything else that was going on, I guess we weren't exactly a priority, just more patients loose in the asylum.

After a while, especially for us oldies, pain and discomfort began to overwhelm adrenalin and we were forced to stop, gasping for breath, begging the old ticker to calm down. Jimmy tried to be smart, to freewheel on the moving sidewalk, but it stopped the moment he got on and wouldn't start again 'til he got off (it scans you, looks for your credit implant, usually on your wrist or behind your ear).

I started searching for signposts and the quickest way out of the City, though actually, apart from what happened on the waterfront, things hadn't been anywhere near as bad as I'd expected. Most streets were more or less functioning as normal. On the other hand, it was disturbingly quiet and I wondered if, maybe, we hadn't come across the main event yet.

As we approached the commercial district and the up-market shopping area I began to realise how right I was. You could feel the atmosphere starting to change. There were more people, a simmering clamour, and gradually, one sound that overwhelmed all others. I didn't recognise it at first. It was like a plague of insects, the cry of a thousand cicadas on a warm summer evening, but as we got closer, it finally hit me. It was a mass accumulation of alarms, hundreds and hundreds of them, all different notes, different kinds, all futilely signalling their premises had been breached, crying out for help that plainly wasn't gonna come. And as we turned the corner into one of the main shopping streets, finally we saw where everyone had gone.

From one end to the other, as far as you could see, it was bedlam, with store after store being looted. People were using baseball bats, sledgehammers, scaffolding poles, anything to smash their way in. Within minutes, sometimes seconds, they re-emerged laden down with so much stuff they could barely carry it. Their first few steps outside were always that bit tentative, taking a quick glance up at the sky, just to reassure themselves the satellites really weren't working any more.

'Jesus,' I groaned, my thoughts immediately going back all those years to the Good Behaviour Riots, when the state stopped paying the kids to stay out of trouble.

'Quite a party,' Delilah croaked.

I turned to Lena to explain what was going on, but she cut me short.

'I can guess.'

'You're better off not seeing this,' Delilah told her.

I don't know why, but I glanced at the kids, concerned how they would react. I wasn't altogether surprised to see Gordie looking just that little bit interested.

'Anything you fancy?' I asked.

He just shrugged and looked away, and I realised I'd gone too far. 'Sorry,' I said, patting him on the shoulder.

Again he shrugged. That kid's got a whole dictionary of them, and each and every one's got a different meaning.

'I was out of line,' I added, but he still didn't seem that bothered.

The one good thing about what was going on, leastways as far as we were concerned, was that, amongst it, the presence of a small group of Detainees was unlikely to be noticed. And you know, I don't condone such behaviour – no matter what I used to get up to in the old days, I've now come to see all crime as wrong – but as we made our way down that street, and despite all the mayhem, I couldn't help but feel that little bit relieved, that if that was it, their generation's version of anarchy, then maybe we were getting off lightly. But I should've known better.

We hadn't gone more than three or four blocks before we heard it – a different sound this time, more potent, more threatening. In fact, it reminded me of being on the Island on a foggy night. There were the same wild shouts, the same frightened screams, the same summoning of madness.

I guess we could've worked our way round it, but our curiosity got the better of us. There was an open area, set back from the street, and something was really burning away in there. As we approached you could hear this kind of low grumbling, like an explosion that couldn't quite reach its detonation point but was furiously trying, and finally we came face to face with a scene which was much more in line with what I'd been expecting.

There was this shiny new shopping centre – it couldn't have been open for long, but all eight or nine floors of it were blazing away like it was made of rice-paper. And dancing all round, high on drink, drugs or merely adrenalin, thousands of rioters were, not only looting everything in sight, but burning it down as well.

Most of the outside of the building was glass, and just as we rounded the corner some of its huge panes reached a point where they simply exploded, showering debris down on those below.

'Jesus! Not cool!' Jimmy cried, instinctively backing away.

All around us flames were leaping into the air the way they might when you light a barbecue – the same curve and character – but a thousand times higher, a million times more potent. The whole world was alight. Worse still, there was a pitched battle going on. People were fighting all over, and it didn't take long to work out why. Looters were wrestling with looters, trying to steal what had already been stolen. A lot of them were armed with clubs or knives. I actually saw one guy stabbed to death by a gang of girls. I was going to get over there, try to stop them, but it was too late. They just grabbed up his stuff – shoes, a handbag, maybe for his

14

girlfriend or something – and ran off. Not going far before they spotted someone else who had something they wanted, a teenage couple, and immediately surrounded them. Everywhere we looked people were being beaten, even slain, for something that was never theirs in the first place.

'Let's go,' I told the others, though they were almost too stunned to move. 'Jimmy!'

'Can't we help?' Lena asked.

I turned to her, saw those sightless eyes registering such confusion. 'No. We can't.'

When I took her hand there was a moment of resistance before I managed to persuade her that there was no other choice, that anything else would only be putting us all in danger, and we took off as quickly as we could. The kids having to be told to keep up, as if they would like to have stayed a little longer, that what we witnessed wasn't much more than entertainment to them.

I mean, that was it, that was what I feared more than anything, that the loss of the satellites would result in total breakdown, and I should've known that was where it'd be, in the home of designer labels and luxury goods. We saw two bodies on the sidewalk, still lying where they'd thrown themselves out of burning buildings, but we just kept going. This might've once been my city, my *home*, but having seen what I had I didn't want to spend so much as a night there. I wanted to wake in the morning in a quiet country lane, or at the very least a leafy garden suburb, on the threshold of the countryside and freedom.

What I didn't appreciate was how hard I was pushing everybody, including myself, to achieve that goal.

A little later, Jimmy came pegging up to Lena and me, his limp worse than I'd seen it in a while. 'Big Guy, we have to stop soon,' he told me. 'Lile can't go much further.'

'We gotta get out of this city,' I told him.

'Tonight?' he exclaimed.

'Uh-huh,' I replied, not letting my pace drop for a moment.

'Clancy,' Lena protested. 'We're too tired.'

I was about to argue the point, but looking at her, realising how much more difficult it must've been, that she'd been hanging onto my hand running into nothingness ever since we left the Island, I saw I had no choice. 'Okay,' I sighed, a little reluctantly. 'Just for a few hours.'

We took a couple of side streets into an unfashionable area where things were a bit more downmarket, less likely to be of interest, and eventually came across this old abandoned carpet store. Lord knows how long it'd been since it was in business – long enough for rust to have melded shut the padlock and grille. I forced them apart, wrenched the wire aside, then kicked the front door open.

The first thing we saw was the welcome sight of a pile of carpet offcuts, in all colours and sizes, that we could use to sleep on. Lena and me grabbed a handful and retired to the back office, Jimmy and Delilah pretty well flopped out where they were, whilst Gordie and Arturo did the same. Only Hanna spent any time choosing exactly where she wanted to be, ending up at the far end of the room, as far away from those boys as possible.

The moment I lay down, I realised I was every bit as tired as everyone else. Every muscle and bone in my old body seemed to be setting up a chattering protest. And yet, with Lena asleep in my arms within minutes, I was wide awake, thoughts whipping around my head like trash in a typhoon.

What do they say about never going back? This was supposed to be my home. Okay, so we were nowhere near my patch, but I had the feeling that even if I was, even if this was my old street, I still wouldn't feel warmly disposed towards it.

To think we imagined this place would be heaven – okay, so not our idea of heaven exactly, but someone's, maybe. Only a few hours ago we'd been making our way across from the Island, so excited to be free at last, at where we were going. Now look at us. So far we've confronted addicts, looters, arsonists, murderers – though all of them pale in comparison with Infinity. I mean, what the hell's going on with them? Have they taken over law and order? And what does that mean for us?

Just at that moment, Lena stirred in my arms, almost as if she could sense my fretting. 'You okay?' she mumbled out of the dark, plainly only half awake.

'We're only stopping for a few hours,' I reminded her. 'I want to be away from this place as soon as we can.'

I waited for a protest that I was being obsessive, but there was none, and I realised she'd already fallen back to sleep. I kissed her on the forehead. I mean, whatever or wherever, I'm still the luckiest dumb old big guy in the world. No question.

The last thing I reminded myself before I finally succumbed to that unfamiliar darkness was that it was up to me. I would have to get everyone up at first light, ignore their inevitable grumbling and get them out on the road. Too bad if they hated me for it. Above everything, we needed to get away, out into the country, and res-urrect our bid for freedom and a better life.

Though, in fact, did I but know it, it was already too late.

CHAPTER TWO

Sometimes I wonder if it's sleep that won't come to me, or me that won't allow it, that I don't care for what it brings. Maybe it was being back in the City, my memories getting all stirred up, but I dreamed it was the old days and I was driving Mr Meltoni.

I could see that proud smile of his in my rear-view mirror as he gazed out the window at his domain, the streets he owned, people nodding and bowing as we went by. As his main muscle and minder, I had it pretty good, I can tell you. Fancy lifestyle, plenty of money . . . plenty of R.E.S.P.E.C.T. And yet, somewhere along the line, I dunno why, and no matter how much I loved the guy, I began to feel that what I was doing wasn't right. That nothing was worth what was going on, and especially not money. Even before he died, I'd stopped getting my hands dirty. When he did finally pass on, well, it was an easy decision: I was going straight, off to start a new life. The only problem was, my timing couldn't have been worse. The world economy hadn't had another hiccough, more of a damn cardiac arrest. A combination of greed, demographics and straight-out stupidity meant that even governments had gone broke, and could no longer afford to look after the needy, or the old, or the sick, nor could they provide any of the essentials like hospitals or schooling. If you couldn't pay for it, you couldn't have it, and that was it.

The pension I'd contributed to every month for all those years got 'lost' somewhere, probably in some fat cat's pocket. I was classified as an 'unsupported retiree' – an old person with no money or family – and sent out with the rest of society's waste to live on the 'Island': a mountain of landfill in the middle of a polluted sea.

I never dreamed I could hate life the way I did out there. No chance of escaping, not with those punishment satellites – if you tried, you got zapped. The only other inhabitants apart from us old folks were the kids. Kids who never got to go to school; who'd always been told that old people and their selfishness were to blame for the world's misfortunes, some who'd got into trouble and whose parents couldn't afford to pay for their incarceration. And boy, did they have it in for us. Though the real bane of our torturous existence was the Wastelords.

The Wastelords were the dyed-in-the-wool Island survivors, young offenders, now adults – who abused the smaller kids in every way. They fed them drugs when the fog came down and the satellites weren't working and encouraged them to go up to the Village and 'have a good time' – in other words, to run amok, butchering us, burning us out . . .

I guess there's a worse life somewhere in this world, but I can't imagine it. However, if there's one thing I do know, it's to never give up hope. One day I stumbled on this blind young woman living alone in the old subway tunnels, and from then on everything changed. Lena saved me, she took care of me, and finally, she gave me something I never thought I'd know in my sad old big-guy life: love. The two of us lived underground with Jimmy and Delilah, later joined by Gordie, Arturo and Hanna: the kids we captured, who became our friends – well, more like family really.

Eventually the day came when we were forced into fighting the Wastelords – but Jimmy had other, much grander ideas. He may be in his seventies, but when it comes to original computer geniuses, you won't find any better. He's always tinkering with stuff, pulling it apart, putting bits with other bits so it does something else, things I wouldn't even begin to understand. He found a way of destroying the punishment satellites, which is how we all ended up out on that ocean last night.

I don't know when exactly, but somewhere along the line my subconscious must've decided that Lena had earned the right to be as present in my dream world as she is in my real one. And I guess as we've kept each other company just about every minute of the day and night since we became an item, that's not exactly surprising. What *is* surprising – and I can think of any number of people who'd raise an eyebrow or two – is that this level of companionship should happen to *me*. I'd always seen myself as a loner, someone who prefers his own company to that of others. But I guess the truth is, there aren't too many who want to admit to being lonely, and I'm no exception. There's a stigma attached, an implication that you ain't so much lonely as a loser. I mean, I'm sure there are people out there who prefer being on their own, 'course there are, but contrary to appearances – contrary to what I'd always assumed myself – I ain't one of them.

And don't get the idea that Lena's around just to alleviate that condition either. Nothing could be further from the truth. That woman's taught my tone-deaf old heart to sing. I'd give my life a thousand times over for her – and that ain't just talk either. I'd die happy knowing I prolonged her existence for just one single day. And as I sit here, holding her in my arms, both of us silently gazing out across the lake in the park to the shimmering warmth of the trees on the other side (it's gone now, they built on it twenty-odd years ago), I know two things: one, that I'm dreaming, and two, that when I awake, when I make that transition from this world to the other, she'll be there beside me too.

My eyes slowly blinked and batted their way open, instantly filling my mind with confusion: what the hell? Where was I?

The first penny to drop was that I really was off that Island, that I hadn't dreamed it; the second was that I hadn't woken at dawn as I'd promised myself; there'd already been a big bite taken out of the day.

I grabbed my watch, cursing when I saw it was nine-fifty, and sat up with a real jolt. Lena woke but didn't say anything, just tried to pull me back down, to keep me with her a little longer.

'No,' I told her, 'we gotta go!' I released myself from her grip and struggled to my feet, aware that I was painfully stiff from last night's activities, that my old body was again complaining about being asked to do the work of a young one.

Stumbling through to the showroom, I found the others also still asleep.

'Let's go!' I shouted, jolting Jimmy's shoulder. 'Kids, come on! We gotta get moving.'

I was about to go back and check Lena hadn't returned to sleep when it occurred to me that there was something odd about the light – it was kind of dull and purplish. I went to the front of the store and took a look out.

At first I thought it was fog. I mean, they don't get a lot on the Mainland, not like we did out on the Island, but it does happen. However, I soon realised it was something else: a thick gauze of smoke that I saw first, and then smelled, kind of hot and dark and strongly chemical.

I threw back the door and rushed out. One look was enough to see we had real trouble. There was a building burning further down the block, but it wasn't just that, the possibility that the flames might spread to us; more this feeling that during the night we'd somehow got trapped.

I hurried back inside. 'Come on,' I shouted, frustrated by everybody's slow progress, particularly the kids, who didn't even seem to have the energy to get themselves upright. 'Let's go!'

'I'm hungry,' little Arturo whined.

'Me too,' agreed Gordie.

'Later,' I told them. 'Now, come on!'

As we emerged from the store, the nearby blaze exploded across the narrow street as if from a flame-thrower, instantly setting another building alight.

'Jesus, Big Guy!' Jimmy gasped. 'Did you see that?'

I never commented, just took Lena's hand, the two of us locking together now like it was second nature. A dozen or so paces on, I glanced back and found Jimmy still gaping at the fire. 'Jimmy!' I shouted, and he turned and started to peg after us, soon catching up with the dawdling kids. Little Arturo was still complaining he wanted something to eat and Delilah had a consoling arm round his shoulder.

Lena kept sniffing the air, almost like she was taking in random samples for analysis. 'I can smell it again,' she told me, 'that odour I noticed on our way over from the Island.'

'It looks a bit like the Island,' I observed, gazing around, ''cept this is smoke.'

'How far can you see?'

'I dunno – maybe forty, fifty yards? It depends.'

Again she sniffed, shaking her head as if she didn't quite understand. 'What is it that's burning?'

I looked at her for a moment, then back at the fire now disappearing into its own smoke. 'Everything,' I told her, only in that moment realising that was true, that there didn't seem to be a thing in that City that wasn't flammable.

She was about to say something more but fell silent when I stopped at a junction, looking this way and that, trying to work out which way we'd come the previous evening.

'That way,' she told me, and without questioning it for a moment, I set off in the direction she indicated.

When we got up to the main street and turned in the direction of the hills – though with the smoke, of course, you couldn't see them – it felt like we'd joined an assault course. Everywhere you looked it was as if madness had been set free and told to do whatever it wanted. All manner of stuff had been discarded, Lord knows why. Maybe they saw something better, or just couldn't carry as much as they'd thought. I noticed this irradia-fry, still in its box, covered in blood, more smeared handprints on the sidewalk nearby as if someone had been forced to crawl away on their hands and knees. Every possible window, every outdoor screen low enough to be reached, had been smashed. And fires, of course, still burning all over: some big, some small. To Jimmy's continuing fascination, a couple actually exploded in front of us, swear to God, again shooting out streams of flame.

It reminded me of those images you see of the surface of the sun: everything just bubbling away one moment, erupting with rainbows of fire the next. The front walls of several buildings had given way, spilling out across the sidewalk, whilst the blackened hulks of automatic buses were skewed all along the street, leastways as far as you could see. But you know, despite all the destruction and chaos and the fact that it was probably gonna kick off again later, there were still those determined to carry on with their normal lives. Off to their places of work, the office or store, hell-bent on making it 'business as usual'.

The worst thing was the bodies. I don't know how many we saw – it didn't occur to me to count – but it's a sure sign that civilisation's breaking down when you see corpses in the street. When no one's come to clear them away. I guess if the kids had come from anywhere but the Island we would've done everything we could to shield them from it. But they've seen stuff like that all their lives. I don't think they gave it a second thought.

There were a few looters already out and busy, very different animals from those who'd rampaged through the previous night. Most of them looked to be old folk, though I didn't notice any Islanders, which made me wonder how many got away from those Dragonflies. There was something almost apologetic about their behaviour. They were skulking from one place to another, their heads held low, as if they really didn't agree with what they were doing but had realised they had no other choice, that this was just the latest version of survival.

At one point Hanna stopped, peering into this quaint but rather run-down little store that like a lot of the less impressive-looking places hadn't been touched. I went back to see what had caught her eye and was met by a slightly faded display of ballet clothes. More particularly a pair of shiny pink satin shoes.

To be honest, I'm not sure I would've said anything if she'd picked up the nearest brick, smashed the window and taken them. For sure I don't know anyone who'd put them to better use. And amongst all that ruckus, everything that was going on, what would it have mattered? But she just had her fill of looking, turned, smiled at me and carried on.

The further out we went, into the old migrant suburbs – Chinese, Greek, Italian – the more we got into, well, not exactly home territory, but certainly more familiar. Eventually, despite the dense smoke and the years I'd been away, I began to recognise places: a couple of businesses I used to collect money from for Mr Meltoni, a pool hall where I used to play as a kid.

It might sound odd, but in a way I was waiting to see what my reaction would be, how I'd take to my first real memory. But do you know something? No matter where we were, or what we saw, there was nothing. I really didn't care I'd spent the majority of my life there, that it was my hometown. For sure it didn't feel like it any more. All I wanted was to get out into the open spaces, to see a whole horizon contributed to by no one but Nature, and until that happened, I wasn't going to feel truly free.

By mid-afternoon the road began to ascend and we realised we'd reached the more affluent suburbs, that though we might not be able to see them, we'd started to climb the hills that half-cup the City.

I was reckoning on another three or four hours to get to the other side, but the higher we got, the more difficult the smoke became. It started to really sting our eyes and gouge the back of our throats, and poor old Delilah, with her one lung, was hacking away fit to burst.

'Clancy,' Lena warned.

'I know.'

'She can't go much further.'

I turned to Jimmy and he gave me this look, like he didn't want to say anything but couldn't put it off much longer.

'As soon as we're over the hills, you'll be fine,' I reassured Delilah, feeling a little guilty. 'The cleanest, purest air you'll ever breathe.'

Jimmy ignored my attempt at lightening the mood. 'I don't think she can make it, Big Guy.'

'I'm all right – keep going,' Delilah told us, but she was coughing so much no one took any notice.

'You go on,' Jimmy said. 'We'll go back down. This smoke's gotta clear sometime. We'll follow you.'

'*No!*' Delilah protested.

I didn't know what to do. If things got any worse, I wouldn't bet on any of us getting through – yet it meant everything that we did.

'We should stick together,' Lena said. 'Whatever we decide.'

I suggested finding some water, maybe wetting a handkerchief or something for Delilah to cover her nose; it might see her through. However, at that moment we saw this small group coming down the hill, emerging out of the smoke, coughing and spluttering, obviously in some distress.

I didn't know whether to speak to them or not – who knows who you might be getting mixed up with? But as they got closer, I thought I recognised one of them from the Island.

'Hey!' I called over.

They slowed but didn't stop, I guess every bit as suspicious of us as we were them.

'You're Detainees, right?' I asked, a look of recognition coming to one guy's face. 'What's it like up there?'

'There's no way out,' he told us, breaking off from the group. 'The City's completely surrounded by fire.' He just stood there for a moment, then kind of nodded apologetically, as if embarrassed to be the bringer of such bad news, before hurrying after his companions as they began to disappear down the hill into the smoke.

For a few moments none of us could bring ourselves to say anything; the only sound was Delilah's sporadic breathless hacking.

'Shit!' I groaned.

'At least that makes the decision for us,' Lena said, though there was real concern in her voice.

'Why don't I take a look?' I suggested. 'There's gotta be some way out.'

'Clancy!' she said, a little irritated by my stubbornness.

Again there was silence. I mean, she was right, of course she was. The only trouble was, we had no Plan B. Nor C or D, come to that.

'This is worse than the Island,' Hanna suddenly ventured, as if she felt it was about time she gave her verdict.

I almost burst into laughter. That kid rarely says a word, but when she does, she has a habit of hitting matters right on the head.

'Just swapped fog for smoke,' Delilah complained, again starting to cough.

'And we're prisoners again,' Gordie added.

'Hey, hey – come on,' I said, not wanting to hear all this negative talk. 'How long can fires burn?'

'These fires?' Jimmy answered. 'Who knows?'

'Nah! Bit of rain, change in wind direction, they'll be gone. And so will we.'

Nobody replied, and I knew why. It might not be that far away, but the weather on the Mainland's completely different to the Island. Over there you can get four seasons in a day; here, with the surrounding hills, high pressure, things can get really locked in. This time of year, we might not see a change for weeks, maybe longer.

'I'm hungry!' Arturo complained again, the way kids do, as if all this life-or-death stuff is of no consequence compared with the demands of their bellies.

I paused, my eyes resting on him, my thoughts elsewhere, until it occurred to me that probably it wasn't such a bad idea, that things might look better if we got a little food in us.

I ain't got an ounce of pride, not any more, not after living on the Island knowing the sorts of things we had to do to survive, some of the stuff we had to eat. Thing is, if you're not too fussy, you'd be surprised what people throw away. We know that better than anyone.

I'd noticed this little restaurant on the way up: Il Pomodoro Rosso, recently painted but now looking a little smoke-stained, the big Italian flag needing a wash. The windows had been boarded up – I guess as protection against looters, though I couldn't imagine it would be much of a deterrent to those we saw rampaging through the City the previous night. We retraced our footsteps, headed up the side alley, found the trashcans and started to pick our way through them.

Okay, so hunger is the best sauce, but I still gotta say a lot of what we dug out was a helluvan improvement over what we ate on the Island. The only thing was, we'd assumed the place was empty, but while we were busily chomping away, the back door suddenly burst open and this guy came out pointing a fancy-looking hunting rifle at us.

'What are you doing?' he demanded.

I put my hands up, more in a gesture of apology than anything. 'Sorry. We were really hungry. We got kids with us. We thought . . . you know, it's just garbage.'

He stared at us as if we were some kind of new lowlife he hadn't come across before and didn't have a name for. Bearing in mind the way we looked, I guess that was understandable.

'Get the hell out of here,' he said, choosing to level his weapon at me.

I wasn't going to argue, especially now there were no satellites up there to stop him. I apologised again and led the others up the alleyway, the guy still squinting down the sight of his rifle, his trigger finger looking like it might twitch at any moment.

'Friendly,' Delilah commented, once we got back up to the street. 'Very.'

We walked on in silence, the full impact of our situation weighing heavier by the moment. What the hell were we going to do? How were we going to survive? This place *was* worse than the Island – maybe a whole lot worse. And, of course, the irony was, we were partly to blame. It was us who took out the satellites, who started the fires (or some of them) that caused all this smoke.

'Clancy?' Lena said, interrupting my thoughts. 'We gotta find somewhere safe for the night.'

I grunted my agreement. Without satellites, there was no reason why those looting and burning should confine their activities mostly to the night, but for some reason, you knew they would. That as if responding to some primaeval call, they'd keep the very worst of their excesses for darkness. The hardcore, those we'd do best to avoid.

A lot of properties looked beaten up and deserted, but when you got closer, peered in the window or something, there were people inside. Those who'd already been the subject of intruders and were pretty hostile towards any more. We got chased by this armed gang, who might've made a real mess of us if they hadn't been distracted by an intact sports store with a window full of sneakers.

Night was rapidly starting to fall, pressing down on the smoke, compounding its darkness. In the far distance, deep in a remote fold, you could hear the sound of something starting up you'd rather not know about. None of us had spoken for a while and there was this sense that hope was dying with the remains of the day when Jimmy spotted this ruined church set back from the street.

All of us stopped and peered through the railings, even Lena, though she was sniffing rather than looking. It didn't appear that inviting – just a few walls, as crumpled as Christianity, in the middle of an overgrown churchyard; the odd gravestone poking out of the surging undergrowth like debris through floodwater. But at least it had the advantage of being isolated from other buildings, so that there'd be no chance of a fire spreading to it.

'Stay here,' I said, thinking I'd check it out, but Lena had other ideas.

'Isn't it dark?' she asked.

'Getting there,' I admitted.

'Then you need me.'

I thought about refusing, saying I preferred to go alone, but it was obvious how important it was to her. 'Yeah. Sure.'

Slowly we began to pick our way through the tangle and whip of the undergrowth, expecting an angry shout at any moment, ready to turn and run. There was a path worn through there where someone had been in and out many times. However, Lena stopped, sniffed the air several times and finally gave it the nod.

'It's okay.'

I trusted her senses. I breathed a sigh of relief and made my way into the building.

Actually it wasn't much more than flagstones and mud, with walls on two sides, a little bit of roof, but most of it open to the elements. I was right; at some point quite recently it'd been someone's home. There was garbage everywhere, and the remains of a fire, and they'd used one corner as a latrine.

I sighed as if to indicate that maybe we should keep looking, but Lena put a hand on my shoulder. 'It's okay,' she said. 'If it was nice, everyone would want it.'

'You sure?'

30

'Yeah.'

I went outside, headed back towards the street and waved the others in. The moment they entered, Delilah and the kids started complaining about the smell.

'I'm sorry,' I told them. 'The palace was fully booked.'

'Well, I'm not sleeping anywhere near that,' Delilah croaked, gesturing at the corner.

'Me neither!' Arturo chimed in.

'What about down below?' Lena suggested.

There was a slight pause, no one really understanding. 'What d'you mean?' I asked.

'The cellar or crypt or whatever it is.'

It always amazes me what she smells, senses or hears. Really, it's like she's some superior being. And sure enough, on closer inspection, in a corner, barely discernible in the dark – plus someone had made a bit of a half-hearted attempt to disguise it with a couple of broken gravestones – we found a flight of steps.

I squatted on my haunches, peering down, but all I could see was black.

'No!' Delilah croaked, backing away. 'No, thank you!'

Without saying a word, Lena pushed past us and began to feel her way down.

'Hey!' I protested, but she was already disappearing from sight.

We just stood there, helplessly waiting, yet again reminding ourselves that for her to stumble around in the dark was nothing unusual, that that was all she ever did.

'Are you okay?' I called, but there was no reply. 'Lena!'

'Come on down,' she shouted at last.

With some difficulty I made my way down, the point that there wasn't a lot of room painfully emphasised by my head bumping on the overhanging stonework. One by one the others followed, the last a grumbling Delilah. I guess we were hoping for better things, but together we created nothing but chaos, everyone blundering round in the pitch-black, bumping into each other, tripping over, and yet again it crossed my mind that it was a valuable insight into Lena's world.

'Just settle down where you are,' she told us, with a touch of impatience. 'At least it's dry.'

We tried to do as she asked but ended up falling over each other, sitting in each other's laps, getting in a real tangle.

'There's more room over here!' she shouted. 'Hey!'

The kids started getting in an argument, accusing each other of all sorts of things, Hanna whopping Gordie, who promptly threatened to 'lay her out, girl or no girl'.

'Okay! Okay!' I shouted. 'That's not helping.'

Finally, we sorted ourselves out, but no matter how tired we were, how long the day, I don't think anyone was in the least bit comfortable. After a while I became aware that there was the tiniest glow of light spilling down, but initially I felt like I was being asked to bed down on nothingness, to fall back until I came across something solid to support me. Not to mention that our sudden departure from the Island meant we hadn't brought a thing with us – no blankets, no matches, just the clothes we were dressed in. And it wasn't long before we realised how cold it was.

The night started with everyone feeling out their own little space, making themselves as comfortable as they could, but it wasn't long before I heard Arturo snuggle in with Delilah and Jimmy. To my surprise, a little later, not only Hanna joined Lena and me, but eventually Gordie as well, though the tough little guy did stick it out as long as he could and, by the time he gave up, was trembling like a leaf. It took us for ever to warm him up. But slowly our weariness and the endless hours of walking over-whelmed us and one by one we fell asleep.

Couple of times in the night Gordie kneed me in the back, which I guess was his way of telling me I was snoring. Mind you, I gotta say, despite not having a clue as to my surroundings, just what that darkness held, I did sleep unusually well.

However, in the morning, with a little daylight filtering down, I gotta bit of a shock – we all did. I suppose we should've guessed. It was a church – what would you expect in the cellar of a church if not a crypt? I opened my eyes to find myself surrounded by any number of graves and carved inscriptions – around the walls, the floor – and when Delilah stirred, I tell ya, she practically screamed the place down.

'What the hell?' she cried, gaping all round.

'What is it?' Jimmy asked, waking with a jolt.

'*Look!*'

He took a couple of moments, but then just shrugged. 'They're not going to do you any harm,' he said, though you could see he wasn't entirely comfortable with the situation himself.

However, at that moment Delilah realised not only had she been sleeping in a crypt, but her actual bed, the flagstone she'd been lying on, was a grave.

'For the love of God!' she shrieked, leaping up with an agility I wouldn't normally associate with her. 'I been sleeping with the dead!'

'Lile!'

'In the arms of a skeleton!'

'Listen,' I said, 'I'd rather lie with the dead than leave myself open to those who'd make me that way.'

I was kind of pleased with that, but she didn't even notice.

'This place must be jam-packed with ghosts. I bet they had a real party last night jumping in and out of our souls.'

'Delilah! You're scaring the kids,' Lena told her.

I don't know how she knew it, but she was right. All three of them were starting to look just that little bit uneasy, especially little Arturo – maybe 'cuz he kind of regards Delilah as his ma now, and don't like to see her upset.

'I'm going outside,' she said, making heavy weather of the steep stone steps.

'Don't worry,' Jimmy told Arturo, the moment she was gone. 'There's no such thing as ghosts.'

'There is!' the little guy came back. 'We saw them!'

'When?' Jimmy frowned.

'On the beach!'

'They weren't ghosts!'

'Zombies!' Gordie cried.

'Gordie . . .' I warned.

'They were!' Arturo insisted, and promptly headed off upstairs, as if to make it perfectly clear whose side he was on in this.

A few moments later we went up to join them, and found it was substantially warmer outside than in the crypt.

'Probably the damp,' Jimmy suggested.

'That ain't what's chilling my bones,' Delilah complained.

But gradually it became less of a griping session and more of a meeting. There was a lot to discuss, the most pressing subject being whether we should try to find somewhere else to stay, or just stick it out where we were.

Delilah, of course, was all for moving on – in fact, she swore she'd rather swim back to the Island than spend another night in that damp ghost-infested pit. However, as Jimmy pointed out, it was relatively safe and in the end, and despite a lot of grouching and grumbling, we managed to convince her to stay at least one more night.

'Thing is, if we're staying,' Lena said, 'we're going to need stuff. Food, water, blankets.'

Delilah grunted dismissively, as if the plan was breaking down already.

For a few moments there was silence, no one caring to voice what I thought was obvious.

'Well,' I sighed, knowing it had to be said, 'I guess that don't leave us with a great deal of choice.'

'What?' Arturo asked.

'We have to go looting.'

Again there was a pause. Going on what we'd witnessed the previous night, I don't think any of us fancied it very much.

'I'll go,' Lena volunteered.

'No,' I told her.

'Course!'

'Lena!'

'What?'

I hesitated. I didn't want to say it, but I didn't have a great deal of choice. 'You don't know the area,' I eventually told her, both of us well aware that wasn't exactly what I was saying.

She went all quiet, maybe trying to come up with some logical argument why she should go, but there wasn't one.

It made me feel really bad. We'd only been on the Mainland a day or so but her blindness had already become more of an issue. Taking her looting with us, in a strange area, with all manner of broken and smashed debris around – it was out of the question.

I wanted to say I was sorry, but I knew it would be a mistake, that she'd get angry with me if I even hinted at it.

'Jimmy?' I asked the little guy.

'Sure,' he said, as if there'd never been the slightest doubt.

'Me, too,' Gordie chipped in.

I turned and looked at him. He may only be a kid, but surviving for so long on the Island means he knows how to take care of himself. My only concern was he was a fairly recently rehabilitated member of the enemy and there were a lot of temptations out there.

'Okay,' I said, not wanting him to sense any hesitation.

'And me!' Arturo piped up.

It took a while, and a fair amount of argument, but in the end I managed to convince the little guy to stay by telling him I needed someone to take care of the women.

'Do I get to tell them what to do?' he asked.

'Yeah, sure,' I told him, silently wishing him good luck with that. I mean, I wouldn't try giving Hanna orders, let alone Lena or Delilah.

I went and put my arms around Lena, still feeling bad about her not being able to come and not knowing what I could say to make it better.

'Be careful,' she warned, as if that was the only thing that mattered.

I gave her a big hug, squeezing her against my body. With what was out there, I needed all the strength she could give me.

CHAPTER THREE

Really, all we needed to do was to keep a low profile, not to attract attention in any way, to fade in and out of the smoke. I mean, yeah, technically we're on the run – we committed a Crime Against the State, after all – but amongst everything else that's going on, I didn't think that would be a priority. People've got more important things to worry about. Turns out it's not easy to mind your own business where looting and lawlessness is concerned, and it didn't take long to realise. As soon as we arrived in the shopping district there seemed to be nothing but fights going on all over.

I saw a couple of old ladies wrestling with each other over toilet paper. Can you believe that? They must've been eighty if they were a day. Both of them ended up coughing and wheezing, having to sit down, almost having a heart attack over a roll of ass-wipe. People were arguing and fighting over all sorts of stuff as if they were worried stiff there might be a shortage, whether it was something they used or not.

Looting – and I'm talking about the essential kind here; I got no truck with the other – ain't just a matter of going to the nearest store and helping yourself. Like I said before, a lot of people were doing their best to carry on with their usual lives. You gotta search for an area where you know law and order's broken down, somewhere mostly trashed and burned, but where there's still the odd thing left to be taken.

It took us a while, especially as we had to detour around what was probably the biggest and most ferocious fire we'd seen, exploding and popping away, ripping through everything, plainly not gonna stop 'til it took out the whole block, but eventually we located this one department store which had still been looted but looked like it had a few bits and pieces left inside. We hung round in the street for a few minutes, conquering our nerves – none of us had done anything like that before – then cautiously entered through one of the many smashed windows.

The atmosphere inside was surprisingly subdued. You could sense something had happened, that emotions had run riot, but now everything was just drained and cold. There *were* a few looters at work, but it all felt a bit half-hearted. People were picking over stuff, dragging things out from beneath mounds of rubble, then considering them seriously, deciding whether it was worth bothering with or not.

We climbed the motionless escalators to the fourth floor, where signs pointed the way to the bedding department. We weren't very hopeful of finding anything useful but actually scooped up a few discarded blankets and pillows that'd obviously been dropped, maybe by someone rushing to get out. Then we went down to the basement food hall, but our luck had run out. It was stripped completely bare, with not so much as a drop of water or a single potato chip left. My stomach was starting to remember how long it was since it'd last been full.

We left the building the same way we entered, relieved at how easy it had been – that there hadn't been any trouble. Not to mention the fact that we'd all be sleeping a little more comfortably that night.

Most of the big stores had been ransacked, so a block or so further on we thought we'd try a different approach and started venturing off down the side streets. It wasn't long before we came across this traditional old camping store. Someone had already paid them a visit and it took us a while, but eventually we managed to find enough useful stuff: a couple of backpacks, parkas, sleeping bags, all ideal for our situation. Gordie even found a hunting knife, which, to his annoyance, I immediately pocketed. I thought it was far better with me than him.

Unfortunately though, the search for food and water turned out to be another matter altogether. We tried store after store, always with the same result: endless bare shelves and nothing but maybe a little melted ice in the freezers. I didn't know where else we could look, and Jimmy wasn't being a great deal of help. He was forever getting distracted by all the technological innovations there'd been while we were away on the Island. I kept hearing him whistling over and over at how 'cool' something was – particularly the screens. It looked like they could now 'read' people as they pass by, not only addressing you by name, but directing targeted adverts towards you, based on your hobbies, make of phone, choice of shampoo, any damn thing.

But not us, of course. Just like the moving sidewalk, the first screen we came across immediately realised we had no credit implant, that we were 'non-persons', and it occurred to me that maybe somewhere a warning bell might be sounding, that if we had no status or record, they might guess we were escaped Islanders. Not that it worried Jimmy, every few moments he would stop, scrutinise something, nod his head and smile when he'd worked out what it was. He was like a kid in a candy store. And yet as the day wore on and still no sign of food or water, he might've preferred it if that candy store had been real. All three of us were not only hungry ourselves, but were starting to worry about those back in the church.

We did manage to pick up a few useful items in a drug store where Jimmy went to find something for Lile's cough. We got some organi-plasters and bandages and painkillers, that'd fallen down behind the shelves and been missed by earlier looters. Even so, it wasn't much more than a diversion and we all knew it. What we really needed was food and water, and if we didn't find some soon, we were in real trouble.

Slowly, as that realisation bit ever deeper, our conversation went from concerned to sporadic to a dull nothing. Jimmy lost all interest in new technology and suddenly looked both tired and ten years older. I mean, okay, sleeping bags, warm clothing, medical, all useful stuff, but the first priority had to be something in our bellies. We tried a few more places, supermarkets, delis, but it was no use, and with the night now starting to lock down, the atmosphere was beginning to change. The shadows were growing deeper and darker, the smoke wrapping itself ever tighter around everything. The time had come to get off the streets, to leave them to the real evil-doers, and as much as we dreaded returning without food or drink, we began to retrace our footsteps, heading back to the church.

I was too immersed in my disappointment to pay much attention to this guy approaching from the opposite direction. There was a fire behind him, all cracking and exploding, so that all I could really make out of him was a dark silhouette. As he got nearer, I could see he was well dressed, round about forty, plainly a well-to-do Mainlander. It did cross my mind it was a little odd, that he wasn't someone I'd expect to see wandering the streets, but nothing more. He slowed and looked us up and down, two oldies and a kid, like he was assessing us for something, then he resumed his previous pace.

As he went by, he muttered something out of the corner of his mouth: 'Food and drink. Victory West. Superfood-7.'

He was gone before we could even react.

'What did he say?' Jimmy asked.

'Food and drink,' Gordie repeated.

'D'ya know it?' Jimmy said, turning to me.

'If it's still the same place, yeah.'

'What d'ya think?'

'Let's go!' Gordie urged.

I turned to Jimmy. 'Can't do any harm.'

It was amazing what an instant spring to our steps that little piece of information brought – we began chatting again, speculating on where we were going, if there really was food there. I'll admit we were a little concerned at how we'd got the information, but when you're that hungry, I guess the thought of eating overrides everything else.

Course, we didn't just march up to the place – we're not as dumb as all that. We approached cautiously on the other side of the street, stopping to lurk in the shadows, to see what was going on. And actually, the answer to that was a big fat zero: the place was in complete darkness. No entry had been made, nothing was broken, and the doors and windows all seemed to be intact.

'You sure this is it?' Jimmy asked.

'Unless they opened another one.'

We just stood there, something not feeling quite right, but Gordie was all for a little action. 'Come on. Let's go,' he said, turning to head across the street.

'Whoa! Whoa!' I cried, grabbing him by the shoulder and tugging him back. 'Let's just check it out first, shall we?'

He gave a rather impatient sigh and slumped back against the wall. The three of us waited in silence, really not sure what we were dealing with, though it wasn't long before we realised we weren't alone, that there were others watching from the shadows.

'*See?*' Gordie whispered angrily. 'The moment someone makes a move, there's gonna be a stampede.'

Despite how cautious I felt, I knew he had a point. If we were going to get everything we needed, we had to be some of the first through the door. 'Okay. I'll get water,' I said, knowing it would be the heaviest item. 'You two just grab whatever you can.'

He was right: the instant we broke cover all the others came rushing out of their hiding places – far more of them than I'd been expecting. I immediately started to run, knowing it was going to be a free-for-all, that having cast their doubts aside, everyone was gonna grab what they could.

In the absence of any kind of heavy instrument, I hit the door with my shoulder. There's a moment I always get these days – if I'm forced to throw a punch or something – when I wonder if my old bones have become too brittle for that sort of thing, but the door gave way surprisingly easily, its frame crumpling, the glass popping out and smashing on the floor.

'Quick as you can,' I said to Jimmy and Gordie, aware of this jostling mob rapidly converging behind us.

Despite it being almost dark inside, I could see there was plenty of stuff to be had. The fridges were still working, which was kind of strange, bearing in mind the lights weren't, but as the store behind me erupted with angry shouting, I ran over and stuffed as many bottles as I could into my new backpack, grabbed a large container in each hand, then headed back to the exit, calling across to Jimmy and Gordie. Something was telling me to get out of there as quickly as possible.

Some guy tried to grab one of the water containers from me and I had to release it momentarily so I could hit him. I mean, I'd got no choice, not the way things were, with water more precious than gold. The funny thing was, as he went down, I suspected I might know him, that he was a fellow Detainee. Not that I cared, not in that moment. I leant forward and wrenched the water container back, and as I did so, I noticed this guy crouching down behind a display.

He was young – I don't know, in his twenties maybe, with long dark hair and one of those masks people wear to avoid infection. But he was too well dressed to be a looter – and why the hell was he hiding? What was that in his hand, a weapon? I immediately lunged forward, knocking the display aside so as to get a better look, and as he tried to scrabble away I saw what he was trying to hide: it was a camera: a movie camera, and by the look of it, infrared.

'What the hell's going on?' I demanded. Everything about his manner was exuding guilt.

He never answered, just glanced nervously up over my shoulder in an involuntary gesture, as if looking for help. I turned and followed his eyes and caught a glimpse of another guy with a camera in the upstairs office window, also, for some reason, wearing a mask. Behind him I could see the dark shapes of several others. What the hell was this? Were they filming us?

I hesitated, but only for a second. Something was very wrong here. I turned and ran after Gordie and Jimmy in their dash to the exit. '*Move it!*' I cried

They were probably waiting for some kind of signal, but as soon as they realised someone was onto them, those dark shadows in the office sprang forward, sliding the windows back and aiming their weapons, and a hail of laser-fire spat down on us. All around there was that now-familiar screaming, the stench of burned flesh, the explosions of light as person after person was cut down.

I think the idea was it was supposed to be a complete turkey-shoot; that no one would make it out of there alive. There were two uniformed guys just outside the entrance, I guessed to cut anyone down who tried to escape, but we were there sooner than they'd anticipated and I barged one over as he was still setting up, dropping the water containers, trying to grab his weapon but losing it in the dark. His buddy joined in and I found myself having to grapple with both of them. Gordie was repeatedly punching one in the back, Jimmy kicking the other in the leg, and somehow, in all the confusion, we managed to get away. I fell over some boxes but still managed to grab my goddamn water containers before setting off down a service alleyway. Several laser shots were directed at us, scoring the brickwork, starting a fire, but with everything else that was going on, no one bothered to give chase.

Jeez, I should've known – maybe I did know, deep down. It was a set-up, of course it was. We were too desperate, too hungry, like starving animals lured into a trap. The cameras had obviously been there to record the whole thing and use it for propaganda: *Look what happens when you loot* – and maybe far more importantly, *Look who's still in control, even without satellites.*

'I don't like these Infinity people. Not one little bit,' I muttered.

'Looks like they're the law now,' Jimmy said.

'Mm.'

'And in which case, who the hell's government?'

I turned and looked at him. 'Good question.'

We walked on a little further, both of us turning that over, but it wasn't such a dilemma for Gordie.

'The guys with the biggest sticks are always in control,' he told us.

I mean, you can dismiss it, you can mount all kinds of arguments based on politics and democracy, but in the end, he wasn't so far wrong. Which was a helluva worrying thought when you related it to our situation.

We hadn't been walking more than thirty minutes when the screens cleared of 'individual advertising' and all came up with the same thing: *Infinity News*. Sure enough, the first items up were the looting, the anarchy on the streets and the way the authorities were dealing with it. Over and over they showed the extermination of those in the supermarket, sparing us nothing: looters being lasered and cut down, getting exactly what they deserved. Bleeding corpses sprawled on the ground, close-ups of the most horrific injuries and of the shock and agony of those who suffered them. Mind you, they were careful not to show what kind of store it was, or suggest that people had been trying to take food and not, as one clip led us to believe, luxury items. Not to mention pointing out that some of the dead looters were Detainees, that these people had already committed a Crime Against the State punishable by death. It was pretty fearsome stuff, and if Infinity's aim was to frighten the hell out of faint-hearted looters, to convince people how uncompromising they intended to be, I imagine it worked.

We must've walked a mile or more watching the same images being played over and over 'til it reached a point where I could pretty well tell you what was gonna happen next. Where I knew that that woman was about to be blasted to pieces and her partner would throw himself on top of her a second too late. Where those two people would get melded together with the same shot. And where that young girl died just as she was putting a piece of chocolate into her mouth. It was a bit like being beaten senseless over and over, and even when I told myself to turn away, within seconds I was looking back again – we all were.

Finally they must've felt the point was well and truly made and they moved on to the next item – though it was connected. At first it was such a shock I really couldn't take it in. Some stretches of street it can be as much as a couple of hundred yards to the next screen, and with the smoke you can't see anything, but as luck would have it, the next story came up just as we were approaching a profusion of screens, big and small.

I turned to Jimmy, then back to the screens, then back to Jimmy again, hardly believing my eyes.

'What the hell are you doing up there?' I asked.

CHAPTER FOUR

They were images taken from a satellite, looking down on his freckly bald head with his trademark straggle of a ponytail, some with him using his stick, others not, around the Village mostly, though there were a couple out on the tips. It made me wonder if they had photos of us all or if he was picked out later – if they'd been doing a little investigating.

'What've I done?' Jimmy protested.

We paused by a screen so we could catch what was being said, though I think we both had a pretty good idea. Sure enough, having shown how they deal with looters – those hell-bent on civil unrest, the 'anarchists on our streets' – Infinity were now revealing the person responsible for this situation, the 'monster' who destroyed not just the satellites, but Life, Law and Order, and the very fabric of our society. Viewers were advised that 'this evil man, this master terrorist with a death sentence on his head' must be apprehended, and that a substantial reward was being offered to anyone who had any information as to his identity – or, even better, could bring about his demise.

47

I turned to Jimmy. Even in the murky light, I could see all the colour draining from his face.

'Oh, Jeez!' he whined. 'Not cool!'

Without saying another word, he put his head down and began to peg it away from us as fast as he could. For some reason Gordie found the whole thing highly amusing; he just stood there laughing and pointing after him.

'Jimmy!' I called out.

He stopped and turned round and hurriedly retraced his footsteps. 'Big Guy!' he hissed, 'are you *crazy*? Don't call out my name like that!'

I apologised – then had something of a brainwave. I dug into my backpack and tugged out one of the parkas we took from the camping store. 'Put it on.'

He looked at it for a moment as if I'd lost my mind, then realised what I was getting at: as long as he kept the hood up, there was every chance he'd go unrecognised.

'I'm not scared,' he kept saying as he was zipping it up. 'Just aware I'm an irreplaceable part of the team.'

Nevertheless, all the way back to the church, he kept a real watchful eye out. Withdrawing his head as far back into his hood as he could whenever anyone approached, then extending it out again to check all around once they'd gone. In and out, in and out, like some turtle on speed.

When we finally descended the steps into the crypt, the others were so relieved by our return, and what we laid out before them, our meal turned out to be a bit more of an impromptu party. We'd found a couple of wind-up emergency lanterns that, at first lit the crypt just fine, but as they began to run down, they created some disturbing shadows that kept little Arturo looking around as if he expected to see a ghost appear at any moment.

Gordie, surprisingly generously for him, handed out some of the candy bars he'd brought back, not only to Arturo but to Hanna as well; while Delilah started modelling her new parka as if it was an expensive fur, parading up and down, looking about as pleased as she could be. I couldn't help but wonder how long it had been since she'd had any new clothes. Or maybe she'd never had anything but hand-me-downs.

Jimmy'd asked Gordie and me not to say anything about him being on the screen, that it would only cause ructions with Lile. As long as he lay low, it'd be fine, and once the fires died down, we'd be out of this city and it wouldn't be an issue anyway.

For his sake, I hoped he was right, though I gotta say, those Infinity people really worry me. They're not like the Wastelords: a disorganised rabble united only by a love of cruelty and violence, they go deep into everyone's lives, with a power and position they're utterly ruthless about enforcing. They might not know Jimmy's name, but the fact that they were already broadcasting his image just two days after our escape was a real cause for concern.

Lena gave me a big hug when I first got back. I thought it was 'cuz she was so pleased to see me, but she hung on for so long I realised there might be more to it. The rest of the evening she never once left my side. It wasn't like her at all. I mean, we're talking about someone who spent four years alone underground, who had self-sufficiency down to an art form. But over here, on the Mainland, she doesn't look so comfortable. I mean, it's only natural it'd take time to get used to it, but I gotta admit, she was starting to worry me.

Later, warmly ensconced in our new sleeping bag, whispering to each other so the others couldn't hear, I asked her if she was okay.

'Of course,' she replied, a little surprised by the question. 'Why wouldn't I be?'

For a while I left it at that, not wanting to make matters worse, but in the end I couldn't stop myself. 'Sure?'

'What do you mean?'

She waited, as if she wanted me to clarify what I was saying, but she knew what I was talking about.

'Clancy . . .' she sighed.

'I'm worried about you.'

'Well, don't! It's my problem.'

'So there is a problem?'

'No!' she said, turning over, repositioning herself for sleep, getting used to the confines of the sleeping bag.

She didn't say any more, but I could tell she was still awake. I gave her a squeeze but she didn't respond. 'Lena?'

Eventually she gave a long sigh and turned back over, I guess realising I was going to keep on 'til she told me.

'I'm no use here. Not to you, not to anyone.'

'What d'ya mean?'

'Oh, come on! It was fine on the Island, down in the tunnels, but over here . . . I'm just another mouth to feed, slowing you down, complicating things.'

'Are you serious?'

'Yes! You might not want to admit it, but the truth is . . . you'd be better off without me.'

'Whoa, whoa,' I said, tugging her towards me, no longer worried the others might hear. 'There are no circumstances in this world in which I'd be better off without you. None whatsoever. D'you hear me? . . . Lena?'

'Yes.'

'Please. Never ever talk about this again. Not for any reason.'

She gave a long sigh, as if she really wanted to say more.

'Promise?' I persisted.

Eventually I felt her nod, but it was a long way from convincing. The two of us opted to pretend the subject was closed and returned to our search for sleep, but I knew the issue was far from resolved: she was still troubled, I just didn't know how deep it went. And you wanna know something? The worst part of it? It's left me with this awful feeling that maybe – just maybe – I can't trust her any more. Not 'cuz I'm worried she might do something wrong – more 'cuz I'm worried she might try to do something *right*. She might think about sacrificing herself for us, slipping away, heading off on her own, under the impression that it would be what's best for everyone. And to be honest with you, try as I might, I can't think of one thing in this world that frightens me more than that.

I spent almost the entire night turning things over in my mind, thinking of what I could do or say to put her mind at rest, to convince her she was as valued here as on the Island. Once we got out of this damn city and found ourselves somewhere to live, far away from all this, everything would be so much simpler. Well, maybe that's not doing her situation justice, I mean, no matter how strong she is, it's always gonna be a battle she'll have to fight.

It was just as the daylight was beginning to spill weakly down the stone steps that the idea came to me. At first I kind of played with it, running this way and that, waiting for the jolt when I hit the wall, when I ran up against the obstruction that told me it couldn't be done. But do you know something? I never reached that wall. I couldn't think of any reason at all why I shouldn't at least explore the possibility.

I lay there until the day had well and truly arrived, still churning over what I had to do, and eventually came to the conclusion that, as always with my ideas, the best thing was to just go ahead and do it and that there was no time like the present.

I managed to untangle myself from Lena, unzip the sleeping bag and make my way across the crypt without waking anyone. Later I'd tell them I thought of something else we needed, that we forgot the previous day. Maybe I could pick something up just to support my story? For sure, I wasn't gonna let any of them know what I was really up to. Especially not Lena. I mean, it wasn't gonna be easy, and, actually, I probably wasn't the best guy for the job, schmoozing ain't exactly my speciality. On the other hand, if I did succeed, it would change our world.

Despite my new green parka, I'm aware I don't cut much of a figure these days. I remember when I was working for Mr Meltoni, I had eleven suits hanging in my wardrobe. Can you believe that? All handmade by a little Moroccan guy down on Union and set off with genuine French or Italian silk ties. Actually, that was Mr Meltoni's idea. He thought his boys should reflect his status, especially his Number One minder, but after a while, I kind of got into it myself. You feel good when you're wearing nice clothes. They move with you, instead of against you. And I'll tell you something else too, a big guy badly dressed is nowhere near as impressive as one done up to the nines. You get more respect, which means you don't have to get your hands dirty so often.

Now, of course, apart from the parka, I'm just about dressed in rags, which ain't that surprising given that there was rarely anything in the Island's garbage big enough to fit me. I knew I needed to smarten up if I was going to get where I wanted to go. Not that I had a great deal in the way of options. All I could think of was trimming my beard with the knife Gordie found, then wetting and combing my hair back with my fingers. There wasn't a lot I could do with my pants, but I did clean my boots and give them a bit of a polish on the lining of my parka.

It was better, but not a whole lot. Maybe the most persuasive thing I had going for me was my absolute determination not to let anyone fob me off, but if I thought that was going to intimidate people, I was wrong, 'cuz whether it took ten seconds or ten minutes, in the end, I was still shown the door.

There was one other place to try, and a name that had cropped up several times already that morning. Dr Evan Simon had his own private clinic but worked two days a week at St Joseph's – and fortunately for me, that day was one of them. He was one of the new breed: 'techno-doctors', they're called, though compared to those we had when I was a kid, I don't reckon they're doctors at all. There are no medical specialists any more – far as I could see, some of them know little more about the human body than I do. What they do specialise in is programming; it's computers do all the work now, diagnose, treat, operate. You don't need the knowledge of years of medical school, just cutting-edge data. The really gifted ones are those who create their own programs – and apparently, when it came to gifts, Dr Simon was 'the man', or even something a little *higher*. He certainly required you to fall to your knees when he entered the room, far as I could work out. Whatever, all I knew was, if I wanted a miracle, he was the most likely source, so I headed off through the smoke and debris to St Joseph's.

I got directions from this young guy at reception who kept looking me up and down as if I'd accidentally rolled in dog crap and he didn't know whether to tell me or not. I knew the first thing he'd do once I was out of sight would be to warn security, and that meant I had to get to Dr Simon's office as quickly as possible, otherwise I wouldn't get there at all.

I just sailed past his clucking secretary, pushing some assistants out of the way, and barged straight in. He was on the screen, talking to someone – maybe his PA at his private clinic? It sounded like he was going over his schedule for the week. I gotta say, one look was enough to know I was in the presence of real twenty-four-carat-gold success. I might've enjoyed dressing up when I worked for Mr Meltoni, but this guy oozed his own brand of aftershave: traditional English shirt, country-club tie, gold cufflinks, metallic midnight hair with polished silver sides: the very picture of success.

'What do you want?' he asked, immediately looking over my shoulder for someone to come and rescue him.

I came right out with it. 'I need you to look at my partner's eyes. She's blind. I wanna know if there's any chance of her seeing again.'

He just stared at me as if he couldn't believe my nerve. 'Have you got an appointment?' he asked, plainly not having heard a word I said.

'She's been blind for four years – got caught in an explosion,' I told him, determined to tell him everything before I was thrown out. 'She can't see a thing, but there's no visible damage.'

'Make an appointment. My secretary will tell you my fees and availability,' he told me, again looking to the door.

'I don't have time for that!' I growled, knowing I'd never get back in again, that this was my only shot. 'I need you to see her right away.'

'I'm afraid that's impossible,' he replied, getting that look about him, that tone, as if he'd just realised he was dealing with a madman – one who might have to be pacified.

I heard someone enter behind me and saw his look of relief. Security had arrived. 'Please,' I begged, 'you gotta help her!'

Two guys grabbed me and one stuck a taser in my back and told me to calm down. They half-wrestled, half-shoved me towards the door, ignoring my efforts at digging my heels in.

'Please! Dr Simon, you have no idea what she's been through. She's the bravest woman I've ever known – she lived all alone for four years in the old subway tunnels on the Island,' I cried out, willing him to listen. 'Can you imagine? Could you've done that? Please, give her a chance!'

There was a pause and I realised that not only had the security guys stopped pushing me towards the door, but Dr Simon was actually listening.

'I know I shouldn't've come here like this, but she's everything to me. And she deserves to be helped, more than anyone you'll ever meet.'

Dr Simon took a deep breath and told the security guys to release me and wait outside. 'You've got five minutes,' he told me.

That was all I needed, a chance – and I tell you, I was as persuasive as I've ever been, assuring him over and over what a wonderful person she was, that if he met her, he'd know what I meant . . . 'course, he realised straight off we were Detainees, but that didn't seem to worry him – in fact, oddly, it seemed to make Lena that bit more interesting to him.

'She's perfectly healthy otherwise?' he asked.

'Yeah, she's fine,' I told him – and she is; whatever her sight problems, and maybe 'cuz of her change of circumstances, these days Lena looks so much more healthy.

He asked me a lot more questions, mainly about her surviving underground: what she ate, where she got water – but after a while he started glancing at his watch and I knew my time was up.

I had just one more question. 'How much would it cost?'

'Do you have money?' he asked, unable to stop himself looking me up and down.

'I'll get it,' I said, though I didn't have the slightest idea how.

'I've been doing research into the growing incidents of blindness in the City – she might fit into that program. I could waive my fees but my support staff would have to be paid. They're not a charity. Probably somewhere in the region of eight to ten thousand.'

It was a lot of money, but it had been *his* fees I'd been really worried about. Thanks to Mr Meltoni, I knew how much these guys charged. 'Thank you,' I said, and I meant it. 'That's really kind.'

He just shrugged as if it was nothing, but I was genuinely moved. A few minutes later, having made an appointment for Lena for the following day, I was in the elevator, smiling to myself, ignoring the lingering doubt that I was getting into something I didn't understand. It was the first real act of kindness I'd experienced since we arrived in the City, and I gotta say, it made me feel a little better about the place.

However, when I got to the ground floor, I was in for a shock. There was a whole room jam-packed with those zombie-sick, just like the ones on the beach. In fact, there were so many, people were queuing out into the corridor.

I walked by, moving to one side to let a couple of nurses pick a guy up who'd collapsed, taking the opportunity to snag several bottles of water that'd just been delivered and stuff them in my backpack.

As I got to the door, I glanced back. What the hell was wrong with those people?

It was well into the afternoon before I got back, and the amount of sidewalk-crunching I'd done, I should've been exhausted – but I wasn't. I was too excited at how things had gone, what it might mean, and it was all I could do to keep it inside.

The others were sitting round up-top, slowly appearing out of the smoke as I approached like a circle of stones.

'Clancy! Where've you been?' Lena asked, obviously having heard my approach. .

'Sorry. I went looking for more water,' I said, taking out the bottles I'd liberated from St Joseph's. 'All I could find . . . Oh, and I got something for Jimmy.'

I thought bringing the little guy back a mini-screen was a real brainwave, a distraction from my behaviour, but he didn't react the way I'd expected.

In fact, it was Delilah who eventually took it from me. 'Oh God!' she groaned. 'I thought things had been peaceful.'

No matter how she might feel about reuniting Jimmy with his precious technology, she still started to look for the power switch.

'Don't turn it on,' he told her.

'Why not?' she asked.

There was a pause, then little Arturo started giggling. 'He doesn't want you to see him.'

'Gordie!' I groaned, realising he must've told Arturo the whole story.

'What?' Delilah asked.

Jimmy knew he had no choice, that he had to tell her. 'They know it was me who brought down the satellites,' he admitted sheepishly.

'*What?*' she cried.

He played it down, like it was nothing, that there was no way they could be sure – and anyways, as soon as the fires died down and we got away, what would it matter? But Delilah was a long way from happy, especially when Arturo blurted out there was a price on his head.

'*Jimmy!*'

'Public Enemy Number One,' he nodded, with just the faintest suspicion of pride.

'How much is it?' she asked. "bout time I got something for all these years of aggravation.'

'Nowhere near enough,' he told her.

Delilah stood there for several moments, glaring at him as if ten cents might be a temptation. 'Where's that knife?' she asked.

He knew what she had in mind immediately. 'I'm not cutting my ponytail off – not for you or anyone!'

'You'll cut that stupid thing off and shave what little other hair you got,' she told him.

'What?'

'Clancy?' Delilah implored. I raised one hand in a gesture of submission and used the other to tug Lena downstairs to the crypt. I couldn't go another moment without telling her.

'What's the matter?' she asked, once we were alone.

I hesitated for a moment, suddenly not sure how she'd take this. 'I been to see someone.'

'Who?'

'A techno-doctor . . . Dr Evan Simon.'

Just for a moment there was this expression on her face, like a close friend she'd fallen out with a long time ago had walked into the room. 'Why?'

'You know why.'

'Clancy! I'm never going to get my sight back—'

'Are you sure?'

'What do you mean?'

I told her the whole story, all the places I went, the way Dr Simon's name kept cropping up, and finally, about barging into his office, and most important of all, that he thought there might be a chance of restoring her sight. 'But first he has to see you – do some tests.'

It was like all the rigidity went out of her body. She gave this kind of little whimper as if the subject was just too painful, and slowly slumped down the wall to the floor.

'I did it for you!' I told her, not understanding her reaction. 'I don't care if you're blind – well, I do, course, but . . . on your behalf. I want you to be happy.'

'Oh, Clancy,' she sighed. 'I *am* happy. With you—'

'You *were* happy. On the Island.'

'Yeah. What does that say about me?' she replied. 'Everyone else's life was hell.' Again there was silence. She reached out, took my hand and tugged me down next to her.

'You gotta give it a try,' I said. 'You got to.'

'What about money?' she asked.

'He's doing some research. He said he'll make you part of it,' I told her, deciding not to mention the other costs for the moment.

She just sat there, gently shaking her head, as if it was all too much.

'Just see him, Lena, please? If there's nothing doing, well . . . But if there's any chance . . .'

She kissed me on the cheek. 'You're the most wonderful man in the world.'

'I know,' I joked.

'I'd do anything to be able to see you.'

I hugged her, kissed her head, burying my lips in that warm profusion of thick brown hair, aware that, actually, that was probably the last thing I wanted to hear her say. All I could do was to try to put it out of my mind, but it wasn't gonna be easy. See, if she does get her sight back – and I know that's a big *if* – but if she does, what the hell's she gonna think when she comes face to face with this big old bag of sad wrinkles and bent bones?

*

The next day, as arranged, I took Lena to Dr Simon's private clinic. He had patients all morning, but he'd assured me he'd do his best to fit us in at lunchtime. We didn't tell the others, not yet, not with so much hanging on it.

Dr Simon's clinic was at his home up in the hills, where the smoke smelled a little more like wood instead of giving off that chemical odour she hated so much. It was one of those swanky enclaves, with security so tight they can read the whole place at any given moment and tell you how many people are in there, where they are, even what they're doing.

When we got to the gate they really gave us the once-over: initially 'cuz of our appearance, I guess, but then 'cuz they discovered we had no implants – we were non-people. They made us wear those bracelets that not only monitor you, but damn near take your hand off if you're caught doing anything you shouldn't, officiously informing the driver Dr Simon sent down that they weren't happy about 'non-people' in the compound and it would have to go down in the records.

The guy drove us the few hundred yards up to the house without a word, obviously no more relaxed about the situation than security were. He kept glancing in his rear-view mirror at us, as if he couldn't wait to get this odd-looking couple on his back seat out and give it a damn good clean. Mind you, it was a nice limo: long, shiny as a dinner plate and clearly bullet- and laser-proof, just like the ones Mr Meltoni used to have. As for the house, well, it was every bit as huge and imposing, every bit as stylish, as you'd expect from someone like the Doc.

Naturally, we weren't taken to the front door where we might embarrass one of his wealthy patients but ushered round the back and in through a side entrance, then hurried into his office.

'The doctor will be with you shortly,' the receptionist said, as

Lena immediately started to find her way round the room, feeling the large expanses of shiny minimalism, stroking some pretty expensive-looking ornaments, checking the acreage of the Impressionist originals.

'How much did you say this would cost?' she asked.

'It's not a problem,' I told her. 'Just, er . . . a few thousand for the staff.'

'Clancy!' she protested.

'Nothing for him . . . I said, he's doing some kind of study.'

She groaned as if having second, or even third, thoughts.

'Just see him,' I begged. 'What've you got to lose?'

It's funny: there was this moment when Dr Simon first entered the room when I felt really uncomfortable, almost like he'd forgotten something – the quality that made me trust him the previous day. He seemed much more businesslike, and probably 'cuz it was his private clinic, looked even smarter in a silver-grey sharkskin suit with swirly blue silk tie and soft leather slip-ons.

'Clancy.' He nodded at me, making no attempt to shake my hand. 'And this must be Lena?'

She didn't say anything, which slightly surprised me – normally she's pretty friendly.

'Take a seat,' he told us, and Lena immediately headed for the two chairs in front of his desk. 'Very impressive,' Dr Simon noted.

He proceeded to ask Lena an almost endless list of questions – not only about her blindness, but also every aspect of her background, feeding every detail into his computer.

Lena was plainly reluctant to fill in so many blank spaces, particularly when he asked her about her time living with the Wastelords. On more than one occasion she simply refused to answer and he was forced to move on.

At last he stopped talking and started to examine her, shining attachments into her eyes, using a scanner over her head to draw across her, over and over, as if taking the thinnest slices of salami. The screen was showing all kinds of colourful images – hot-spots, stimulated areas. It meant nothing to me, but the Doc was concentrating as hard as could be. Meanwhile, Lena did whatever he asked without comment or reaction. Her face was a real study of seriousness; I couldn't begin to guess what was going through her mind. Finally he got a nurse to take blood tests and a bunch of different scans, more standard stuff.

At last she resumed her seat and the Doc sat across from us scrolling through the initial information.

'Mm. Interesting,' he commented.

I turned to Lena, expecting her to ask the obvious question, and when she didn't, I did. 'In what way?'

'Well, as best as I can make out, it *is* possible.'

'What are the odds?' I asked, wanting to hear it in layman's terms.

He made a face like he really didn't want to reduce it to simple terms, but eventually he hit a few keys on his computer as if checking something before saying, 'Well, my programme, her profile – it's not complete but . . . I've got a provisional forecast of eighty-two per cent success with a corneal graft. It would be greater, but there's always a risk of infection and perhaps even rejection.'

'That doesn't sound good.'

'The computer minimises it, of course, but in cases like these the possibility of rejection one day never goes away completely.'

I turned to Lena, again expecting her to make some kind of comment, but still she said nothing.

'It's up to you,' Dr Simon continued, 'but . . . at the very worst, you'd be no worse off.'

'How much would it cost?' Lena asked, finally joining in on the conversation.

Dr Simon hesitated, looking to me as if he expected me to say something.

'We'll talk about it later,' I told Lena, in something of an aside.

'Clancy, we have no money,' she reminded me, obviously irritated by my continued refusal to discuss the subject. 'And we have no way of getting any.'

I took her hand and squeezed it. 'Let's wait and see, huh?'

She sighed and turned away, and I could see she was as much bemused by my behaviour as annoyed by it.

Faced by her obvious doubts and degree of antagonism, Dr Simon visibly softened, even resorted to a little persuasion himself. 'Well, talk it over,' he said. 'I always programme in a degree of caution – it avoids disappointment later. The odds are probably a little better than I said.'

'Wow,' I commented, trying to wring a little enthusiasm out of Lena.

'As for the cost, I've already told you, I'm happy to waive my fee. Maybe some of my technicians, too . . . it's possible.'

There was a pause, as if he felt he'd just delivered his knockout blow and was giving us a chance to appreciate it, then he checked his watch and announced, 'I must go.'

Realising I had no way of receiving a link, he pulled out a drawer and started hunting through until he produced an old appointments card and wrote the details on the back. 'I can fit you in on the weekend.'

We said our goodbyes and declined the offer of a lift back to the security gate. Lena was still surprisingly mute, despite him repeating his more optimistic prognosis. Plainly she had her doubts about the guy, and in a way, I could see why. He was certainly smooth, but there was this suspicion that he saw her as nothing more than an intriguing specimen.

'Clancy?' she said, as we neared the gate.

'What?'

'It's out of the question, you know that, don't you?'

'Why?'

'We don't have any money!' she repeated. 'No matter how little it costs—'

'It's not a problem.'

'You wanna run that by me again?'

'We can get money.'

'How?'

I didn't answer, mainly 'cuz I'd been thinking about it all night and still hadn't come up with anything that resembled a solution.

'I'll adjust,' she told me firmly. 'Once we find somewhere to settle and I get to know it, I'll be just fine.'

'Why should you have to if you can see again?'

We made it to the security gate and had our bracelets removed before we were allowed to leave.

'You heard what he said. There's a good chance,' I persisted, as we walked away.

'Clancy,' she begged, 'just leave it, huh?'

But of course, I couldn't, not for long. Later, back at the church, I waited for my moment, then told the others. It wasn't exactly fair: I knew they'd be on my side and start pressuring her. I guess I was just hoping that weight of numbers would eventually tell.

Sure enough, they all got stuck into her, telling her that even if there was only a *one* per cent chance, she should grab it.

'We don't have the money!' she cried, yet again.

'We'll get some!' Delilah reassured her.

'How?'

Delilah looked at Jimmy and the little guy at me. Instantly I cut Gordie and Arturo off before they could start going on about robbing a bank again. That whole interchange must've occurred a dozen times in various different versions, but it always died at the same point – with no one having the slightest idea how we could get our hands on *any* money, let alone something approaching ten grand.

Tell the truth, I didn't know what to do. The one person you'd think would be most enthusiastic about the idea, who had everything to gain, was the one dead set against it. Several times she reassured me she was perfectly happy the way she was, that it was just her new surroundings making her insecure. In fact, she was so persuasive, I almost got to believing her. It was only later, waking up and finding her crying beside me, that I realised how she really felt.

She hadn't been showing any enthusiasm 'cuz she couldn't bear to get her hopes up and be disappointed. We had no money – and even if we did manage to get some, the operation wasn't guaranteed. It was easier for her to cope with what she had, to go on as she was.

I pulled her towards me and kissed away those tears, tasting their salty sadness on my lips. I'd gone over and over this a million times and I could think of only one way of coming up with the money. It was madness – in fact, it was damn near laughable – but it was all I had.

I was gonna have to come out of retirement and find myself one last job.

CHAPTER FIVE

The following morning I was awakened by this commotion up-top, a lot of screaming and whooping. I struggled out of the sleeping bag and went up to investigate. I was immediately confronted by the apartment block across the street burning away like a billboard for Hades. Flames were leaping into the air so high they disappeared into the smoke, feeding into the general fug; occasionally exploding out in bright orange unfurling ribbons.

Jimmy and the kids were already up there; Gordie, Arturo and even Hanna were letting out squeals of delight every time there was a new eruption, as if they were watching a fireworks display or something, whilst Jimmy just looked on, a puzzled frown on his face.

'That ain't normal,' he told me, his old eyes bloodshot from the smoke.

'So you keep saying,' I commented absently, my thoughts still locked on finding a job and getting some money.

'Something causes that.'

I nodded, watching as a tongue of flame suddenly shot in our direction, invading the churchyard. He was right: it wasn't normal. Then again, what was, these days?

'Listen, Jimmy,' I muttered, making sure the kids couldn't hear, 'I gotta go somewhere.'

'Well, don't look at me,' he said, mindful of the fact that Infinity had put a price on his head.

'No, I mean, alone.'

He stared at me, only then appreciating just how worried I was. 'Where?'

'It don't matter,' I replied, glancing behind me, checking Lena hadn't followed me up, 'but . . . listen, you know, if for any reason I don't come back . . . take care of Lena, won't you?'

'Whoa! Big Guy!' he said.

'No, no, it's nothing,' I told him, pulling him a little further away. 'It's just in case.'

'Where you going?'

I paused for a moment, then sighed. 'Places I haven't been in a long, long time.'

'Where?' he persisted, but I refused to tell him. 'I don't like this, Big Guy. Not cool. Not cool at all.'

'Jimmy,' I groaned, getting a little impatient.

'Okay, okay—'

'Just look out for her . . . It'll be fine.' I gave a bit of a sigh, wanting to change the subject, to make out it really wasn't that serious. 'You looked at that screen?'

'You're kidding, right?' he asked.

'Why not?'

Jimmy shook his head in that infuriating way he has when he thinks the answer should be obvious even to a preoccupied two-year-old.

'The reason I didn't want Lile to turn it on was nothing to do with *me*,' he said, pausing to emphasise my ignorance. 'You know why they don't know who I am? That even with a photo they still can't identify me?'

I shrugged, wishing he'd just say it instead of going through the usual humiliating exercise of trying to wring it out of me.

'It's 'cuz we're "non-people". You seen what happens when we pass a screen or get on the moving sidewalk . . . *nada!* We dropped off the database long ago. No one ever dreamed Islanders would ever come back. For all intents and purposes we no longer exist. It's our one great advantage, and the last thing we should do is give them any kind of information – if we turn on something stolen, it might put a search program in operation. So, no cells, no GPS, no pacemaker or implants, nothing that would help them identify us.'

'So the screen's no good?'

He shrugged. 'If I can get hold of a couple of things, make some modifications, then maybe.'

Just at that moment, Lena came up the steps. At first she looked a little put out that I hadn't returned to her and our sleeping bag, but as soon as she smelled the smoke and felt the heat of the fire opposite, she forgot all about it.

'That's close.'

'Yeah, and big,' I agreed. 'I might take a look round the back. See what's behind all those brambles. Maybe we'll need another way out of here. Should've done it before – in case of unexpected visitors.'

'Good idea,' she said, sounding like she was planning on coming with me.

'Only trouble is, those damn things are gonna rip me to pieces,' I told her, making it sound as if it would be impossible for *me* to get through, let alone someone who couldn't see.

Actually, it was the perfect alibi. I could explore out back where the undergrowth was thickest and hopefully find somewhere to hop over the wall. Later, when I returned – presuming nothing had prevented me – I'd just say it had taken me longer than I thought, that I'd gone on to check out the immediate area.

As it turned out, my comment that the brambles might rip me to pieces wasn't that far off the truth. Several times I thought I'd found a way through, only to come up against a massed army of razor-sharp needles. My new parka got ripped up good and proper before I finally managed to reach this empty space up against the wall, Nature's no-man's land, all brown and quiet, where the sun wasn't able to reach.

The only problem was, the wall out back was considerably higher than the ones at the front and sides of the churchyard. I worked my way along it, looking for somewhere to get over, and was almost on the point of giving up when, right down in the far corner, I came across this tree that had fallen across it, creating a fairly precarious bridge.

Twenty years ago I would've been up and over there in a matter of seconds; now it was more like negotiating the tricky side of Everest. Nevertheless, I finally managed to make it to the top and found myself looking into an abandoned builder's yard – or maybe even something a bit more specialised, like a stonemason's. I slid awkwardly down the other side, trying to make my landing as gentle as possible, but still collided with the ground with a real thump. I picked myself up, made sure nothing was broken, and soldiered on into the acrid gloom.

I really didn't know that city any more. It wasn't so much that it had changed – though, of course, it had – more that we didn't recognise each other. Okay, so the last time I saw it, it wasn't enveloped in smoke, there weren't fires everywhere, all this chaos and destruction, but it wasn't just that. It's like when you bump into an old friend you haven't seen for a long time and now you can't remember what you were to each other, how your relationship used to work. And the further I went in the direction of the old neighbourhood, the more familiar the surroundings became, the less comfortable I felt. Mind you, bearing in mind what I was planning on doing, I guess that wasn't so surprising.

If it hadn't been so desperate, it would've been funny – me, nigh-on a senior citizen, hoping to get back into the muscle business. I guess I did work out on the Island a little, and yeah, no matter what, I'm still a big guy – but unless someone was planning on putting the frighteners on the residents of the local old folks' home, it was hard to see what job I'd get.

Not that that was my only concern about being back in the old neighbourhood. I'm a pretty peaceful guy these days, but working in the business I did, you're gonna make yourself enemies – you're bound to, once you've sworn loyalty to one particular gang. I could think of several people over there I wouldn't want to run into. Mind you, it was a long time ago, and I could only hope that most of them had moved on – in one way or another. Or maybe, like me, they'd got a bit more forgiving in their old age.

I'd been going over and over it: the people I could look up, those who might help, and I gotta say, it was one helluva short list. There were a couple of guys I reckon would've been there for me, but they had to be dead, or near as damn it. In fact, the more I thought about it, the more I realised my only real chance was the First Original Sushi Bar.

Bankers probably have a favourite bar where they collect, cabbies a café, but anyone involved in crime in this city, certainly when I was living here, ended up in the First Original. It was partly the food, partly the location, but mostly, I think, the owner. Yoshi was the perfect guy for that sort of operation: welcoming, agreeable, kept his ears open and his mouth shut and occasionally even acted as broker, putting client and criminal together – usually the younger ones, those who hadn't found a gang yet, out to make a name for themselves, or even the occasional freelancer who, for one reason or another, liked to work alone.

Can't tell you how relieved I was to see it still there, a little older, in need of a lick of paint, but as I drew closer, I could see the usual gang of young hopefuls hanging around inside. There were a lot more women than there used to be, which, as an old-fashioned guy, I didn't feel entirely comfortable about, but I guess that's just the way it is now.

I entered hesitantly. Even in a place like that, where no one stares at anyone, a lot of people were staring at me. I hoped it was only out of curiosity and not remembering some age-old grudge, but after taking a quick look around, I realised it was unlikely anyone there would have a problem with me – there wasn't a soul within thirty years of my age. I heard a couple of comments about my appearance and smell but just kept my head low and made for the bar, which meant Yoshi was able to sneak up on me.

'How are you, sir?' he cried, suddenly standing in front of me with that big beaming smile of his. 'How *are* you?'

He'd gone a bit grey and put on a lot of weight, but he was still wearing those crazy game glasses he liked so much, and I gotta say, I was really pleased to see him.

'You remember me?' I asked, with some surprise.

'Of course!' he said, beckoning me over to a stool at the bar.

I sat, feeling cripplingly uncomfortable as people looked over as if a mangy stray had just been offered a bowl of something expensive.

Apart from the clientele, nothing much had changed; like the outside it'd just got a little older and less shiny. The same conveyor belt was clicking and clacking its way round, tempting the customers, but its progress was a lot jerkier now, at times threatening to throw the food onto the floor.

'You escape from the Island, sir?' Yoshi asked, going behind the bar and standing in front of me.

I took my time answering – I mean, he used to be a good guy, but who knew how this place worked now. 'Yeah,' I eventually replied. 'We all did.'

Almost as if he thought I deserved it, he immediately gave me a couple of plates off the belt, amazingly, after all that time, still remembering my rather conservative taste: a slice of fresh salmon on plain rice, a little soy and hold the wasabi.

'I don't have any money, Yoshi,' I told him.

'Next time,' he said, again with a beaming smile.

I devoured what he gave me almost before his hand had retreated to the far side of the counter. Bearing in mind what I'd been eating, especially over on the Island, a couple of plates of sushi was a helluva luxury. 'Wow,' I said, my mouth exploding with delight.

'Good, huh?'

'You said it . . . Actually, Yoshi,' I went on, thinking I might as well get this over with, 'money's why I'm here. I badly need some. Like *really* badly.'

To my surprise, he didn't look shocked, nor did he burst into laughter, but that might have had something to do with him coming from a culture that's always been well versed in hiding emotions.

'Ten grand,' I continued.

'Not a lot of money these days,' he commented.

'It is to me, more than you can ever imagine.'

He stared into my face. I think he realised just how desperate I was, but it never seemed to cross his mind to ask why. 'What do you want to do?'

'No killing.'

He nodded his head. 'Let me think,' he said, taking a few dirty glasses off the bar and stacking them ready to be washed.

A few moments later, two guys in suits sauntered in with 'something sinister' woven into their pinstripes. At the far end of the bar there was a stampede to vacate what were obviously their usual stools. They were so young there was no fear of them knowing who I was, but I have to admit, I felt that bit intimidated myself. The bigger guy – Afro-Caribbean, a diamond stud in his ear – ran his eyes round the room, going from one face to the next, stopping when he got to me.

'What's wrong with him?' I muttered to Yoshi.

'Oh, you're new,' he whispered out of the corner of his mouth. 'Nothing to worry about.'

He immediately went off to greet the two men, to give them the big hello: shaking their hands, pouring complimentary drinks, while I just quietly sat checking out those around me. With their sharp clothes and cool haircuts they couldn't have contrasted more with my reflection in the mirror on the far side of the room if they'd wanted to. Despite my efforts at tidying myself up when I went to find a doc for Lena, I still looked like a wild man. No wonder I'd attracted so much interest when I walked in. Mind you, it wouldn't harm my ability to put the frighteners on someone. As I ran my eyes along the bar, person after person averted their gaze – until I got to Yoshi and his two new companions. They were looking over, obviously in discussion about me.

A few moments later, Yoshi returned. 'Maybe I have a job,' he muttered, making sure no one overheard.

'Yeah?'

'Not so difficult, but delicate: letting someone know they're not wanted any more, time to move on.'

'Okay,' I said. It sounded a little odd, but I was grateful for anything. I also realised that Yoshi must've vouched for me.

'They'll take you to their boss.'

'Sorry?'

'The client.'

I frowned at him, now not understanding. If they had a boss and there was a job, why weren't they doing it? 'Who is it?'

Yoshi gave me that fixed smile I remembered so well and I nodded my head, knowing I shouldn't have asked.

For some time I just sat there, waiting for the two guys to finish eating, wondering what the hell I was getting myself into. Why would these two need someone else to put the frighteners on? The big guy was as tall as me but probably weighed twenty or thirty pounds more – and it wasn't fat, either. His companion, a sharp-faced little Latino, looked as if he killed people all day just for fun.

Eventually, they finished – no bill, I noticed – and made their way to the door, giving me the slightest of nods to indicate that I should follow.

Out in the street I saw them get into this big black limo. I think you must have to have some kind of permit to drive in the City now. You see plenty of official cars, Infinity vehicles, public transport, but I just realised private autos were few and far between. Which means whoever I was dealing with had influence.

They started the motor before I could get to them and slid down the road forty or fifty yards. I guessed they didn't want anyone in the First Original seeing me getting in their vehicle. I caught them up and the big guy opened the back door, neither of them responding to my muted greeting. The Latino floored his foot almost before my ass touched the seat.

74

Being driven through the smoke-filled streets of the City was to truly appreciate what kind of world we'd come back to. We went for block after block and there was nothing, just islands of burnt debris with ash swirling around them, blackening people's faces and clothes. Occasionally we were forced to make a detour, even turn around once or twice, as fires exploded into the sky before us. You wanna talk about Hell? The City fitted the description perfectly. And to think I'd once believed nothing could be worse than the Island.

The other thing it was impossible to ignore was the number of zombie-sick around. I don't know what percentage of the population they represented, but in some areas they were obviously the majority. They looked so weak that even the effort of stretching one foot in front of the other was too much for them; I watched one slowly move his leg forward and hit the ground, looking as if he thought his foot might break. I also couldn't help but notice that a lot of the 'authority' figures, even everyday Specials, were wearing masks like the camera guy in the supermarket had, presumably to protect them from contracting 'zombie-sickness'.

But all this was no more than a backdrop to what was going through my head: I'd jumped at the chance of this job partly 'cuz I'd feared it was the only one I'd be offered, but now I was starting to wonder if I'd been a little too hasty. Who knew who these two worked for? I hadn't met anyone from the old days, but that didn't mean they weren't around, and actually, when I stopped and thought about it, there were some worrying possibilities. If I'd wanted the money for any other reason but Lena's operation, I wouldn't have gone anywhere near this.

When we arrived at the house of the client, I felt even more uneasy. It was massive and forbidding, with two huge and hungry-looking dogs patrolling the garden. Whoever I'd come to see was obviously someone feared and respected.

For the second time since returning to the Mainland, I was escorted in through the tradesmen's entrance; through the kitchen to a hallway, where I waited while the bigger guy went to talk to his boss.

He didn't make any attempt to lower his voice. I heard him quite clearly making a joke at my expense, saying I was just the man for the job, that I'd frighten the hell out of anyone.

There was a pause while I waited for the boss' reaction, to hear what he had to say.

'Okay. Bring him in.'

In that moment, it felt as if a sinkhole opened up inside me, that all my insides were sucked down into it. *No* . . . It couldn't be—

CHAPTER SIX

It says a lot that I hadn't thought about him, hadn't so much as mentioned his name, in more than ten years. I mean, the way things have been, all that time the satellites were in control, I thought he would've moved on, maybe even died, but obviously not.

It's a weird thing having a half-brother, especially when he's the only family you've got. It's the part you don't know that makes you distrust him, and the part you do that confirms your suspicions. I was thirteen before I even knew he existed. He just came up to me one day in the street, leant right into my face and sneered, 'Hey, I'm your big brother.' I didn't have a clue what he was talking about. He was quite a lot older than me, and twenty or thirty pounds heavier, and shit to admit, pretty intimidating. I didn't know what to say, ended up just shrugging and walking on, hoping he wouldn't follow. The next thing I knew I was flat out on the ground, blood pouring from my forehead, with him on top of me yelling about showing my 'big brother' respect.

I thought he was crazy – an escaped inmate from the local nut-house, until I got home and told Ma, who immediately went all quiet and thoughtful on me. She headed off to her bedroom and I realised there was more to this than I'd imagined.

I never saw the old man as the cheating kind – the beating kind, sure, the bitter-and-twisted kind and, on the odd occasion, the joking and crooning kind, but then again, if you get drunk that often, I guess at some point you're gonna be just about every kind going. Turned out he'd had his fair share of affairs, most of them no more than a block or two from our home. He was never the most energetic of individuals, couldn't be bothered to play further away – perhaps he preferred to save his strength for lovemaking. During that period, he managed to father a couple of kids with different mothers. Ma never actually knew what was going on, not for certain, though for sure she had her suspicions, but she decided just to turn a deaf ear to all the whispering. After he died, it became even more important to her that she didn't *know*, that she didn't have her whole life undermined. It was my misfortune to unknowingly put an end to all that make-believe.

I don't know what it was about Ray, maybe he had a hang-up about being illegitimate, but once he'd introduced himself – once he'd started to terrorise and torture me – he just wouldn't stop.

Every day on my way home he would catch me somewhere and give me a good beating. It got so bad you could actually follow the trail of blood on the sidewalk to my home. But, no matter what he did, how hard or often he hit me, I always tried to get him back, feeling that bit better if I could get in one good shot, maybe even give him the suspicion of a bruise. Though that was a problem too: if I did, it just made him even more angry, even more vicious.

I stuck it for a while, in the way you often do when you're a kid, 'cuz you think you got no choice, then one day I got these books from the library, 'bout working out and different martial arts and stuff. It took me almost two months before I finally managed to nail him. That afternoon, I used this move I'd been working on over and over and not only dumped him on his ass but gave him a black eye too – a real big, bright purple shiner. 'course, he went crazy, beating me up so bad I had to go to hospital, but at least I had a brief moment of revenge.

The only problem then was, how was he going to react? The next time I saw him, was he going to maintain this new level of fury? 'cuz I gotta tell you, I wasn't sure I could take it, not on a regular basis. A couple of days later he brought a friend with him and they beat me up good and proper – split my lip, blacked both eyes, cracked my ribs – but, do you know something? It didn't matter. In fact, I almost smiled my way through it, you know, 'cuz I knew I had him, that if he needed a friend to help him deal with me now, it could only be a matter of time.

I can't tell you how sweet my eventual revenge was, the day I left him lying unconscious on this patch of waste ground, still cursing him as I walked away, even though he couldn't hear me.

I didn't see him again for ten years and by then I was working for Mr Meltoni, learning the tricks of the trade, running some pretty sweet little numbers, or so I thought. Though actually, at that age, you're not really thinking, just enjoying the ride.

There's only one problem with being top dog – there's always someone sniffing around, baring their teeth, wanting to take a piece out of you.

We got to hear about this new gang moving into the area, real mean sons of bitches, prepared to do anything to get themselves a reputation. They carried out a couple of high-profile killings – well, more like massacres really, taking out Mr Meltoni's clients' restaurants as well as the customers who happened to be in them. But it wasn't that that upset so many people, it was Francesca Cassano. She was only five, cute as hell, the daughter of a banker. They kidnapped her, and when he didn't come up with the ransom fast enough, hung her from the bridge over the expressway for everyone to see. In fact, the suspicion was that they never intended to nego- tiate, that all they really wanted to do was enhance their bad-ass reputations.

When we found out who was to blame, I was pretty sickened to hear Ray Ormerod's name – I mean, no one was sure who'd *actu- ally* done the deed, but I knew that son of a bitch well enough to know he was capable. In no time, a turf war broke out; they'd take out one of ours, we'd take out two of theirs and vice versa. It could've gone on forever if Mr Meltoni hadn't come up with this really smart plan. He knew their boss, 'Frenchie' Martin, had a few horses and that he doted on this one in particular – Dancing Boy. He really loved that animal; nothing was too good for it. It had a stable a dozen Detainees would've been proud to call home. If it'd been Dancing *Girl*, I reckon he would've slept with it every night.

Mr Meltoni managed to get one of their stable boys and have Dancing Boy poisoned – 'course, it wasn't that that was so clever, it was knowing how Frenchie would react. He was heartbroken and insisted on a massive funeral for the horse, with all the pomp and ceremony of a king or president. The only thing was, that same stable boy scooped out some of Dancing Boy's insides and stuck a bomb in there.

You ain't ever seen anything like it. There was this special grave- yard up in the hills, complete with church and properly ordained minister, for the pets of very rich owners, and every one of Frenchie's guys was ordered to turn up to say goodbye to Dancing Boy. It needed a dozen of his strongest, including Frenchie himself, to act as coffin bearers.

Mr Meltoni detonated the bomb from his limo up on the highway. There was the most almighty explosion, this loud *kerrump!* and, not to put it too indelicately, body parts flew everywhere, horse, human, who knew? God knows how they put them all back together, how they divided things up for all the funerals that followed. Maybe they didn't bother, just did it by weight.

It became a bit of a joke round the neighbourhood – horsemeat salad and French dressing – yeah, I know, not exactly in the best of taste, but that's how we people are, we like to make jokes about death, to prove it don't really frighten us.

We thought that would be an end to it, but it's times like that, when there's a power vacuum, that those not prepared to do the work to fulfil their ambitions sometimes seize the initiative.

It didn't take him long. Within six weeks, Ray – who, at the moment the bomb went off, had been behind the church taking a leak – took over what little remained of Frenchie's operation. A year later no one was mentioning Frenchie Martin any more; it'd become Big Ray's gang. And yet, to my surprise and I guess, his credit, he didn't return to the path of confrontation; he let it be known he wanted to talk to Mr Meltoni.

I had no choice but to go along and listen to their discussions, to see that piece of shit try to elevate himself to the same level as my boss, my only comfort being that I was sure Mr Meltoni would put him in his place.

But do you know something? Crime is just another business. When it comes to making money, to doing the right thing for the 'company', people are prepared to overlook anything. It's the same with politics. International relations, beliefs and morality are one thing, but money always speaks a damn sight louder. People will lie down with anyone and forget all manner of evils and atrocities as long as there's something in it for them.

They worked out a deal where they could focus their energies on taking care of their individual businesses and not on trying to kill each other: Mr Meltoni let Ray have the parts of the City he never really got to grips with – places like Chinatown, where he felt cultural differences made it too difficult – and from then on, they became the best of friends – well, like I said, this is business, so they *acted* like the best of friends. Nevertheless, there was no choice but for me to go along with it, to occasionally welcome Ray and his boys to Mr Meltoni's home, even pour him drinks and stuff.

You can imagine how much he enjoyed that – how he went out of his way to humiliate me whenever he could. I never told Mr Meltoni he was my half-brother, I mean, as far as I was concerned, he wasn't; I would've denied it to anyone, God himself couldn't have tortured it outta me.

The last time I saw him was when Mr Meltoni died, right after the funeral. He approached me in the parking lot, came over to offer me a job; said it would show continuity, that his rivals would be less likely to wage war against him if I was involved.

I don't think he believed me when I said I'd had enough, that I was going straight. Maybe he thought I had ideas of my own, or perhaps he was just incensed at me having the gall to turn him down. One way or another, he got really ugly, telling me I was too stupid to do anything else, that I had no education, no other experience, that I'd end up on the street. Which, did he but know it, turned out to be right on the button. That was the reason I got sent out to the Island – but I'd still rather have what I had over there than carry on living the life of a criminal.

In the end I just turned and walked away from him, like I did that first time we met, leaving him screaming after me, cursing me from the window of his limo as he was driven away, telling me that if I didn't join him, I was against him, and I'd be taken care of.

I never saw him again. Not from that day to this.

*

I thought about turning round and running out of there, getting away from that place as fast as I could, but I guess I hoped I was wrong, that after all those years how could I possibly be sure it was his voice?

I was beckoned into this rather palatial room, all gilt-edged this and velvet that, and in the middle of it, like some unwelcome sore denying the existence of all beauty, sat this huge old man I instantly recognised.

He looked utterly grotesque, slumped in this wing-backed chair, his heavy chin on his chest, a few strands of long, greasy hair flopped across a flaky scalp – a comb-over he'd given up on long ago. His complexion was so red he looked like he was covered in a rash. But none of this mattered in comparison with the leg he had propped up before him. You wouldn't have believed the size of it: it was like some monstrous bandaged mummy. I could see his left leg was also swollen, but the right one was almost twice its size.

I just stood there, waiting, knowing my appearance, the changes over the years, could only hide me from him for a few seconds. It was almost comic: one moment he was staring at me like I was a cross between a curio and a clown; the next this expression had collapsed to be replaced by recognition.

'*What the fuck*, Van?' he yelled.

The Afro-Caribbean guy looked at the door, as if he thought someone else had come in. 'What's the matter?'

'Is this who you brought me?'

'Yeah.'

'*Jesus!*'

'I thought he was perfect—'

'What the fuck do you want?' Ray demanded, turning on me.

'A job,' I said simply, deciding to bluff it out.

'You gotta be kidding.'

There was a long silence, no one quite knowing how to react, Ray expelling these grunty little noises while he tried to collect himself.

'You said someone unknown who looked like he'd frighten the hell out of anyone,' the Afro-Caribbean guy protested.

'Fucking idiot!' Ray snarled. He paused for a moment, staring at me, taking in my appearance. 'What the hell happened to you? Where you been?'

'Around.'

'You stink,' he said, wrinkling up his nose as if he'd just caught his first whiff of me.

I never said anything, but a look came into his eyes and I knew he'd worked it out. 'You're an escaped Detainee!' he exclaimed.

I didn't deny it, which was all the proof he needed.

'All this time you been out on the Island!'

'So?'

'Jesus!' he cried, somehow managing to heave the many folds of his face into a twisted smile. 'You ended up on the Island! After all those high-and-mighty words! Best news I had in years.'

To my surprise, he started to laugh, this kind of sickening gurgling, like he was rolling rocks round in his throat, and his two guys, plainly relieved to see it, joined in.

'What happened to your legs?' I asked.

He immediately stopped, glaring at his propped-up leg as if it was something alien to him. 'Rotting,' he told me. 'Rotting and poisonous. One day they reckon they might swell up so much they explode.'

'Isn't there anything they can do?'

He shook his head. 'It's not just my legs – it's taking over my whole body. Nothing can stop it. Germs have developed a resistance to our resistance. Less than twenty-five per cent of antibiotics work now.'

'I'm sorry,' I said, with very little conviction.

'Sure you are,' he said, adjusting his leg.

There was a pause in which I realised that was probably as civil as either of us was going to get, and if I had something to say, it had better be now. 'Whatever this job, I promise you, it'll be done to your satisfaction. All I want is ten grand.'

Yoshi might've thought it wasn't a lot of money in this day and age, but Ray wasn't happy about it at all. Though whether that was 'cuz he thought it was too much, or 'cuz he didn't want to pay it to me, I don't know.

'I know I'm older, and . . . yeah, we had our problems, but at least you know I do things right.'

He paused for a moment, taking in a lungful of ragged air and expelling it, apparently giving it some thought.

'After all, business is business,' I added.

He nodded as if I'd just cited a universal truth that no one could deny. Or maybe it was more that he wanted the job done urgently and I was just right for it. 'You look the part, that's for sure,' he said begrudgingly. 'Seen better-looking things crawl out of my ass.' He laughed at his own joke, as did Van, the Afro-Caribbean minder. I even smiled myself, just to keep things moving along.

Eventually he sighed and gestured to Van to pass me a photo. 'There's this guy, bothering someone I used to know, making a real nuisance of himself. I want him to leave her alone.'

I immediately understood what it was all about – an ex had got herself a new man. Ray couldn't have her any more and didn't want anyone else to either. He wanted whoever it was frightened off, but just in case they ever told her, it couldn't come from him, or from anyone known to associate with him. It had to be utterly anonymous – which was why they'd made sure no one saw me get in the limo.

'I don't want him dead,' Ray insisted, though obviously with a degree of reluctance. 'Fucking bitch'll only blame me. I want him out of the picture, but still visible.'

'Okay.'

'Give him the address,' he told Van.

I was out of there five minutes later, barely able to believe my luck. Of all people, Ray would've been last on my list – and yet, just like when Mr Meltoni made peace with him, we'd come to an arrangement. He still hated me, he made that plain, telling me never to go to his house again, that I'd stunk it out, to collect my money from Yoshi. But when all was said and done, I could be useful to him – and business is business.

Out in the street, I took a look at the address they'd given me and realised it wasn't that far away. I could go down there and check it out – if the guy was around, maybe even get it over with: go back to Yoshi's, collect my money, and with a bit of luck be home by nightfall.

Just the thought made me pick up my pace. I was feeling pretty pleased with myself now; after all, when I'd set out that morning, I hadn't known what to expect. As it turned out, it couldn't have gone better.

What is it they say about pride before a fall? The job turned out to be a complete fiasco. Ray's ex's lover lived in one of those fancy apartment blocks down by the river: I managed to sneak in with a furniture delivery, went up-top and just knocked on his door. I had no idea what I was going to say, only that I was going to be highly persuasive and get it over with as quickly as possible. If I could get the money that night, Lena and me could be on our way to Dr Simon's in the morning.

I don't know who the guy was expecting – Ray's ex, I guess – 'cuz he came to the door with a rose between his teeth, an open bottle of champagne and an even more open dressing gown, showing off something his woman might've wanted to see, but I sure as hell didn't.

And, of course, I wasn't exactly what he expected to be confronted by either: this wild, hairy Sasquatch blocking out the light. He tried to slam the door but I already had my foot in it so he ran to the bathroom and locked himself in. I beat on the door, ordered him to come out, and when he wouldn't, gave him my lecture through it – telling him exactly what I'd do to him if he didn't leave this woman alone, that he wouldn't be displaying his wares at anyone else in the future, and if he told her – or anyone else – about my visit, all this would be as nothing compared to my retribution.

I don't know, maybe I overdid it, I was a bit rusty, after all. It seemed about right at the time, but somewhere amongst what I said he must've panicked, 'cuz he climbed out the window and tried to crawl along to the next apartment. Trouble was, he slipped and fell eleven floors to his death, screaming all the way down, trying to get all his life out before he hit the ground. I broke down the door, looked out and saw him lying there and legged it out of that building as fast as I could.

I mean – shit, I hadn't wanted that, not for one moment. Anyone who'd taken Ray's woman couldn't be all bad. It also presented me with a real dilemma: did I do the job right or not? For sure, the guy wasn't gonna be making whoopee with Ray's ex any more. On the other hand – and ironically, 'cuz I didn't want to anyway – I was told 'no killing'.

I guess the point was, I *didn't* kill him. It was an accident. So maybe Ray would regard it as the best of both worlds.

In the end, I decided to just go back to the First Original and say the job was done, that Ray's 'friend' wouldn't be bothered by the guy again and leave it at that. They didn't need to know the details, just that it was taken care of.

Yoshi was astonished when I walked back in – I'd only left a couple of hours before, after all. The good thing was that my reputation obviously still lingered, 'cuz when I told him the job was done, he was more than happy to take my word for it.

'No problems?'

'Nope.'

He disappeared out back, and returned a few minutes later with a takeaway carton. 'Something for you,' he said, with a big smile.

I squashed the carton into my backpack, accepted a complimentary glass of sake and sipped it as he wiped tables. I actually wanted to get going but felt that would be rude. Outside, the smoke continued to ghost past and as I watched, a couple ran by on the other side of the street, disappearing into the murk. Seconds later a gang appeared, apparently chasing after them.

'What the hell happened to this place, Yoshi?' I asked.

He stopped what he was doing and turned to me. 'You were better off on the Island.'

It was weird; that was the very last sentiment I'd expected to hear from anyone once I got back; now I was hearing it all the time.

'Why?'

He shrugged. 'The world coming to an end maybe.'

I waited for him to say more, to explain, but he didn't. 'Are you serious?'

'Everything is burning, everyone is sick, the crazy people have taken over. What else can it be?'

'What crazy people?'

He grunted, like I had a lot to learn. 'You'll find out,' he said. 'One night when they come for you.'

No matter how pleased I was about what I had tucked away in my backpack, how eager to give Lena the news, I still gotta bit of a shock when I finally struggled across the fallen tree and made it back into the churchyard. It was late and I thought the others might've been starting to worry, but as it turned out, they'd had distractions of their own.

I don't know whether she'd been trying to prove a point or what, but Lena had gone out with the kids – not so far, just across the road and down a couple of side streets, but they'd brought back a few odd bits and pieces: chewy bars, soda, sticky tape for some reason – I don't know, I guess they just grabbed what they could. The other thing they'd brought back, which, it turned out, had been the reason for their trip, was scissors and a razor.

The kids were all sitting round up-top, enjoying the last of what had apparently been quite a show. Somehow Delilah had managed to convince Jimmy that a ponytail on a man with barely ten per cent of his head covered in hair was distinctly 'uncool', that a shaven head would suit him better.

'Whoa! Who's this young whippersnapper?' I joked.

'Everyone needs a change of image now and then, Big Guy,' he told me proudly. 'You should try it.'

'Yeah. I'll give it some thought,' I said dryly. 'Where's Lena?'

Delilah gestured to the crypt. After exchanging private little smirks with the kids I made my way down and found her sorting through our food, trying to work out how much longer it would last.

'I was beginning to wonder where you were,' she said.

I never said a word, just walked up and put the takeaway carton in her hands. She frowned and fumbled with it for a moment, finally getting it open.

'What is it?' she asked.

'What does it feel like?'

She put her hand in and knew immediately what it was. '*Clancy!* Where'd you get it?'

'Does it matter?'

She paused, as if not sure what to say. 'Yes . . .'

'From a guy I used to know,' I told her, knowing that if she thought her operation had been bought at the cost of me committing a crime or putting myself in danger, she wouldn't be happy.

'What for?' she demanded.

In the end I told her the whole story, even about Ray being my half-brother, and the unfortunate accident.

'What's he gonna say?' she asked.

'Don't matter. I got the dough.'

'He might come after you.'

'Yeah – amongst all this madness, a sick old man who can't walk is gonna find us down here,' I joked. 'I did his job.'

She was plainly concerned, but I suspected it was more than that: that fear of the operation and what it might mean was already starting to set in.

'In the morning we'll go and see Dr Simon,' I told her.

'What if it doesn't work?'

'We go on as we are now.'

'You won't be disappointed?'

I put my arms around her and gave her a hug. 'Only for you,' I told her.

I don't know what time I woke up; we'd gone to bed early, but I couldn't have been asleep that long. There was this noise some way off, over in the direction of the centre: a kind of rhythmic rumbling echoing into the night, like the clatter of machinery, and yet it covered such a wide area, as if a major part of the City was vibrating. It went through my head that it was an earthquake, but then I heard something else even more disconcerting: this massed chorus of shouting. How far away it was, I don't know, but I didn't get the impression that whoever was making it was being pursued – more like they were doing the pursuing.

'What is it?' Lena asked. The insistent pounding rhythm and the deep, ground-shaking pulsation plainly unnerving her even more than me.

'I dunno.'

We both lay there, silent and still, holding our breath, unable to make any sense of what we were hearing and all the more disturbed 'cuz of it.

Eventually I couldn't take it any longer, I got up and stumbled over to the steps, Lena not far behind me.

Arturo's sleepy voice came to us from out of the darkness. 'What is it?' he mumbled.

'It's nothing. Go back to sleep,' Lena whispered.

Once outside, I realised that whatever it was wasn't as far away as I first thought. It's hard to tell in the City, especially with the persistent blanket of smoke deadening everything down, but I guessed not much more than half a mile.

Still it continued at the same pitch, this insistent rhythm: *thump-thump-thump! thump-thump-thump!* The mass yelling now interspersed with the occasional scream. And just for a moment I got the impression that it was moving, spreading through the City like an army on the march.

I turned to Lena. The soft smoky glow of the continuing fire across the street just enough for me to see how worried she looked.

'I never heard anything like that before,' she said. 'What the hell is it?'

As if in answer, there was the sudden sound of gunfire – a couple of single shots, and then, as if whoever else was involved had been waiting for that signal, a huge, seemingly never-ending volley, dozens of weapons being repeatedly fired.

Jimmy came hurrying up the steps, followed by Gordie and Hanna. 'What's going on?' he cried, as if he thought it might have something to do with him, that Infinity were closing in.

'Beats me,' I said. 'But I don't like the sound of it.'

There was another massive discharge of weapons, a sporadic spluttering of loud shots crackling across the night, and Jimmy looked even more frightened.

'Sounds like a war,' Gordie said.

'You need two sides for a war,' Hanna commented, and then, as if she couldn't bear it a moment longer, that it only confirmed what she'd said, that this place *was* worse than the Island, she turned and went back down to the crypt.

Course, she was right: it ain't a war if no one's firing back, and by the sound of it, this was another massacre: Infinity shooting looters again. And yet, I had this nagging feeling there was more to it than that, and that difference was really unsettling me.

It went on for quite a while; the repeated beating and baying like some battle tactic designed to put the fear of God into the enemy, followed by the occasional crackle of gunfire; 'til, when it finally started to die down, Lena decided she'd also had enough and went back to bed. Jimmy gave a sigh of relief that it wasn't coming our way, muttered something about Lile probably having seized the chance to get Arturo into their sleeping bag and followed on behind, leaving me alone with Gordie.

For a while he just sat there, idly gazing at the fire across the street. 'When can we leave?' he asked.

I turned and looked at him, only then realising it wasn't an issue any more: that even if the fires did die down, I still couldn't go.

'I gotta stay, Gordie – I gotta see if I can help Lena get her sight restored,' I told him. 'You can go – if you can get through. All of you can.'

'Nah,' he said. 'We'll wait.' And as if that put a seal on it, that it was all decided, he also turned and made his way back down the steps.

I smiled to myself as I watched him go. He might be just a kid, but sometimes his simple approach to everything was really reassuring.

I waited another ten minutes or so, just to see if the noise would start up again. When it didn't, I too returned to my sleeping bag: slipping in beside Lena, doing up the zip every last quarter of an inch and putting my arms around her.

I don't know what the hell happened out there, but it'd heightened this feeling that the threat to us was growing by the day. For some reason it reminded me of what Yoshi said earlier, about the crazy people coming for us – and that maybe it wouldn't be much longer.

CHAPTER SEVEN

The following morning, almost at first light, I was up and out. Lena and me were heading up to see Dr Simon later, hopefully for the operation, but first I wanted to know what had gone on the previous night.

If you turned left at the entrance to the churchyard and headed up the hill, you eventually got to Victory Square and all the many streets that led off from there. If you turned right, it was a bit more leafy, more residential, though not the nicest part of town. All the commotion the previous night had been somewhere up near the Square – and even if it hadn't been, it was a pretty good place to pick up a rumour or two.

In fact, I didn't need to ask anyone anything. One of the streets leading off the Square was cordoned off by Specials and I promptly took the next street over and followed it down. Block after block, every time I tried to turn, finding it was still closed off, which was kind of frustrating. I was about to give up and head back to Lena when I saw this empty office building and figured that if I broke in on this side, I should be able to make my way through to the other and maybe get a look at what had gone on.

There was a sturdy chain and padlock clamping the door handles together, but the hinges are generally the weak point and after a few minutes of searching I found a scaffolding pole I used to lever the doors apart.

I went up a couple of flights of stairs and made my way down a long corridor that plainly hadn't been used or cleaned in quite a while. Eventually I found myself in an office on the far side of the building.

I looked out on this sort of pedestrian precinct, with a few potted trees and a lot of benches dotted about. It looked like the sort of place you might eat your packed lunch – but not that day. It was thick with Infinity Specials all busily clearing up, taking stuff away, hosing things down. You didn't have to be a genius to work out why, not with those dark stains everywhere. On the far side there was a line of slightly sinister-looking white trucks: like field ambulances, windowless apart from heavily tinted slatted screens, and as I looked, a body-bag was disappearing into the back of one of them.

So that was it; Infinity had been wielding its iron fist again. And yet, still something didn't feel quite right. This was where the shooting had happened for sure – the buildings were pitted and scarred, windows had been shot out, fires were still burning – but the variety of the damage set me wondering. Normally, if there's a force involved – army, Specials, whatever – you'll see damage caused by two or three types of weapons at the most. But all kinds had been used: I could see the scoring of lasers, the dotted lines of automatic weapons, even the precision of high-powered hunting rifles. What the hell had happened? It looked like some kind of wild come-one, come-all bloodfest.

As I watched I realised there were far too many Specials round for my liking, and who knew what kind of surveillance they'd set up? They could've been scanning the building for life forms at that very moment. The last thing I needed on the day I was taking Lena to the doctor was to get picked up. And taking one last glance out, I quickly hurried away.

A little later, with noticeably few words being exchanged between us, Lena and me were once again making our way through the smoke to the hills, arriving at the security gates and asking them to inform Dr Simon, being made to wear pressure bracelets again, the same disapproving driver coming down to collect us. This time, I gotta say, the doc didn't keep us waiting – in fact his attitude was altogether more friendly, more positive: maybe 'cuz we had the money, 'cuz he realised we were serious about this.

The first thing I did was to insist on paying him, handing over the entire ten grand – well, less a few hundred I kept back for emergencies – even though he told me it wasn't necessary, that he didn't even know what the final cost was going to be. But I just wanted it out of the way, for his staff to know that, no matter how we looked, we paid our bills.

All the tests were really encouraging. He'd matched up a program to her profile and told us he was convinced he could give Lena back partial sight at the least – and that was something he'd never mentioned before. The only disappointing news was that he wanted to keep her in overnight.

'It's a fairly standard operation but the computer needs to monitor her for at least twelve hours, run its checklist,' he told us. 'It's also critical her eyes aren't allowed to dry out. The last thing she needs is to go out in that smoke.'

'Can I stay with her?' I asked.

For a moment he just stared at me, tugging his shirt cuffs out from beneath his jacket sleeves, as if subconsciously wanting everyone to see his gold cufflinks. 'No, Clancy, I'm sorry. She'll need to get all the rest she can.'

'I'll be fine,' Lena said, taking my hand.

'Stay for the operation,' Dr Simon suggested, 'just to put your mind at ease. After that, you'll both need a good night's sleep.'

It took a little bit of rescheduling, but in the end – as good as his word – he booked her in for the final operating slot of the day.

I stayed with her as long as I could, even though as the day wore on neither of us knew what to say. I had no idea what this really meant to her – how could I? I'd never been blind; I didn't know what it was to be in endless darkness, missing all the colours of the rainbow, the sun setting over the sea, the expressions on a child's face. Nor could I begin to imagine the torture of trying to find your way around somewhere utterly unfamiliar, having no idea if you were about to collide with something or what repercussions there might be. And maybe that was the reason why I was even more nervous than she was. For sure, I wasn't helping matters, so when they finally came to tell me to leave, I think both of us were that bit relieved.

I waited out in the corridor, leafing through magazines I didn't have the concentration for, making the situation worse by going to the restroom and catching sight of myself in the mirror.

The next time I saw Lena there was every chance this was what she'd be looking at: a sad-faced, dull-eyed, greying old bag of bones. I took a deep breath, determined to ignore it; this wasn't about me, it was about her.

It was surprisingly quick. Dr Simon came out less than three-quarters of an hour later, smiling as he approached, which I hoped was a good sign.

'Everything's fine,' he said. 'Couldn't have gone better. Now we just have to wait.'

'Can I see her?'

'Clancy, no,' he told me, as if we'd been over this before. 'More than anything, she needs to rest.'

'Just a look – I won't even let her know I'm there.'

He shook his head, and I guess he thought I was being a bit of a pain in the ass, which was probably true.

'Go home. Come back tomorrow. With any luck she'll be able to go home with you.'

In all my life I don't think I've ever felt as alone as I did when I finally forced myself to walk away from that clinic. I kept glancing back, hoping she'd appear at a window somewhere, but of course I was being foolish. From what the doc said, she was probably fast asleep.

Oh God, keep her safe, will ya. Let me come back tomorrow and find everything the way she'd want it to be; just for this one night, forget everyone else on this planet and devote all your time to her.

When I got back and told the others the whole story – about the money, where Lena was – they were a little put out: Jimmy and Delilah at being kept in the dark, at not being able to at least wish her good luck, and the kids, I think, at not getting to see all that dough. Nevertheless, they were quick to understand how worried I was; repeatedly reassuring me she'd be fine, that I'd done the right thing.

And maybe it was the fact that I was so preoccupied, that I couldn't settle to anything, that prompted Jimmy to suggest we went out after dinner.

I was a little surprised. He hadn't left the churchyard since Infinity put a price on his head. 'What for?' I asked.

'I gotta do something, Big Guy,' he complained. 'It's driving me crazy.'

'Jimmy!' Delilah protested.

'It's okay. They're looking for an old man, not a young cool one,' he told her, indulging in his new habit of stroking his shiny bald head from forehead to nape.

'I'm not living with junk again,' she warned, obviously having a fair idea what he had in mind.

'Not junk – new stuff.'

'Jeez!' I muttered, no more enthusiastic about the idea than Delilah. 'What for?'

'I want to block their ability to locate that screen so we can use it,' he said.

I gotta admit, put that way, it was pretty hard to deny him. Delilah groaned, but I could tell she was also conceding it made sense.

'I'll be fine,' he told her.

'If you're going to a computer store, bring me back a game,' Arturo begged.

I started to shake my head, but he threw himself at me, pleading, looking up with those big brown eyes – I tell ya, all the old tricks.

'Clancy!' Delilah joined in.

I half-wrestled with the little guy; after all, I was almost as fond of him as Delilah. As I did so, his sleeve rucked up and I caught a glimpse of something on his arm. 'What's that?' I asked.

He gave this fanfare, like I'd just discovered his buried treasure. 'Taa-da!' he cried, pulling his sleeve right up and revealing a large picture of Mickey Mouse on his arm.

Gordie sneered, like it was too pathetic for words, then promptly pulled up his own sleeve to reveal an Asian-style dragon on his rather more developed bicep.

'Are they tattoos?' I asked.

'Just transfers,' Hanna told me, in her 'boys will be boys' voice. 'They got them when we were out with Lena.'

99

'Whose is best?' Gordie asked.

'I dunno,' I replied, not in the mood for diplomacy.

'Arturo's,' Hanna ventured.

'Mickey Mouse!' sneered Gordie.

'I like it,' she told him.

'You would.'

'I've always liked Mickey Mouse,' Delilah chipped in.

'Big Guy?' Jimmy interrupted, still waiting to go out.

'Yeah, yeah, okay,' I replied. 'But no kids.'

For a moment Gordie didn't get it; he just sat there nodding as if he was in complete agreement, glaring at Arturo and Hanna in case they got any ideas.

'That includes you,' I told him.

'What?' he protested.

'I'm not taking any of you out at night.'

'I can take care of myself!' he said, pulling his sleeve back up, flexing his muscle, showing off his dragon.

'Not this time,' I said, and he got really angry with me, as if I was disrespecting him somehow, giving me that sharp stony look that reminded me of the crazed little animal he used to be out on the Island. He threw down his food and went storming off up the steps.

'Keep an eye on him,' I said to Delilah.

'I'll try,' she said, attempting to get her arms around little Arturo, as if he would always be her first responsibility, but he wriggled free and ran after Gordie.

'Let's go,' I said to Jimmy, anxious to get away before Dragon Boy and the Mickey Mouse Kid came back and started giving me the evil eye.

There's this street, Melville Highway, they nicknamed Hi-Tec Alley, it's anything to do with technology, computers, screens, scans. It's all there, as well as spare parts stacked up to the ceiling, some so old you couldn't believe anyone would still have a use for them. Fortunately, it wasn't that far – less than thirty minutes even at Jimmy's pegging old pace – so I was kind of relieved to hear that was where he wanted to go.

The story of the City at night was pretty well still on the same nightmare page: a fathomless sea of smoke, fire after fire, gangs of looters and muggers frequently fighting with each other, having to watch your back all the time. Though there was this sense that in some areas everything that could be taken had, and that the new strategy was to try to frighten functioning streets into closing down, abandoning everything to the mob.

Mind you, it depended on what you were looking for. If you wanted a good read for example, you were in luck, 'cuz wherever looters got their ideas, it wasn't from the printed or electronic page – I hadn't seen one bookstore broken into – well, not until we made our way to Hi-Tec Alley.

Out on the Island, I'd really got into reading, not just for the story, but also for the appreciation of the words, the way the writer used them. Yeah, I know that don't sound like a big guy, but I'd never really had the chance before. Tell the truth, I was really missing it, and when I saw that smashed window, all those books just lying there and no one seeming to care, I couldn't help myself. It'd been a display of classics and I grabbed some titles I recognised but had never read: *For Whom the Bell Tolls*, *A Tale of Two Cities*, *The Grapes of Wrath* and *Dr Zhivago*.

Jimmy kind of frowned at me as I stuffed them in my backpack, like I was wasting his precious time, but I just waved him on. 'Let's go.'

There wasn't a lot left of Hi-Tec Alley. I wouldn't've minded betting it was one of the first places visited when the satellites came down. Jimmy and me went from store to store, but the theft and destruction were pretty well total. Arturo could forget all about his computer game.

If it'd been me, I would've given up then and there, but Jimmy wasn't there for laptops, game glasses, screens or whatever, he just wanted some parts, and down the side alleys, some of the little repair shops were still relatively intact.

I shouldered open one door for him and he swept in like an overeager ant, going from shelf to shelf, actually trying to climb up to some of the higher ones, until I pointed out that there was a ladder. Every now and then he'd let out a little whistle or cry of appreciation.

'I ain't carrying nothing,' I warned him.

'You won't have to. It's micro.'

In the end, he filled a bag and came up to me, proudly holding it open for my approval.

'Don't mean a great deal to me,' I told him.

He grunted like I was letting him down as usual, and turned for the door. 'It should do,' he told me.

As soon as we set off back to the church, our task completed, I found myself worrying about Lena again, about leaving her alone like that. I hated having to trust Dr Simon. It was completely against my nature. If the circumstances had been different, I wouldn't have even considered it, but as it was, I had no other choice.

I was that concerned, I gave out with one of those long sighs we all expel when we want a friend to ask, 'What's up?' but Jimmy was too preoccupied to notice.

We were on the corner of Melville and a couple of kids had just passed by, looking like they had something on their minds, when he grabbed my arm, looking back at where they were going.

'What's the matter?' I asked, but he never answered.

They turned off down this narrow alley and he immediately set off after them.

'Jimmy!' I shouted but he ignored me. More than a little irritated, I tagged along behind him tagging along behind them: down the alley, round a corner, then up a fire escape and through a door. The little guy pegged it up there after them, hesitated for a moment and then, making sure I was right behind him, he entered.

Actually, in a way, it was kinda amazing: he's in his seventies and those two kids were in their teens, but somehow he'd recognised kindred spirits. They were a couple of gamers who'd unknowingly just led us to what looked like a makeshift games parlour, stocked with what I guessed were looted machines.

I don't know how many kids were playing, maybe twenty or so. I thought they'd take one look at us and kick up a fuss, that there might be trouble, but they were too engrossed with what they were doing to even notice.

Jimmy stood there gazing around like he was in the Games Room of the Gods, practically licking his lips at all that technology and the different types of games, while I was more concerned with what the deal was here.

'Let's go,' I told him, feeling uneasy.

'Are you kidding?' he cried.

This sleazy-looking guy, overweight and unshaven, approached us. Presumably he was running the show. He asked Jimmy if he wanted some change.

'You didn't keep any of that money?' the little guy asked, turning to me.

I gave him a short hard burst of The Look, just to let him know how unimpressed I was. 'Nope.'

'Just one game!' he cooed, somehow knowing I was lying. 'For old times' sake.'

He got such an expression about him, such a longing, a cry of nostalgia, that – call me soft, call me stupid, call me whatever you will – I took out a ten and handed it over.

'*One* game!' I insisted.

'Hey, Big Guy, you're the coolest, man,' he said, immediately changing the note into coins.

'For chrissake, Jimmy, be careful,' I muttered, as soon as we were alone. 'What if someone recognises you?'

He didn't even reply, just stroked his bald head as if that answered everything.

I followed behind him as he went from game to game, looking over kids' shoulders, peering into their booths, his eyes twinkling like they might catch fire, determined to make his one game count. One girl didn't like it, you could see that, this old guy closely studying what she was doing. Eventually she got all twitchy, shooting sideways glances and flicking her hair 'til in the end she got wiped out and promptly stormed away. Jimmy was in her seat before it had even lost the impression of her butt.

'Know what you're doing?' I asked, and the kid on the other side of him gave this kind of cruel snigger.

'Yeah. It's just a variation of an old favourite,' he said with supreme confidence, immediately getting himself wiped out. The kid started giggling, nudging his neighbour and pointing at Jimmy.

Jimmy made this face like he'd missed the obvious, then started to play again. The two kids waited to see how long he'd last this time, their laughter threatening to erupt at any moment.

The only thing was, that was it. That was the only occasion he got himself wiped out. I mean, it's not something that's ever interested me, not in the least, but I could see I was in the presence of a grand master. He whirled his hands through the air like he was conducting an orchestra, his movements rapid and smooth. In no time he moved onto the second level, then the third, with the machine congratulating him all the way. The two kids just gaped, their mouths getting ever wider, and others started stopping their own games to stare over at us. I guess I'd seen a little of it out on the Island, but I had no idea just how much in tune he was with that stuff.

I kept an eye out for any hint that someone might've recognised him – not that I thought they would've done anything if they had. I mean, you could see it in their faces: disbelief, shock, but more than anything, absolute and overwhelming respect. I couldn't imagine any of them informing on him.

He finished up, got what I suspected was the maximum possible score – the machine was practically throwing itself at his feet – but he had one more trick up his sleeve. There was this kid a few stations down, on a bit of a run himself and refusing to let this old man's antics distract him. Jimmy saw him, got a bit of a twinkle in his eye and dug something out of the bag of stuff he'd taken from the repair shop. Don't ask me what it was, but he fiddled around with it for a few moments, lodged it into the machine, and then started shifting icons left, right and centre. A few moments later, the kid still playing let out a cry of protest, plainly having been wiped out.

'*What?*' he wailed. 'I never even seen one of them before!'

I don't know how he did it, but obviously Jimmy had taken control of the kid's game. The others burst into laughter, cooing with astonishment and admiration, and with a few more quick manoeuvres, he not only managed to invade everyone else's game, but to gain access to every computer in the place, linking them together and using their joint capacity to create a super version of what he'd been playing before, one that practically covered the entire wall. I tell you, little old bald guy with a limp he may be, but in a matter of seconds he'd transformed himself into a superhero to every kid in that place.

He paused for a moment, making great play of flexing his fingers as if limbering up, then gave them all a proud little smile, as if they hadn't seen nothing yet.

'One game,' I reminded him.

'Big Guy!' he protested.

'*One game!*' I repeated.

He sighed and reluctantly followed me to the door, I swear those kids were every bit as disappointed as he was.

'See you, guys!' he called back. 'Another time, huh?'

We descended the steps of the fire escape, Jimmy pretty pleased with himself, repeatedly stroking his newly acquired shiny bald head, and actually, I could see why. We all need to remind ourselves who we are occasionally, what we're capable of and how it might affect others. He had this quiet little smile about him the whole way back – at least until we came to that last clutch of screens just before the Square.

Suddenly he stopped, staring up at the closest one, his face falling like a landslide. 'Oh shit!'

I looked up at the screen. It was the usual thing: somehow it identified you, knew all about you, and immediately personalised the ads for your attention. Though not for us, thank God – or leastways, not 'til then.

Tired of your friends' jokes, Jimy? Of being 'Mr Slaphead?' or
Jelly Bean'? Make an appointment with one of our hair surgeons
and be a real man again.
Lion's Mane Studio – 25% off all this month

It seemed so everyday, so comic, and yet we both knew what it meant.

'They know who I am!' he wailed. 'They *read* me!'

If he was on the commercial database, then it could only be a matter of time before he was on the security one, too. And you didn't have to tell either of us what that meant. Immediately we both started to run, the next screen also reading him, trying to sell him software.

Hey, Jimy! How fast is fast? Organo 9
– anything else is the slow lane

'How the hell did they do it?' he cried, trying his best to run quicker, to get back to the crypt and underground.

At that moment, an Infinity Dragonfly, presumably alerted to Jimmy's presence, took off from the roof of a nearby office building – I guessed they must keep them up there in various locations, ready to swoop down whenever they were needed. Jimmy immediately let out this long wail of alarm.

'Move it!' I shouted, though I had a fair idea he was already going as fast as he could.

It was over us in a matter of seconds, lights blazing, engine burbling, so close I could actually see scratches in the paintwork on the bottom.

I had no idea what they had in mind, whether they intended to capture us or not. For sure, if they did, he'd be quite a prize; they could parade him onscreen; people like someone to blame: 'This is him, the guy who wrecked all our lives.' Maybe it would calm things down? But it soon became apparent that that wasn't their strategy, that they wanted a more immediate end to the situation.

They opened up with just about everything they had as we

ducked down an alleyway. Laser cannons and automatic weapons made the walls and sidewalk around us erupt, deluging us in shards of brick and concrete.

I kept trying doors, back entrances to places, finding them all locked; having to jump back at one point as the brickwork next to me was melted by a laser, sending flames up the wall and setting fire to the whole building.

The Dragonfly was within a whisker of the roof of the building opposite, hovering at just the right angle to be able to squeeze out the occasional shot. A laser almost clipped Jimmy's heels as he ran, but somehow we made it to the other end of the alleyway and out onto the relative safety of a main street, where there were enough people around for us to merge briefly, if not actually disappear. I looked both ways, scanning for taller buildings, a city canyon, somewhere where a Dragonfly couldn't operate, then beckoned to Jimmy to follow.

'Big Guy!' he complained, almost bent double with exertion.

I practically had to carry him. My arm was locked round his shoulders, stopping him from tumbling over as the Dragonfly continued to shadow us, its spotlights – and no doubt lasers – locked onto their target. Neither of us could go much further, not at our age. We came to some looted stores with their windows smashed and slipped inside to rest, but there was no sanctuary: the Dragonfly just waited outside, hovering there, no doubt going through the building with heat-seeking scanners to pinpoint exactly where we were.

We found the back exit into this service alleyway but hadn't gone more than thirty yards before they were over us again, opening fire almost before they'd picked us out with their spotlights. More concrete and brick exploded round us, more buildings burst into flame, and in the distance I could hear sirens – Infinity ground vehicles maybe, coming to join the chase. I turned a corner and led us down yet another alleyway and it looked like the lasers were trapping us in a cat's cradle of deadly beams of light.

Jimmy fell over, almost taking me with him, exhaustedly protesting as I yanked him back to his feet and dragged him on. I had no idea what the hell we were going to do.

Suddenly there was this loud metallic crunch behind us, and we heard the shriek of a distressed engine. Jimmy and me turned around, barely believing our luck – the Dragonfly had struck the top of a building and somehow become entangled in its superstructure.

'Keep going!' I told Jimmy, pushing him on, the noise of the screaming Dragonfly's engine behind us almost deafening.

As we approached the junction with the main street they must've realised we were getting away 'cuz they opened fire again, even though there was no clear shot. I guess up to that point it had never occurred to them that we might escape, but now they were determined to finish the job, to eliminate Jimmy once and for all. But it was too late. We left them there, on top of the building, pinned and helpless like some huge insect on display.

CHAPTER EIGHT

Dr Simon had told me to get to the clinic for ten, but I was at the security gates before nine, waiting for him to send my clearance. I hadn't slept a wink all night – in fact, I hadn't even bothered going to bed. Jimmy and me had stayed up for a while, talking over what had happened. Neither of us could work out how he'd been read, how he'd ended up on the database. It couldn't be from the Island, 'cuz we'd all been there and they didn't have anyone else's name – and anyways, he hadn't been 'recognised' when we first got over. Something must've happened in the last few days – or maybe they'd just manually fed him in, adding as much information as they could to the photos taken on the Island? But that couldn't explain where they'd got his name, even if they hadn't spelled it correctly.

Eventually we got tired of speculating, of worrying what it might mean, and Jimmy went to bed, telling me to do the same. I was too embarrassed to say there was no point, that I simply wouldn't be able to sleep without Lena beside me. I did try, lying there in the dark for a while, staring at nothing, but eventually I returned up top; leaning against one of the church walls with my sleeping bag draped around my shoulders, gazing at the fire still burning across the street, thinking about all manner of stuff.

I never said anything to Jimmy – 'course I didn't – but I'd been really shocked by how badly Infinity wanted him taken out of the picture. I mean, yeah, destroying the satellites, taking away their system of control, that'd make anyone Public Enemy Number One, but I couldn't help but feel there was more to it than that. The amount of firepower they laid on us, for one – and for sure, most of it had been directed at him. For some reason this was personal: they wanted him removed from the face of the earth and the sooner the better. But I just didn't get why. What could Jimmy possibly know or discover that would do harm to Infinity?

I shifted position and a slight waft of Lena came off the sleeping bag. I smiled, tried to chase it, to get it back into my body, but it was gone, swallowed up by the stifling smoke. How I wished that night was over so I could see her, make sure she was okay, find out if she'd regained her sight.

The trouble with dealing with medical people is that they automatically got this thing going on; this professional aura. You're almost too scared to ask them questions, to meet them head-on, and they know it. Perhaps we were being conned? Maybe Dr Simon was just going to take our money knowing we were in no position to kick up a fuss? Not to mention the fact that every operation, no matter what it might be, has its dangers – what if Lena ended up not only blind but damaged in some other way?

And it wasn't just the failure of the operation I was worried about, it was also the success. What would happen if she *could* see? Would it change things? Would it change her? Would she want to do something different with her life? And, Jesus, sorry to keep going on about this, but what was she gonna think when she saw me?

I don't know whether he was trying to prove a point, or maybe there were just things to do, but the Doc didn't arrange my clearance 'til nine fifty-five precisely. Nor was the driver sent for me. By the time I got through security and walked up to the house it was ten past ten.

He came out to greet me, bidding me good morning, looking all fresh and polished, dandy and dapper, but I wasn't in the mood for exchanging pleasantries. 'She okay?'

'Yes. Of course she is,' he said, a little taken aback by my abruptness.

'No problems?'

'Clancy . . . No! None whatsoever.'

I hesitated for a moment, never so afraid to ask a question. 'Can she see?'

He smiled. 'Let's go and find out, shall we?'

'Don't you know?' I asked.

He never replied, just took me through to her room.

I couldn't help myself: I stopped dead at the doorway, too afraid to enter, letting him go in first, just kind of easing myself into the room.

Maybe I seen too many movies, but I assumed she'd be sitting up in bed with bandages round her eyes, that we were going to unwrap her and she'd tell us what she could see. She *was* in bed, but there were no bandages and she was staring at the door, waiting for me to enter.

Again I stopped dead, unable to go so much as an inch closer, waiting for some kind of reaction, in that moment feeling like I was nothing, that she was bound to reject me.

'Clancy,' she whispered, opening her arms.

I tell you, big guy or no, it was just too much. I went to her, grabbing hold, fighting tears every step of the way.

'You can see?' I whispered.

'Kind of,' she said. 'Not clearly. You're very blurry.'

'Well, that's for the best,' I told her, not altogether joking.

'But I can make things out. Shapes . . . people,' she said, her excitement threatening to bubble over.

'That'll improve,' Dr Simon assured her. 'Quite quickly.'

I might've been a bit sparing with the pleasantries when I first arrived, my mind elsewhere, but I tell you, not then. I thanked that man from the bottom of my heart. I mean, he might see it as a fairly standard operation, but as far as we were concerned, it was a damn miracle.

'Just one thing, Clancy,' he told me. 'I'd like to keep her here.'

I turned to him, a little surprised. 'Sorry?'

'The first seventy-two hours, she really should be under observation.'

'You told me she'd be able to come with me.'

'I said I "hoped" . . . Best not take chances.'

I looked to Lena. I know it was crazy, but I just couldn't bear the thought of having to spend another night without her.

'I'm coming with you,' she said, swinging her legs round to get out of bed.

'Lena! Please!' Dr Simon protested. 'Just for a couple of days.'

It's funny, for both of us her sight was the most important thing in the world, but being together suddenly seemed almost to rival it.

'I'm going with Clancy,' she told him.

'Lena!' he repeated, sounding just that bit angry. 'Really. I've got to insist.'

'Sorry,' she replied. The image of her searching for her clothes, actually trying to find something by looking, almost stopped me in my tracks. Were we being foolish? Shouldn't we take every precaution?

'Maybe . . .'

'I'm coming with you!' she insisted.

'I can manage.'

'Well, I can't. Where are my clothes?' she asked Dr Simon.

In the end, and despite how unhappy he was about it, she got her way. He did ask where we were living, just in case anything went wrong, but Lena refused to answer – it was only when I faithfully promised that, no matter what, I'd bring her back on Friday to check everything was okay, that he finally let her go.

I think we both felt kind of guilty as we were leaving, a bit like rebellious teenagers. That man changed our world; he'd been so generous, but he couldn't understand how much we wanted to be together, to explore the gift he'd bestowed.

The whole way back to the churchyard was spent kind of stumbling in wonder; stopping every now and then, letting her take things in, listening to her almost childlike cries of joy. I mean, it had been more than four years.

When we finally descended the steps into the crypt everyone went crazy. She took them outside into the daylight, so she could get as clear a view as possible: standing in front of them one by one, looking them up and down, so thrilled to finally put faces to voices. Arturo insisted on showing her his transfer, rolling his sleeve up as far as it could go so she got the full effect, moving his arm and giggling when Mickey Mouse moved with it. Lena's delight, her excitement, were utterly infectious. You never heard such a lot of whooping and laughter and helpless crying.

'course we celebrated; using up the last of the food, knowing we'd have to get more the following day, that it was probably going to be even more difficult. But do you know something? In that moment, we didn't really care.

Delilah took the opportunity to sing; none of her usual chilly blues stuff, more gospel, praising the Lord, praising every possible entity who might've assisted in any way in restoring Lena's sight. And though I couldn't help but deliver the odd note of caution, reminding them that we couldn't be certain her sight would improve, that we shouldn't forget the possibility of rejection, I think I was saying it more for my benefit than theirs.

The kids joined Delilah in singing, even Gordie, without the slightest hint of a sneer or protest, and all of us ended up dancing round the crypt in our own individual manner (which for me is a kind of internal thing that you might not even notice too much from the outside).

As ever, Delilah had her arms round Arturo, the Mickey Mouse Kid, teaching him how to waltz as if he was to be her partner at the summer ball. She loved him more than if she'd had one of her own. For sure, Jimmy was convinced she loved him more than him. Sometimes he got a little jealous, asking her stupid questions like which one of them she'd save in a fire. Mind you, I gotta say, she never gave him an answer.

Later that night, as quietly as humanly possible, Lena and me made love in our sleeping bag, keeping every movement so gentle and slow, our breathing shallow, stifling our moans. I don't know why, but for some reason the silence makes it even more intense, as if the discipline of keeping quiet, of not being able to let our passion fully go, mingled a little pain with the pleasure. Afterwards, we lay there silently cuddling, feeling a little naughty, wondering if the others had heard and were just indulging us.

'It's the same,' Lena whispered.

'What?'

'The crypt. I can't see any more than before.'

'Can't see that much myself,' I told her. 'Give it a few days and you'll see a damn sight better than me.'

She never bothered to reply, just grunted, maybe 'cuz she caught the slight tone in my voice, 'cuz she feared which direction those words would take us in. As much as I hated myself, and I truly did, I knew it'd have to come out at some point.

I went silent for a little while, pretending disinterest, though, in fact, I was frantically wrestling with this madman, trying to shove him back into his room and lock the door.

'So was it a shock?' I eventually asked.

She paused for a moment, knowing all too well what I was talking about. 'It was the nicest thing my eyes have ever seen.'

'Really?'

'Yes.'

I forced a bit of a chuckle. 'Find that a little hard to believe.'

'I've run my hands over this body a thousand times,' she said, with the first hint of impatience.

'Feel sorry for you,' I said, knowing even before the words were out that it was a step too far, that I'd crossed the line.

There was one of those expectant kind of moments, like the world had shifted on its axis and something profound was about to happen, then her fist slammed into my stomach, air literally exploding out of me.

'Jesus!' I gasped.

'Goodnight, Clancy,' she said, turning over as if she'd just given me the fondest of pecks on the cheek.

'Lena!' I protested.

'And thank you for spoiling such a special moment.'

I gotta say, that hurt me even more than her punch. Mainly 'cuz it was true, 'cuz I'd pushed her into that, knowing it would make me feel better.

'You're right. I'm sorry,' I said, putting my arm round her.

'Never again, Clancy,' she warned, shrugging me off. 'Never again!'

Sometime in the night she must've forgiven me, 'cuz I woke with her nestled in my arms. Mind you, that wasn't what disturbed my sleep; it was feeling how tense and concentrated she was, like the prey sensing the approach of the hunter.

'What's the matter?' I asked.

'Can't you hear?'

I guess I hadn't been fully awake 'cuz when I really listened I could hear the same noise as the other night: this kind of rhythmic beating, an echoing clatter, and as it began to grow, the yelling and shouting too.

'What the hell *is* that?' I said, more confused than actually asking the question.

And suddenly Lena was panicking, scrabbling frantically at the zip on the sleeping bag, desperate to get out.

'What's the matter?' I asked.

'It's coming this way!'

I listened again. At first I couldn't hear any difference. It sounded more or less stationary to me. However, after a few moments I began to think she might be right: it was growing in volume – and yes, it was coming our way.

'Jimmy!' I shouted, struggling up. 'Kids!'

'What is it?' Jimmy asked, immediately going quiet, realising what was going on. 'Oh Jeez!'

I stumbled across to the steps. Lena was already up to the entrance and I followed on behind. Just as before, the noise was a lot louder outside: *Boom-Boom-Boom! Boom-Boom-Boom!* Not to mention those cries scything through the night like the raw emotions of creation.

Jimmy, Delilah and the kids followed us up and all of us just stood there, gaping out into the huge smoky darkness.

'What is it?' Arturo cried, looking from face to face, as if at least one of us grown-ups should know.

Whatever it was, Lena was right, it was coming our way. Through the smoke, I could just make out the shapes of people running past in the street, heading in the opposite direction, doing everything they could to get away. A guy stumbled into the churchyard, looking for a hiding place and almost immediately decided it wasn't safe, that he was better off running, which was kinda ominous.

I made my way over to the street, ignoring Lena's shouted warning, thinking that even in this visibility I might get some idea what was coming our way.

More and more people came scurrying past. Some were kids, younger than any I'd seen on the Mainland up 'til that point – where the hell did they come from? An old couple dashed past, the man coughing from the smoke, and I was pretty sure they were Islanders so I called out, asked them what was going on, but they just kept running.

Whatever was scaring them, it wasn't that far away. It sounded like the beating of a thousand different drums, a hundred different surfaces, the mass crying of countless angry emotions. I also realised there was a glow beginning to colour the night, not of fire, but lights. I promptly turned and ran back to the church. Whatever was coming, it was going to roll right over us.

'Go back down!' I shouted.

Delilah and the kids didn't need a second bidding, Jimmy followed them down, wailing to himself, convinced it had something to do with him. But Lena hesitated, trying to get her eyes working, squinting through the smoke.

'Can you see?' I asked her.

'Something,' she told me, repeatedly blinking. 'Maybe we should make a run for it?'

'It's too late,' I told her.

We went down after the others and I dragged the old gravestone that had been used to disguise the entrance when we first arrived back into place. The only thing was, it left us in complete darkness; our wind-up camping lights had run down as usual and hadn't been rewound.

Moment by moment, time-slither by time-slither, the sound and that heavy vibration grew. It was starting to take form now: there were vehicles amongst it, heavy ones, by the sound of it. I could hear the straining of an engine being asked to do a difficult task, another one joining in, revving, roaring, then a loud crash. That was something going over – a wall or a building. Jeez, maybe Lena had been right, we should've made a run for it. The pounding was getting ever nearer, and that war cry of a chorus, and then we heard the wall tumble over at the far end of the churchyard.

We huddled together for strength in the darkness, fearing the church walls, maybe even the ceiling, were about to come crashing in on us. Delilah started to weep, sparking off little Arturo. Gordie told them to shush, but they were only silenced by the screaming of an engine, growing louder and louder, 'til we realised something monsterous was right overhead, lurching this way and that, colliding with everything in front of it, 'til finally something big must've given way. The impact on the stone floor above us was like the deep-throated shuddering of an avalanche.

'Shit!' I gasped, convinced we were about to be buried alive.

The yelling and shouting came next, and more drumming, and for the first time I realised that whoever was doing it wasn't only beating something they were carrying but also everything they passed, as if they were marking their territory, hitting everything before them: buildings, walls, trash cans, posts, anything that would resonate to their threat.

It crashed over us like syncopated thunder whilst we waited help-lessly below. Lena buried her face in my chest, hugging me with all her strength, as if determined to crush us into one before that last moment came. All of us were waiting for the crack, the first specks of dust that would tell us the floor was about to give way – and yet slowly, so slowly that at first I couldn't be sure, the noise started to recede. Whatever it was was moving on into the night.

I waited 'til I was sure whatever it was had moved on, then fum-bled my way up the steps, forced the gravestone off the entrance and peered out.

There wasn't a lot left of the church, just a few stumps of wall, the rest piles of rubble. Jeez, we'd been lucky: bricks and stones had fallen almost everywhere but on top of the entrance. Just a few more inches our way and we would've been buried under several tons of rubble, and the crypt would've played host to more lifeless bodies.

I scuttled across a pile of broken stones, keeping as low as I could, anxious to see who our visitors had been. No prizes for guessing: there were hundreds of Infinity Specials, all in a line stretching from this side of the street to the other, every one equipped with riot gear and beating their shields and anything else they came across, shouting at the tops of their voices. They were so loud they could be heard above the massive earth-moving equipment in front of them. Overhead, spotlights blazing, were a couple of Dragonflies. I tell ya, it was a full-blown army.

Through the smoke, I could just make out the silhouettes of those fleeing before them. It was like they were being herded, driven like sheep. Infinity were forcing them out of the area, clearing the City of those they didn't want, and yet, even when I'd come to that conclusion, even though it was the only possible explanation, I knew it didn't entirely fit.

I started to follow, keeping at a safe distance, my curiosity well and truly aroused. Something about this seemed somehow familiar. A time long ago . . . when I was a kid . . .

And then – oh God! – finally I realised what was going on.

I glanced behind me. Gordie and Arturo were following and I frantically waved them away, telling them to go back.

Jameson Circle is three-quarters of a mile or so down the street from the church. In the old days, and I mean long before I got sent out to the Island, it was an impressive address. Now, just like the rest of this area, it's all a bit run-down: the grand houses have been allowed to deteriorate, divided up into apartments, or mostly just rooms for those who never stay for more than a month or two. In the middle there was once a well-tended communal garden, but now it's just an open grassless area with a few dying trees – nowhere you'd want to visit, day or night, but I had a strong feeling that was where this circus was headed. And sure enough, as we approached the swell in the street, an order was given and the Specials stopped their beating and shouting and formed themselves into a wall several persons deep – a move, I noticed, that was being replicated on the far side of the Circle, where there was another access – and all those caught inside were trapped. There was a moment of sickening silence, like the feeling of nausea just before you vomit, and I realised my fears were about to come true.

Once when I was a kid visiting relatives in the country, I was asked if I wanted to go beating. They were paying a few notes, so yeah, I volunteered, despite having no idea what it was. The following day we were up before dawn, dozens of us, and driven out into the middle of nowhere, where we had to form this long line right across the hillside and slowly advance, beating everything with sticks, shouting at the tops of our voices, making a helluva racket. The aim was to flush out any game in the vicinity, to drive them towards the guns of the hunters waiting ahead. I had realised that was what was going on here.

There was nothing I could do, had no way to stop it. I wouldn't have even made it through the wall of Specials. Another signal was given, a couple of shots rang out, and then all hell broke loose. It was deafening, partly 'cuz it was echoing away inside the enclosed circle, bouncing off the walls, but also 'cuz of the sheer weight of weapons being discharged – hundreds, maybe even thousands of them. It went on for the longest couple of minutes I've ever known, then finally came to a sporadic spluttering halt. The smoke from their weapons added to the smoke already there, making it impossible to see anything. Into that brief and terrible silence other noises started to be heard: people screaming for mercy, the wailing of the wounded and dying. Those still able ran at the Specials' shields, trying to force their way out, but they were clubbed and thrown back to await the next spattering round of gunfire. They were helpless. On the nearest roof and in the windows of surrounding buildings I could just make out men and women equipped with firearms, all kinds, eagerly taking aim at those hemmed in below.

It was a straight-out massacre. I guess they couldn't get rid of those they didn't want by sending them out to the Island any more, so they'd started culling them here, taking advantage of what was going on to 'cleanse' the Mainland.

I don't know how many were killed; with all the smoke I couldn't really see. Certainly there wasn't a lot of movement amongst those lying on the ground. As I turned and slipped away they were already bringing up the white trucks and the clear-up operation was underway.

Jesus, this place *was* worse than the Island. Far worse. A lot of those shooting didn't look to have the faintest idea about guns; I'm not even sure they'd held one before. They were just wildly blasting away, shooting randomly like it was some kind of fairground attraction.

I turned and hurried back towards the churchyard feeling shocked and bewildered, the way you do when you're forced to realise the gap between you and other members of the human race is far wider than you ever could've imagined. It was so ironic: on the very day that Lena regained her sight, she could've been witness to this.

A little ways down the street I came across Gordie and Arturo hiding in a doorway.

'I told you two to go back!' I said, turning to check no one was following.

'What happened?' Gordie asked.

'Nothing.'

'Did they kill them?' Arturo asked, looking a little distressed.

'Just get back to the crypt, will you,' I said, really not wanting to answer that question.

'Why did they kill them?' Gordie persisted, knowing my anger was a sign of admission.

'I don't know,' I replied, leading them away. 'I guess they don't want some people in their city . . . It don't matter. As soon as the Doc gives Lena the all-clear, we're going anyway. Even if I have to put out every fire myself.'

For a while we walked in silence, both kids looking very thoughtful.

'It's like us back on the Island,' Gordie eventually commented.

'Nah. You didn't know any better,' I told him, glancing back to see Arturo starting to lag behind. 'Hey! Come on!'

'Can I have a horse in the country?' he asked as he caught up, his thoughts a million miles away from where I expected.

'What?'

'A black one, with a white star here,' he said, pointing at his forehead.

I shrugged, a little perplexed. 'I dunno.'

'You never even seen a horse,' Gordie said dismissively.

'Seen pictures.'

'I seen one,' Gordie told him.

'When?' Arturo asked, with obvious disbelief.

'In the park, when I was a little kid.'

'Did you ride it?'

'Nope.'

'I'm gonna ride mine,' Arturo said, as if he'd regained the upper hand.

It's quite something the way kids do that, draw you into their world, their values. Scores of people had just been massacred but these two were far more interested in which of them had ever seen – or ridden – a horse. Maybe, in a way, it's kind of comforting; as if, by hanging on to a little of their innocence, we can stave off some of our harsh reality.

We were almost back to the churchyard, Arturo still telling us about all the other animals he was going to have once we got to the country: pigs, sheep, a tiger. In a way, I s'pose it was that sense of normality, of listening to the kind of conversation I'd heard a thousand times before, that made me relax a little, maybe even forget something of what I'd just seen.

Suddenly there was the sound of a powerful engine roaring up behind us. I turned around, hoping it had nothing to do with us, but in that precise instant we were hit by a bank of spotlights.

'Run!' I shouted, knowing it meant trouble. '*Run!*'

I protected them as best I could, keeping myself between them and our pursuers, but I realised immediately we couldn't go into the churchyard, that it would endanger everyone. 'Don't go in there!' I screamed, 'Keep going!'

That was a helluva thing to have to say: I mean, we were utterly exposed, caught in those spotlights with nowhere to go – and I'd just run past our only possible refuge.

We skirted round the edges of a pile of rubble that had spilled out across the street at a junction, giving us the opportunity to slip down a side road, but whoever was chasing us just bumped over the rubble and accelerated after us and was soon only yards behind, holding station, as if to make it perfectly clear that they could run us down any time they liked, that this was just a game. I felt, rather than saw, this big white pick-up. The driver was repeatedly revving the engine as loud as it would go. I shepherded the kids closer to the wall, hoping there'd be some shelter somewhere, but suddenly a shot rang out. I glanced back at the pickup, looking for something I could do, some way of stopping them. There was a group of four men and two women in the back, all taunting us, guffawing away as they drunkenly swayed around, trying to aim their rifles.

'*Move it!*' I screamed at the kids, hoping to put the fear of God into them, to make them run faster than they ever had in their short lives. There was a sudden flurry of gunfire, as if someone had given the order, and bullets were flying everywhere, ricocheting and whining through the air – and one of the kids gave a little moan.

I turned to Arturo, the youngest, the most vulnerable, but he was running as fast as ever. Gordie also appeared to be moving freely. I was just on the point of assuming it was nothing, of urging them on even faster, when suddenly Arturo faltered, clutched at his side and fell to the ground, rolling over and over.

I stopped and ran back; in the street the pick-up screeched to a halt. Arturo was just lying there, making this kind of gurgling sound, his eyes rolling back in his head, blood spreading out from his body at an alarming rate. I squatted down, took him in my arms and went to stand up but there was another volley of shots and I got clipped in the shoulder.

I'd dropped the little guy before I realised, but I recovered enough to try to scoop him up again – but there was so much fire coming my way I had to scramble into this small recess in the wall, next to a tree. Again and again I tried to get out to grab Arturo, but each time I was met by more bullets snapping and pinging round me.

Gordie had managed to scramble over the wall a few yards further on, but he must've worked his way back 'cuz suddenly his voice came from behind me: 'Clancy!'

'Yeah!'

'Is Arturo okay?'

'I don't know,' I told him, though I had a really bad feeling.

I was about to try for the little guy once more, at least to get him out of the line of fire, when the pick-up suddenly mounted the sidewalk and drove straight at me, lights blazing, while automatic weapons were indiscriminately discharged. I thought they were going to run Arturo over and maybe settle with me, but the driver screeched to a halt, the passenger door was thrown open, and someone reached down and grabbed Arturo's body. He gave this cry of triumph as he dragged it inside like he was landing a prize fish or something.

Then they were gone, accelerating away into the smoky night before I even got to my feet – but I did catch a glimpse of the sign on the back:

Join the Infinity Clean-up Campaign.
Beer, burgers and your choice of weapon.

'What happened?' asked Gordie, suddenly appearing at the top of the wall.

For a moment I just stood where I was, in a state of shock, again recalling Yoshi's warning about people coming for us in the middle of the night. 'They took him,' I said dazedly.

'Kidnapped?' he said, scrambling down the wall, staring at the pool of Arturo's blood.

I didn't know how to reply. In the end, I knew he would demand the truth so I just came right out and said it. 'No . . . They took his body.'

For a moment I thought he was going to cry, but he was a tough little guy and even at a time like that, not the sort to let himself go. 'You sure?' was all he managed.

I nodded. I've seen death enough times over the years to be able to make a positive identification. 'Yeah.'

Don't ask me why, but we both turned and stared into the smoke where the truck had disappeared, stunned by the brutal sudden-ness of it, I guess. Only minutes ago, a few hundred yards away, we'd been listening to Arturo telling us what animals he'd have as pets in the country. Now we couldn't bring ourselves to walk away from the spot where he'd been killed.

'Why did they take him?' Gordie asked.

'I dunno,' I replied. I'd been asking myself the same question. Why did they?

His bottom lip started to quiver and I wondered if he was going to lose it after all. 'What's Delilah going to say?' he wailed, as if he was only upset on her behalf.

God, yeah – what was Delilah going to say? Jeez, I couldn't begin to imagine . . .

It was an irony, but just as we couldn't bear to leave, soon we couldn't bear to stay. With one last look at that pathetic pool of blood, all that remained of Arturo, we silently walked away.

It was beyond all comprehension . . . Gone. Just like that. Arturo, everyone's favourite, our mascot, our talisman, didn't exist any more. I found myself thinking about that transfer – Mickey Mouse – and the first of what I knew would be many tears came to my eyes. It'd been so typical of him: wanting to be a little hard man – at times *having* to be – but inside he'd been just a normal, everyday kid.

Gordie was right: Delilah was the one who was going to be hit hardest. She loved that little guy more than life itself, and I can't tell ya how much I was dreading giving her the news.

Slowly we descended the stone steps of the crypt, our hearts so heavy it was all we could do to bear them. Jimmy had wound up a camping light, I guess 'cuz no one could bear to be in the dark any more.

'Clancy!' Lena cried, noticing the blood on my shoulder where I'd been winged.

'It's nothing,' I said. 'Plaster'll fix it.'

Delilah peered round us, waiting for one more person to come trotting down those steps. When he didn't, it was like these shadows started erupting out of her. 'Where's Arturo?' she asked, slowly getting to her feet.

There was a long and deathly silence. I couldn't bring myself to meet her gaze.

'Clancy?' Lena asked.

All I could do was to shake my head. I couldn't say the words.

'Dead,' Gordie told them, like he wanted to prove he was man enough to say it, but his voice cracked as the word left his mouth.

Delilah just stood there, her mouth slowly falling open, her eyes filling with a pain that almost hypnotised me.

'Oh no—' Lena moaned.

'They got this new form of "entertainment",' I told them. 'Call it

"Cleaning up". Looks like people pay to get drunk and shoot as many "undesirables" as they can.'

'*Why did you take them?*' Lena wailed, her restored sight fixing me with a look that cut right through me.

'He *didn't!*' Gordie told them. 'We followed him.'

But everything was lost after that: there was no more conversation, no more questions or answers; everything was drowned out by Delilah collapsing to the ground and weeping so loudly and with such pain it was all you could do not to turn and run from it. It filled that crypt to overflowing, and though there must've been all manner of grief expressed for the dead there over the years, I doubt any of it compared. Delilah howled with such force, such complete abandon, it made me fear for her frail old body.

'Lile! Lile!' Jimmy begged, trying to get a hold on her as she writhed from side to side, but within seconds he too was crying – not so much for Arturo, I didn't think, but 'cuz he simply couldn't bear to see her in so much pain. Hanna started to weep too, as silent as ever, the very opposite of Delilah, just sitting in the corner, her head in her hands, not making the slightest sound as tears ran out through her fingers and fell to the floor.

For a moment Gordie stood there, staring, then he turned and ran up the steps.

'Be careful!' I shouted after him.

Lena went to Hanna and squatted down, comforting her, all the while holding my gaze. For the first time in our relationship we were able to exchange consoling looks, and I wished to God we hadn't had such a reason.

'I hate this place,' I told her, 'more than anywhere I've ever known.'

'Why don't we go?' she suggested.

'As soon as Dr Simon gives the all-clear.'

'I can see; it's improving already.'

I was tempted, but for the matter of a couple more days, it didn't seem worth it, not with something so important. 'Give it 'til Friday. Then we're gone. No matter what.'

Suddenly Delilah stopped wailing, raised her head and looked at me with strained and bloodshot eyes. 'Where is he?' she asked.

Jesus. That was the other question I'd been dreading her asking. 'I don't know.'

'What d'you mean?'

'They took him.'

'What?'

'I don't know why.'

'I want to see him!' she protested.

'Lile!' Jimmy said, again trying to put his arm around her, but getting pushed away.

'I want to see him!' she repeated, even more desperately.

'He's gone, Lile,' Jimmy told her, and she resumed her sobbing, though this time she did allow him to put his arms around her – or maybe she was just oblivious to anything else.

There was nothing anyone could say. That was our world, both out on the Island and here on the Mainland; nothing and no one was permanent, anyone could disappear, just like that, and it was up to each individual to decide how to deal with it: keep everyone at arm's length, 'cuz feeling for them was merely an invitation to pain? Or dive in and take whatever might be going?

In a way, it was a bit like getting drunk. You could be the loud guy, laughing, singing, living every emotion to the fullest, pulling down the walls and saying all the things you always wanted – or you could just sit there, quietly sipping, never overdoing it, never willing to risk any kind of hangover.

CHAPTER NINE

You gotta move on; in your mind, in your heart, if you don't, sadness will nail you to the floor, crush you wherever you choose to lie. Mind you, that's easy for me to say, I never spent as much time with Arturo as Delilah did. She cried right throughout the night while Jimmy tried to comfort her, but no one could ease that pain. The rest of us just lay there helplessly, hearing every word but pretending we didn't, not reacting or commenting, as if that gave them a degree of privacy.

Occasionally Lena would bury her head deep into my chest, maybe to shut out Delilah's grief or to seek some comfort for her own. It was the suddenness as much as anything: just a few hours ago this place had been echoing to the sound of Arturo's laughter, Delilah chasing him round, the pair of them screaming in excitement until she finally managed to tug him into an embrace. Death might be the most natural thing in the world, but it's the hardest to accept.

Not a word was spoken in the morning as we stirred, one by one. The only sound was Delilah's usual early-morning hack, and even that sounded grudging, as if she just didn't want to make the effort.

The first thing I saw when I opened my eyes was Arturo's sleeping bag. I stared at it for a while, sickened by its emptiness, then, with the others still dozing, slipped over and grabbed it. I was gonna take it across the street and toss it on the fire, but with the way the world was it seemed like an awful waste. In the end, I took my secret path through the thorns to that empty space alongside the back wall where no one else went but me and hid it there.

When I got back, Delilah was staring at the space where the sleeping bag had been. She looked at me with a hint of betrayal as I entered, but never said a word.

'Sorry,' I muttered, but she remained silent.

The rest of that morning was one of the longest and saddest of my life. No one really knew how to react or what to say. Tell the truth, it got a bit much for me. As lunchtime approached, I remembered how little food we had and suggested Lena and me went out to look for some.

She paused when we got to the churchyard gate. The fire across the street had burned down to almost nothing, and yet there was still something fuelling those flames.

'In a terrible way, that's a beautiful thing for me,' she told me.

'Guess so.'

She wandered across to get a better look. 'I see what Jimmy means,' she said, when it flared up again.

'Are you all right getting this close?' I asked, remembering Dr Simon's warning about the smoke and her eyes.

She nodded, but I pulled her away anyway, just in case, and we both walked slowly on, heading up towards the Square.

The further we went, the more I started to wonder if maybe I'd been wrong to suggest she came with me; actually seeing all the destruction was very different to being told about it. On the way back from Dr Simon's most of the City had still been intact. Here it was nothing but destruction and burned-out buildings, with the occasional twisted corpse left lying for everyone to see. But she took it all well – almost too well – 'til I began to wonder if maybe, as she hadn't been able to see, her mind had conjured up something even worse. Though that was a pretty hard thing to imagine.

We didn't have to go that far in the end: by exploring the more unfashionable-looking streets we found an area where a few stores and restaurants were still functioning and did our previous trick of rummaging through the garbage. I'm not sure what sort of food it was – Asian, maybe Vietnamese or Korean – but business obviously wasn't that good 'cuz we scooped out enough to last us several days.

I would've liked to have kept going, to have shown her more, but we were both feeling guilty about leaving the others for so long, so we headed back.

'Do you think it's getting better?' I asked, referring to her sight.

'Yes. Things are becoming clearer all the time.'

'That's a shame,' I said, kinda teasing myself.

'Clancy!' she groaned wearily.

'Only joking!' I said, grabbing her arm and pretending to restrain her fist in case she took a swing.

'I'm not laughing.'

'Okay, okay, fine,' I said, putting her hand back at her side with the care of a loaded weapon.

We wandered on, both of us trying to be as normal as possible, to wordlessly withstand the crushing weight of Arturo's death, or maybe just beginning to learn to live with it.

'So is that it then?' she finally asked. 'Now that I can see my own way you're not going to hold my hand any more?'

I chuckled and immediately took her hand. 'You don't get rid of me that easy.'

'Clancy,' she said, stopping for a moment to face me, 'you have no idea how wonderful it is to actually *see* you.'

I smiled at her, grateful for the reassurance, but also delighted to indulge in the simple pleasure of gazing into each other's eyes.

And there, in the middle of the sidewalk, with passers-by staring as if there had to be something wrong with us, we stood and held each other for several minutes, letting the world go by and the pain subside, knowing that, as long as the doc gave the okay – and we could find a way through the fires – by this time the following day we'd be away from all of this.

The following morning, Lena and me took what was becoming a familiar route up into the foothills to Dr Simon's clinic. Both of us were feeling this odd mixture of optimism tempered by sadness; we were excited at the prospect of going to the country, but oh-so-painfully disappointed that Arturo wouldn't be with us.

This time we were shown straight into the doc's office, though he didn't appear for a good twenty minutes. When he did, he looked unusually flustered.

'So? How is it?' he asked Lena, immediately booting up his computer before scanning her eyes with this scope attachment.

'Fine. They're improving by the day.'

'That's good,' he said, obviously pleased with what he was seeing on the screen. 'No pain or discomfort?'

'No, none.'

He studied her eyes for a few moments longer, taking in every detail, then pushed the attachment away. 'Fantastic. You can see again,' he announced.

'That's it?' Lena asked, a little surprised.

'Yes. Everything's fine.'

'But the rejection?' I asked, wanting to get it straight in my mind. 'That could happen at any time, right?'

'Well . . .' he said, as if dismissing the thought as one of no consequence, 'in theory, you're never free of that possibility, but it's minimal. A serious bump might do it, some kind of violent disturbance, but that could happen to a normal-sighted person.'

For a moment Lena just sat there in silence, as if with this final confirmation that she really had regained her sight, she was only now allowing herself to take it in.

'Thank you . . . thank you, thank you!' she said to Dr Simon, and after a moment, as if she'd been considering it, she jumped up and gave him a hug.

'It's my pleasure,' he told her, looking like a man who didn't like being touched – or maybe he just didn't want his suit creased. 'Now, there's just a couple of final tests, and something I want to give you . . . Will you excuse us a moment, Clancy? Then she's all yours. You won't have to come back again.'

The news that we were finally free to go had prompted as big a smile on my face as it had Lena's. In fact, left alone, and despite being the clumsiest old big guy in the world, I was tempted to leap up on the doc's desk and do a little dance. All we had to do now was find a way out of the city – a corridor, maybe, where the fires had burned themselves out and we could slip through and out into the wilds to somewhere altogether sweeter.

I can't tell you how good that sounded. For sure it would've sounded a whole lot better if Arturo had been coming with us – and I knew his shadow was gonna be there for a very long time – but I reckon he would've been as pleased as anyone to know we were about to go free.

Five minutes waiting for Lena and Dr Simon to return became ten and I started to pace a little, becoming impatient. I wanted to get going, collect the others and find a way out of that shithole, but I told myself it was only right that the doc should do everything necessary.

I went to the window and took a look out at the garden, noticing how some of the manicured vegetation was starting to feel the effects of the smoke; even the obviously expensive and well-tended plants were becoming a little brown and withered. It was just as I went to turn and resume my pacing that I saw Dr Simon being driven away in his limousine.

I was too surprised to react – I couldn't get my head round it at all! It couldn't have been— No way! My eyes must've been playing tricks on me. For a moment I just stood there, watching the limo disappearing down the drive, my face frozen in a frown . . . *What the hell?*

I rushed to the door and took a look out. 'Hello!' I shouted down the hallway, but nobody came. 'Hello!'

I started opening other doors, finding room after room empty. What was going on here? Had there been some kind of emergency? Had he had to leave in a hurry? Is that why he'd been so preoccupied earlier?

'Lena!' I shouted. '*Lena?*'

I found a kind of laboratory, the sort of place where you might've expected her to be, but again there was no one. I was just about to head out to look somewhere else when I noticed an empty syringe on the floor.

What kind of doctor does that, just leaves a syringe lying around? Weren't there rules about that kind of thing? I squatted down, picked it up and studied the couple of drops of clear liquid left inside as if I could tell what they were. Finally, I slipped it into my pocket. I was starting to get a really bad feeling about this.

I went to stand up and found my stiff old joints a little reluctant to straighten. Only at the very last moment did I hear this kind of low swish behind me.

I started to turn but never made it, colliding with something that hit me with real uncompromising force, propelling me straight out into the centre of a dark universe and leaving me there to perish.

I came to slowly, blearily, as if all the life left in me was trickling out of one barely open eye. I was in the dark – I didn't know where, but it certainly wasn't the crypt. The space was far too small. One thing was for sure, wherever I was really stank. In fact, the stench was so overwhelmingly obnoxious, it made breathing difficult. At first I thought it was fish – bad fish, old fish, left to putrefy in some forgotten corner, then I realised it was something else, something far worse: the smell was rotting flesh. Rotting *human* flesh . . .

I started to pant. I desperately needed fresh air, but something was on top of me: a sprawling, inert, suffocating weight – in fact, it wasn't just on top of me; I was surrounded on all sides. It was only when I tried to move, to force myself free, that I realised what my cheek was pressed up against, and I tell ya, I damn near threw up.

I was crammed into the middle of a pile of corpses. There were bodies all around me, layer upon layer of dead people. That was the weight I could feel pressing down and from all directions. They weren't quite decomposing yet – though those at the bottom were obviously well on their way – but fluids were leaking out, dripping down onto me. Blood was everywhere: I couldn't see it, but for sure I could smell and feel its salty stickiness.

Again I tried to move, wriggling and pushing this way and that, all the while trying not to panic as I battled this overwhelming feeling that I was locked into some ultimate nightmare – but I couldn't. It was as if I was jammed into this big tin can, sealed in with as many bodies as could possibly fit in with me. I pushed again, as hard as I could, trying to give myself some space to manoeuvre, and then – Jesus, the worst thing of all – I gave the body next to me a real shove and my hand disappeared inside. I wrenched it back out, feeling a broken bone, a rib maybe, scratch my skin, and I realised I'd pushed through into nothingness – that body was empty.

My fear must've generated some sort of primitive instinct 'cuz I pushed upwards as hard as I could, trying to shift those on top of me, and at last there was a squeak somewhere, the grinding of metal, and just for a moment I saw a tiny slither of the smoky night sky. Then whatever it was – and I guess it was some kind of lid or door – slammed back down and I was entombed once more.

It was that metallic clank that made me think about what I was inside – I knew that sound, it was really familiar. And finally it hit me: it was a dumpster, a big industrial one, by the feel of it, and Jesus, you wanna talk about karma? I'd dumped the odd body in a dumpster myself in my time. I'm not proud of it, and I hope for their sake they hadn't still been alive like me, 'cuz it was about as a bad a fate as I could imagine anyone suffering.

There was no way out of there other than by sheer brute force, focusing down into the very deepest depths of me and mining whatever was left to push and shove, fighting my way through ruptured bodies, torn flesh, discarded organs, things I didn't dare think about, ignoring the blood and bile and slime and faeces that coated my body, until finally I managed to punch my way through to the top of the pile and heaving the lid back, gasped in something closer to fresh air.

God only knew what I must've looked like as I tumbled out of that thing. Thankfully, there was no one to see me. I found myself in a deserted service alleyway at the back of some empty buildings, and by the look of all the crap around, it was a favourite dumping place for locals. I spotted some old paint drums nearby filled with murky rainwater, and believe me, nothing could've been more welcome. I tried to rub my face clean before rubbing myself down, but eventually I just poured every drop I could find over me, anything to remove that noxious slime.

What the hell happened? How in God's name had I ended up in a dumpster? Did I die? Or did someone think I was so close it was only a matter of time? And where had all those bodies come from? Women, men – and though it sickened me to say it, there were kids there, too. How'd they died? For sure some had been operated on . . . just thinking that reminded me of that sickening feeling when I'd plunged my hand through the ribs into that empty cavity . . .

The longer I stood there the more things started to open up in my mind, like someone popping that bubble wrap stuff: Dr Simon – the laboratory – and—

Oh my God! '*Lena!*'

I was running even before I knew it, no matter I felt all weak and shaky and was still wanting to puke my guts up, and with a pain in my head like I had an axe sticking out of it. I could see a glow in the sky and realised it was early morning – somehow I'd lost the best part of a day. Where the hell *was* she? What had happened? And *why*? Why had Dr Simon cured her blindness only to kidnap her?

When I emerged out onto the street at the top of the alleyway, I realised I was in the bay area. Immediately I turned towards the hills: I had to find her and the only place I could think of to start looking was back at the clinic.

*

I knew security would be a problem, but I was so desperate, so scared for Lena, I just charged up there anyway. They were fine when I first arrived, when they saw me looking through the gate, but then this woman came over and when she got a closer look and saw I was still damp from my 'shower', when she realised how agitated I was, her attitude changed – particularly when I told her I had to see Dr Simon. I had no clearance but I begged her, over and over, 'til eventually she agreed to talk to the house. She returned to the gate office, perhaps to unwittingly give them the unwelcome news I was still alive.

After a while, she came back out. 'Dr Simon's not there.'

'Who is?'

'No one – the housekeeper,' she corrected herself.

I stopped and thought for a moment. 'Did you see Dr Simon yesterday? Round about lunchtime? With my friend?'

She stared at me, obviously concerned by my manner, trying to work out what the hell was going on here and who was involved. 'No.'

'In his limo?'

'No.'

'You must have!'

She stood there for a moment, then sighed and went back inside, returning a few moments later. 'Dr Simon left here yesterday at 12.08 with his driver. There was no other life form in the car.'

I shook my head, more to myself than to her, and gazed through the bars of the gate to the clinic. 'Can I just go up there for a few minutes?'

'Not without clearance,' she said, her patience obviously wearing thin.

'Well, I'm not budging from here 'til I do,' I warned her.

She glared at me, obviously not too impressed at the prospect of having a threatening-looking crazy at the gates on her watch. I guess she realised that I could create a fair amount of embarrassment before I was taken away. Eventually she sighed and went back inside. Returning a short time later she said, 'If you wait for a while, the housekeeper's just got to do something then she's going to come down to let you in.'

'When?' I demanded.

'Five minutes!' she snapped, walking away, and left me standing there with my hands gripping the bars, looking for all the world like a prisoner. She didn't go far but stationed herself on the steps of the office – I guess she wanted to keep an eye on me.

I'd seen Dr Simon's housekeeper once, but never spoken to her. I had no idea how willing she'd be to talk about her employer – who knew who was involved? Though the news that there'd been 'no other life forms' in the limo worried me far more: what the hell did 'no other life forms' mean? Dr Simon wouldn't have just knocked Lena out and left her, surely? He would've had to've taken her with him – in which case, maybe these people were lying? 'cuz if they weren't, I didn't want to think what that might mean.

As I waited there, pacing from side to side of the gates, repeatedly checking to see if the housekeeper was coming, I had a sudden thought: the last time I was asked to wait a few minutes round here it hadn't worked out that well.

Was it instinct or what? The moment the thought occurred to me I just turned and ran, leaving the security woman calling after me. I hadn't got more than a couple of hundred yards into the smoke before I heard a Dragonfly go over. I ducked off into this little gully that followed the path of the road and hid in the trees when it returned a few minutes later and started circling. They turned on their searchlights, trying to pierce the gloom, but I remained well hidden.

I was on automatic, in survival mode, not wanting to think any further than that. I didn't know if it was the security woman or the housekeeper who'd called for backup, but whoever it was, it meant I could forget all about Dr Simon kidnapping Lena 'cuz she was some kind of medical miracle. Our good doctor was working for Infinity, and I would've been willing to bet anything it was them holding her prisoner.

When the Dragonfly finally gave up and thrummed off into the smoke, I broke cover and began to make my way back to the church-yard, partly 'cuz I needed to tell the others what was going on (after all, we'd been missing more than a day) and partly 'cuz I couldn't think of anywhere else to go.

I felt sick to the stomach. Jesus, what a fool! What a first-class dumb-assed stupid old big guy! No wonder I was only ever employed for my muscles. How could I have allowed myself to be taken in by that smarmy bastard? Lena had been right: the moment he told me he'd waive his fees I should've known something was wrong. Instead, I guess he had all that time plotting, waiting for his oppor-tunity – but why hadn't he kidnapped her when she'd stayed at the clinic? None of it made any sense. And what the hell did Infinity want with her anyway?

Was it something to do with Jimmy? Were they trying to get to him through her? Didn't seem very likely. I didn't think Infinity even knew the two of them were connected.

Not that any of this mattered. There was only one thing my dull old heart was insistently repeating: *I'd lost her!* The woman I'd waited my whole life for had been taken from me. And as I passed yet another scene of blazing destruction, of life reduced to lifeless-ness, it momentarily went through my head that maybe normal order had been restored, a wrong had been righted; that there was simply no place in this hell for an angel like Lena.

When I reached the sad remains of the church, wearily climbed across the piles of rubble and down the steps into the crypt, the others just looked at me. I guess they knew that me and Lena's absence meant something had gone terribly wrong, and the fact that I was alone meant they were just too afraid to ask what.

For a moment I just stood in front of them, unable to get the words out, wanting to tell them but knowing that if I tried, tears would flow.

'I think Infinity have got Lena,' I eventually managed.

Of all the things I could've said, that was plainly the one they least expected.

'*What?*' Delilah cried, as if the death of Arturo made her less able to take such a blow; that it could be the final straw.

I told them the whole story – well, as best I could. Dragging it up from my consciousness and fashioning it into any kind of sense felt a bit like sticking my fingers down my throat and puking my guts up.

'It must be me,' Jimmy said. 'They're gonna torture her, find out where I am.'

'How do they even know you're connected?' I muttered.

He thought for a moment, but came up with nothing. 'I don't know . . . What else could it be?'

'Maybe it's got something to do with the syringe?' Gordie suggested. 'They experimented on her.'

I handed the syringe to Jimmy to look at. 'Something to knock her out, d'you think?' I ventured. 'Make sure she didn't make a fuss? Even then, I reckon she'd've put up a fight.'

'She still would've shown up on the gate scan,' Jimmy pointed out.

'Maybe she did?'

There was a pause. I couldn't bear the thought that while Lena had been fighting for her freedom – maybe even her life – I'd been only a few yards away, oblivious to the whole thing.

Delilah sagged slowly down onto her sleeping bag. 'What are we going to do?'

There was a long silence. What could we do, three unarmed old folk and a couple of kids?

'I dunno,' I said eventually, 'but I'll tell you one thing: Lena's everything to me. If it's a choice between living without her or dying trying to get her back, I'm gonna choose the latter every time.'

Hanna slipped over and put her arms round me – the last person I would've expected to do such a thing – and though she never said anything, like always, I could feel her unspoken emotions.

'We'll get her back,' Jimmy said, and the others all muttered agreement.

And yet, no matter how brave their words, how reassuring they all attempted to be, it was impossible to ignore the sense of despair, of hopelessness, that settled over us. We were already grieving for Arturo and now here we were, stricken by further disaster.

Even if I'd been run over by a truck, I couldn't've felt any more squashed. Everything inside me was knocked out or shut down, and as our conversations became progressively more desperate and the fact that I really had lost Lena sank in, I began to feel more and more frustrated. I had to *do* something.

Eventually I headed off out, ignoring Jimmy's plea that we should start looking for somewhere else to live. All I cared about was getting Lena back, and if Infinity really did have her, then there was only one logical place to start looking.

The night we escaped from the Island I'd been aware of the Infinity building and how dominant it was, but I hadn't really studied it. That afternoon as I made my way round the perimeter, I began to see exactly what I was up against. I ended up in this patch of scrub at the front that led down to one of the many rocky inlets in the bay, finding myself a little cover and just sitting there scrutinising the complex, trying to work out how I could get inside. The side that faced the sea looked impregnable, yet somehow aloof. From the front it was a whole different matter: it was a lot more 'in your face', with concrete bollards lined up like soldiers on parade, fences which looked like they might well be electrified and a gate protected by double automatic barriers and armed guards. There was no way into that place other than perhaps flying in and landing on the helipad on the roof.

No sooner had I come to that conclusion than a Dragonfly came whooshing over, its arrival triggering spotlights that even in daylight picked it out of the smoky sky, and a whole bank of laser cannons swivelled into action, primed and ready to bring it down at a moment's notice.

The one thing that puzzled me was the arrival of a line of half-a-dozen or so of those sinister white trucks – what the hell were they doing here? They just dumped bodies, didn't they? In convenient dumpsters down dark alleyways, apparently. Whatever the reason, they got the same treatment as everyone else: they were searched, swept and scanned every which way. Not until the security guards were entirely satisfied were they allowed to enter.

I expelled a lungful of tired air. The longer I stayed, the more intimidated I became. I also realised something else: I'd been so busy taking in all the major stuff that I hadn't registered this constant background noise. It was a kinda rolling, sliding sound, travelling up and down, and when I saw the source, I knew I should've noticed it before.

That top wire on the fence wasn't electrified; it was a trolley-way for cameras. Every thirty seconds or so one whirred by, looking out for any possible intruders.

I didn't know exactly where those cameras were pointing and I wasn't gonna hang around to find out either. I got to my feet, dusted myself down and stretched, hoping I looked like some hobo who'd been looking for a few hours' sleep but had found his chosen spot unsuitable, and headed off. The last thing I needed was them taking a special interest in me.

As I wandered away, my eyes went to the endless rows of windows on that huge building. 'Lena, are you in there?' I whispered. 'Don't worry. I'm coming for you . . . Promise.'

But that damn place was so big, so damn formidable, even if I did somehow manage to get in there, it might take a day of searching to find her. I needed information on the layout, to know where she was most likely to be . . .

Then again, who was I kidding? I needed a damn sight more than that. I needed a miracle to get me in there, and then something even bigger to get the two of us back out again.

CHAPTER TEN

I tried, but there was no way could I sleep without Lena next to me, though in terms of my thoughts, she never left my side all night. Jimmy kept telling me I had to stay calm, to think before I acted, 'cuz my impulse was to just get hold of the biggest weapons I could and blast my way into that place. It wasn't exactly the best plan anyone'd ever come up with, but it sure as hell didn't stop me wanting to do it.

I had this real empty ache inside that wouldn't let go for a moment; like someone'd ripped out my heart and all my other vital organs as well. What I'd said to the others was true: I didn't want to live without Lena, I'd done it for more than sixty years and believe me, I knew just how damn pointless it was. If she was gone forever, then I needed to know so I could do something about it.

And yet, in the odd few moments when I did manage to calm down – when I tried to take Jimmy's advice and think things through – it occurred to me that maybe, just *maybe*, there was just the tiniest glimmer of hope. They had to have taken her for a reason, not just to kill her, and hopefully that meant that for the moment at least, she was safe. On the other hand, how long would that last? If it was information they were after, then they might torture her – and that was one helluva disturbing prospect. But what the hell could she know? What information could she have that Infinity wanted? And really, that was the crux of it, the question I kept asking myself a hundred times an hour: *why had they taken her?*

Later that day I went out with Gordie. There was a permanent need for food, which made it a good excuse to go somewhere, but actually, I didn't need one. I think the others all sensed not only my pain, but also my helplessness too. I didn't know what to do, and didn't want to be questioned about it either.

I thought about going down to the Infinity building again, taking another look, but even in the depths of my despair I knew that wouldn't make a great deal of sense: being seen hanging around, acting suspiciously, would blow any tiny chance I might have had of getting into that place. And anyway, I still didn't know for certain she was in there. So instead, we just wandered the City, blindly hoping that we might see or hear something that would help us understand what had gone on.

There weren't as many fires as there had been, though the smoke didn't appear to have thinned at all. It felt like it had permeated everywhere and everything. We couldn't go anywhere without smelling that odd acrid stench Lena had complained about. I guess that went for us, too, if we could've smelled ourselves: we were probably just as smoked as any smokehouse ham or herring.

Gordie and me hadn't exactly been deep in conversation – in fact, I was so lost in my thoughts, we'd exchanged barely a word. It wasn't 'til he started complaining that I realised just how hard I'd been pushing us on.

'Clancy! I'm tired – we can't cover the whole city,' he whined.

It took a moment for me to absorb what he'd said, to appreciate that he had a point, and also to grasp that I'd led us somewhere I didn't recognise at all.

'Where the hell are we?' I muttered.

'The sun's that way,' he replied. Like everyone who lived on the Island he was pretty good at working out that kind of thing.

'So . . . down there,' I said, pointing left at an upcoming junction, though I wasn't anywhere near as confident as I was making out.

It wasn't an area I knew at all, and we hadn't gone that far before I began to wish I could've kept it that way. They would've had to have spent an awful lot of dough on it to convert it into a slum, and worse still – maybe 'cuz it was an underprivileged area – there were a lot of those zombie-sick around, slumped in doorways, reclining on stoops, draped out of windows, all as pale and lifeless as the moon. And just like when we'd been down on the beach, they started to take a real close interest in us, particularly Gordie.

'Shit!' I muttered, noticing we were collecting a following.

'What do they want?' Gordie asked, looking nervously over his shoulder. 'Suck my blood?'

Funny thing was, it might've been an attempt at humour, a little bravado, but I could almost believe it. They looked so weak and drained I could imagine a glass of Gordie and tonic doing them a power of good. Not that I said as much to him.

I hesitated for a moment, considering turning back, but now there were more behind than in front. 'Let's cross over,' I said, seeing it was quieter on the other side.

They all followed, starting to crowd in and surround us, with even more appearing, stumbling out of houses, rising up out of basements. I mean, a few of them, no problem, they were so weak you could just push them aside, but thirty or forty was another matter . . .

This one old man made a clumsy grab for Gordie, trying to get hold of him, but the little guy sidestepped him easily. 'No, thank you,' he said, trying to make it sound like he was well in control, but I could hear fear starting to whittle away at his voice.

The old man reached out again but this time I pushed between them, putting my arm on Gordie's shoulder and leading him away.

It wasn't so much of a problem when we were out in front of them – we were much quicker and could easily outpace them – but the more that appeared, the more the excitement grew, and they started calling to others to come out, too. It felt like we were slowly being swallowed up by a sea of wailing white faces with smudged inky thumbprints for eyes.

'Get outta the way,' I growled, shoving a little knot of them aside.

Even then, despite their number, I thought we'd be okay – but then there was a shout and I looked around to see this guy emerging from an apartment block with a machete.

I guess old habits die hard even if you're sick. There was this immediate scramble away from him and people started looking up into the sky, obviously expecting instantaneous punishment to rain down, but thanks to Jimmy, there was nothing.

'Let's go,' I muttered to Gordie, wanting to take advantage of their momentary lapse in attention. I mean, I had no idea how much danger we were in, but I didn't intend to hang around and find out either.

The guy with the machete started after us, people moving out of his way as he swept it in this slightly feeble arc. He was shouting at others to stop us and some tried, tugging at our arms and grabbing at our clothing. I snarled at them, told them to leave us alone.

The machete guy might've been making heavy work of it, but he was starting to gain on us, mainly 'cuz people were getting out of his way but not ours. I tell ya, it felt as if we'd blundered into a street party for the living dead, only there seemed to be some misunderstanding about what was on the menu. Gordie's face was almost as pale as those around us and he was keeping as close to me as he could – and yet, I still didn't think there was any real reason to fear them; they were as weak as kittens, and I could already see our crazed pursuer was starting to tire. I barged more people out of the way, shoving and pushing harder and harder until we finally broke free.

I checked behind us to see the guy with the machete had stopped and was draped over a hydrant looking as if he'd just run a marathon. And you wanna know something? That mean, scary machete-wielding punk who'd looked like he'd wanted to cut and dice us both, started to cry like a lost child.

'D'you see that?' Gordie sniggered, suddenly full of himself again.

'This whole city's one giant damn asylum,' I muttered as I led him away.

Once we got back on track, we began to make a slow sweep in the direction of the Square. I don't know what I thought I was achieving – guess I was just trying to pretend I wasn't helpless, or maybe I was reverting to old habits, stratagems that'd served me well in the past. Back when I was working for Mr Meltoni, if I thought there was information being held from me, I'd walk the streets 'til I found out what it was – forget about your limos, you gotta get out with the people. I remember him insisting I took his wife's dog with me – Mitzi, this little Yorkshire terrier with a pink bow in her hair, can you believe that? A big guy like me with that fancy furry flea. He said it made me look less threatening, less conspicuous. Well, 'threatening' – he might've had a point about that. But 'conspicuous'? I never stood out more in my life. People didn't want to talk to me 'cuz they were too embarrassed, or laughing too damn hard to pass on any information.

We'd been making our way along the main road for a while when Gordie pointed down a side street, reminding me of the other reason we were walking the City: food. There was this market that had just finished for the day and everything that hadn't been sold was being thrown away (I never did get that: in a city where half the population was starving, the other half were still chucking stuff away.).

'Grab those crates,' I told him, starting to gather up as much as I could, knowing it wouldn't be long before others spotted it. Gordie lugged over a couple of empty apple boxes and I began to fill them rapidly with whatever I could.

'Not carrots!' Gordie whined.

'You'd rather starve?'

'Any time.'

'That can be arranged,' I told him.

'If I gotta eat green stuff, at least make it fruit.'

I sighed and ignored him, stuffing whatever looked freshest into the boxes. I'd filled one for me and was halfway through his when I straightened up to rest my aching back and glanced up the street. I saw this big black limo appearing out of the smoke.

'Jesus!' I gasped, grabbing Gordie and forcing him to duck down behind a pile of broken crates.

'Who is it?' he asked.

'Someone I'd rather not see.'

The car crept slowly by, windows down, music playing; the passenger's head swivelling left and right, as if scouring the streets for someone.

'They look mean,' Gordie whispered. 'Specially the big one.'

'Stay down,' I told him, my hand heavy on his shoulder.

I waited 'til they were some way down the street and had started to disappear into the smoke, then slowly stood up. It was Van and his sidekick, and it might've been just coincidence – they could've been looking for anyone – but I wouldn't have minded betting it was me. Ray was probably pissed off at how that job had worked out, the guy ending up dead. Jeez, with everything else that had been going on, it was the last thing I needed.

'Let's go,' I said to Gordie. We picked up the boxes and I led him away, hugging the storefronts, ready to duck into a doorway at any moment if the limo returned.

I saw one other odd thing on our way back to the churchyard. The fire across the street had died right down at last, leaving a few jagged sections of slowly cooling walls, and someone had sprayed graffiti on one of them – not that there's anything unusual about that, there's always been graffiti all over the City, but the words kind of gave me a jolt.

There's none so blind as those who will not see

Why I thought that meant anything, I don't know. I guess, the way things were, I just couldn't resist. It was the only graffiti in the street and someone had picked out that particular wall, right opposite us, to spray it.

'Weird,' I commented, resting my crate of vegetables for a moment.

Gordie grunted, puzzled by my reaction 'Why?' he asked.

'Don't you think it's strange?'

He looked for a moment, then gave his 'highly unimpressed' shrug. 'Nope,' he replied, and turned and headed into the church-yard.

I stood there for a few seconds, then picked up my own crate and followed him. He was probably right; my tortured old imagi-nation was starting to run away with me again.

Everyone was pretty impressed with the amount of fresh food we'd brought back. Even Jimmy momentarily stopped working to give an appreciative little whistle. He'd been fiddling with that screen for days, trying to use those parts he'd brought back to make it untraceable so we could watch what was going on. One look at his frustrated expression was enough to tell me he still hadn't cracked it.

'No luck?' I asked.

'It's not a case of "luck", Big Guy,' he said, somewhat put out by my terminology. 'If that was all it was, anyone could do it.'

'Don't know why you're bothering,' Delilah grumbled. 'They'll only tell you what they want you to know.'

The little guy never commented; partly I guess 'cuz he knew she had a point, but also 'cuz of how down she still was about Arturo – and now Lena, and he knew he had to tread lightly.

Delilah, as if reacting to his concern, started to hum tunelessly to herself as if to make it clear that no one needed to worry about *her*.

Later, after we'd eaten and Gordie and Hanna had argued end-lessly about whether or not people were meant to consume fruit and vegetables, I went back up-top. It was getting late, but that graffiti was still on my mind and I wanted to take another look before it got dark.

There's none so blind as those who will not see

It was just a scrawl, hastily written – as if whoever had done it wanted to get away as quickly as possible. Why on earth did I think there was any connection with Lena? 'cuz of the use of the word 'blind', maybe? But she wasn't blind any more, leastways, not as far as I knew. I sighed, checked up and down the street that no one was watching me and where I was going, then crossed back over and entered the churchyard. Clearly I was searching for answers in places where there were none. I mean, what wouldn't she want to see? Her captors? What they were trying to make her say or do? That didn't make any sense – and most senseless of all: if it was about Lena, who could've written it?

The following day I lost it altogether. I missed Lena so much – there was a terrible ache where she should've been. I've told you before, I'd give my life for hers anytime. If someone had told me then and there how to do it, I would've been happy to. But it was the not knowing that was killing me, and the longer it went on, the more my mind played tricks on me. Every time I went out I thought I saw her, even chasing after people sometimes, calling her name, frightening them and embarrassing myself. I had all sorts of stupid thoughts going through my head, including that maybe she hadn't been kidnapped at all – she'd run away.

I was out 'skulking around', as the others called it, talking to people, asking if they'd seen her, when I spotted someone who looked just like her entering a looted department store. I mean, yeah, it was smoky and this woman was on the far side of the street, but the way she was dressed, the way she moved – I could've sworn it was Lena.

I rushed over, entering through the same smashed window she had, trying to pick her out from the scavengers, but she'd disappeared.

I scoured the entire floor and still hadn't found her, so I made my way over to the escalator. I went up level by level, searching all round, but still there was no sign. When I reached the top, my frustration got the better of me and I went and hung over the rail.

'Lena! *Lena!*' I cried, my voice sounding all empty and strained, but still there was nothing. I turned and started to make my way back down, this time searching each floor more thoroughly, even checking the restrooms – I mean, in my heart I guess I knew it wasn't her, but I still had to be *sure*.

I was descending to the third floor when I came across this commotion: a couple of Infinity Specials were struggling with the woman I'd been looking for, and you know, with her back to me, it still could've been Lena. I gave this cry of outrage, but when the three of them stopped and turned, when I got a better look, I could see how wrong I'd been, that actually, she was older and shorter; in fact, there was barely any likeness to Lena at all.

She was trying to keep hold of this dusty overcoat she must've picked up whilst the two Specials were attempting to snatch it away from her. They were a pair of big muscle-heads, dressed in laser-reflective gear, black gloves, helmets and dark glasses, and I guess they reckoned fear alone should've been enough to subdue her.

It was a strange kinda coincidence that the person I'd mistaken for Lena was being mistreated by the very organisation I suspected of kidnapping her – too much so for a man in my state. Suddenly I wanted to defend that woman as much as anyone in my life, and I leapt down the last few steps of the escalator, shouting at them like a maniac. The woman gave out with this awful animal-like yelping; in fact, I reckon she might've been a little crazy herself.

The few people around immediately scattered, not wanting to get involved in anything that involved violence and Specials, but it was me who was completely out of control.

'What d'ya want, old fuck?' one of the Infinity men snarled.

Okay, so I know I'd become touchy about my age, but that's never been a good conversation opener with me.

156

'Leave her alone,' I told them.

He looked around as if checking to see if anyone was watching. 'Look, we got enough nut-jobs to deal with. Just get the fuck out of here, will you?' He turned back to the woman and angrily wrenched the coat out of her hands as if determined to get this over with.

She wailed all the louder and I shouted again, 'Leave her alone!'

The same guy turned back to me and sighed, like he didn't want to do this but I'd given him no choice. 'Some of you old fucks just don't want to go on living, do you?'

He was quick – too quick for a man of my age – but luckily for me, he wasn't that accurate. He hit me with his clenched fist and though it was only a glancing blow, an awful tingling resonated through me. He was wearing shock gloves.

But you know, no matter how young and fit they were, or well-equipped, it wasn't a fair contest 'cuz they didn't have one ounce of my rage or frustration. I just leapt at them, in such a fury, growling like a bear, throwing punches left and right, immediately knocking one down and then kicking him for good measure. I turned to the other as he was going for his laser, making a grab for it myself 'til the two of us, wrenching it back and forth, somehow managed to break it. I took a swing at him, but hadn't noticed the guy on the floor getting back up. The next thing I knew, I was flat on my back, twitching and shaking, feeling that electricity zipping through me. He hit me again, on the left side this time, just on the bottom rib. I can't tell you how painful those damn things are, each new blow, each new electric shock, slicing you into a trillion pieces.

The only drawback with shock gloves is that they have to be recharged. It only takes a moment or two, but for that brief period, whoever's using them's disarmed. He pulled away from me, I guess thinking his partner would have me covered with his laser, and I'd just about got to my feet as his gloves gave off that shrill 'charged' sound and I caught him on the cheek as he went to turn, knocking him to the floor.

From then on there was no stopping me. I was like an old familiar beast bursting free of his chains; any hope I had of doing the sensible thing was gone. All the loathing I had for this organisation finally had an outlet. I jumped on the guy and jerked his head back, wrenched off one of his gloves and stuffed it into his mouth. Then I put on the other glove so I was insulated and rammed his jaws shut, triggering the electric charge. He screamed and went all limp, and when he started to come round, I did it again, and again, each time his screams getting weaker. I maintained my grip 'til I was certain he was dead, then turned to deal with the other guy. He was up on his feet, but backing away, making for the escalator.

I'm not sure I would've caught him, but as luck would have it, he was in such a state of panic that he cannoned into the woman as she was also making for the escalator, the coat bundled up in her arms. I grabbed him and as the woman took the opportunity to scamper away, I dragged him to a nearby office. I didn't want anyone else to overhear what I was about to say.

I'd calmed down a bit by the time I threw him into a chair, maybe 'cuz I finally had a chance to ask someone the question I'd been asking myself every moment since I fell outa that dumpster

'Where's Lena?' I said, the words almost tripping over each other.

'Who?' he asked.

'Lena!' I shouted.

'Who the hell's Lena?'

'You got her prisoner. Thirty-something, long brown hair, hazel eyes.'

He shook his head and I hit him, hard, on the side of the face, once and then again. 'Tell me!'

'I don't know what you're talking about!' he cried, blood starting to trickle from his lip. 'I'm just an ordinary Special – from the barracks behind the main building. We don't get involved in that sort of stuff.'

'Where would they keep her?'

'*I don't know!*' he said exaggeratedly, like I must be hard of hearing or something.

'Jesus,' I growled, and grabbing him by the collar I jerked him up out of his seat, gave him a real blast of the look, face to face, then threw him back down again.

For a moment I just stood there, slowly becoming aware that my loss of control had meant me making a mistake, playing it wrong – or leastways, taking a gamble that hadn't paid off.

Eventually he met my gaze, regaining confidence, maybe taking my preoccupation as a sign that I'd lost my nerve. 'I'd start running if I were you, old man,' he said. 'Killing an Infinity Special? The way they'll torture you, you'll beg them to end your life.'

I sighed. He was right. The only thing was, he hadn't thought it through properly either – 'course he was right, I shouldn't've killed his partner, but now that I had, I'd be a fool to leave a witness.

I grabbed him and wrestled my way over to the full-length window. As he began to guess what I had in mind, he started struggling even harder, elbowing me in the face with such force I thought for a moment I was going to black out. But I clung on, determined to maintain my grip as I dragged him ever closer, 'til finally I was able to manoeuvre him round, release his hold on me and shove him as hard as I could. The glass exploded outwards and for one absurd moment he just hung in mid-air like a cartoon character, then he let out this long, loud wail and disappeared from sight as he plummeted to the street below.

I took the emergency stairs and slipped out the back of the building, having no wish to be seen by the crowd I was sure was gathering at the front. I headed back to the churchyard as fast as I could.

As I was crossing the Square, this Dragonfly suddenly dropped down out of the smoke, flying so low I thought they were going to land. It hung there for a few moments, then slowly began to circle, ever wider, 'til eventually it disappeared into the smoke again. I mean, it wasn't unusual, but it didn't do a lot for my peace of mind. I was feeling pretty guilty about what I'd done – I didn't do that sort of thing any more, and even back in the day, I'd never been one for mindless violence – and yet really, what were we talking about? A couple of Specials, guys who'd repeatedly massacred help-less people – and who knows, maybe two who were on duty the night little Arturo got killed? They might even've assisted in some way.

I turned the corner off the Square and was just about to head down to the churchyard when I noticed something. I stopped, back-tracking several paces.

It was here, too, written on the wall in even bigger letters than opposite the churchyard:

There's none so blind as those who will not see

CHAPTER ELEVEN

The graffiti was written in exactly the same way, and presumably by the same person. It was also quite fresh, maybe even from that morning. Immediately it set me thinking: this was another place I frequently passed, where someone might just leave a message they were hoping I'd read. But no, I knew I had to stop thinking that way. It had nothing to do with me, just someone who wanted to share something with the world. It was sheer coincidence Lena used to be blind and wasn't any more. In fact, it wasn't even coincidence, just me trying to make something out of nothing . . . There's none so all-seeing as those out to torture themselves.

To my surprise, when I got back to the crypt I found everyone sitting round watching Jimmy's mini-screen.

'Is that okay?' I asked Jimmy.

'Yeah,' he replied, a little smugly, 'if they're searching for its location, they're currently sifting street by street though St Petersburg.'

I'd do anything but tell him, but his skill with that sort of thing never failed to amaze me. 'Anything interesting?' I asked, a little concerned in case there was any mention of the two Specials or the monster who'd taken them out.

'Ask "The World's Most Wanted",' Delilah rasped drily.

'Really?'

Again Jimmy looked a little pleased with himself, though he did attempt a degree of modesty. 'It's just a title,' he said. 'Something snappy for people to remember me by.'

'All the other channels the same?' I asked.

Jimmy grunted. 'What other channels?'

I stared at him. There'd been hundreds of different channels when I'd left for the Island, mostly little independents, but a dozen or more big players too.

'There *are* other channels,' he told me, 'but Infinity or its affiliates appears to own them all. We were right: they're in total control now. What government there is – well, nothing more than a figurehead really – went bust long ago. Same old problem: too much going out, not enough coming in. The satellites were their last hope, though Infinity even paid for them. Private enterprise – and for sure I didn't have to dig far to find Infinity – called in their loans and shut them down.'

'Huh. No one told us that at the time.'

'They talk endlessly about democracy but have complete control of all media – and we know what that means, don't we. Oh yeah, and they provide free Internet, too. To *everyone*.'

'What's wrong with that?'

He gave this kind of disgusted snort. 'Manipulate so-called competition laws to get rid of the opposition, then when it's just you, use it for whatever you like: censorship, spying, propaganda; invent stuff, erase it, take people out, remove their records, say they never even existed. Not cool.' He paused for a moment, then started ranting again, 'No one ever stopped to think . . . it's Lemmings'

Law: if everyone's doing it, it must be okay. We were seduced into becoming utterly reliant upon the media, and while we all went along blindly trusting in the idea of the greater good, Infinity was hell-bent on its own evil agenda. In truth, we lost control almost immediately.'

He gestured at the screen. 'Look what they're saying about me,' he protested. '"The biggest threat to our society we've ever known!" *Me!* . . . I can barely put my socks on in the morning.'

'They must be pretty open about it if you found all this out,' I said, looking for some consoling factor.

Jimmy stared at me as if I was even stupider than he'd thought. 'What d'ya think took me so long? I had to hack in all over the place.'

'Oh,' I said. I should've guessed that, and probably would have, if my mind hadn't suddenly shot off in its most-travelled direction. 'What about Lena? D'you find anything out about her?'

He shook his head. I guess he'd known that would be my first question. 'I did try, but . . . no, sorry.'

'Nothing at all?'

'I'll keep looking,' he told me. 'There are holding cells in the Infinity building, I can tell you that.'

That didn't really mean much – maybe she wasn't even being held in a cell. 'What about a hospital?'

'I think they've got pretty much everything in there.'

I went quiet for a moment, absently looking at the screen. There was an ad on there for some new chocolate bar – I mean, what could've been more normal? But in the context of our lives, it felt like an obscenity.

'I need you to see the place,' I told him. 'It's too hi-tech for me.'

'I can't go down there,' he protested, 'not if it's as secure as you say.'

'Jimmy—' I begged, and though I never actually said *Lena*, I knew he heard it all right.

'It's not going to help anyone if I get caught,' he told me.

Delilah turned to him and raised her eyebrows, like she wasn't so sure about that, but the little guy had obviously had a thought. 'Mind you . . .'

'What?'

'If I could take the camera out of this', he said, pointing at the screen, 'there's a mini-monitor amongst that stuff I brought back from Hi-Tech Alley . . . a microphone . . .'

I just sat there, no idea what he was talking about, but knowing any interruption would be dismissed.

'Maybe . . . just maybe,' he went on, those wheels almost visibly spinning away in his head. 'Be a bit crude, but it might do the trick.'

'Jimmy?' I asked, my curiosity getting the better of me.

'You could be my eyes and ears . . . I can't go, but you can.'

I stared at him as I finally got some idea of what he had in mind. 'I'm gonna be your cameraman?'

'Yeah! I tell you what I want to see, and all you gotta do is point.' He paused for a moment as another problem occurred to him. 'If it's as sensitive as you say . . . it's probably got some kind of image-jamming going on.' I thought that was it, he'd run out of ideas, but no, this was *Jimmy*. 'There'll have to be two of you – one with the camera, one with a shield.'

Gordie felt my eyes upon him and jumped to his feet. 'No problem,' he said, acting all big and hard.

'I wouldn't,' Jimmy said. 'You've probably been recorded somewhere as a grouping – appear down there together, it might set alarm bells off. You're better off with someone else – a female.'

'Lile?' I said, not wanting to offend, but fearing she really wasn't up to it.

Jimmy gestured at Hanna, and Gordie immediately let out this howl of protest. '*No way!*'

I turned to Hanna – I mean, she's a great kid, and fearless too, but I really wasn't sure about taking her to the Infinity building. She glanced up from the screen, apparently not in the least bit fazed. 'Okay,' she trilled, immediately returning her attention to whatever it was she was watching.

But Gordie was a long way from happy; him and Hanna never had got on that well, and without Arturo round to act as a buffer, their antagonism had become that much more noticeable.

'You can't take *her*,' he sneered. 'All she does is dance.'

'I can fight . . . if I have to,' she said, with the hint of a threat.

'As long as it's set to music,' he scoffed, but Hanna ignored him, concentrating on the screen, like he was a stupid child and she'd expected no better from him.

'Clancy!' Gordie protested.

'There's not going to be any fighting,' I told him. 'Leastways, I hope not.'

'*Nooo!*' he cried, turning his back on the screen, sulking, or until he realised the only person he was punishing was himself.

In the end, Jimmy's logic prevailed. Even in the middle of the twenty-first century a man accompanied by a young female was much less threatening than two men together. And he was right about me and Gordie possibly having been logged as a group already, and covering a suspiciously wide area of the City in the last couple of days. As for the 'equipment' we needed, he eagerly rose to the challenge, promising us he'd come up with something by the end of the day, and that with a bit of luck, we'd be able to head over to Infinity the following day.

He was just about to turn off the screen and start dissembling it again when he was confronted by his own image.

I tell ya, they sure had it in for him. I couldn't believe all the stuff they came up with. They'd guessed he might've disguised himself so ran through all the possibilities, ending up with making him look like the devil, with horns and all. But it was what they *said* that was truly offensive. There wasn't a thing they didn't throw at him: his senility, the money his 'terrorism' was costing everyone, the fact that his parents were illegal migrants, that he was in a relationship with a prostitute (how the hell did they even know that?), that he kept the company of young children – and all reported so heavy with innuendo that it damn near fell out the bottom of the screen. By the time they'd finished with him he was an arch-terrorist, a mass-murderer, a whoremonger, a paedophile, the bastard son of illegals – and worst of all (and the charge they kept repeating over and over, as if they knew it would have the most influence), he was gonna cost every man, woman and child thousands and thousand of dollars. There wasn't one emotive rabble-rousing button they didn't press.

And yet I couldn't help but feel there was something a little desperate about it, almost as if this huge all-powerful organisation was afraid of him. I turned and looked at Jimmy: this wizened, bald old guy limping round the crypt, getting all sparkly-eyed at the possibility of using that resourceful brain of his. What the hell was there to fear in him? I guess he did take out the satellites, but that was just to escape the Island. We never really thought about the repercussions. This ceaseless vendetta against the little guy didn't make any sense at all.

Jimmy sent me out shopping. I had to trek around for some old-fashioned wire coathangers, tinfoil, all kinds of stuff I'd normally associate with setting up a home rather than embarking on a dangerous operation.

When he finally got everything finished – well, he sure was right when he'd said it'd be 'crude'. He gave me this little bundle of techno-junk held together with insulating tape, and Hanna had a kind of large tennis racket that he proceeded to take apart and show her how to reassemble before taking it apart again and stuffing it into her pockets.

We talked the plan through and decided the best time would be late afternoon, just as the light was starting to fade. Even with the pall of smoke hanging over the city, broad daylight hadn't seemed like a great idea, but we needed enough light for Jimmy to get detailed images. Mind you, we were kidding ourselves if we thought less light would hamper Infinity's security in any way. I couldn't imagine there'd be any time they'd be at a disadvantage.

Gordie didn't wish us luck or even say goodbye; just made more of his acid comments. Mind you, it did feel kinda strange going off with Hanna. I seen her fight over on the Island and though she might not've looked it, underneath all that slender grace she was a real tough kid. But counting on her as my buddy, to watch my back? That was something else.

I never minded that she didn't say a lot – in fact, I preferred it. I've never been much of a talker myself, so it was pretty relaxing being with someone who didn't feel the need to constantly pick up the slack. I wouldn't've have expected us to exchange more than the odd word all the way over. However, when we got to the church-yard entrance and were about to head up towards the Square, I noticed another message, sprayed on a smaller scrap of burned wall but not far from the original. This time there were just three words:

LOVE IS BLIND

'What the hell?' I exclaimed.

Hanna stopped and followed my gaze across the street.

'What is that?' I exclaimed. 'Always this thing about being "blind".'

We crossed over, me straining to see into the smoke just in case whoever had done it was still around. By the time I reached the other side, Hanna was already inspecting the graffiti.

'Still smells,' she said. 'Must be recent.'

'Do you know what they mean?' I said, looking from one message to the other.

Hanna shook her head. 'Not really.'

'"There's none so blind as those who won't see" . . . "Love is blind" – I just don't get it.'

'Do you think it's Lena?' she asked.

I must admit, that had been one of a thousand thoughts that'd passed through my mind but I'd never really entertained it. 'Why d'ya say that?'

'Could be.'

'Wouldn't she just come to the crypt?'

'Maybe she can't for some reason.'

It's weird, but as I stared into that kid's face, with its prettiness still somewhat watermarked by what she'd endured out on the Island, I realised yet again what a complete original she was – and how useful it was having someone like her around.

'Why not?' I asked.

'I don't know,' she said, turning to walk on in that assured manner that always made me think she was making her entrance onto a stage and about to dance.

I stayed where I was, thinking it over. Even if Lena couldn't return to the church for some reason – if she was worried about leading others here, or something – she'd find a way, wouldn't she? Sighing to myself, I hurried after Hanna, afraid of losing her as she began to disappear into the smoke.

We arrived at Infinity just as the falling sun was giving the building a pink rinse, though it didn't look any less intimidating for all that. I found myself scouring those endless rows of windows again, hoping to catch a glimpse of Lena. It was pretty stupid: from that distance, and through the smoke, it was like looking for a needle in a haystack blindfolded – but still I tried.

Between the fence and road at the front of the building there was a lawn, eighty yards or so wide: a human touch in an otherwise inhumane place. We'd already checked the entrance out as we sauntered by, trying not to look interested but taking in everything we could. There was all kinda stuff there: what looked like shields, scanners, maybe even automated weapons. That was what I needed Jimmy for – to be certain.

We found a bit of cover amongst the scrub and I explained to Hanna about the cameras – that you only got thirty seconds or so before the next one came along. What I didn't know was whether they were computer- or human-monitored, which'd make a big difference: computers can only be programmed for a finite number of actions, while humans are much better at interpretation. On the other hand, if a computer concludes you're up to no good, it's pretty hard to talk your way out of it.

She waited for the next camera to pass, then took out her coathangers and began to shape them, dropping the arrangement to the ground when the next camera approached. Piece by piece she worked on assembling this kinda large saucepan, wrapped with tinfoil, adding the battery and gizmo Jimmy gave her to make a shield. She did it with such precision, followed his instructions so coolly, I gotta admit, I was already more comfortable with the decision to bring her. Meanwhile, I took out my so-called 'camera and communicator'.

'I'm ready,' Hanna told me, turning on her shield so it was working before I operated my camera. Jeez, I really hoped Jimmy knew what he was doing.

'Jimmy?' I muttered into my apparatus, keeping my voice low. There was no answer, so I tried again. 'Jimmy!'

I looked at Hanna. 'Doesn't work,' I muttered.

'Worry about your end of things – not mine,' came this barely recognisable, rather automated-sounding squeaky voice.

He appeared on the mini-monitor, for some reason looking unnaturally red. Before I could speak, I had to conceal the apparatus from yet another passing camera.

It certainly wasn't ideal, what with Hanna and me having to hide our stuff every few moments and Jimmy not always able to hear us, but slowly we began to make sense of each other.

'Okay, just start by panning the whole thing for me, one end to the other,' Jimmy asked. '*No!* Too fast – go slower!'

'Jimmy,' I complained, seeing another camera bearing down on us, 'I gotta be quick!'

The little guy kept thinking out loud about what he could see, going through an inventory, barely taking any notice of me apart from to give orders.

'Okay, yep, that's pretty standard – hey, can you focus in on the roof? By the helipad there . . . Nah, can't see – no, no, wait! . . . *Whoa!*' he cried. '*Heavy!* I won't be landing my private jet there any time soon. I wonder what an average everyday respectable conglomerate wants with heavy-duty laser cannons? . . . Clancy, where you gone?'

I covered my makeshift apparatus yet again as a camera slid past, pretending to be searching the waste ground for anything of value while Hanna did the same. I tell you, she was doing really well. Nothing seemed to fluster her.

'Wow! Cool!' gasped Jimmy, impressed more than intimidated by the hardware on display.

'So what d'ya think?' I asked.

'I dunno,' he said. 'The roof's heavily guarded, and as for the entrance, well, forget it. I don't get the lawn though.'

'What d'ya mean?'

'What's the point of it? Every thing else is there for a purpose . . . Try chucking a rock.'

'What?'

'Heave a rock over there. But get ready to run.'

'Are you kidding me?'

'I doubt anything'll happen outside the fence.'

'You sure about that?'

'More or less.'

'Thank you, Jimmy,' I said, glaring at that tiny red representation of him on the monitor. Maybe Infinity was right and he was the devil incarnate.

Though I say it myself, rock throwing is one of my few talents, and one was winging its way over there in no time. It landed on the grass while I trained my makeshift camera on it, watching for any reaction. There was none.

'Try a bigger one,' Jimmy said.

'What?'

'It might have a heavier trigger point. Otherwise anything would set it off. A bird could drop a twig.'

With a pointed sigh, I picked up a larger rock and lobbed it over. This time there *was* a reaction: a rabbit appeared from nowhere, ran around in a couple of circles, then just sat there.

Hanna gave out with all these 'cooing' and 'ooohing' noises, and it occurred to me that she'd probably never seen a live rabbit in her life.

'There you go,' I said to Jimmy, as if the whole thing had just been declared safe by an expert. But he still wasn't happy.

'I don't know,' he said. 'Maybe it needs to be even heavier.'

'Jimmy!' I protested.

'It don't make sense, Big Guy! All those open areas unprotected. Where did that rabbit come from?'

'A hole, I'd guess,' I rather sneered.

'Mm . . . That must be the dark areas I can see,' he said, obviously splitting his screen and pulling up a second image.

For a while he said nothing as he studied and played with the other image. I couldn't see his face that well, but he looked worried. Several cameras passed by, sliding and jerking on their wire, and I realised what they reminded me of: the dishes in the First Original Sushi Bar, trundling by on their belt.

'There's something wrong here,' Jimmy muttered to himself. 'I just don't know what.'

'You want me to hop over the fence and go for a walk?' I said sarcastically.

'Ideally, yes,' he replied.

'Yeah, well, you know what you can do.'

I was so intent on that tiny monitor I didn't notice what Hanna was doing until I glanced up: she'd left her 'shield' propped up in a bush and was bounding over to the fence.

'Hanna?' I called, wondering what the hell she had in mind.

It was like watching a champion athlete do something you wouldn't have even thought possible. She kinda leapt up, rebounded off the fence about halfway up, then sailed over the top, slithering under the wires and down the other side, landing on the ground with barely any impact.

'Hanna!' I shouted again, but she took a few steps away from the fence, hopefully avoiding the gaze of the oncoming camera. 'What do you want me to do?'

'Christ! Jimmy, can you see this?' I said, directing my makeshift camera at her.

'Tell her to just walk round naturally,' he said.

'What?'

'She's in there now,' he said, perfectly logically.

When I looked up again, Hanna was already off, moving towards the squatting rabbit, doing her best not to frighten it, taking a few gliding steps forward at a time.

'*Big Guy?*' Jimmy suddenly said, his voice lower, worried.

'It's okay, she's fine,' I replied, glancing over at the main building to make sure there was no sign of any activity.

'What the hell's that?' Jimmy muttered.

I turned to the monitor. He was looking at his other image and obviously something that was really unnerving him.

'What's the matter?'

'There's something going on there.'

'What?'

'Get her out!' he suddenly shouted.

'Why?' I said, looking over and seeing nothing.

'Clancy! *Get her out!*'

'Hanna! *Hanna!*' I called.

I tell ya, it was one helluva shock: suddenly sections of the grass started to rise up, mounds split open, doors slid back and something began to emerge.

'*Hanna!*' I screamed.

It took an age for me to realise what they were. Two of them came bounding out of one opening and several more from another: shiny, silver, moving like some kind of animal – but how could they be? Then I heard this sound, a sort of slurping, pneumatic galloping, and I realised they were robots.

I guess they looked closest to a dog, a much chunkier version of those pit bull things I used to see around when I was a kid. Their heads were almost entirely comprised of jaws, with huge, pointed metal teeth and a couple of slashes for eyes that I guessed were cameras; and all of them were giving out with this snarling mechanical roar, louder and more chilling than any real animal could ever be.

Hanna turned and started to run back to the fence, but it was obvious she wasn't gonna make it. There must've been half a dozen or more of those things converging on her. Worse still, there was nothing I could do, no way could I get over that fence in time . . . Two of them came streaking in from the side, emerging from bunkers only yards inside the perimeter, snarling and snapping, their eager jaws ready to rip into her.

It was weird, almost miraculous. I swear, how fast those things moved, she didn't stand a chance, but she kind of changed mode and started to move in a different fashion, and in a lull amongst the growling and snarling, I realised she was actually humming to herself. She started to dance to the music, leaping into the air time and time again, pirouetting, leaving their jaws snapping at nothing. Two of them collided with each other, one ending up on the ground, kicking its legs in the air whilst the other resumed its pursuit.

Now more and more mounds were rising up, their exits spitting out further silver monsters, all running at her with their pneumatic *slurp-slurp*. As she neared the fence, there was a whole pack waiting for her and I had no idea what she was gonna do, but she just ran at them full speed and leaped into the air, using their backs as springboards, bouncing from one to another, eluding their snapping jaws until she was finally able to jump onto the fence, scramble up it and slide through the gap, leaving them growling and snarling down below.

She ran over and threw her arms round me, giving me a grateful hug.

'You okay?' I asked, hugging her back.

'Yeah,' she said, forcing a slightly nervous smile. 'It was fun.'

Just at that moment we heard these kinda howls of pre-programmed victory and celebration: the rabbit had been chased and caught and was being systematically torn to shreds, piece by piece, like they'd keep going 'til there was nothing left.

Hanna looked a little sick, maybe 'cuz of what happened to the rabbit, maybe 'cuz it was a graphic demonstration of what might've happened to her.

'That's horrible,' she moaned.

Jimmy's voice suddenly crackled into life. 'Big Guy, get out of there,' he said. 'Somebody's coming.'

We didn't worry about the cameras any more – I reckon they were computer-monitored anyway. We just ran, disappearing into the smoke and gathering darkness, ignoring the sirens coming from the direction of the main building, the sound of a Dragon-fly's engine starting up on the roof.

When we got back to the crypt everyone was sitting round looking a little worried, even Gordie, though I reckon we'd've had to've dragged it out of him by his back teeth. Hanna made light of what had happened, answering almost every question simply, like it was an everyday thing to be chased by a pack of mechanical jaws on legs.

'What the hell are those things?' I asked Jimmy, knowing he'd be the only one who might have a clue.

'Growlers.'

'What?'

'Dogs of war, or a version of them. Thought they were only allowed on the battlefield. Officially they've never been used, but there were rumours. They were supposed to be a more humane, more convenient way to fight,' Jimmy said, with some irony. 'Tearing your enemies apart, incurring no domestic casualties, made them politically popular. They'll attack anything they're told to; they'll plant bombs, blow themselves up – they can even rebuild each other if they get damaged, work out how to divide their parts to keep the maximum number functioning, so instead of three four-legged growlers and a heap of nothing, you got four three-legged ones coming at you.'

'Jeez,' I gasped.

'Never thought I'd see them in civilian use.'

Delilah gave this long, weary sigh, the kind she often gave out with since she'd lost Arturo, as if everything that had subsequently happened was merely confirmation of how bad this world had become. If the Infinity complex hadn't looked unbreachable before, it sure did then. I'd been no use at all to Hanna earlier – by the time I'd've got my arthritic old bones over that fence she'd have been torn into bits no bigger than postage stamps. I thanked God she was young and strong and full of spirit . . . but me . . . I was a dinosaur, a washed-up old big guy. I didn't even know what I was up against any more. *Dogs of war!* What the hell next? In my day you fought *people*: you saw the whites of their eyes, even heard what they had to say; a lot of the time there was even a sort of respect. Now we got jaws on legs: *Growlers*. And yet I knew that if I was ever gonna see my Lena again, somehow I had to find a way of dealing with them.

I don't know if I got up in the morning or just didn't go to sleep at night, but shortly after dawn I made my way up the steps as quietly as I could. I didn't want the others to see me in the mood I was in. I'd been churning all sorts of stuff over all night and it hadn't done me a helluva lot of good.

There was a little bit of an early-morning mist mingling with the smoke and the light of the day was slowly seeping through both of them, creating this rather eerie and unreal world, like a no-man's-land between this existence and the next. Maybe that was why I started to meander round the churchyard, reading the occasional gravestone, tributes to those on the other side.

I don't know when she did it – for sure she never said anything to me – but I came to this very plain, simple stone cross with no carved inscription, but someone had recently scratched something on it.

FAREWELL THE MICKEY MOUSE KID
– OF WHERE AND WHEN, I DON'T KNOW,
BUT YOU'LL ALWAYS LIVE IN MY THOUGHTS

It was Delilah, of course, and I have to say, not only did it bring a tear to my eye, it also shamed me. This was no time for feeling sorry for myself: I had to get on with it, contribute in some way. Maybe I could go out and find some decent leftovers at an all-night diner, have breakfast ready for the others when they got up? I turned and started to make my way over to the street, filled with a sudden purpose, but then I stopped in my tracks.

It was the graffiti. There was no new message, nothing cryptic for me to try to work my way through, but it was all perfectly clear now. Someone had added a word. One single word, but it changed everything.

CHAPTER TWELVE

LOVE IS BLIND, CLANCY

Finally, I understood: all that time I'd been dismissing the messages, saying they couldn't have anything to do with Lena's blindness, and I was right. They didn't. It had been *my* blindness they were talking about.

They'd been trying to tell me that I was missing something! That somewhere there was a two and a two that needed putting together, and I hadn't identified them.

Maybe it had something to do with the Island? The fact that – though I hated to say it – Lena'd had a 'relationship' with the head Wastelord? He'd trusted her with a lot of his secrets, and everyone always reckoned there was Mainland involvement in what went on with them, shipping organs, all that, so maybe she knew something that could prove embarrassing to Infinity? Though what that might be I couldn't begin to imagine. Or maybe it was what I said about Jimmy: they knew there was a connection and were determined to exploit it.

I went back down to the crypt and got the little guy, dragging him over to take a look almost before he was awake, but he just confused me even more. 'It's an Islander, Big Guy,' he said dismissively, looking like he wanted to go back to his sleeping bag. 'Gotta grudge. They're messing with you.'

'What d'you mean?'

'Love is blind! You love a blind woman. They don't know she can see now.'

I stopped for a moment, staring at it, trying to see it from his point of view. 'Nah . . .'

'Come on! Who else would it be?'

'Jimmy! It's someone who knows where I am – they're following me!'

'Probably just walking by and happened to see you, or maybe they seen you around and know you live in the general area. It's a coincidence.'

I just stared at him, disappointed by his reaction.

'Big Guy!' he groaned. 'You know what some Islanders were like, they didn't call that place the Village for nothing – it was full of idiots.'

I got a little annoyed with him, without another word spinning round and heading off, going up to check out the Square. The message had been altered up there too, just as I'd expected, though this time they didn't put my whole name, just my initial.

LOVE IS BLIND, C

Somebody knew something; it wasn't just gossip, some Villager from the Island taking an unhealthy interest in my relationship. There was something they thought I should know – the only trouble was, they were hopelessly overestimating my intelligence.

I hung around for a while, hoping to see someone I recognised, someone who might do such a thing, and came across another sprayed message. I must've missed it before, 'cuz again it looked like the 'C' had been added later – so maybe Jimmy was right, they weren't sure where I was? They just had a vague idea and putting the message opposite the church *was* a coincidence?

The more I drifted around, the fewer ideas I got on who I was looking for. I mean, even after all these years, I still had a finely tuned survival instinct and I was sure I was followed at some point – though they were pretty good at it. It did briefly occur to me that maybe Ray was involved, that he was planning something, but if he'd found me, I reckoned he would've let me know.

I moseyed around for the rest of the morning, never going too far from the Square, doing my best to make myself visible but actually using all the old tricks when you think you're being followed: ducking into doorways and waiting, doubling back, all that stuff. I never saw a soul, and actually, began to worry I was letting my imagination run away with me. That kinda thing can drive you completely crazy. I remember several guys in the old days, promising young ones who might've been able to make something of themselves, but they blew it all 'cuz they became obsessed with the idea of being plotted against – they developed class one paranoia. They were forever looking over their shoulders, checking underneath their cars, accusing all kinds of people of all manner of things – and what made it worse: there was no chance of any kind of respite, they couldn't possibly have a relationship 'cuz they didn't trust anyone. One guy I knew, Donnie Davis, got so fixated on the notion that everyone was spying on him, he stopped going out altogether. In the end they found him backed up against the wall in a cupboard in his apartment. The place was wrecked and everything that might possibly have been used for spying on him – even his two cats – had been pulverised to nothing. He blew out the back of his own head, as if worried someone behind him was still watching.

When I finally got back to the crypt, I was greeted by Jimmy with that look about him; the one where's he's about to astonish me with how clever he is, and, by implication, how stupid I am.

'I know what happened to Lena,' he said. The others immediately turned from what they were doing.

'What d'you mean?'

'I know how that doctor was able to get her through the gate scan.' Again he produced a homemade contraption that incorporated the screen, but this time as something even more elaborate. He'd been using that thing as a basis for all manner of stuff; taking it apart, rebuilding it, a bit like Lego, that old kids' toy.

'Know what this is?' he asked, well aware I didn't.

'Nope,' I replied.

'It's a kind of poor man's spectroscope. It measures the properties of light emitted or absorbed by chemical elements.' He looked at me and saw my eyes had already started to glaze over but he was determined to have his moment of glory. 'It worried me that even if the people on the gate lied to you, that doctor would still risk the limo being scanned in a spot-check. I thought he must've left Lena behind. Even that she might be . . .' He grunted and picked up the syringe I'd brought back. 'There was just enough for me to analyse.'

'You don't say,' I muttered, though actually, shit to admit, I was pretty impressed yet again. Mind you, I wasn't ready for what came next.

'He poisoned her.'

I just gaped and Delilah let out a gasp. 'She's dead?'

'I never said that,' he said with a smirk.

'Screw you, Jimmy,' I growled, not caring for the way he was going about this.

'She might've died . . . but she's not dead,' he told me. 'Leastways, I don't think so.'

He paused for a moment, savouring the looks on our faces.

'Okay. So what?' I asked impatiently.

Again he held up the syringe. 'It was developed for space travel. Very loosely based on a drug called tetrodotoxin – an emergency alternative to freezing, if you were really low on juice or something. With the right equipment, it can be surprisingly accurate. On a six-month journey, they reckon they can get you to wake up within a few hours of your allotted time.'

'That's what he gave her?'

'It shuts everything down: there'd be no life signs to monitor.'

I collected my thoughts. I mean, apart from the relief of having confirmed what I knew all along – that Lena was alive – I was slightly disappointed: it was another piece of the puzzle, but not, as far as I could see, one that advanced us in any way.

'So she's alive?' Gordie said.

'If they went to those lengths,' Jimmy said, 'yeah, I'd say so.'

Gordie gave a loud sigh, almost a cry of relief, and I realised that he, like the others, had had his doubts.

''course she is!' I told him, touched by just how pleased he was. 'Have you seen the graffiti?'

'Big Guy!' Jimmy protested, plainly thinking we hadn't spent anywhere enough time appreciating his discovery, but I was already on my way up the steps.

'I want his opinion.'

Despite still being deadly enemies, I took both Gordie and Hanna, the pair of them getting these expressions on their faces when they first saw the graffiti, the new additions, like they were more impressed than they thought they were gonna be.

Part of the reason I took Hanna was 'cuz of that individual way she has of looking at things – but she applied herself in a much more practical fashion, stepping up to the graffiti and going along the letters one by one.

'I've seen this "s" before,' she said.

'What d'you mean?'

'People often have a signature letter. With this person it's the "s". I seen it over on the Island. In the Camp.'

'You sure?'

'Yes!'

'Bullshit,' Gordie sneered. 'It's everywhere.'

'Where?' I asked.

'All over! It's real common.'

'Not like that,' Hanna said, indicating the bottom curve.

Gordie gave this highly contemptuous snort, as if he would laugh at her but she wasn't worth the effort.

I paused, not knowing who to believe, and eventually, without another word, Hanna just turned and walked back to the church as if she'd given her verdict and now it was up to me to decide who to believe.

Gordie and me followed on behind. I glanced back at the graffiti a couple of times, still a long way from understanding. But if I really wanted to find out who was doing this, and what it was all about, there was only one way.

I hid myself behind a bush not far from the churchyard gate so I could be across the street in a matter of moments. The fire, what little remained of it, was giving off just about enough light for me to see by. It was more or less the same wherever I went now: the fires had wreaked pretty much all the damage they could, and though there were still new ones erupting, I felt the end might well be in sight – not that that was any cause for celebration or optimism; more just the understanding that there was nothing left to burn.

A little later Delilah came out to see me. She was seeking me out more and more; as if she felt there was an affinity, that we were both in the same boat, grieving for those we dearly loved and missed.

'You'll find her, Clancy. Don't worry,' she told me, talking rather louder than I cared for, nor making any attempt to hide herself.

'I know,' I replied, keeping my voice to not much more than a whisper, hoping she'd take the hint.

'Thing is,' she continued, not dropping her volume one bit, 'we so rarely savour life . . . spend a whole lifetime mourning its loss . . . I keep thinking about all those times I scolded Arturo, or was too tired for him—'

'Delilah,' I interrupted, 'I'm hoping to surprise someone here.'

For a moment she did go quiet, but I knew it wouldn't last for long. 'How often do we take the time to think, "Today I'm happy, I appreciate this for what it is"? Instead we just cry when it's gone.'

'You got that right,' I agreed.

'When you get her back, Clancy . . . savour the moments.'

'Oh, I will,' I told her, absurdly grateful for the 'when' as opposed to 'if'.

She started to cough, a real full-blooded hack that echoed all around the churchyard, the smoke getting to her single lung again.

'Delilah! If anyone does come, you're gonna frighten them off.'

'Okay, okay,' she said, punctuating almost every word with breathless splutters, 'I know when I'm not wanted.'

'Go and savour your man,' I joked.

'Now there's someone who does appreciate every minute – not with me, but with his goddamn junk. One day he's gonna invent himself a beautiful robot lady and I'll be shown the door.'

'He wouldn't dare.'

'A real male fantasy; programmed never to complain, stand up for herself or need foreplay.'

'Delilah!' I protested. Way too much information for my liking!

'Oh, I'm sure you're different, Clancy.'

No way was I going to add to that discussion, and finally taking the hint, she shuffled off, sniggering away to herself, leaving me slightly puzzled as to what the real subject of the conversation had been.

I sighed and settled back down. I'd brought my sleeping bag up, ready to stay there all night if had to – but as it turned out, it wasn't necessary.

Maybe an hour or so later the occasional individual or group were still passing but by and large, most people had found somewhere safe and battened down hatches for the night. I was just starting to think I should do the same, that our graffiti artist wasn't coming, when suddenly a figure slipped out of the smoke on the opposite side of the street.

What with my old eyes and the poor visibility I couldn't make out if they were male or female. They were quite small, and it occurred to me that maybe it was a kid, which would've explained why they didn't want any contact with an old person. They were dressed in a slightly bizarre fashion that gave them a kinda shapeless look. One thing *was* certain; I could forget any wild notions Hanna had put in my head. It wasn't Lena.

Whoever it was paused at the graffiti'd wall, staring over at the churchyard so intently that for a moment I thought I'd been spotted. I ducked down. I mean, I'd only caught a glimpse and it wasn't the best of circumstances, but you know, I didn't recognise them at all.

I could've made my way over then and there and grabbed them, demanded to know what the hell he – or she – thought they were playing at, but I thought I'd bide my time 'til they started work. That way not only would I get to see what they were gonna write, but they'd be so preoccupied it'd be much easier to sneak up on them.

Man or woman, boy or girl: whoever it was slid a can out of their pocket and started spraying.

I gotta admit, there was a kind of tension to it, watching those words slowly appear, letter by letter . . .

IT'S A

It's a what?

IT'S A FOGGY

What the hell?

IT'S A FOGGY NIGHT

It was only when they stuffed the can back into their pocket and checked up and down the street that I realised they'd finished. *That was it?* That was all they were going to say? What did that even mean? *It's a foggy night* – it wasn't even correct: it was smoke, not fog.

I stood up, about to make my way over and exercise a little frustration, when I stopped dead . . .

Foggy night!

Jesus, no! It didn't mean a great deal here on the Mainland, but it sure as hell had out on the Island: it meant we were about to be attacked!

186

And at that precise moment, almost as if someone'd been waiting for that thought to trigger it, a familiar yet terrifying noise echoed out across the City, instantly turning the hairs on the back of my neck to icicles. Maybe 'cuz it was quite close – possibly in the Square – I could clearly hear each separate component: the shattering rhythm of the beaters, pounding everything they came across, yelling into the night; the hullabaloo of the heavy machinery, the thrumming Dragonflies. There was an army gathering, hell-bent on genocide, on eradicating all those who represented an inconvenience to them, and don't ask me how, but I just knew they were coming our way.

I turned back to see my graffiti artist hurrying off in the opposite direction. 'Hey!' I hollered, '*Hey!*' but their only reaction was to start running.

I chased after them, calling out again, but it soon became apparent that they were way too fast for me – and more importantly, that I needed to get back to the churchyard.

'Hey!' I shouted one last time as I stumbled to a breathless halt, and then, 'cuz I could think of no other way to do it, I cried, 'Thank you!'

But they'd already gone, lost somewhere in the loudly erupting night.

I stood there for a moment, trying to get my breath back as people started emerging out of the smoke, panicking as they ran round me. In the distance I could just about make out the glow of an advancing wall of discordant light. They were going to run through and over everything again, mopping up those they'd missed the other night, and this time I was sure the crypt wouldn't survive.

I started to run back, a swimmer against the tide, ignoring the many people who tried to tell me I was going the wrong way. Panic was spurring me on, urging me ever faster, the realisation that with half the buildings already flattened, the Specials would arrive a lot quicker this time.

I found the others already outside, gaping in the direction of the advancing army, Delilah looking like she was about to start screaming – and I didn't exactly blame her either.

'Big Guy! What we gonna do?' Jimmy begged.

'Grab what you can,' I told them, directing everyone towards the crypt. *'Quick!* We gotta go.'

'Where?' Delilah asked.

'Not far,' I told her, in my haste almost pushing her down the steps.

We took everything we could, scrabbling around in the dark, so aware the noise was getting closer by the second, fumbling our way back up. All but one of us, that was: Jimmy was still down below.

'Jimmy!' I screamed down the steps as the Dragonflies emerged out of the smoke, breaking ranks and flying forward like the pilots couldn't wait to start shooting. *'They're here!'*

'Okay, okay,' he shouted.

'We're going!' I told him.

Finally he came tottering up, carrying, not the last of the food or essential supplies but as much of his damned techno junk as he could manage.

'Come *on!*' I yelled as the Dragonflies started to sweep their searchlights from side to side.

I showed them the way through the jungle of razor-sharp black-thorns, stopping to move the branches I'd used to disguise the path. I'd always known the day would come when we'd need that place, and finally it had.

Jimmy was so determined not to drop any of his stuff he got his arms badly scratched, but not even the growing noise, the approaching lights of the Dragonflies, could persuade him to discard anything.

'Where we going, Big Guy?' he kept repeating, though he didn't look like he was in any fit state to register an answer. 'What's the plan?'

'Keep moving,' I told him.

Finally, we made it to that sheltered area I'd found right up against the wall, protected by ramparts of nature's spikes and spears. I couldn't see even Infinity beaters being game enough to try to get through there. 'course, they might've sent the dozers over – but if they couldn't get in, I was praying they'd assume that no one would get flushed out.

They were right behind us. Another few seconds and we would've been seen. There was that same crashing tsunami of noise: walls being toppled, a cacophony of wayward crying and screaming, the occasional shot, and it frightened the hell out of us – it'd frighten the hell out of anyone. They flattened almost everything in their path, anything that might possibly have offered refuge or provided a hiding place, and just as I'd feared, the floor of the church gave way, one of their machines almost disappearing into the hole.

Everything stopped, the Specials paused in their relentless rhythm, and several people came to peer down. An earnest conversation took place with the Dragonflies hovering overhead, illuminating the scene. Eventually someone picked their way down into the crypt, disappearing for a moment, and it went through my head that maybe they'd known we were there – that they were looking for us. The guy climbed back out and I couldn't tell whether he'd guessed anyone had been living down there. Whatever, they bulldozed the remains of the church into the hole so no one could ever seek that particular sanctuary again. I turned to the others and saw the fear frozen on their faces. I put my arm around Hanna.

When they were finally satisfied no one would ever make that place a home again, the order was given, the noise resumed, and everyone slowly moved forward. I heard Delilah give this little moan. I thought at first it was relief that we'd escaped again, but then I saw they'd run over Arturo's memorial stone, the one that she'd so lovingly scratched out, smashing it along with all the others.

I waited till I heard them clear the churchyard, then began to tentatively pick my way back out through the blackthorn bushes. Seeing the last of the Specials disappearing into the smoke, try as I might, it was impossible not to think of the last time they'd paid us a visit; when we'd lost our little Arturo.

'Shit,' Jimmy muttered, appearing at my side, looking at the further devastation around us.

'They wanted to warn us,' I told him.

'Who?' he asked, mystified.

I pointed towards the other side of the street, but Infinity had done an equally thorough demolition job over there and very little was left standing.

'Whoever's been leaving the messages.'

I told him the whole story, but I guess he didn't think it mattered much in that moment. With no more than a grunt he returned into the bushes: our new home.

It must've been another thirty or forty minutes before we finally heard the noise we'd all been dreading. Not one of us spoke as volley after volley rang out. Hanna put her hands over her ears to try and shut it out, rocking back and forth, just the way I used to sometimes when the kids were raiding us out on the Island. But again it was Delilah who took it the hardest, sitting there with a thousand ghosts playing on her face, every shot a reminder of the one that had killed Arturo.

'Sick,' was all Jimmy could say, as he sat there cleaning his scratches. 'Sick society.'

After we'd all positioned and repositioned our sleeping bags several times over, trying to work out the driest and warmest places, we bedded down for the night. As it turned out, it was that bit more comfortable than the crypt – softer underfoot, without that invasive cold and damp – and Gordie wanted to know why we hadn't moved over there sooner. Despite what we'd been through, everyone fell asleep remarkably quickly.

Everyone, that was, of course, 'cept me. Once again I was left just lying there, listening to their various nocturnal noises: Jimmy's wheezy creaking, Delilah's heavy sawing, Gordie's precociously loud snore and, if you could pick it out, the absolute silence that surrounded Hanna.

I felt a little sad that we'd moved. It might've been forced on us, but if Lena came back she'd find everything wasn't exactly the way she'd left it, and that made it feel like she was just that bit further away.

I also couldn't stop thinking about our phantom artist. Who the hell was it? For sure I didn't recognise them – and yet whoever it was knew something about Lena – about both of us. And the way they'd tried to warn us, they were apparently on our side. But did they know where Lena was? Did they have any real information?

I sighed and turned over, for a moment enjoying the slight disturbance of the outside wafting over my face. Whoever this graffiti artist was, they represented my only hope. Somehow I had to find them.

*

People are never one hundred per cent consistent one hundred per cent of the time – after all, it's a boring person who can always be predicted. Jimmy might say I respond purely to instinct, that I'm some kind of animal who never thinks things through, but I have my moments, even if they ain't that frequent.

The following day I walked slowly up to the Square, then turned round and walked back down again, checking what little remained after our second visit from Infinity. The answer to that question was . . . not a helluva lot. There was barely a building that hadn't been rendered to rubble by the Specials, smashed to bits and obliterated, completing the job the fires had begun. In fact, it reminded me of the Old City out on the Island, the way it had been left after the riots. Just like over there, there was still the odd finger of a building left standing – a doorway that refused to topple, an occasional stubborn slither of wall – and as I made my way back to the churchyard I made a mental note of each and every one.

The way I saw it, if this mystery person was still of a mind to communicate with me, the chances were that with the walls across the street gone, they'd look for the nearest alternative stretch of brickwork between here and the Square – a place they knew I regularly passed. Which didn't leave too many possibilities, since most of what was left wasn't big enough to write a word on, let alone a message. However, I did find one section, five or six yards long, partly slumped over like some old sleeping dinosaur, and only a few minutes along the street.

That night I stole up there and hid amongst the rubble, concealed by the wall itself, on the other side to the street but ready to jump out at a moment's notice. For hour after hour I sat there, ignoring the bricks biting into my squidgy old ass, repeatedly telling myself that no one was gonna come, that they'd either been frightened off or fallen victim to Infinity, 'til finally, with the first faint smudge of smoky light fanning out from the East, I got to my feet slowly and stiffly and walked back to the churchyard, not only pained and aching but fearing that whatever opportunity that artist had presented had now gone.

I spent the rest of the day trying to improve our little shelter as much as I could: weaving black garbage bags into the overhanging branches so that at least a part of our lair would stay dry in the event of bad weather, digging out a pit for a fire so we could attempt a little cooking

Jimmy got his screen back performing its intended function and everyone stopped to see what had been going on. However, it didn't take us long to get fed up with all those endless clips of 'crazed looters, degenerates and anarchists', and up against them, the 'gallant Infinity Specials'; there to watch over us, to protect and maintain the status quo, prepared to give their very lives in our defence. According to the reporter, seven Specials had been brutally slain whilst performing their heroic duty – though much to my relief they didn't go into detail. They also went on to show a gang of executed looters, laid out at the scene of their crime, though I wouldn't have minded betting they were 'Clean-up' victims; that this was just more Infinity propaganda.

At the end of a long and predictable sequence about 'the battle between good and evil being played out on our streets', they went on to show us the villains' gallery. Jimmy was still Number One, but according to the report, they anticipated his eradication 'any day now'. I glanced across to see how the little guy was taking the news, but his only reaction was to repeatedly shake his head. He just didn't get how they'd managed to 'read' his name – what they used, how they went about it – and I'll tell you, if he couldn't work it out, there wasn't much point in me even trying.

I didn't plan on going to watch for the graffiti artist that evening

– I mean, they probably wouldn't risk it again, I even said as much to the others. The only thing I was searching for that night was a good few hours' sleep. But as soon as it got dark, it started to nag at me and in the end I gave in, promising myself I'd just go for a short while, an hour at the most.

Three hours later I was still sitting there, telling myself to go back to the shelter where there was a comfortable sleeping bag waiting for me. But I kept giving it another five minutes, then another, and another.

Where he or she came from, I dunno; wherever it was, they sure came quietly. The first I knew was hearing the hiss of the spray on the other side of the wall. I slowly got to my feet, determined not to let whoever it was get away this time, tiptoeing over the rubble, making sure I didn't dislodge any and give myself away. As long as that hissing kept on going, I had every chance of catching them cold.

I slipped out into the street, tip-toeing up behind them, immediately realising it was a kid, and why I'd thought they were oddly dressed: multi-layered clothing, feathers in their tousled hair – but you know, I still wasn't sure if it was a boy or a girl.

I grabbed whoever it was, lifted them up in the air and a voice, unquestionably that of a girl, started demanding I put her down. I did as asked, but kept a real firm grip, studying that scowling and dirty face, but Jeez, I didn't know her at all.

'Who the hell are you?' I demanded.

She hesitated for a moment as if slightly puzzled, then resumed trying to wriggle free. 'Get *off* me!' she demanded, but I maintained my hold.

'What's this all about? Why're you writing these messages?'

This time she just shrugged, in typical teenage fashion, in fact, it kinda reminded me of Gordie. 'Do I know you?' I asked, for some reason starting to feel that bit unsure.

'No,' she grunted, but in such a way I knew there was some kind of story.

I guessed she was somewhere in her mid-teens, though her face was so caked in dirt and soot I couldn't be certain. Her hair, apart from the feathers, was a bit like Lena's when I first met her in the tunnels, when she hadn't seen anyone in years; it was all rats'-tails and tangles.

'What d'you know about Lena?' I asked.

She paused for a moment, then, 'Nothing.'

'Oh, come on!'

'I don't know nothing!'

I turned and checked out the wall, seeing what she had to say this time.

TO LAY DOWN AND LET LOVE DIE

'So what does that mean?' I asked.

'Nothing.'

'You wrote it!' I said, utterly frustrated. What the hell was going on here? 'Were you on the Island?'

Again she shrugged, but this time it appeared as if she was indicating the affirmative. I tell ya, those kids gotta whole alternative vocabulary of such things.

I continued to stare at her; something was glimmering in a far-off corner of my mind. I *did* know her – I just couldn't remember from where.

In the end she could see I was gonna get there anyway, so she decided to put me out of my misery. 'I fought with you against the Wastelords. We met on the way down into the Camp. I'm a friend of Gordie's.'

'*Gigi!*' I said, the name suddenly wrestling its way to the front of my mind.

She just nodded, and yet, with the introduction of her name and the memory of what we shared, her attitude did appear to slightly change, as if she was trying to be that bit more human.

'So what's this about?' I asked. 'Why are you leaving these messages?'

At first I thought she wasn't gonna say anything, then eventually she said, 'I don't trust grown-ups.'

'I know that,' I said – it's a pretty common sentiment amongst kids, especially those who were out on the Island.

Eventually she gave a long drawn-out sigh, like she was far from happy about it, but on balance, was prepared give me the benefit of the doubt. 'How much d'you know?'

I gave a kind of snort. 'Nothing.'

She paused for a moment. 'Infinity've got her.'

'Shit!' I groaned, the last glimmer of my hope finally crushed.

'I didn't know if you knew. That's why I left the messages.'

'Shit!' I exclaimed again. '*Why?*'

'I dunno,' she commented. 'Thought you might.'

She checked up and down the street, looking a little nervous, and I took her arm and led her back to my hiding place beside the wall so we could talk. 'Is she okay? They're not torturing her?'

'Not really,' she replied, in such a way it sounded like there was a story to tell.

'What?'

'She's staying in their private hospital – guarded twenty-four/seven but living real five-star. I tell ya, she don't want for a thing.'

For a moment I just stared at her. That wasn't what I'd been expecting at all. 'How d'you know?'

She hesitated, and I guessed she was trying to conquer her

instinctive reaction not to trust adults, to decide how much to tell me. 'I know . . . some people . . . They know some people.'

'Can I get in there?' I asked immediately.

She scoffed, as if I was talking utter insanity. 'No one can get in there!'

'There's gotta be a way.'

'There ain't, believe me.'

'I just need a little information – maybe someone to turn a blind eye.'

Again she shook her head like there was no point in this conversation and we both fell to silence. Eventually, it was her who broke it. 'Is she special in some way?'

'She's special in *every* way,' I told her.

Gigi couldn't help herself; she gave this rather rusty, almost dirty, laugh. 'Must be love,' she commented. 'I know she is to you, but, I mean, is she special to the world, d'ya think? Unique somehow?'

I stared at her, wondering what the hell she was talking about. 'No,' I said, 'she can see now but . . . I don't know what that's gotta do with anything. I got no idea why they'd want her . . .'

'Well,' Gigi replied, suddenly sounding that bit older than her years, 'for whatever reason, they're taking care of her as if she's a goddamn miracle.'

CHAPTER THIRTEEN

I hesitated over it, but in the end took her back to the shelter. She was a friend of Gordie's and had gone out of her way to try to warn us about Infinity, so I reckoned I could trust her. Mind you, it gave the others a bit of a shock, especially as they were fast asleep when we got back and I asked her to stay 'til morning, said that she could sleep in Arturo's sleeping-bag.

You should've seen the looks of absolute mystification on their faces when they awoke. Gordie was pretty pleased, you could see that, but he'd never really been one to gush. He just hung out a bit of a grin and gave her a dig in the ribs when she got close enough. Delilah was plainly put out to see someone else in Arturo's sleeping bag, but after a few minutes of looking like she was on the point of objecting, I guess she decided the time had come to try to move on. The only one who didn't react in any way was Hanna, which wasn't that much of a surprise, I guess – but to be honest, this felt a little different and it went through my head that maybe those two didn't get on. Not that there was anything I could do about it.

Gigi told us everything that'd happened to her since she'd

arrived on the Mainland, expanding on what she'd already said to me: that she'd joined this underground group. At first I didn't quite get it, I mean, how the hell could she've met them so quickly? But apparently when she was on the Island, she was befriended by one of the guys on the garbage boats. He'd even given her an address in case she ever managed to escape. She had no idea how many were in the group – Infinity security was that good, they never dared collect in the same place at the same time. Could be ten, could be a hundred, but again she hinted that they had people on the inside, that there were sympathisers working in Infinity, which, I gotta say, I found pretty hard to believe.

'But they're taking good care of Lena?' Delilah asked again, like the rest of us, still finding that hard to believe.

'Yeah, but . . . like I said, no one knows why.'

I'd spent most of the night turning that over, trying to make some sense of it, but I tell ya, I was stumped. What made Lena special – not just to me, but to everyone?

'Maybe it's got something to do with the tunnels,' I suggested.

'Whaddya mean?' Gigi asked.

'The only thing I can think of that used to make Lena different in any way was her ability to see, to function in the dark.'

There was a silence that I waited to be filled with dismissive comments, but actually, everyone was looking that bit thoughtful.

'What good is that to them?' Delilah asked.

I made this gesture, like I had no idea, but Jimmy obviously wasn't short of them. 'Well, for example . . .' he started to say, but suddenly he stopped and turned away.

'What?' I asked.

'Oh, nothing. Just . . . thinking it through,' he replied, though he didn't sound that convincing.

'Jimmy!'

'No, really – it's nothing.'

'If you don't tell me—' I threatened.

'I don't know!' he cried. 'These people are definitely uncool – I wouldn't put anything past them.'

'So what could they be up to?'

He sighed rather helplessly. 'I'm not sure how much more work's been done on it but . . . years ago, there were rumours – I mean, biotechnology's where it's at, it has been for years . . . It's just possible they've reached a point where they can take some facets of the human brain and integrate it into a chip . . . '

'Go on,' I said, a fear beginning to grow deep in my stomach.

'If they can stabilise the synthesis enough to clone it . . .' After a pause he said, 'Sky's the limit.'

I just sat there, not really understanding but the words still somehow mesmerising me, waiting for him to go on.

Jimmy gave a long sigh. 'In theory, they could give every Special her ability, either externally, through some kind of headgear, or internally, through an implant.' Again he stopped, looking distinctly uncomfortable, wanting me to let him off the hook – but I'd just thought of something.

'When I first went to see Dr Simon, I kinda barged into his office. I thought he'd have me thrown out, right away. Security were there in seconds. But when I told him all about Lena, about her life, that she'd lived underground for years, blind and without any assistance, his attitude changed: suddenly he wanted to help.'

There was a long silence, no one quite knowing what to say.

'Don't mean nothing,' Delilah eventually mumbled, though plainly she was as worried as the rest of us.

'So they keep her alive, as healthy as can be, 'til they've taken whatever they want from her brain and then . . . ' I said. I couldn't complete the sentence.

Nobody commented, I guess 'cuz they didn't like the thought of that any more than I did.

'If I ever see that doctor again . . .' I muttered.

'He's in Infinity,' Gigi told me, 'looking after Lena.'

I grunted. 'That's another good reason to get in there.'

Gigi said she had to go, people would be wondering where she was, but we insisted on her staying for breakfast. That's the thing with folk now – ex-Islanders, the homeless, anyone – if you're offered food, you don't turn it down. Who knows when you might next get a chance to eat?

Whilst we were all sitting there, slurping some stewed fruit, Gigi reminiscing with Gordie about stuff that'd happened in the Camp on the Island, Hanna pointedly not joining in, she suddenly stopped. 'I thought Arturo was with you?'

There was a really heavy pause, so heavy, she instantly knew what it meant. 'Oh,' she said. 'How'd that happen?'

'Infinity Clean-up,' I told her.

'They took his body – can you believe that?' Delilah grumbled, almost as if she was pleased to find someone new to tell.

'Yeah, I can,' Gigi replied.

'What d'ya mean?' Delilah asked, a little aggressively.

'What it's worth.'

We all turned to Gigi, waiting for an explanation. 'What are you talking about?' I asked.

She stared at us one by one. 'You really don't know anything, do you?'

'No,' I cried in frustration, 'we don't!'

She gave this long sigh, like she really didn't see why this particular duty fell to her. 'You seen all those sick people?'

'Zombies,' Gordie said, weakly managing to make a face.

'They got this mystery illness – causes all kinds of shit: blindness, burning, headaches, nausea . . . *organ failure* . . .'

With that pause, the underlining of those last two words, a look of revulsion slowly spread across Delilah's face. 'Is that why they took him?'

Gigi nodded.

'Oh no! *No!*' Delilah moaned, her bony and veined hands clasped to her mouth, her horror-stricken eyes staring out from above them. For several moments there was silence, no one wanting to talk over her grief.

When Gigi finally continued, she spoke in little more than a whisper, as if to show her respect. 'Remember how they used to transport kids' bodies back over from the Island?'

I flinched. That was one of the main reasons I'd wanted to destroy that place.

'Well,' she said, almost matter-of-factly, 'no more supply – and a helluva lot more demand.'

'Is that why they get all excited when they see kids?' Gordie asked.

'We're just walking displays of spare parts,' she informed him.

'Which is why you so rarely see any kids in the City,' I said.

'Everyone's after us – especially enticers.'

'What the hell's an "enticer"?'

'Nice name for not-nice people: back-street butchers, organ-pushers – they got all these ways of tempting kids into going with them: money, drugs, food, sometimes just candy. Next thing they know they wake up somewhere with one of their kidneys gone. If they're really unlucky, both of them.'

'Like to see them try,' Gordie said defiantly.

'I wouldn't,' Gigi warned, 'not from what I heard. And it ain't just kids either: some'll steal organs already stolen. The same kidney might get transplanted into several different bodies. You gotta watch out: if they think you got something worth taking, they'll cut you open now and ask questions later.'

'Jesus!' Jimmy gasped. 'So what's the sickness?'

'No one knows,' she said. 'Some people – especially Infinity – give their staff masks, but whether they do any good—?' She shrugged again, her 'who the hell knows?' shrug.

We sat there for a while trying to take it all in. The fact that blindness was one of the symptoms was causing me an understandable measure of concern. 'But it's got nothing to do with Lena?'

'I dunno,' Gigi answered.

Nope, and I didn't either. It was just one unbearable possibility after another. Bad enough that Infinity might be about to steal from her mind; now there was a chance they were out to steal from her body as well.

When we'd finished eating, Gigi got up to leave. She thanked us for the food and we said our goodbyes, told her she was always welcome but to be careful how she entered the churchyard, then Gordie walked her out.

I think we all felt kinda exhausted having to absorb all that new information, like a typhoon had just swept through us.

'Can we trust her?' Jimmy asked.

'Think so,' I replied.

Hanna hesitated in that way she has when you know she's about to speak. 'Maybe,' she eventually said.

'Why d'you say that?' I asked.

'No reason. Just . . . maybe.'

I stared at her for a moment. I'd never heard her say a bad word about anyone before, apart from Gordie, of course. What the hell did she know about Gigi?

*

I didn't do a great deal the rest of that day, just hung around the churchyard thinking things through. I got it into my head to hunt through the rubble for Arturo's cross. I knew it'd been smashed into an uncountable number of pieces, but after a lot of searching, I finally found a fragment with the 'Kid' of 'Mickey Mouse Kid' on it. I held in my hand, the stone slowly warming. For some reason it gave me a small measure of comfort.

This situation had been daunting enough before, but now it was an oncoming flood laden with all manner of dark flotsam. Would it really be possible for Infinity to steal Lena's ability to function without light? I could understand why they'd want to: if the Specials could see in the dark, they'd be even more formidable. Or was there something else they wanted from her? Did this have more to do with the zombie-sick? I just didn't know, and nothing really fitted together, not neatly, not so's you couldn't see the joins.

The most chilling question was: how long would it take them to get whatever they wanted from her? And, of course, what would they do with her afterwards?

I sighed to myself, repeatedly tossing the 'Kid' a few feet into the air and catching it, for one absurd moment thinking I heard Arturo's shrieking laughter in that spit-second just before he didn't know if you were going to catch him or not.

Thank God Lena was apparently safe for the moment, 'cuz sure as hell I didn't even have the scent of an idea how to bust her out of that place. Everyone was saying it was impossible, and going on what I'd seen, they were probably right – but that didn't mean I shouldn't try.

The problem was, everything was inside that building: Lena, Dr Simon, the reason why they took her . . .

Suddenly I stopped, a thought so preoccupying me I let the 'Kid' fall to the ground. Just a goddam minute: there was one thing . . .

*

I love setting Jimmy problems. You know instantly if it can't be done 'cuz he looks at you as if you just failed a sanity test, like you should surely know no one can do that, not even him. On the other hand, when he makes that screwed-up face, takes in that long breathy whistle, like you're talking about uncharted territory but he just might be the one person prepared to venture there, you know you gotta chance, that once he's made sure you appreciate just how difficult it is, he might actually be able to pull it off.

We'd already discussed hacking into Infinity, what problems that might present – and the risks were just too great – but what we hadn't considered was Dr Simon's private clinic. Maybe we could grab a look at Lena's notes, get some more idea why they took her.

'With this?' the little guy said, snatching the screen from Gordie mid-game, inducing a long, mournful groan.

'If anyone can do it–' I said.

Jimmy gave a dismissive chuckle, recognising some clumsy schmoozing when he heard it. 'Yeah, yeah.'

'That's a good idea, Clancy,' Delilah chipped in.

'It might be linked to Infinity,' Jimmy told us, just in case we hadn't realised what he'd be up against.

'You can do it!' Delilah said, making it sound so easy, such a small challenge, I was worried he might walk away 'cuz it wasn't worthy of his talents.

I don't know if it was that, his need to play up the task, but when he finally did get down to it, he really took his time, forever complaining about having to 'break down this, configure that, and, Jeez, there are encryptions everywhere!' Occasionally he'd cuss and shake his head, like it was high time he gave up, but I didn't know if it was genuine or if he was just setting us up to appreciate how clever he was when he finally triumphed.

Now and then he'd turn to me, just to confirm some information. 'Dr Simon?'

'Yep.'

'Evan Simon?'

'That's him.'

'Whoa,' he said, studying his screen. 'Cool.'

'What?'

'Got more letters than the alphabet.'

'Are you in?'

'Not to patients' records – not yet.'

And then you knew he wasn't going to speak for a while, that it was useless trying to keep the conversation going. He would talk again when he had something to say and not before.

That went on for the best part of the day. I forced myself to go out for a while, returning an hour or more later, but I don't think he'd even noticed my absence.

Finally he turned to me. 'What's her name?'

'You know her name—'

'Surname!'

'Oh . . . Oh Jeez, I dunno – how many Lenas are there?'

'None.'

'Shit! No record of her?'

He shrugged. 'Maybe – some odd names here. Could be he's the soul of discretion. Or maybe he's just covering his tracks.'

'She told me once she was of Swedish extraction,' I suddenly remembered. 'Does that help?'

'Mm,' he said, obviously looking through a list of names. 'Karllson?'

'Maybe.'

He handed me the screen. The name Sonia Linekar was highlighted.

I shook my head, not understanding. 'What's this?'

'It's a crude kinda encryption. He alters the syllable order, then plays around with the letters, like here. Lena Karllson: the "son" at the end goes at the front and she becomes "Sonia". "Lena Karll" becomes "Linekar".'

Jesus, I was impressed – if it'd been left to me, we would've been there 'til Doomsday.

'Take a look,' he told me. 'It's private – I don't think I should.'

I tapped the screen and up came a lot of details: age, description, medical notes. Much as it pains me to say it – exasperating little cuss that he is at times – once again I was reminded that the guy was a genius, no two ways about it.

'What does it say?' Gordie asked.

I looked up and realised four eager faces were staring at me, waiting for my news.

'Nothing very interesting.'

'Must be something,' Delilah said.

I went over it again. No allergies, no problems, no . . . 'special talents or gifts'. Then suddenly I stopped and started laughing. *Well, well. So Jimmy does get it wrong sometimes.*

'It's not her,' I said.

'Must be,' he said, immediately on the defensive.

'It's not,' I said, handing him back the screen.

I sat there while he studied it, smirking to myself, waiting for him to see, but he didn't react the way I'd expected.

'Jimmy, it's not her!' I said, annoyed that he always found it so hard to admit to his mistakes. 'It can't be, can it?'

'Well, obviously I don't know her as well as you do, Big Guy,' he replied, his words fairly dripping with sarcasm, 'but I certainly remember the cut she got on her throat from that kid who broke into the tunnels.'

I stared at him for a moment, at the expression on his face, then grabbed the screen back, scrutinising every little detail.

'Well,' Jimmy said, 'are you going to tell them, or am I?'

In a world of bombshells and bolts from the blue, a society where nothing surprised me, I gotta say, that really took the ground out from beneath my feet. I mean, dumb old big guy or what? I'd been saying for ages how well she was looking, that she was blooming – I'd subconsciously put it down to escaping from the Island . . . If I hadn't read that screen, it would never have occurred to me, not for one moment, but there it was: Lena was pregnant . . .

Pregnant! . . . Jesus, she's gonna have a baby!

My first reaction was shaming – believe me, it said everything about me and not a thing about her.

'Who's the father?' I asked.

They all stared at me like they couldn't believe their ears, then Delilah burst into laughter and Jimmy swiftly followed suit.

'Who the hell do you think the father is?' Delilah cackled, and Gordie had the cheek to say he'd tell me the facts of life one day.

'Ten weeks pregnant,' Jimmy said, reading off the screen.

I just continued to gape, knowing my mouth was wide open but unable to close it. Like I said, my reaction was all about me, nothing to do with Lena. I wasn't accusing her of lying or sneaking out the tunnels to meet someone, or anything like that – never even crossed my mind – I just – well, I'm gonna say this just the once and please do excuse me – I just didn't think I had it in me any more!

I admit, we'd never used a condom. I'd never even seen one on the Island – well, not a new one; 'course, there were plenty of used ones around but I wasn't going there, washed out or not. In any case, neither Lena nor me had slept with anyone in years, so there weren't any dread diseases we could pass between us. And – well, like I said, I didn't think I was up to getting anyone pregnant.

Jimmy looked at me, the biggest smile I ever seen on him spreading across his face like a sunrise. 'You're gonna be a dad, Big Guy.'

It was the most disturbing thing anyone'd ever said to me, and for any number of reasons. I never dreamed I'd have a kid – not at that stage of my life. And yet, there I was, a father-to-be, but a father who might never get to see his baby, nor see again the woman he created it with.

And it wasn't just me who didn't know how to react either. Jimmy mentioned about getting out this half-bottle of whisky he took from the Superfood-7, proposing a toast, but Delilah shook her head at him. Instead she came over and putting her long, skinny old arms round me, told me it was going to be all right. And yet once again it was Hanna who came up with the most comforting words.

'I think it's great,' she said. 'It'll make you stronger. More able to fight.'

And you know, the moment she said it, I did feel stronger, more focused, more determined. It wasn't just Lena being held in that place now, it was *our child* too – and come hell or high water, I was gonna get them both out.

It immediately set me thinking. Years ago, when the economy was entering its final death throes and the government was forced into selling off the family silver, they started phasing out the army and getting rid of its hardware. As long as you had the dough, they'd pretty well sell you anything, no questions asked. At the time, Mr Meltoni was having a bit of a problem with this new gang of Eastern Europeans trying to move in on us. He knew it was heading for a showdown and decided to go out and get something to even up the odds a little.

You should've seen those guys: mean as hell, standing in a line across Union North, stony-faced and scowling, all holding these big businesslike automatics, forbidding us to enter 'their territory'. Then they heard something approaching: this creaking and clanking, getting ever closer, all of them starting to glance nervously at one another. Finally, Mr Meltoni came swinging round the corner, dressed in a general's uniform, ribbons and medals all over his chest, at the head of a column of four M1 battle tanks, 120mm guns pointing directly at those determined not to let them pass. I tell ya, you never seen negotiations concluded in such rapid fashion. By the weekend they'd all gone, just melted away.

That was what I needed to get me into Infinity: reinforcements of a truly spectacular nature. And yet, even if I'd had those M1s, I'm not sure how confident I'd have been. The whole situation was so fraught and frightening and I didn't have the slightest idea how to go about solving it.

What I didn't know was that Fate was about to throw one more ingredient into the mix.

I decided to go out, to give the others some talking space, intending to take another look at Infinity. If I could've found just one weakness with that place, no matter how small, you have no idea how much encouragement it would've given me.

I said the fires were starting to die down, but there were still plenty around – plenty of everything bad: fires, smoke, looters, mob rule, and everywhere I went, more and more corpses – always the elderly for some reason, as if, even in death, no one could be bothered with them, they had no value.

I thought I'd seen just about everything in terms of the fires, but I still gotta bit of a jolt when I turned a corner and was met by this burning office block. It was a tall, thin column of flame that had somehow ignited the same two adjacent floors in buildings on either side, so I was confronted by this huge burning cross. Christianity doesn't mean much any more but you still couldn't help but see it in those terms, like it was some kind of sign. I stood there for several minutes, not only looking at the fire, but also at the expressions on the faces of the crowd gathering around me. It was as if they were still a touch bitter that God had let them down, at the way he'd disowned them all those years ago.

I was just about to turn around and head off when something hard was pressed into my back. 'I wouldn't have taken you for a religious man,' someone said behind me.

I turned slowly. I hadn't recognised the voice, but I did the face. It was Van, Ray's main man, with his greasy little sidekick.

'And talking of religion,' he continued, 'I know someone who'd love you to make a Second Coming.'

CHAPTER FOURTEEN

Talk about Fate conspiring – as if I didn't have enough to worry about. They handcuffed me to one of the armrests in the limo – no way was I going to be allowed out of their sight again. I spent the entire journey trying to think of a way to escape, but in the end accepted there just wasn't one and I might as well shut down and try to conserve my energy for whatever was waiting for me at Ray's.

They must've let him know they were about to pick me up 'cuz he didn't look in the slightest bit surprised when I was brought in – on the other hand, I've rarely seen a human being look more furious, more venomous towards another. He wasn't sitting in his armchair but in a hi-tech wheelchair, squat and powerful-looking with really thick tyres, with his bloated legs cocooned in a weird projecting, almost pointed metal frame.

The moment I walked in he started screaming abuse at me, ramming his joystick forward and coming at me so fast I didn't have a hope in hell of getting out the way. My shins took the full force of the blow.

'You stupid fucker!' he screamed.

'Jesus!' I groaned, feeling like he'd swung a sledgehammer at my legs, but he just reversed back and accelerated forward again, this time hitting me so hard, I ended up on the floor. Jeez, that was why he was in that damn contraption: it was the Wheelchair of Death and he was going to ram me into oblivion.

'I told you not to fucking kill him!' he screamed, and suddenly he was that crazy kid again, all those years ago, beating the hell out of me, pounding me senseless on the sidewalk.

'I didn't kill him,' I protested. 'He fell!'

'Fuck you!' he shouted. 'Do you know how much fucking shit you got me into? She knew it was me straight away.'

'It was an accident—!'

'Yeah, and so's this,' he sneered, hitting me with such momentum, I skidded across the polished floor and slammed into the wall, blood instantly running from a cut on my head.

'Boss,' Van muttered, plainly a little concerned that Ray appeared to be bent on killing me then and there.

Again that wheelchair whirled towards me and though I tried to scramble aside, it slammed into me once more, almost dislocating my shoulder.

For a moment I teetered on the edge of unconsciousness, the sound of his screaming voice, ironically, the only thing that stopped me from passing out altogether. I opened my eyes to see this slobbering mouth only inches from me, a rubber band of spit hanging from top to bottom lip, projecting over me as if he was about to vomit. The bile he was expelling was coming from somewhere much deeper and even more noxious than his body, as if all the shit – all the poison – he'd accumulated over the years had been building up to that one moment.

'Where's my fucking money?' he screeched, his bulging face redder than a baboon's ass.

'Gone,' I managed to grunt.

I wouldn't have thought it possible, but he got even angrier, reversing back as far as he could go, then racing towards me and slamming me up against the wall, pinning me to it, revving his motor as hard as he could, trying to crush me.

'You useless fuck! I'll turn you into a fucking blood-and-bone smoothie!'

Plainly he still hated me as much as ever; time hadn't mellowed him one bit. He went back and fired himself at me again, the projecting front of that thing making it look like a damn missile was coming my way.

Van kind of cleared his throat, trying to calm Ray down, maybe to remind him that they didn't want a body on the premises.

I opened my mouth to speak, to beg for mercy, but it was full of blood and I started choking. 'Stop!' I eventually managed to gurgle.

There was a momentary pause, but I couldn't clear my eyes enough to see why; was he trying to calm himself down or merely out of breath? Either way, I knew I couldn't take any more of this, that I had to save myself somehow, and suddenly words started pouring out of my mouth that I swear weren't mine, like the first I knew of them was when I heard them along with everyone else.

'I can get you more money than you ever dreamed of.'

'Fuck you!' Ray sneered, and reversed again, ready to slam into me once more.

'Billions.'

He just sat there glaring at me, joystick in hand, clearly wanting to launch himself again, but momentarily checked by the mention of such an enormous sum of money.

'It's the biggest heist in history, and only I know about it.' I'd overdone it – I knew that as soon as the words were out of my mouth. He shot forward again, pounding into me even as I yelled, 'It's true!'

Again he paused. 'Tell me – and if I think you're lying, this is gonna feel like a massage compared to what'll follow.'

'There's this woman,' I managed to croak out. 'In the Infinity building.'

'Oh, fuck you!' he groaned at the mere mention of Infinity's name.

'She's blind – or she was.' I was panting now, trying not to rush my words, grateful for whatever respite I could get. 'She lived underground on the Island for years – kinda developed these skills . . . They want to clone them and give them to the Specials—'

I didn't actually know if that was true, but I thought it the most likely thing for Ray to believe. 'I was going to kidnap her . . . They'll pay anything to get her back.'

'*Infinity?*' Ray sneered.

'Yeah.'

'You wanna kidnap someone from Infinity?'

'They're not so great,' I told him, trying to summon up at least a pretence of confidence.

'Have you seen that place close up?'

'I've pinpointed a few weaknesses,' I lied. 'All I need is a bunch of guys, some decent hardware.'

Ray didn't want to give the idea a moment's thought, I could see that, but his greed was already starting to nag. He glanced at his two guys but they remained expressionless. I didn't know what was going to come out of that snake hole of a mouth of his next – whether he'd take the bait or not – but at least I'd given myself a chance.

In the end he waved a dismissive hand and just reversed away from me. I grabbed the arm of a nearby chair and attempted to pull myself up, but it was a real struggle.

'Watch the blood!' he shouted, and I fell back to the floor rather than stain his furniture. 'Whaddya think?' he said, turning to his two boys.

Van shook his head, like it was completely out of the question. 'Place is a fortress,' he said.

Ray turned to the other guy, Van's moody little sidekick, but obviously decided his opinion wasn't worth waiting for. 'If it's true . . . ' he said, glaring at me, daring it to be otherwise.

Again Van shook his head. 'Infinity?'

'For sure they wouldn't be expecting anything.'

Van grunted. If it had been up to him I wouldn't have stood a snowball in hell's chance, but Ray always was a greedy sonofabitch.

'Show us,' he ordered, and a screen started glowing up from one of the walls. He gestured for Van to help me up. 'And don't think it gets you off the fucking hook either.'

I'm no expert when it comes to technology, and my case wasn't helped by trying to pull up a map of the Infinity complex and getting an immediate 'NPI' (not in the public interest) classification. I had to draw it, best I could, but at least it gave me a few moments to recall all the stuff Jimmy'd told me. I went through the whole thing and it soon became apparent that they were grudgingly impressed by my thoroughness as I started telling them about the trolley-cameras on the fence, the laser cannon on the roof and of course the dogs of war, the growlers.

'Shit! Shit!' Van kept muttering every time I came up with yet another deterrent.

'So where are these fucking "weaknesses"?' Ray asked, looking as daunted as his henchmen.

For a moment I just stood there, wondering what the hell I was gonna say. After all, that was exactly what I wanted to know, what I'd been trying to find out ever since I first clapped eyes on the place.

I took a deep breath. 'First off,' I told them, 'you're right: they won't be expecting anything. They're pretty good at throwing their weight around, but I bet it's never occurred to them someone might do the same to them.'

'That's for sure,' Van muttered sarcastically.

'The gates aren't that heavily manned,' I went on, clutching at straws.

'No need. All that automatic security,' he commented.

'Not without power,' I countered, again my mouth coming out with something I hadn't been expecting. All three of them turned to me, now looking just that little bit interested. 'If we can knock out their power, they'd lose a lot of their advantages.'

'They'll have fucking backup.' Ray sneered.

'A generator? Sufficient to juice that place and all its equipment? I don't think so,' I said, though actually I had no idea. 'There'd have to be compromises somewhere.'

Again there was silence and this time I could tell they were giving it serious thought.

'They might lose a few things if they have to go to a generator, I guess,' Van conceded.

'D'you know exactly where this woman is?' Ray asked. 'That's a helluva big place.'

'I'm working on it,' I told him. 'Gotta couple of people on the inside.'

That was it: I felt a distinct tug on my line. Now they *were* impressed.

'She's really worth all that dough?' Ray asked, like he wanted to hear the word 'billions' again.

'Yep,' I assured him. 'Think about it: it'd give them one helluvan advantage.'

'Yeah,' he snarled, as if it was his duty to at least make them pay dearly for that privilege.

Again they fell silent. You could see why they were struggling with the idea; a few moments ago I'd been a loose end that needed tying up, now I'd have to become – even if only temporarily – an essential part of their organisation. After all, I was offering them the most lucrative job they'd ever handled.

We talked about it a while longer – I provided a bit more padding and a helluva lot more bullshit; mostly to do with Lena and her special skills, how she could virtually turn night into day – and finally Ray let me go. The last thing he said before I went out the door was that if I screwed up again, he'd kill me in the slowest, most torturously painful manner he could think of, and I didn't doubt it for one moment.

I gave him my word I wouldn't, and left. I mean, it wouldn't have surprised me if that was what he had in mind anyway, that as soon as he got his hands on Lena I'd get a quick couple of bullets or a burst of laser-fire in the back – but it still felt like my best, maybe even my *only*, option. I just had to hope that somewhere in the confusion of the 'rescue' I'd be able to steal Lena away. Oh, yeah, and that I'd never see Ray again as long as I lived.

With the inducement of a couple of the notes I'd been keeping back for emergencies, I persuaded a delivery guy to give me a lift almost back to the churchyard. He wouldn't go the whole way – he refused to enter the destroyed neighbourhoods – but took me as far as he dared. I didn't want to spend any of that money, but I'd tried walking and it was just too damned painful.

The expressions I was greeted with as I entered the shelter told me I probably looked every bit as big a mess as I felt.

'Clancy,' Delilah cried, 'what the hell happened to you?'

'You been to Infinity?' Gordie asked.

I slumped down on my sleeping bag, doing my best to keep any expression of pain off my face. Hanna jumped up to get me some water.

'I'm fine,' I lied, all four of them staring at me with obvious concern. 'I met Ray.'

'Whoa!' Jimmy gasped. 'Not cool.'

'You know what families are like,' I commented, pausing before making my announcement, 'He's gonna help me get into Infinity.'

The little guy just stared. 'You serious?'

'I've thought of a few things – cutting off their power supply.'

'They'll have backup,' he said, as if a child would know that.

'I know, but I'm betting it'll still leave them short in some areas.'

He sighed, neither agreeing, nor disagreeing. 'Big Guy!'

'I don't have any other options!'

'How many men does he have?'

'Not sure. Twenty or so maybe.'

'And how many in Infinity?'

'They won't be expecting us,' I replied, a little weakly.

Jimmy got this look about him like he was wondering how best to go about patronising me, but I shut him up by asking if he could find out how to cut off Infinity's power – somewhere away from the actual building. I just wanted to get it over with in case Lena's time was even more limited than we thought – not that I could push Ray any more; in fact, I was worried that when he stopped and thought about it, he might just change his mind about the whole thing.

'I gotta talk to Gigi,' I told Gordie.

He shrugged. 'I don't know any more than you. She won't say where she lives.'

I thought for a moment. 'Then I guess I gotta get her to come to me.'

The state of the City, it shouldn't've been that much of a surprise, but it took me forever to find a store with any spray paints. And for sure it didn't help that every step I made was dogged by pain. I had no broken bones, but a whole bouquet of bruises, and my head felt like a boiled egg that had had the top sliced off. That damn wheelchair, I tell ya, it was a one-man armoured vehicle – and not something I wanted to face again.

I went up to the Square and sprayed a message at the same place where Gigi used to leave them for me. It wasn't quite as artistic, but it got the point across.

The blind want to see

On my way back, I sprayed it again, just along the street from where I'd first confronted her, then I returned to the shelter, my body still aching and telling me it needed to rest.

Presently Jimmy came to see me, mini-screen in hand. 'There's a substation just along the beach.'

'Great.'

'But—'

'What?'

'Can't find out anything about their generator. Nothing. Whether that's deliberate or not, I don't know.'

'Maybe they don't wanna advertise a weakness?'

'Mm. Maybe,' he replied, doubtfully.

'Even if they have to go to emergency lighting, it'll be something.'

He gave a slightly begrudging nod. 'So whaddya want me to do?'

I hadn't wanted to push him – in fact, I hadn't been planning on saying anything at all, but I should've known he'd want to get involved. I hesitated for a moment, but he was way ahead of me.

'I could blow it,' he said, plainly referring to the substation. 'Me and Gordie, Hanna too, if she wants.'

'She will,' I told him.

'I don't think Lile's up to it.'

'What d'you reckon they got on the gate?'

He sighed. 'Scanners. After that, could be anything.'

'What are they looking for?'

'Weapons, explosive materials, hidden life forms – all sorts of stuff.'

'There don't seem to be many guards.'

'Yeah,' he agreed, 'which is kind of worrying in itself.'

I admit, I shared his concern. I needed to know more, much more, which was why I had to speak to Gigi.

She appeared that night, a few moments after everyone had zipped up, sneaking in and damn near frightening us all to death. I wasn't sure what she'd have to say, or if I wanted the others to hear, so I took her outside, Gordie trailing on behind us.

'What's up?' she asked.

'You know people on the inside, right?'

Immediately she went on the defensive. 'Well . . . kind of.'

'Will they help us get in there?'

'No!' she replied, scoffing at the idea.

'Why not?'

'Too damn scared.'

I paused for a moment, not feeling comfortable about it but knowing I had to tell her. 'There's a gang of us going in there, but we need help.'

'Jeez!' she groaned, like we were crazy to even consider it. 'You just don't get it, do you? Infinity's like, you know, a dictatorship. Everyone's paranoid. The enemy they fear most is the one within. They're watching each other day and night. No one trusts anyone.

The only person who ain't watched is Nora Jagger – she's head of security and the meanest all-powerful bitch you're ever likely to come across. It's her rule that no one knows their roster from one day to the next – not what they're doing, when or who with. Even if you could persuade anyone to help – and that's one helluvan "if" – they wouldn't know if they were going to be in a position to or not.'

I went quiet for a moment. I'd been really counting on this – in fact, I couldn't see Ray going without it. 'Could they at least give us information about what we might come up against? An internal breakdown? What's on the gate?'

Gigi shrugged. 'Maybe. I gotta get a message to them. I mean, they want to, 'course they do, but . . .' She shook her head, as if no other words were necessary.

'D'you know anything about the generators?'

Again she shook her head, now looking that bit embarrassed. 'I'll try and find out.'

'Lena's pregnant!' Gordie suddenly blurted out, I guess wanting to be the first to deliver the killer news.

'What?' Gigi cried, her voice filled with such astonishment, such disbelief, I was a little put out.

'You gotta problem with that?'

'No! I just—'

'What?'

'Hey, you gonna jump down someone's throat, take your big boots off,' she said aggressively, reminding me she was an Island kid.

'I just don't see what's so amazing.'

She paused for a moment like she didn't know whether to go on with the subject or not. 'How many babies you seen on the Mainland?'

I stared into her grimy little pixie-like face, immediately getting a really bad feeling. ' . . . none—'

She never commented, just waited for the information to percolate on down inside me.

'Where are they?' I eventually asked.

'I dunno.'

Again there was silence, I had another question but it was a while before I could ask it. 'Is that why they took her?'

Gigi sighed. 'Could be.'

I thought I'd felt bad before, but that made me feel a whole lot worse. I mean, was that really what this was all about: the baby's organs? That something about Lena being its mother meant each and every spare part would be worth a fortune?

Whether the subject just got too uncomfortable for her or what, I didn't know, but Gigi suddenly announced she had to go. The last thing she said as she hurried away was to think long and hard before going into Infinity – that there were good reasons no one else had ever attempted it. And of course she was right – and yet, after what we'd been discussing, the possibility that my partner and baby's bodies would be ransacked, nothing was gonna stop me.

I'd arranged with Ray to rendezvous at the First Original Sushi Bar. I got there nice and early, feeling I should apologise to Yoshi for what'd happened with the job in case it'd caused him any embarrassment, but when I tried to raise the subject he just smiled and waved it away.

'I thought you'd gone,' he said, bringing me miso soup. 'Found a way through the fires.'

'Not yet.'

'You must.'

'You too.'

'No – this is my home. Where would I go?'

'Back to Japan?' I suggested.

'You can travel in distance, not time,' he said. 'I know nobody. Strange country full of strange people.'

He looked at me and we both laughed, each aware of what the other was thinking: that nowhere could be more bizarre than this place.

A familiar limousine drew up in the street and a look of fear immediately collapsed Yoshi's face. 'Ray!'

'I know. We gotta meeting.'

He turned and got busy behind the bar, like he didn't want to be seen talking to me, and I took my soup and retired to one of the booths. Moments later, Ray exploded in, followed by his two goons, his swollen legs caged in the tapered superstructure of his wheel-chair so that he entered like a launched torpedo. Yoshi went into genial-host mode, offering them free drinks, directing them to my table, though I could see he was still concerned Ray might exact revenge for him paying me for the job and not checking it'd been done properly.

As I expected, Ray had done some research of his own. They'd even gone down to the Infinity building to take a proper look. He wasn't exactly encouraged by what he'd seen, repeatedly cursing Infinity, calling them 'fucking animals', as if protecting themselves from someone like him was about as low as you could get.

'What about these people on the inside?' he asked.

Despite the fact that I'd known the question would come and how critical it was, I didn't have my answer off as pat as I'd hoped. 'Yeah, yeah, they're fine,' I said. 'When the power goes off, they'll make sure everything stays that way.'

'Everything?' he asked, a little surprised.

'Well, most.'

'General stuff or just security?'

Again I hesitated. 'As much as they can.'

Ray sighed, his face starting to redden. 'Do you have any idea what the fuck you're doing?'

'Yeah!' I retorted, 'they're good guys. I trust them.'

'You've met them?' he asked.

'Sure.'

Ray turned to Van, saying in a barely lowered aside, 'I must be fucking mad getting involved with this loser.'

There was a long pause. I knew I was on thin ice and was anxious to change the subject. 'I need some explosives.'

'What the fuck for?'

'The substation.'

Just for a moment, I thought that was it: the step too far. His hand actually went to the joystick of his chair.

'We'll teach Infinity who's running this city,' I said, attempting a bit of a rallying cry.

I admit it was pretty basic stuff, but as I knew all too well, the only other thing guaranteed to motivate Ray apart from money was revenge.

He grunted. 'Nothing would please me more than to settle with those bastards.'

From there on, it got a little easier. Both of us had ideas on how it should go and we slowly moulded them into a workable plan. First we would bust our way in through the gate – which, Ray agreed, looked a little undermanned – then split into three groups. The main one would be a decoy, that would go to the general office, steal any cash available and later, if for any reason things went badly awry, take hostages. Another group, just two or three sharp-shooters, would position themselves overlooking the Specials' barracks at the back and prevent anyone coming out. And Van, his sidekick, me and a few others would go to the hospital and grab 'the mark'.

'And don't think I won't be keeping a close eye on you either,' Ray warned.

'You're coming?' I said, much surprised.

'You think I'm just going to let you waltz off with her?'

'No – I thought—'

'I still do jobs,' he said, reversing his chair a few feet and spinning it round, though he had no need to demonstrate to me what a formidable weapon it could be.

After we'd worked out our strategy, we went through what equipment we'd need. I could hardly believe my ears. They might not have had access to M1 tanks, but it appeared they could get their hands on just about anything else – even RPGs to bring down the Dragonflies.

'And something for me too,' I told them.

'I thought you didn't do firearms any more?' Ray commented.

'For this, I'm gonna make an exception,' I said, trying to make light of it, though he knew as well as I did why I wanted to be armed.

In the end, after we'd gorged on Yoshi's sushi, not to mention his special sake – though I noticed Ray gave him the cold shoulder, the decision whether to punish, punishment in itself – we made our way back out onto the street.

'I'll be in touch,' Ray said, driving his wheelchair up the ramp into the limo. 'Oh fuck – you don't have a cell, do you?'

I shook my head. 'Non-people,' I explained.

'Okay, same time, same place. Four days.'

'Four!' I exclaimed.

'There's a lot to organise!'

'I'd hate to go in there and find we were too late,' I told him. 'That they've done what they wanted with this woman and disposed of her.'

He thought for a moment, then conceded the point. '*Two* fucking days,' he said, and motioned for Van to close the door.

They swept away in an effortless purr of power and money, leaving me to slowly make my way back to the churchyard. Not that I would've accepted a lift even if they'd offered – I mean, we were the strangest of bedfellows: half-brothers who couldn't bear each other's company, who'd mount a whole comic opera on the other's grave. He thought he was using me and I knew I was using him, but I had no other choice: for even the faintest possibility of getting Lena back, I would've lain down with the Devil and given him a back rub.

227

CHAPTER FIFTEEN

I returned a couple of days later to the First Original, still worried Ray might've changed his mind, but everything was fine. He had these explosives for me – this new stuff that looks like a pack of gum but blows everything sky-high, that I hoped Jimmy was familiar with. Everything was arranged for Saturday; he'd chosen the weekend 'cuz he thought there'd be fewer people around, which kinda made sense.

All in all, there were gonna be twenty-seven of us, including me and him, which sounded like quite a formidable team. One thing you could be sure of with Ray; all of them would be seasoned professionals familiar with violence. In fact they'd probably killed many times.

We discussed a few of the finer details, me still having to drag him along occasionally when he sounded on the point of baulking, rebuilding the blaze with the tried-and-trusted fuels of greed and revenge. We agreed to rendezvous on Saturday evening at a venue I suggested halfway between the churchyard and Infinity. No way was I gonna give him any clue as to where we were living – who knew how it'd turn out, what repercussions there might be?

Friday night I was that on edge I couldn't sleep at all. If only I could've let Lena know, maybe stretch my arm out across this city and tap on her window, tell her she might be back lying beside me the following night.

I think that must've been the thought I took with me when I finally fell asleep, 'cuz when I woke the next morning, I was that bit disappointed to find my arms still empty. I lay there for a few moments, my head slowly clearing, praying that really had been my last night alone – then noticed we had a visitor.

Gigi must've sneaked in some time during the night and again made herself comfortable in Arturo's sleeping bag. Don't ask me why, but for a while I just lay there studying her. The flurry of wild hair braided with seagull feathers, the sprinkle of freckles, in that moment she was looking what she was: a child, and with all a child's innocence. That was the thing with Island kids: one moment they were laughing and giggling, appearing almost normal, the next they got this real harsh look about them, like they were a pocket-knife and you'd just flicked the blade.

I sighed to myself, knowing all too well why she'd become a temporary object of fascination: I was thinking about Lena and me again, what sort of kid we'd have. I wanted it to have her looks and character – it'd be cruel if it had anything else. And if it turned out to be a boy, well, maybe he'd benefit from a little bit of my strength, though he wasn't gonna be a big guy, not as long as I was around to show him a better way.

I took a deep breath, unzipped my sleeping bag and slowly got to my feet. The aches and pains of my beating were still there, but restricting my movements much less. I had to get the fire going for breakfast.

'You okay, Clancy?' Delilah mumbled, as I poked at last night's embers.

I glanced over to her and Jimmy in their sleeping bag. Neither of them had their eyes open. 'Fine.'

'Sorry I'm not coming tonight.'

I gave a little grunt. 'Not really your kinda thing, and certainly not the sort of company you wanna mix with.'

'Just get her. Bring her home.'

I smiled to myself. 'I will,' I promised.

Slowly, one by one, the others vacated their sleeping bags. Apparently Gigi was there to help Jimmy – or more likely Gordie – blow up the substation, which was a bit of a worry, 'cuz Hanna was also part of that team and I just hoped those two could forget their differences for one evening.

We spent the day going over and over the plan, making last-minute preparations, weeding out any potential unwanted surprises. Jimmy was going to wear his parka and a bandanna Gigi had lent him to cover up his face, which hopefully would mean he wouldn't get read or recorded anywhere. As soon as it got dark, the four of them would be heading off, making their way down to the beach and getting into position to blow the substation at ten on the dot. After that – well, who knew? It was up to us and Lady Luck.

When they set off across the churchyard – three kids and an old guy with a limp – I got that self-same feeling I'd had when Jimmy and Delilah had gone off to demolish the drugs warehouse on the Island; that I was sending people whose rightful place was at home in front of the screen or playing computer games off on a suicide mission. Thank God Delilah was sitting this one out – though it did mean the two of us were left alone for a while, each trying to reassure the other that everything was going to be fine. The conversation rapidly became uncomfortable until it finally withered away to nothing.

I set off thirty minutes early, making up some excuse about not being sure about finding my way in the smoke and darkness. By the time I reached the rendezvous point, and despite taking it easy, I was still a good fifteen minutes ahead of schedule. I waited in the shadows, expecting to see several limos approaching, but what turned up was one limo sandwiched between two trucks.

I walked up to the limo as the window was sliding down, anticipating Ray, but there were a bunch of guys I didn't know.

'Behind,' one of them said, indicating the following vehicle.

As I approached the back of the final truck the door swung open and there, surrounded by a bunch of real hard-looking sons-of-bitches, was Ray, squatting menacingly in his wheelchair.

Tell the truth, it gave me a bit of a fright – that thing had obviously been converted into battle mode: the framework extended all the way round, armour cladding bolted on, so he looked like he was encased in his own private shell. Furthermore, he was wearing a helmet with a computer-screen visor, night-vision glasses and microphone, presumably so he could orchestrate the whole thing.

Sure enough, he handed me an earpiece. 'Put this on. And don't fucking lose it.'

I did as asked, checking out the rest of the gang; no one met my gaze, no one was saying a word.

As we got closer to Infinity I thought it was time to remind Ray he'd promised me a weapon.

Grudgingly he turned to Van's companion and nodded his head in my direction. The guy handed me a laser, a surprisingly modern one, with a heavy power-pack grip, though personally, I've always preferred good old-fashioned bullets.

'Thanks,' I said, just for once happy to be reunited with that reassuring tug on my inside pocket.

We stopped a few hundred yards down the street from Infinity and Ray checked the time again. 'Six minutes,' he growled.

Immediately the tension inside the truck began to rise, as if we'd come under starter's orders; everyone was looking all single-minded and serious, checking their weapons and kit.

'You sure you can trust this guy?' Ray asked me.

'With my life,' I told him.

He grunted like there was no one in the world he'd trust with that. 'Okay, let's go,' he said into his microphone. 'Take it slowly.'

We didn't go as a convoy. The larger truck headed off first, followed by the limo thirty seconds or so later, and we finally moved off another thirty seconds after that. As we turned into the Infinity entrance, the other two were waiting in line and a couple of Specials were lowering their health masks to talk to the guys in the front truck.

I gotta say, Jimmy was every bit as good as his word. We'd synchronised watches before he left and the explosion went off literally to the second. There was a loud *kerrumph!* over towards the sea and the air flashed and rippled out to the horizon and instantly every light in the Infinity building flickered and dimmed.

That was it: the critical moment, the unknown element I'd put so much faith into, that I'd repeatedly assured Ray would give us the edge. Everything depended on what the emergency generator could and couldn't handle – on what Infinity was about to lose. I was hoping for something close to a blackout, panic perhaps, maybe even people deserting their posts, but if I had to choose one moment when I realised our plan was about to go awry, that was it.

Some things *were* extinguished: lights in the main building, spotlights overlooking the lawn, even the gate office was left at the mercy of something close to darkness. At the same time a couple of things came on that weren't there before, and one that I instantly knew meant big trouble.

There'd been this green neon sign flashing as we'd turned in:

Welcome to Infinity
Please be patient whilst the Specials admit you
and if necessary scan or search your vehicle

However, with the loss of grid power, another sign, pulsing bright red, instantly appeared in its place:

RED ALERT!
By the reading of this notice you automatically accept
any security measures taken by Infinity and absolve the
company and its associates of any future legal action

I didn't know exactly what Ray's gadgetry was capable of – what he was seeing on his visor – but suddenly he looked really alarmed.

'Shit! They're scanning us!'

No sooner had he said it, and God knows why, the guys in the front truck panicked and started shooting. The two Specials fell to the ground.

'*No! No! What the fuck're you doing?*' Ray screamed into his microphone. He hesitated for a moment as if not sure whether to go on or not, but when there was no reaction from the office he decided to chance it. 'Go!' he screamed. '*Go, go!*'

For some reason, the first truck – our main one, with most of the guys in it – stayed where it was, and the limo was forced to pull out and go round it. We followed immediately, speeding in the direction of the main building with Ray shouting and cursing at everyone. This wasn't the way it was supposed to have gone: blasting our way in, a fire-fight threatening at any moment. Infinity's loss of power and the ensuing chaos was supposed to have been our opportunity to take them by surprise.

Behind us, the main truck still hadn't moved.

'Frank, what the fuck are you doing?' Ray screamed at the driver. 'Frank . . . ? What? I can't understand a word you're saying! *What?*'

At that moment, and to our utter astonishment, the truck suddenly blew up, spraying fire and wreckage in every direction.

'*Fuck!*' shouted Ray, yanking off his headset as if he'd caught some of it in his ear.

'What happened?' Van asked.

'I don't know! They got scanned and blown up – he was going on about "swelling" or something, then they started screaming—'

The limo in front of us suddenly faltered, coughed and bucked, then came to a halt like it had run out of gas. We almost slammed into the back of it.

Instantly Ray was screaming again, '*Go back! Go back!*' at our driver.

And sure enough, we hadn't reversed more than twenty-odd yards before the limo also exploded with that same sense of erupting from within: as though pressure had been created inside to a point where everything simply tore apart. A piece of heavy debris, maybe the back axle, hurtled straight at us, smashing through the windshield and killing our driver before he had a chance to move.

'Oh fuck!' Ray wailed.

'Get out!' Van shouted, knowing we were next – that the scan was locking onto us and the truck was starting to tremble, to creak and strain.

The incredible thing was, however it was being generated, it worked on *everything*: I could feel this pressure, this sense that the space inside my body was starting to fill, the bones of my ribcage expanding, my skull starting to crack. The back door swung open and I made a dive for it, but I wasn't alone. The floor beneath our feet moved, a ramp projected straight out into the air and landed with a crash on the ground and instantly Ray shot forward, knocking people aside.

One guy ended up on the tarmac, hitting his head with a real thump and lying there out cold, but the others managed to get out safely and started running back in the direction of the gate – however, a group of Specials burst out of the main building, cutting us off with a wall of laser-fire.

For the first time in many years I pulled out a gun and started shooting, and I gotta say, these new weapons are something else. They take all the skill out of hitting your target; you don't even have to worry too much about aiming, just point in the general direction and the software does the rest. Mind you, it wouldn't be a lot of use if you wanted to fire a warning shot at someone. I took out three Specials in the same number of seconds and not one of them was actually in my sights.

There was this loud report only feet behind me – it actually made me jump – and the door from where more Specials had been about to emerge more or less exploded. I turned around and was not in the least bit surprised to see Ray had cannons mounted in the armrests of his chair. That was why that thing was so squat and stable: to combat recoil. He fired again, and this time the foyer of the building took a direct hit. Jesus, perhaps we were going to get out of this after all.

But my optimism was hopelessly misplaced: a large group of Specials suddenly came streaming over from the gate, directing more bullets and lasers our way, and I realised why the gate always looked undermanned: there had to be a tunnel from there to the main building. One of our guys went to the ground, another, right next to me, got just about cut in two.

'Shit!' Van groaned. I thought it was 'cuz he realised we were cut off, that we were on the losing side of things, but then he went down too, that big muscular frame of his as vulnerable as any to a bullet or laser. He must've got off five or six rounds before his face finally collided with the ground and he stopped moving.

'You fuck! *You fucker!*' Ray screamed. I turned, thinking he was angry at the enemy, at how they'd just slain his number-one man, but it was me he was so furious with.

'I should've known! Anything to do with you, you fucking *loser!*'

Thankfully, I saw the way he was manoeuvring his wheelchair to line up the armrests and dived to one side, scrambling away on my hands and knees as two missiles *whooshed* inches over my head and across the lawn, ending up blowing a hole in the fence.

Another of our guys got cut down and as far as I could see, there were now only three of us left. Ray decided he'd had enough, ramming his joystick forward and shooting off towards the breach in the fence, the one other guy left running hell for leather after him.

'*No!*' I called after them, knowing all too well what was about to happen.

Sure enough, Infinity might've only been on emergency power, but they must've decided long ago that under such circumstances, the growlers would take priority, 'cuz once again those mounds began to rise up out of the ground and silver shapes appeared out of the smoky darkness, moving at incredible speed as they went racing towards the intruders.

Even from where I was, and with the spotlights out, I could sense Ray's shock. His chair wobbled for a moment as if he was about to overbalance, but to his credit, he held it together and kept going, weaving from side to side, blasting his cannon. He took out a couple of them, leaving nothing but strewn piles of flaky junk, but the guy running after him wasn't so lucky.

It hadn't really occurred to me 'til then that the guy was Van's sidekick, but I wasn't altogether surprised; he'd always had that look about him, that he'd find a way of surviving, of sneaking away whilst others did all the dirty work or dying. Mind you, he had it all wrong this time. He was frantically following in Ray's wake, doing his best not to get isolated, leaping over the occasional growler wreckage, firing his laser indiscriminately, and it was probably that, a programmed response to any threat, that provoked several of those pursuing Ray to turn on him instead.

He managed to shoot one of them, dodged his way round another, but the damn thing just turned on a dime and sped after him like a heat-seeking missile, all the while making that eerie howling and growling sound.

There's nothing very scientific about it once they get to you: they just rip you to pieces, as simple as that. The pursuing growler was alongside him in seconds, snarling and snapping, then it just leapt at him and with one crunch from those huge metallic jaws took off his leg just above the knee.

Jesus, I never seen anything like it – nor do I want to, not ever again. The guy thudded to the ground, screaming at the top of his voice, and several other growlers were on him at once, sinking their teeth into every part of his body, wrenching with those massive jaws, tearing him limb from limb, stripping him bare, reducing him to nothing but a scattering of finely chopped blood and bone.

A couple of Infinity bullets thudded into the ground beside me, a laser actually singed my parka and I realised I was completely cut off, that I had no other choice but to run the gauntlet myself. I set off towards the hole in the fence as fast as this old hulk of a body could carry me, praying the growlers were sufficiently distracted by dismembering the guy and their pursuit of Ray to worry about me.

Ray'd just about made it to the fence, in fact, I thought he'd gone through, that he'd escaped, but as I got closer, I saw he'd checked, that he was spinning around, lining up those cannons again. He hit a couple of growlers, but they were immediately replaced by others and soon I saw the flash of a laser and realised he'd pulled out his hand weapon and was firing that as well.

I blundered past what remained of Van's sidekick, praying I wouldn't attract the attention of the growlers, but two of them immediately broke away and started to give chase. Jesus, they were fast! I tell ya, it was like having an express train after you.

One of Ray's pocket missiles swept by only feet away – I didn't know whether he was trying to hit the growlers or me. I couldn't under-stand why he hadn't kept going when he'd reached the fence – surely he hadn't stayed to save me? Up ahead, I could see him clearer now, manoeuvring his chair left and right, lining himself up for another shot.

I turned around and blasted one of the two pursuing growlers, blowing its head right off. It stopped dead, there in the middle of the lawn, one foot raised, like some bizarre sculpture. I also managed to shoot a leg off the other one, but you know, Jimmy was right: it just checked for a moment as if reprogramming itself, then continued after me on three limbs. Worse still, behind it, I could see more of the group that had obliterated Van's sidekick leave his remains and join the chase.

The three-legged growler was rapidly gaining. I took another shot at it, and again, desperately trying to keep it at bay . . . and then – Jesus, I almost screamed out in fear! – my laser died on me.

Even in that moment, I knew why: Ray had given me a laser with an almost empty power-pack so that, when the operation was over and the time came, it'd be that much easier to kill me.

Instantly my three-legged pursuer lengthened its pneumatic stride and was at my side. I tried to kick the damn thing, but it dodged me with ease; I made what I thought was a sudden swerve, but it barely hesitated. What the hell could I do? Its huge jaws started to open in a deathly smile revealing four rows of fearsome teeth – and yet when it went to bite me, to tear into one of my legs, its mouth wouldn't open enough and it just kind of nudged me. It tried again, but with the same result. Obviously there was a malfunction somewhere – maybe it'd been damaged by laser-fire? Whatever the explanation, I couldn't tell you how grateful I was for the occasional frailties of technology.

Despite the growler still occasionally digging at my leg, I finally managed to reach the fence as a little wild laser-fire resumed from the main building, I guessed 'cuz they couldn't see that well and didn't want to take any chances. Ray was reversing back and forth, the wheelchair's engine screaming, and finally I realised what'd happened. He hadn't been covering my retreat; the wires from the broken fence had got tangled up in his wheels.

Don't ask me why, but I went to free him.

'Fuck off!' he shouted.

'I'm trying to help!'

I guess he saw it was true 'cuz he shut up, but he was clearly still as mad as hell at me.

I wrenched at the wire, twisting it this way and that and doing my best to tug it free, but all his to-ing and fro-ing had really got it tangled.

'*Come on!*' he screamed, peering over my shoulder.

I glanced behind me to see half a dozen or more growlers bearing down upon us, all gnashing and snarling, obviously having nothing wrong with *their* jaws. I turned back to Ray and out of sheer desperation tried to lift him out of the chair.

'You can't!' he cried, 'not with the armour! I'm bolted in!'

You think about those moments, what you'd do in that position, but you never know 'til it happens. I stared into his horror-stricken face, my half-brother, partially my own flesh and blood, knowing he was about to die either alone or accompanied by me, and turned and ran through the fence towards the bushes at the far side of the road.

I *had* tried to save his life, but if I thought that counted for anything, I was wrong, 'cuz I suddenly felt this real thud in my right buttock, like someone had kicked me as hard as they could, and I knew he'd shot me: that his last action in life had been to try to kill me.

I fell to the ground but I guess he must've known I wasn't dead 'cuz he kept on firing, and yet within seconds all that pneumatic *clank-clank*, the growling and howling, converged behind me and there followed the kinda high-pitched scream I would never have associated with Ray.

They were all over him, tearing at his body in a frenzy of flashing teeth and snapping jaws. I tried to struggle up, knowing I'd be next, but I was in too much pain to do more than wriggle a few inches, then an inch or two more, the noises behind me – the crunching of bones, the ripping of flesh – spurring me on. Yet suddenly I heard a noise unlike any I'd ever heard before: it was like a giant balloon popping underwater, or a hugely overweight jumper smacking against the sidewalk. I knew immediately what it was: the growlers had bitten through those swollen legs of Ray's and the damn things had exploded.

I drove myself forward another few inches, pivoting on my elbows, straining with every muscle, but it was hopeless, as soon as they'd finished with Ray they'd be over for me.

Again I glanced over my shoulder. Jesus, you've never seen so much blood – the whole surrounding area was awash with the stuff, and it was dripping off everything. The growlers had ripped through the armour as easily as they had Ray's body and now, their job done, were just standing there and scanning for any other threats to their masters. As one they turned and moved towards me with that familiar slurping pneumatic clank and a renewed chorus of howling, and I scrabbled and scratched at the ground, my fingers bleeding, trying to will my damaged body away.

It was the weirdest thing: all of them, a pack of maybe fifteen to twenty, stopped dead the moment they had to cross the fallen fence. They were just standing there, motionless and silent. Had they lost power or something, maybe used up all their emergency reserve?

They were facing in my direction, but I couldn't make out if they were still functioning or not.

After a few agonisingly long seconds, as one they just turned around and clanked back in the direction of their burrows.

What the hell . . . ? What happened? And finally it hit me: they were only programmed for the complex, nothing outside, their world ended with the fence.

Over on the concourse, the Specials stopped firing. I wasn't sure how much they'd seen, but presumably the growlers returning to their lairs had put their minds at rest – though they were bound to send someone out through the gate to check. Before they did, I had to somehow make it to the far side of the road and hide myself.

I don't know how long it took – twenty minutes or so, maybe – but I'd just about managed to roll into the long grass and squirm my way up against a bush when a party of Specials drew up.

They didn't stay long; just did some makeshift repairs to the fence, called maintenance and ordered them to fix it properly in the morning. No one bothered to search for me. I didn't get it – they must've seen me running across the grass – but finally I came to the conclusion that it was Ray: the way his body had exploded, going all over the place like that, they must've assumed it was the remains of two people, not one, that the growlers had got us both. Jeez, and how was that for revenge? I wonder how that venomous old bastard would feel knowing that his last action on this Earth hadn't been to end my life but to save it.

Quite a lot of joking went on: comments about what messy eaters growlers were. Someone got a big laugh after looking at what remained of Ray and his armoured wheelchair and quipping that growlers didn't normally like canned food.

Soon they jumped back into their vehicle and returned into the complex, leaving me all alone and utterly at a loss. What the hell was

I going to do? Jimmy and the gang wouldn't have the slightest idea where I was or what'd happened. If Infinity showed any footage of the attack – and that was a big 'if', bearing in mind they wouldn't want to admit to their actual headquarters being attacked – they were bound to make a thing of having killed everyone, and in that case, there was every chance I'd never be found, that I was going to die out there of exposure or starvation.

That immediately sent my thoughts winging across the grass to the Infinity building. How close were we, exactly? Had she heard us? Maybe she'd asked someone what was going on and they'd told her Infinity were under attack from terrorists or something . . .

'Lena,' I groaned, 'don't you believe them . . . I came to rescue you—!'

Jesus, it was humiliating: helplessly lying in the grass with a laser wound to my ass. If I could've found a branch or something, maybe I might've been able to use it as a crutch and get moving – but I couldn't see a thing in that smoke-curdled darkness and I certainly wasn't up to wandering round searching.

Again my eyes went to the Infinity building. Forget the risk, I couldn't help myself, it just came bursting out: *'Lena!'* I moaned, *'Le-n-a!'*

I don't know when I passed out exactly, nor for how long, but at some point the sound of hushed voices somewhere nearby woke me. Jeez, I shouldn't have called out like that. Or maybe they'd been studying random camera footage and seen me crawl into the bushes? I heard the thud of nearby footsteps: someone misjudging the terrain in the dark and almost falling, and tried to shrink further under the bush.

There were several of them, that much I could make out, whispering to each other, searching around, getting ever closer. I thanked God they didn't have torches, though I knew it could only be a matter of time.

'Definitely someone made it out,' I heard a voice say, maybe finding a few drops of my blood in the grass.

'You sure?' came a female voice.

'They're wounded.'

There was silence for a few moments, then one of them started slowly heading my way, tracking from side to side, maybe picking up on more blood.

'Those things are so fast,' the female voice whispered.

'And he's not,' the first voice commented.

I turned my head, trying to hear clearer. Were they talking about me?

'Not at his age,' the first voice added.

Wait a minute: I knew that voice. 'Jimmy!' I whispered.

There was an immediate silence. Obviously I'd frightened the hell out of them. 'Jimmy!' I called again.

Finally he got up the nerve to answer. 'Big Guy?'

'Over here!' I whispered.

They started to make their way over, hesitantly, like they were a little scared of what they might find.

It was Gordie and Gigi who found me and they called to Jimmy, the little guy hastily pegging it over. 'Big Guy! You okay?'

'About as okay as a man who's been shot in the ass can be,' I grumbled. 'Just get me up, will ya?'

With considerable difficulty, all four of them hauled me to my feet, having to pause once they got me there for my pain to subside. 'Okay, let's go,' I eventually said.

With Gigi and Gordie taking one arm and Jimmy and Hanna the other, we slowly skulked away from the darkened quasi-military monolith of Infinity.

'What the hell happened?' Jimmy asked when we'd eventually got into some kind of rhythm.

'Infinity did. That place is a super-fortress. You need a damn army to get in there. I'm the only one to make it out—'

'Shit!' Jimmy exclaimed.

'Did you see the growlers?' Gigi asked.

'Yeah – and what they're capable of.'

'Grab them by the front legs and pull them apart,' Gordie advised, giving a quick demonstration.

Hanna laughed like she couldn't believe how stupid he was and he flushed and told her to shut up.

'You shut up,' she replied.

'Okay, okay!' I said, wondering what had happened for their differences to have reached that level.

I told them the whole story, not just as a way to smooth things over and let tempers die down, but also 'cuz I thought they should know how easily Infinity had dealt with us; the way our vehicles had been blown up, what'd happened to Ray, and, of course, if it even needed saying, the fact that I hadn't got anywhere near the hospital wing and Lena.

'She'll know it was you,' Hanna reassured me.

I turned and tried to give her a hug but ended up squeezing Jimmy as well. 'You think?'

''course!'

Jimmy nodded his agreement. 'Yeah, she'll know.'

I almost managed a smile, only then noticing the little guy'd lost his parka and bandanna. 'Where's your disguise?' I asked.

He shrugged, looking a little reluctant to tell me, and I caught Gigi and Gordie smirking at each other.

'That Ray,' he said dismissively. 'For chrissake! What'd he give you all that explosive for?'

I paused for a moment. 'You used too much?'

'Just what I was given.'

By now Gigi and Gordie were openly giggling, and if it hadn't been them she'd have had to have sided with, I reckon Hanna would've done the same.

'You blew your clothes off?' I asked.

'Not all of them!' he protested.

'And his eyebrows,' Gordie chipped in.

'It's cool,' Jimmy protested, running his fingertips along his singed brows. 'Matches my head.'

'Next you're gonna tell me you did it deliberately—' I commented.

To be honest, I was more than glad of the distraction: Jimmy being Jimmy, the kids giggling and teasing, even Hanna and Gordie having their little spat, 'cuz believe me, I was feeling pretty sorry for myself. Big guys get shot in the arm or shoulder, occasionally even the chest, not the ass. Several more times on the way back I had to get them to prop me for a few moments till the pain subsided. And the situation wasn't helped by something of a competition developing between the two pairs: Gordie and Gigi making out I was no weight at all, whilst Hanna and Jimmy were so intent on proving they were well up to the task that a couple of times I had to ask them to let me down their side a little.

But of course that wasn't the real reason I needed a distraction. It was returning from Infinity empty-handed. I'd been so hopeful, so buoyed up by the thought of having Lena back with me, but now, at least for the foreseeable future, the two of us were just going to have to get used to the idea of being apart.

CHAPTER SIXTEEN

I used to suffer from insomnia regularly before I met Lena. Out on the Island, not knowing who might come for you in the middle of the night, are you surprised? When I started sleeping with her, it appeared to go away, but insomnia's all about establishing a pattern. Even then, if my sleep got disturbed a couple of times, my body-clock assumed that was when it was meant to wake up – every night. And, of course, after Lena got kidnapped, my sleeping routine was burned to hell.

One of the things about insomnia is, you might not get that many opportunities to dream, but when you do, your mind goes a little crazy trying to catch up. It's like three speeded-up movies playing at the same time. I dreamed about Lena, of course, which wasn't exactly a surprise. She'd had our baby, a boy, and maybe 'cuz I was concerned at how long it'd be before I saw her again, he must've been twelve or thirteen, but a real monster, a Wastelord in the making. He killed Hanna. The church was still intact and I walked down the steps of the crypt to find her face-down with a machete in her back, blood seeping out and filling the inscription of the gravestone she was lying on. She had her ballet gear on, tutu and shoes, as if she'd dressed for the occasion. Worse still, when I turned her over, I could see he'd slashed her right down the front and taken all her organs.

Lena wanted me to protect him, to say nothing to nobody, but I wasn't having any of it. I got so angry with her – angrier than I ever could've imagined. At one point I actually accused her of having sex with someone else – I mean, no son of mine could behave like that, surely? In the end, I told her to choose between me and him, and you know, she never even hesitated. The last I saw, the two of them were disappearing into the smoke over by the gate.

I awoke with a jolt, the images dissipating like mischievous genies returning to the bottle. After everything that had happened at Infinity, I was so tired I never imagined I'd have any problems sleeping. On the other hand, bearing in mind the things I'd seen, I guess it wasn't that much of a surprise.

I turned over, seeking a more comfortable position, but it wasn't sleep I craved as much as oblivion. What on earth had I been thinking, trying to get into Infinity that way? All we'd done was to confirm what I'd already suspected: that that place was a fortress and there was no way in there, certainly not by force.

A little later, after managing another fitful hour or so, I awoke feeling even more negative, and sure as hell it didn't help that I'd taken that laser-burn to the ass either. It had to be looked at, cleaned and dressed; 'course, if Lena had been there it wouldn't have been a problem, but it was well into the afternoon before I finally gave in to everyone's nagging and, dismissing Jimmy's sniggering offer, asked Delilah to take a look.

Thankfully, it wasn't as bad as I'd feared, not according to her, anyway. Though she sure didn't help matters by making all these comments about, 'if it had been a little more central and down a touch'– as if I hadn't been embarrassed enough already.

She reckoned it would take a while to heal, even with the organi-plasters. For sure I wouldn't be doing a great deal of sitting in the near future, but I guess I got off quite lightly, physically, that is. Mentally and emotionally, I couldn't have felt worse: I didn't only get my ass lasered, I got it kicked good and proper.

Naturally, everyone came up with all sorts of alternative ways of rescuing Lena: parachuting in, checking if there were any old tunnels under the building, jamming the growlers' frequencies. Gigi even said she'd do what she could to find out how many there were inside Infinity prepared to help.

But it was just talk, and we all knew it: a futile attempt at getting our morale back up, though actually, as the suggestions became more and more desperate, it did quite the reverse.

We didn't watch the screen that often – Jimmy had a solar boost for the battery so it wasn't lack of power, nor that he was constantly playing with it, trying to make it do things it wasn't intended for. It was more that it was *their* world and we didn't want any part of it. But after a couple of days of lying on my side, restless, bored and uncomfortable, I asked the little guy if I could watch it for a while.

I turned it on, glancing at the image and getting the shock of my life. With everything else that'd been going on, I hadn't really given it a thought, but sure as hell I should've.

'Ah, shit!' I groaned

'What?' Jimmy asked, shuffling over to take a look. Gordie and Hanna did too, though Delilah hesitated, like she didn't want to know, only finally joining us when she saw how pale Jimmy went, the expression on his face.

It was him again – on the screen. The big difference was that now they not only had pictures of him with his shaved head, but also his name, or at least the same misspelling of his name as on the commercial data bank: 'Jimy'.

'I knew this would happen,' he moaned as they showed endless footage of him from the night of the raid and from the point that he got his disguise blown off.

'Hey, look! That's me!' Gordie cried proudly, as an enlarged image of the four of them was shown. 'And Gigi!'

Hanna pointedly raised her eyes and shook her head, as if he'd reached new depths of dorkdom.

'I just don't understand where they got your name,' Delilah complained. 'And spelled that way, too.'

'Looks like a game name,' Hanna commented.

'What do you mean?'

'When you play a computer game – most people use a nickname, or a shortened version of their own.'

'He hasn't played a game in thirteen years,' Delilah said dismissively.

And that was it, that was when it finally hit me: Hanna had seen what I should've long ago.

I turned to Jimmy. He had this look on his face like he'd just stepped into something left by a very large dog.

'What's the matter?' Delilah asked.

'Don't tell me—' I said accusingly.

'What is it?' Delilah croaked again as I glared at the little guy, waiting for him to explain. However, he didn't need to, 'cuz the next thing they showed was the video image from the game he'd played at the secret arcade, complete with screen information: 'Highest-ever score and grand champion: Jimy'.

'You put that in?' I cried, barely believing what I was seeing.

'It was a good score,' he replied weakly.

'Jesus, Jimmy!' I groaned. 'Even I wouldn't do that! That's how the screens started to read you.'

'You don't say!' he commented, like I was being annoyingly obvious.

Nor was that the end of our bad news – a world from it. As always, they interviewed a spokesperson from Infinity, the journalist teasing out answers that had obviously been well-rehearsed. Normally it was this no-nonsense career cop-type, reassuring the general public that everything was under control, but this time it was someone else – someone who I immediately sensed we had to respect, maybe even be that bit afraid of, as if Infinity had finally brought out their champion, the worst they could possibly do. I wasn't the least bit surprised to see the name Nora Jagger come up on the screen. Gigi'd mentioned her before: Head of Security at Infinity, and the way things were, maybe the most powerful person in the organisation.

I gotta say, I was that bit transfixed. I never seen anyone look so damn mean, so lacking in human qualities. She had very close-cropped blonde hair, blue eyes that pierced through you even outta the screen, and a face that'd bring down Rushmore.

Mind you, the personnel might've been different, but the message was still the same: all she could talk about was 'Jimy' and how he was the biggest-ever threat to our society. She went on to announce that Infinity was both doubling the reward for his demise *and* removing all restrictions on firearms. Something about the determined way she said it made you think that this was her initiative, her way of settling things, and that she thought it wouldn't take long to get results.

'Shit,' I muttered as the interview came to an end, as much concerned by the messenger as I was the news.

'*Jimmy!*' Delilah wailed in despair.

The thing about the little guy is, he never makes mistakes, or not as far as he's concerned, and on the rare occasion that he does, he always manages to wriggle out of it, to put the blame on someone or something else. But this time, there was no way out.

For a few moments he just stood there like an animal waiting to be tethered to an unbearably heavy load. 'Sorry, guys,' he eventually whispered, turning towards the shelter entrance. 'Not cool.'

'Hey!' Delilah called after him.

'*Lile*,' he cried, 'I screwed up!'

'Where you going?'

'I don't know – to get some food or water. Maybe I can manage that without endangering everyone's lives.'

'You can't go out there,' I told him, worried he was so upset he wasn't thinking straight. 'It's hunting season and you're what everyone's got tattooed on their sights.'

'Well, *you* can't,' he said, reminding me of my injury.

'I'll go,' Delilah said.

'Lile!' Jimmy protested.

'Listen, mister, you take one more step and it'll be your last!' she warned, working herself up into one of her highly volatile states.

No matter how bad he was feeling, the little guy still knew enough not to go up against her. He paused for a moment, then turned and slunk away in the opposite direction, following the wall down 'til he disappeared from sight.

'He is *such* a fool,' Delilah commented.

'It *was* a great score,' Gordie commented, as if that made it more understandable.

Actually, it didn't change things that much. Jimmy barely went out anyway, and never without a disguise. What it did do, though, was to enhance the feeling that Infinity were starting to close in, that with every day their grip was slowly tightening.

It started me thinking: maybe it'd be possible to get through the fires now? The only reason we were all still there was Lena. The others didn't need to stay, especially not Jimmy, with all the problems he had, not to mention Delilah's one lung still sawing away at that solid wall of smoke. Why didn't they just go on and leave me to find a way of rescuing Lena?

But when I tried to raise the subject, no one would even hear me out.

Of course, I was touched, I truly was, but some people might've thought it was a little foolish. Everything felt so hopeless now – even the length of time since I'd last seen Lena was starting to work against me. Maybe she didn't wanna be rescued any more? Maybe things had changed? . . . I dunno. Lying propped on my side on that sleeping bag for hour after hour, I was imagining all sorts of crazy stuff.

Which was why a visit from Gigi, something she brought with her, couldn't have been more timely.

She appeared that afternoon, not bothering with any greeting, just strolling up and handing me a piece of paper.

I stared at her as I unfolded it, having no idea what it might be, but the moment I started to read, it was all I could do not to break into tears.

My love,

I don't know if you'll ever read this. I think whoever's smuggling it out is taking a big risk, but I have to grab this opportunity.

You have no idea how much I miss you. There isn't a minute goes by when I'm not thinking of you. I don't know what's going on, or why they took me. I hear the occasional whisper, but people are too scared to say much. Even Dr Simon won't tell me. All he says is I'm 'special'.

They're treating me okay, don't worry about that. Whatever's happening, I'm sure, when it's over, we'll be together again and finally able to make our home in the country.

I'm sorry, I can't write any more. No matter what happens, Clancy, I will always love you. Nothing can ever change that.

Lena

PS Do you know Nora Jagger? Whatever you do, don't go up against her.

I have to say, for a while there was quite a wrestling match went on between me and my tear-ducts, and I only won 'cuz I was so surprised by something she'd said. 'Doesn't she know?' I said, turning to Gigi.

'What?'

'That she's pregnant?'

Gigi shrugged. 'Dunno.'

'You have to get word to her!'

She glared at me with real aggression – the Island blade abruptly flicking open. 'Do you know how hard it was to get this out?'

'Yeah – sorry,' I said. 'I am grateful.'

'She's a woman! If she doesn't know yet, she'll work it out soon enough.'

I nodded my head, though I wasn't entirely sure what she meant. I guessed she was talking about having a period but . . . I thought . . . if a woman got stressed or went through a big change of routine or something, might she miss the odd one? Which could be confusing. Mind you, I'm just a dumb old big guy who never had a real girlfriend before Lena, and for sure I wasn't asking for clarification from some kid with seagull feathers in her hair.

I read the letter again, studying it more closely. For the first time since it happened, the pain in my ass was entirely forgotten.

'What's with this Nora Jagger woman?' I asked.

It was funny, even though Gigi paused for only the briefest of moments, you knew that somewhere in there was a whole world of information.

'Some people call her "the Executioner".'

'That's legal?' Delilah asked.

'Not officially, but "accidents" do happen when she's around. People die of injuries sustained alone in cells, commit suicide when they have everything to live for, fall outta locked windows, that sort of thing.'

'Jesus,' I muttered. The thought that Lena was apparently familiar with this woman was not sitting well at all.

'She had all her arms and legs cut off,' Gigi suddenly announced.

'*What?*' Delilah grimaced.

'Well, not exactly . . . she lost an arm in an accident – survival training – and had an artificial one specially made. It can do anything a normal one can but it's ten times stronger. She liked it so much, she had her other arm and legs replaced.'

I stared at her, not exactly sure what my reaction should be. 'You don't believe that?'

'Yeah. I do.'

'Come on – it's just talk, people trying to build themselves a demon.'

Gigi firmly shook her head. 'I don't think so.'

I chuckled like I was dismissing it, but not with complete conviction. Just from seeing that face on the screen, those eyes, I wasn't sure I'd put anything past Nora Jagger.

'How'd'ya get the letter out?' I asked, changing the subject.

Gigi shrugged. 'Can't tell you.'

Hanna sniggered, like it was all a bit absurd.

'What?' Gigi demanded, and I immediately stepped in between them.

'Okay, okay! Thank you.'

'I gotta go,' Gigi said, glaring at Hanna as if she was the reason.

Gordie stood to walk her out, the way he always did now.

'What is it with you two?' I asked Hanna, the moment they were out of earshot.

'Nothing,' she said, as if she didn't have a clue what I was talking about.

I thought about pursuing the subject but instead returned my attention to the letter, reading it again, even checking for a smudge of something, a crumb maybe, anything that would connect it with my Lena.

It wouldn't be fair to say that Jimmy (or should that be 'Jimy'?) sulked for the next few days, though he did keep to himself in a way I'd never seen before. He barely said a word over meals, only spoke when spoken to, and the moment he could, sneaked away to be alone. Delilah and the kids did the scavenging, bringing back what they could, though they weren't exactly a formidable team and on a couple of occasions the stuff they'd spent all day finding got stolen from *them*.

My ass was beginning to heal and I started doing some exercises to free it up a little. It wasn't exactly stimulating, but at least it gave me something to think about rather than endlessly brooding on Lena.

I watched the screen a couple more times, as much to get another look at Nora Jagger, to see what she was up to, as anything. She'd obviously decided to take over the search for Jimy herself, suggesting that no one else could be trusted. I tell ya, that woman looked so damn vicious, so cold-blooded, I could see how rumours about her would circulate, and why people would believe them – but surely no one would deliberately have their limbs removed? Especially when you think of those unfortunate enough to suffer that through no choice of their own. It'd be a damned insult.

It's an unusual circumstance for a killer to make it to the top job. Normally they just stay doing what they're good at (the ultimate 'dead-end job?'), hopefully keeping their impulses in check. But if somehow they do manage to reach a position of authority, a place where their power can give vent to their instinct, well, that's where the problems really start. And from what I'd seen of Nora Jagger, that was what'd happened here. I didn't know a lot about her, but I did know enough to see why Lena had warned me.

Yet again, like some mindless mantra, she referred to 'Jimy' as 'Public Enemy Number One, the arch-terrorist, the brains behind this highly destructive anarchy', not the sad little baldy guy who's been hiding out in a corner of a flattened churchyard.

But Jimmy's not the sort of person to hide himself away for long; there's nothing very constructive about feeling sorry for yourself, and I wasn't altogether surprised when he finished breakfast one morning by asking everyone if they had anything to contribute to his new disguise and borrowed a baseball cap from Gordie, a scarf from Hanna and Delilah's parka.

Lile protested, of course, but not that loudly. She knew he had to do something. Like me, she'd never seen the little guy so down, and if that was the cure, then she was prepared to reluctantly go along with it.

After that he went out almost every day – not for long, nor that far, but enough to prove a point to himself, if not others, returning with food or water, some little gizmo that'd caught his eye. Like the rest of us he was getting by but inside feeling hopelessly impotent, no longer capable of making things happen, blinding our faith and placing it in the care of God and the ticking of the clock.

I can't tell you how surprised I was the day Gordie came home with Dorkus. He kind of shuffled in, looking all self-conscious, glancing behind him with this excited little smile. Everyone looked over, wondering what on earth was going on, and suddenly there was this dog peering out from behind a bush: a little grey, wiry terrier-type with big brown eyes staring out from behind a long tousled fringe.

'Ohhh! Where d'ya get him?' Delilah cried excitedly.

'I just saw him,' Gordie said casually, like such things happened all the time. 'Up near the Square.'

'Here, boy! Here!' Delilah called, and the dog slowly made his way over, a little uncertainly, and tolerated rather than enjoyed Delilah's enthusiastic petting.

'This is Dorkus,' Gordie said proudly

'That's his name?' Delilah asked, a little perturbed.

'It's what I call him. He's mine.'

With that, and despite the fact that she made it a strict policy never to show any interest in anything Gordie said or did, Hanna completely melted, leaping across, falling on her knees, cooing and scratching the dog's ears.

'Hey, now just a moment,' I said, knowing I was about to make myself about as popular as the traffic cop who booked Santa, 'we can't keep him.'

'Why not?' Gordie wailed.

'Clancy!' Delilah chimed, joining in the protest.

'No! I'm sorry – it's more trouble than it's worth.'

'A stray dog?' Hanna asked.

'It's okay, Big Guy,' Jimmy reassured me.

257

'No, it's not! Dogs bark,' I told them, just in case they didn't know. 'They don't understand when you tell them to hide or be quiet – and it's another mouth to feed.'

'Clancy! Look at him,' Delilah protested as the dog glanced from one face to another, plainly wondering what the hell was going on.

'I'm not getting rid of him,' Gordie said, and the dog, as if realising he was his most likely saviour, circled around and pushed himself in between Gordie's legs.

'Nooo!' Hanna moaned, siding with Gordie for possibly the first time ever.

'I'm sorry. We don't have a choice,' I told them. 'What if someone comes sniffing round one night? Some "bounty hunter" looking for Jimmy? Can you guarantee that thing isn't gonna give us away?'

'It's a bit unlikely,' Jimmy said.

'It *could* happen!'

'If he goes, so do I,' Gordie said defiantly.

'Clancy!' Delilah protested.

There was a brief silence. I mean, I hate being the bad guy, but I couldn't see why they didn't get my point.

'Why don't we have a vote?' Hanna eventually suggested.

'Yeah!' agreed Gordie, pretty confident he'd win.

'No. We're not having any vote,' I told them. 'He's gotta go.'

There was a long pause, and Delilah kinda cleared her throat. 'Clancy, we've always been a democracy.'

Oh Jeez! I'd known I was open to that charge. I also suspected that something about that dog, his tousled fringe and big brown eyes, just might be reminding her of Arturo.

'Let him stay! The first sign of trouble, he's out of here,' she begged.

'That first sign might be Jimmy with a bullet in his head.'

'Thanks, Big Guy,' Jimmy told me. 'That's made me feel a whole lot better about the whole thing.'

'I'm just trying to get the seriousness of this over to you!'

Again there was silence, only this time it was set a lot harder. You could see how upset Gordie was: his eyes were all wild and staring and he wouldn't meet my gaze at all.

Hanna bent down to pet the dog again. 'He's so cute.'

'Let him stay, Clancy,' Delilah urged.

I just shook my head. As far as I was concerned, I was done with talking.

'Just for the night,' she added.

I knew what she was up to. It's the oldest trick in the book – I tried the same one when I was a kid – but this was different. 'It's asking for trouble,' I insisted.

The fact that I didn't actually say 'no', that my voice softened a little, was taken as sufficient encouragement for Delilah to start looking out some scraps for the animal.

I hesitated, feeling we were far from done but aware of all these pairs of eyes turned on me, about to unleash a salvo of protest and guilt. 'All right,' I sighed. 'Just for the night, that's all.'

I don't think they heard anything else I said. The only thing that mattered was that for the moment at least, I'd withdrawn my objection. For the rest of the day, and the evening too, little Dorkus was treated like canine royalty, passed from one person to another, everyone taking their turn to pat or stroke him, getting this dopey smile about them, though I pointedly declined.

Not that he was that affectionate – he didn't object or nothing, but he did give the impression he could've done without the fuss. I guessed he'd had to toughen up on the streets. Mind you, he was something of a novelty. You gotta remember, you didn't see dogs anymore. Like so many things, family pets had become a liability:

feeding them, vets' bills, all of it contributed towards people, not selling them, 'cuz no one would buy, but just abandoning them wherever they could. And not just dogs either: cats, rabbits, ponies, even large reptiles had been left to wander the City – 'course, they quickly disappeared, most dying of starvation, some of disease, and quite a few getting killed and eaten. To see a domesticated dog wandering around was quite something, especially for kids from the Island, which made me feel even more of a heel.

When we bedded down, Gordie squeezed little Dorkus into his sleeping bag with him, everyone laughing fit to bust, not in a teasing way, but just as an expression of how cute they looked together. Though Gordie took great pains to point out that Dorkus was a survivor, a tough little mutt, and no one should forget it.

'Hey now, look,' I said, getting a little frustrated by this happy family scene, 'just remember: no decision's been made.'

'Clancy!' Delilah protested, like she'd assumed it had.

'No!' I said impatiently. 'We'll discuss it in the morning.'

The last thing I saw as Jimmy turned off the camping light was Gordie disappearing down into his sleeping bag, two bumps, one large, one small, joining together. I mean, he *was* a cute little fella, I could see the attraction all right, but I could also see the risks.

The irony – and it made a rock grow in my heart every time I thought about it – was that by now I looked on Gordie as a kinda son, and there I was behaving in exactly the same manner as my father once had with me: a man whose abilities as a parent I've constantly called into question.

I don't know how old I was at the time – eight or so, maybe. This guy I knew, Lennie, a real down-and-out, had been sleeping on the same bench in the park for as long as anyone could remember, most days just dozing, but occasionally trying to earn a few coins playing his harmonica. He had this dog, Buster, a bit like Gordie's mutt but rangier, with legs that stuck out at odd angles. He was the most loyal animal you could ever imagine. When Lennie died of TB he sat by that same bench every day for months. They sent the dog-catcher, all sorts of people to impound him, but no one could, and the moment they gave up he returned to sit next to his master's bench.

But the thing was, he knew me: he didn't run when he saw me approaching, he even let me pat him, and when I noticed he was getting a little thin, I started to bring him food. It went on for ages; through the summer and into the winter. Then one day, after I fed him and went to walk away, I turned to see him following. That night we had some of the deepest snow in years and I reckon Buster must've known it was coming.

The only thing was, my old man hated dogs – he hated all animals. He used to get so angry when people said there was no such thing as a bad dog, only bad owners, said it was arrogant for us to assume we had one hundred per cent control of how a dog turned out, which actually, does have a certain amount of twisted logic to it. Anyways, he was against Buster from the moment I brought him home, saying I wouldn't take care of him, wouldn't take him for walks, and that there was no way *he* was going to do it for me. I begged and pleaded, and thanks to Ma, he eventually let me keep him, but he was a long way from happy, and after a while I noticed that Buster started trotting out of the room the moment my old man appeared, as if he was being mean to him when I wasn't around.

In the end, when Pa lost his job and money started getting tight, he said I had to get rid of Buster. I wouldn't, of course, but one day, when I got home, he was gone. Pa said he was sorry but he had to do it, that we just couldn't afford a dog any more, and that Buster had gone to a good home. Couple of days later, some kids I knew told me they'd found Buster in a sack floating in the canal. I told them it wasn't him. Even when they took me down and showed me, I still said it wasn't my dog. I just didn't want to admit it – not then, not even now.

It was Delilah who woke me in the morning, shaking my shoulder and screaming into my face, yelling at me to get up.

'What the hell is it?' I asked, angry at being woken in such a manner.

'They've gone!' she said, not backing away from my annoyance one jot.

'Who?'

'Gordie and the dog.'

CHAPTER SEVENTEEN

Jesus, could things get any worse? Lena was being held captive by Infinity, Arturo'd been killed, Jimmy had a death warrant on his head and any number of people hoping to collect it, and now Gordie'd run off. And just at that moment, I gotta tell ya, I couldn't help but feel I had to take more than my share of the responsibility.

I should've known Gordie'd take that dog and run – at his age, in the same situation, I'd've done the same. And suddenly my argument that it would've been dangerous to keep it seemed so trivial, so unnecessary, I couldn't believe I'd ever made it.

'I'll go look for him,' I said, struggling up.

'Oh, Clancy!' Delilah moaned.

'What?'

She made this face, like it was obvious and didn't need to be said, but Hanna wasn't so restrained.

'You made him go!' she cried.

'I didn't make him.'

'You wouldn't let him keep Dorkus!'

'Look, it's okay, I'll find him, I know where he goes,' I reassured them, as if it was just a matter of going there and picking him up.

263

I ended up searching all morning, my right buttock and thigh far from happy at being pitched back into such exercise, but there was no sign of Gordie anywhere. Kids are usually the best source of information about other kids, but there were so few around, and when you did spot one they were pretty swift to slip away. I managed to talk to a couple of young guys – I mean, a boy with a dog, it was pretty unusual – but they hadn't seen a thing, and it occurred to me that if Gordie didn't want to be found, amongst all that chaos there wasn't a lot I could do.

I just couldn't believe I'd fallen out with him over a dog, not after everything we'd been through together. Surely I could've handled it better than that?

I searched everywhere I could think of, for a few brief moments even getting irrationally worried when I saw this apartment block on fire, just in case he might be in there. But no matter how much I wanted to keep going, to scour that whole city, eventually I had to go back to the churchyard to rest. The look on the others' faces as I entered the shelter almost broke my heart.

'Sorry,' I told them.

'Let's have something to eat, then we'll all go out and look,' Delilah said.

'Can he keep the dog?' Hanna asked.

Jeez, that kid never wastes a word. 'Anything,' I replied. 'A whole damn zoo, if he wants.'

I wouldn't let Jimmy come. He wanted to, but I couldn't bear the thought of something else going wrong, another of us disappearing. I also insisted that Delilah and Hanna went out together, no matter how much more ground they might cover separately.

I spent all afternoon searching – street after street, almost going over to the ocean; in so much pain, I almost wished I'd accepted Jimmy's offer to borrow his stick.

It was almost dark when I got back. Delilah and Hanna had already returned. One exchanged look was enough to know that no one had found him, nor heard a word concerning his whereabouts.

'He's gone,' said Delilah, as if she'd previously thought it was all a game, that Gordie had just been trying to make a point.

'We'll find him,' I said.

No one answered or looked my way and I knew they all blamed me, and that they had every right. I eased myself down onto my sleeping bag, trying to relax my aching body, the muscles around the top of my leg threatening to go into spasm. There was nothing more I could do, not that night – though, in fact, within minutes I was forcing myself back up to my feet.

I grabbed the spray can I'd looted and shook it to see how much paint was left, then urged my protesting old body out one more time. I went to the usual places: along the street, the Square, not really knowing what to write, but in the end keeping it real simple.

LOST – ONE BOY

If Gordie read it, he'd know what it meant, that we were missing him. As would anyone else connected with us, including, of course, Gigi.

She didn't come 'til the morning, just as we were discussing how to go about continuing the search. Mind you, she was spitting nails and broken glass. 'Where is he?' she demanded.

'We don't know,' I confessed, fearing I was about to be turned on yet again.

'What happened?'

I let Delilah tell the story, for sure I didn't feel like relating my part in it. When she got to the bit about the dog and my objection to keeping it, I did try to explain my reasons, but Delilah cut me off. Though we were in for a bit of a surprise, 'cuz Gigi didn't react the way we expected.

'A stray dog?' she said, looking decidedly worried.

'Yeah,' Delilah nodded.

'Shit!' she groaned.

'What's the matter?' I asked.

'*Oh shit!*' she repeated, as if the real impact of it was only just hitting her.

'*What is it?*'

'It's not a *stray dog!*'

'What do you mean?'

'I warned you about these people.' She paused for a moment, staring at us, but no one had a clue what she was talking about. 'Enticers! They train dogs to befriend kids! To bring them back to their place, then they drug them and operate, take out whatever they want.'

It was so unexpected, so shocking, that for a moment all we could do was gape at her.

'The dog?' Delilah eventually uttered.

'Yeah!'

It was too much to take in – that cute little dog romping and playing with Gordie was in fact the accomplice of some back-street organ-stealer?

'You sure?' I asked.

'*Yes!*' she shouted. 'I told you, they got all sorts of tricks!'

'Jesus,' I groaned.

'He should've known that!' she cried, that little pixie face of hers displaying more emotion than I'd ever seen before. 'Stupid dumbass.' She stopped for a moment, trying to get her thoughts together. 'What's the dog look like?'

266

Delilah told her, describing Dorkus in great detail, whilst Jimmy turned to me like he couldn't believe it: in this world you couldn't even trust a dog?

'Jesus, Big Guy! That is so uncool!'

I nodded my head, noticing Hanna getting ready to go out.

'There are a lot of fires up near the Square,' Gigi told her, as if trying to put her off.

'I don't care,' she said, making for the entrance.

'Hanna!' I called, but she was gone before I could say any more.

'Where's she going?' Gigi asked.

'I dunno.'

She hesitated for a moment, looking more than a little put out, then rushed after Hanna.

I turned to Jimmy and Delilah. 'What the hell's going on?'

Delilah shook her head. 'Clancy!' she said despairingly, like I was the biggest fool ever.

'What?'

'They're in "love" . . . Both of them.'

I stared at her for quite a while before the thought finally got off the ground. 'Gordie?'

'Yes!' she cried, as if a block of wood would've surely seen that.

And actually, once she said it, it did make perfect sense. That was why Hanna always acted so oddly around Gordie, not to mention how negative she was about Gigi: she was jealous!

'Great,' I sighed. 'That's all we need.'

Once again I told Jimmy he shouldn't go out, and for the same reason, but this time he wouldn't have any of it. He was as fond of Gordie as anyone and was joining the search whether we liked it or not. We argued with him for a while, but eventually gave in, though I did manage to persuade him to at least stay near the churchyard.

I was so stiff from the previous day my ass felt like it had been nailed on, but the more I walked, the easier it became. I talked to as many people as I dared, avoiding anyone I didn't like the look of, concentrating more on the dog than on Gordie – I mean, that mutt must've pulled the same trick any number of times. In a way, it was something of an irony – a scheming, malevolent dog – my old man would've been delighted. But then, when you think about it, the dog had to be trained, so maybe it didn't prove his theory, after all – maybe it *is* all down to the owner?

I searched and searched, streets and buildings, squares and waste ground, wondering if that dog had already completed its task and got Gordie back to its master. Like I said, Gordie'd become like a son to me and I was feeling pretty protective, pretty damn angry. What sort of scum were we dealing with here? Who'd snatch kids off the street, slice them open and steal their organs? If I did find them, I wasn't sure how responsible I was gonna be for my own actions.

And yet, as the day wore on, it looked less and less likely that I'd have the opportunity to vent my anger. God knows how much ground I covered – I got so tired I wasn't even sure I'd be able to make it back to the churchyard – not to mention the fact that my wound was starting to ooze a little.

In the end, I had no choice but to stop and rest. I swear if I hadn't, I would've keeled over. Part of it was the ever-present sea of smoke; my lungs felt almost numb, as if they wanted to close down rather than breathe in any more of that crap. I slumped down onto the steps of a run-down old apartment block, checking my wound for bleeding, but thankfully, there was none.

I guess I fell asleep, though whether for two minutes or two hours, I don't know. Nor do I know what woke me. Maybe it was my sixth sense, but whatever it was, it did me one helluva favour.

I shook my head and opened and closed my eyes a few times,

trying to awaken a glimmer of life in my dull old frame. It was getting late, the light was starting to fade, and I should be heading back to the churchyard.

I was just about to stand up, to get moving, when suddenly this little dark shape came trotting out of the smoke towards me – *that damn dog!*

'You miserable little piece of shit,' I muttered.

My immediate urge was to leap down the steps, run at him as fast as I could and kick the life out of the treacherous mutt, but then I had a second thought and the moment I did, I knew it was the right thing.

I kept as still as I could, not looking directly at him but following his progress out of the corner of my eye. When he finally reached me, I sprang down from the steps screaming at the top of my voice, spreading my arms and legs, trying to make myself look as big and crazy as possible. And it worked: that dog jumped the best part of a foot into the air, let out a yelp of terror and turned and ran off as fast as he could. Immediately I chased after him, all my energy suddenly restored. *Yeah, that's right, you damned little coward: run! Run all the way back home!*

For a little dog, he sure could move. I'd never have managed to stay with him if he hadn't kept stopping and looking back to see if I was still following. He took a side street, scampering down there as fast as he could, but with me still puffing along behind.

Once I thought I'd lost him: I turned a corner and there was no sign of the mutt – Jeez, could he really have disappeared into the smoke that quickly? But I ventured slowly forward, checking out doorway after doorway, until finally I flushed him out and again he bounded off with me screaming along behind. People were stopping and staring, wondering what the hell was going on – even in Senseless City, I was coming across as insane.

Thankfully, less than a mile from where I first saw him, 'Dorkus' suddenly veered off down an alleyway and began to scratch at a door. Above it was a garish but slightly faded sign: 'Body Talk Tattoos – We'll Say Anything'.

This young guy, not much more than twenty, with greased-back hair and cheap but fashionable clothes, opened the door to let the dog in and I jumped in behind it, hitting the little punk, knocking him up against the wall.

I grabbed him by the collar and yanked him into my face, giving him a real blast of the look. 'Where's Gordie?'

'What?' he cried, his face a contortion of confusion.

I hit him again, just to up his concentration levels. 'Gordie!' I growled. 'You got operations going on here?'

Just for the briefest of moments, his eyes flicked to an inner door and I knew I was right. I promptly hit him so hard he'd take no further part in proceedings and left him lying on the floor. The dog scrabbled under the sofa and just managed to avoid the hefty kick I directed his way. I tell you, if that damn thing hadn't been seen to, I was more than happy to offer my services, and I wouldn't be needing any surgical instruments or anaesthetic either.

Out in the narrow corridor I was confronted by several doors. I hesitated for a brief moment, then heard a male voice coming from behind one and kicked it open with as much force as I could muster. I wanted to put the fear of God into whoever was inside, but it was me who ended up being most disturbed.

There were two people, a man and a woman, performing an operation – and if that summons up a vision of white coats and sterilised surfaces, forget it. A young boy, no more than six or seven, was stretched out on an old wooden kitchen table with dark bloodstains all over it. Hanging from each side were these heavy leather straps, obviously for restraining the patient if necessary, though in this case, it wasn't: the little guy was well and truly out of it. The 'surgeon' – stocky, dyed-black hair, maybe even the father of the one I hit outside – had his hand pushed through a six-inch gash in the boy's side and was probing around in an altogether incompetent manner. Next to him, this little dark woman – I guess it could've been his wife – was standing there dressed in blue overalls, also covered in dried blood.

'Who are you?' the guy demanded.

'Stitch him up,' I told him.

'Get out!' he replied indignantly. 'David!'

'I wouldn't bother.'

'*David!*'

'I'm not going to tell you again,' I said. 'Stitch him up!'

With that, the woman promptly turned on the man, leaving little doubt that they were husband and wife. 'We told you! We told you!' she screamed, as if she'd been waiting for this day for a long time.

'Oh, shut up! *David!*' the guy called again, but of course there was no reply.

'Last chance,' I told him, desperate in my disgust to exact a little retribution.

Still the guy hesitated, turning to his wife but seeing no signs of sympathy, then back to me. 'Don't you know how dangerous it is to interrupt a surgeon performing an operation?' he said, trying another tack.

'First off, you ain't no surgeon,' I told him, 'you're a damn tattooist. Secondly, the only person this operation is dangerous for is you. Now, stitch him up while you still can.'

He took a sideways glance at his miserable collection of medical instruments and what appeared to be his one and only scalpel.

'That'd be the stupidest mistake of your life,' I warned him.

'All right!' he said impatiently, picking up a different instrument. 'All right.'

'Where's Gordie?' I asked.

'I don't know any Gordie.'

I couldn't be bothered with him any more. I returned to the corridor and started opening doors. The next room along was just junk: piled boxes, tattoo catalogues, that sort of stuff. The final one, at the end, was locked and I had to put my shoulder to it. The first time it cracked encouragingly; the second, it burst open.

I tell ya, I just stood there, for a moment too shocked to even enter.

There must've been half a dozen or more bunk beds crammed into the room, all of them occupied by children, the youngest no more than five, the oldest maybe fifteen or so. Each one was covered by a single grubby, bloodstained sheet. Several of them were staring at me, but they didn't seem able to take anything in, their eyes were all lost and lifeless. But it was the sense that they weren't human, that this was just an organ production line, that was most sickening. One little girl, probably no more than eight or nine, looked at me with the most haunted expression I've ever seen in my life, like she didn't know if I'd come to do good or bad, and didn't really care either.

'Gordie?' I called, but there was no answer and I started to check through the beds, one by one, searching face after face.

'You can go,' I told them. 'Go on, get going! . . . Get!'

I was just about to give up when I found him lying on the top bunk in the corner. He looked so unbelievably childlike and vulnerable, it took me a moment to recognise him.

'Jesus!' I gasped. 'Gordie?'

He just stared at me as if he couldn't believe it, when he finally did speak his voice was noticeably slurred. 'Where'd you come from?'

'Tell you later.'

He tried to get up but gave a kinda tremble halfway and fell back again. Thank God, I found him when I did – I figured his turn at being 'operated' on couldn't've been that far away, that he was in that state 'cuz they'd prepped him already. I reached underneath his pale, wiry body, knowing I was gonna have to carry him. I just about got my hands around him when I felt it.

I released my hold, pulled up his T-shirt and there it was: this ugly scar, about six or seven inches long, caked with dried blood, slashed at an angle across his side and crudely stapled together.

'Fuck!' I cursed, unable to stop myself.

Gordie just looked at me, on the point of tears, like he wanted to apologise for being so stupid, for causing me so much trouble, and it was that as much as anything that prompted me to turn and make my way back into the other room.

They must've known how I'd react 'cuz I met them at the door about to make a run for it.

I hit the guy really hard in the face and he fell back against the doorframe. 'You fucking butcher!' I screamed. 'How dare you do that to them!'

'I just take kidneys! I just take the one kidney!' he cried, as if that made him one of the good guys.

I was so angry at what he'd done, and that he didn't even seem genuinely contrite, that I got hold of him and threw him onto the kitchen table, securing him with the straps.

'No! No!' he kept shouting, and his wife started joining in.

'Please, mister!' she cried. 'He'll never do it again!'

'You bet he won't,' I told her, picking up the filthy-looking scalpel beside the table. I knew I was out of control, that what I was doing wasn't right, but every time he begged for mercy, every time I thought about stopping, I remembered all the pain and distress he must've dispensed over the years – and most of it to children.

His wife tried to stop me, but I just kept shoving her away 'til finally she couldn't take it any more and ran from the room.

I don't think I'll ever make a tattooist, not going on my efforts that day: I cut 'ENTICER' across his forehead, as large as I could, the letters spilling into each other.

'You ever touch another child, I'll write this a thousand times all over your body,' I warned, as he lay there crying. 'You got it?'

'Yes! Yes!' he wailed, and I turned to go, leaving him where he was.

Gordie was leaning against the doorframe and I picked him up and pushed my way gently through the other kids as they dazedly made their way outside.

'Clancy?' Gordie asked.

I knew what the question was going to be and didn't want to disappoint, but I had no choice.

'Sorry, Gordie. Not this time.'

'They got nowhere to go . . .'

Thankfully, at that moment he more or less passed out on my shoulder and I didn't have to explain why, that we already had enough problems of our own.

In the small reception area by the front door I found the mother taking care of her son, both of them in tears.

'He's not a bad man,' she told me. 'Just greedy.'

'How many kids?' I asked her, and she turned away. 'How many?'

She shook her head, like she didn't want to think about that, that it had never been her idea.

As I went to leave, out of the corner of my eye, I saw 'Dorkus' scrabbling under the sofa again, anxious to get as far away from me as he could.

'If I ever see that animal again there'll be fresh meat free in the City that night – you got it?'

She nodded and I stalked out carrying Gordie with me. He was gonna be quite a weight all the way back to the shelter, especially with the pain still in my leg, but I'd get him there if it killed me. I gave the little guy a hug, taking advantage of the fact that he was sleeping, knowing if he'd been awake he probably would've given me an earful.

I was so damn pleased to have him back, so relieved he hadn't ended up the same way as Arturo. Something else too, that I *hadn't* expected: for once it felt like I'd achieved something, that we'd scored a rare victory. I guess I was getting a little carried away with myself, but I could've almost believed the tide was starting to turn.

One down . . . one to go.

CHAPTER EIGHTEEN

The only problem was that the 'one to go' was a different prospect altogether. It had been a real slice of luck finding Gordie that way, but compared to what I needed to rescue Lena, it was an ice cube to an iceberg. For sure, no dog, real or mechanical, was gonna lead me to her, and even if it did there was still the little matter of Fort Infinity and its attendant army to deal with.

If I was told this story about someone else, the plight I was in, I guess I'd just think that they had to accept it, that there was no other choice. Not that I'd give that advice – nor take it. No matter how hopeless it seemed, almost every minute of my day was devoted to thinking about rescuing Lena, while at night the problem stole the vast majority of my sleep. How could I get into that place? How could I reach her? *How?* There had to be a way – they couldn't have thought of everything.

I was still more or less confident she wasn't in any immediate danger, that for whatever reason they were taking good care of her – but for how long? If it had something to do with the baby, we were probably talking around six months. If it was more to do with stealing what she had in her head, it could've been any day.

Somehow I had to give it another shot – and yeah, what'd happened with Gordie had given me just the slightest cause for hope, that despite all the terrible things going on, maybe miracles did still occasionally happen.

I was really surprised at how quickly Gordie started to mend. Though I guess at his age you do. He did still get tired and have to take the occasional nap for a while. As for his scar, well, it was never gonna look pretty, not the way he was butchered, but once the risk of infection's gone, the best thing for a wound's fresh air, and it was amazing how rapidly it improved. Mind you, being a kid – and one who'd always regarded himself as a real little tough guy – he never wasted a single opportunity to show it off to somebody.

You should've seen the way Hanna reacted when he first got back. She did her best to hide it, to feign disinterest, but there were tears in her eyes, really big soulful ones that I had to look away from in case they triggered my own. I just couldn't see how I'd missed that. It was so obvious she had a crush on him – the way she sneered at everything he said, constantly rolled her eyes in disapproval, and how she made such a big thing of not being any-where near him – she was a teenager in love!

Then there was her arch-rival: Gigi was hard as the bullet coming out of a gun most of the time, a real uncompromising no-nonsense female, but if Gordie wanted some water or something, you could've been killed in the rush. I mean, all due respect to the kid and every-thing, and I love the boy as my own, but it was something of a surprise. With that sharp little ferret-face, part of an ear missing, the bald patch just behind, he sure wasn't my idea of an object of teenage desire. And you couldn't even say he made up for it with charisma either: that missing part of an ear must've been where he stored his charm and politeness, 'cuz sure as hell he didn't have none.

Mind you, with everything that was going on, teenage love tussles weren't exactly high on my list of priorities, nor Jimmy and Delilah's ongoing spats neither. She was still angry with him for how he gave his name away, though to be fair, she wasn't beating him up any more than he was beating up himself.

People were searching for him all over, enjoying the relaxation of the gun laws, buying themselves weapons and pretty well popping off at whoever they liked, all the while knowing they were unlikely to be arrested even if they did accidentally kill someone. We were definitely hearing a lot more indiscriminate gunfire – in the day as well as night – and seeing more bodies in the street. But Jimmy was still going out whenever he could, no matter how risky it might be, or how angry it made Delilah. Heavily disguised, of course, and he'd added a pair of sunglasses to the parka, scarf and baseball cap, so that now he actually did look like a terrorist – though of the senior variety.

It was his pride that sent him out as much as anything: a need to find a way of making up for what he'd done, to redeem himself in our eyes. I often went with him, the two of us just wandering around, checking things out; occasionally stopping to look at a new fire, Jimmy going on again about how he didn't understand why they burned the way they did, not that I was paying that much attention. The truth was, we were both searching for something out there, though neither of us knew exactly what.

A couple of times bounty hunters got a little too close for comfort. A group set up this unofficial roadblock, stopping everyone and checking for disguises. We had to queue up, all the time whispering to each other, wondering what the hell to do. Fortunately, we were saved by another couple making a run for it. Lord knows why they ran, but they both got shot in the back for their trouble and by the time the excitement had died down, Jimmy and me were long gone.

Another time, something was burning that was making the smoke even more toxic than usual; hitting the back of my throat like someone scratching at it with a fork. I think Jimmy had a bit of a cold anyway and he started coughing and spluttering so much he dislodged not only his bandanna but his hood, too.

It was only for a second but this woman got real suspicious, pulling out a gun, pointing it at him, shouting into this looted store for someone called 'Frank'. When he never appeared and she looked on the point of panicking, we figured there was no way she was going to shoot and ran. We'd made it about thirty yards down the street when finally she got her act together and started firing, bullets flying around like they'd been panicked out of the gun.

We ducked down an alleyway and into a partly demolished building, hiding under the stairs, all the while praying that the woman and 'Frank' weren't following.

But do you know something? Even then, with the real risk of being cornered and killed, I didn't use that breathless silence to think of ways we might escape, but of asking out loud the same question I asked myself almost every minute of the day and night. 'What am I going to do, Jimmy?' I whispered.

He glanced at me, taking but a moment to register what I was talking about.

'I can't just give up,' I told him.

'We'll think of something,' he replied, though he didn't sound that hopeful.

'I gotta get into that place, even if it means knocking it down brick by brick.'

'You gotta *think* your way in there,' he told me, pausing for a moment, ensuring he hadn't heard someone approaching. 'It's not gonna happen any other way.'

I gave a little grunt, figuring that put me at something of a disadvantage.

Neither of us actually said anything, but eventually we came to the conclusion that it was safe and emerged back out onto the street, turning in the direction of the churchyard.

'You can't do nothing with their computers?' I asked, knowing if there was anything, he would've said by now.

'Are you kidding?' he said, his voice impossibly high. 'I gotta mini-screen. They got more technological muscle than anyone in the country. Decidedly not cool.'

For the rest of the journey we barely said a word, and I had to shake off this growing feeling that this period wasn't about coming up with a solution at all, but more just accepting the inevitability that there wasn't one.

Later, when we were all in our sleeping bags, in the first deep chasm of darkness, we were awakened by a familiar sound. It was some way off, over towards the ocean, but somewhere they'd started beating.

'Oh God,' Delilah groaned, turning over, trying to block it out.

It was this eerie mixture of the monotonous and menacing: a persistent, pervasive beat building to an inevitable climax, a drum-roll for a mighty leap of death.

'Are they coming this way?' Gordie asked.

'Nah. We're okay,' I told him.

'You sure?'

'Yeah,' I said, trying to sound as confident as I could.

After a while it faded away, but none of us could get back to sleep. We just lay there, our nerves twanging like piano-wire, knowing it would eventually come and unable to relax until it did.

I guess it was about thirty minutes later, faint, some way off, but the unmistakable sound of heavy gunfire.

Jesus, but I hated this place.

The following morning, exasperated by the usual familiar scraps of sleep, I awoke still in the same black mood. Don't ask me why, but after I'd eaten, I went and dug out those four novels I took from the bookstore and headed off into the churchyard. I guess I was looking for an escape, giving my mind a rest from going over and over the same problem.

I wasn't sure which one to read first but eventually decided on this Charles Dickens guy and *A Tale of Two Cities*.

I didn't get very far. In fact, I couldn't get past the first line: '*It was the best of times, it was the worst of times . . .*'

I couldn't help it; I just burst out laughing – not real laughter, but more just kind of mocking me and my situation. No words I came up with could describe my situation better. After thinking all my life that it wasn't an option, I'd finally found love and apparently I was about to become a father, but in a world where such things could be ripped from you in the blink of an uncaring eye.

In the end, I knew I wouldn't be able to concentrate and returned to the shelter, asking everyone – including the kids – if they had any jobs they needed doing, hoping I could lose myself that way. Delilah got me fetching and carrying – reorganising stuff – but when I complained I was looking for something more demanding, she made me fill in the old latrines and dig new ones. Though in truth, I was grateful even for that, anything to give my tortured mind something else to think about.

But I was just holding back the inevitable – like that King Canute guy and the sea – 'cuz the moment I found myself at a loose end again, all those thoughts of Lena rushed back over me. I had to do something, no matter how futile, and the only thing I could think of was taking another look at Infinity.

The first thing I noticed when I got there was that they'd beefed up their security, presumably in response to our attempt at a raid. For the life of me, I couldn't see why; they weren't ever under any kind of real threat, but there were definitely more Specials around.

I made my way along the road outside the perimeter fence as casually as I could. Now that I knew the growlers were there, I could see these slight mounds dotted round the lawn. Jeez, what a thought that was: those damn things down there, lined up in the dark, waiting for the signal to be snapped back into life.

The gates were obviously out of the question, knowing what they were capable of, how they could scan and destroy. I also couldn't help but notice how little traffic had gone through since I'd arrived – maybe they'd imposed some kind of emergency restrictions? All I'd seen was a couple of lightly armoured Infinity vehicles and yet another short convoy of those white trucks.

The constant *clickety-clack* of the observation cameras passing by in monotonous regularity eventually persuaded me it was time to go. It hadn't exactly been encouraging, just like always. I'd gone there looking for hope, but was returning laden with even more despair.

When I got back to the churchyard, kicking my way across the rubble, Jimmy appeared out of the bushes like he'd been waiting for me for some time. What was more, he had a real look of excitement about him, more so than at any time since we'd left the Island.

'Big Guy! Big Guy!' he cried, keeping an eye on the shelter in case any of the others appeared. 'I need your help.'

'Jimmy!' I groaned. 'Honestly, I'm not in the mood—'

'No, no, Big Guy, this is really important. Trust me.'

I studied his face for a moment. As down as I felt, I was still intrigued to know what had brought back these signs of his old passionate self. 'What is it?'

'Come and see,' he urged.

I gave a long sigh, and realising I was about to give in, he turned and, slightly to my surprise, led me into the shelter. Once there, he hesitated, not wanting to look too eager in front of the others.

'Just er . . . wanna show Big Guy something,' he muttered, though not one of them exhibited the slightest interest; Lile was giving her hair its weekly brush, Hanna and Gordie playing a game on the mini-screen

Jimmy beckoned me on, all the way down into the corner of the churchyard where the fallen tree straddled the wall. 'You ever been here?' he asked, starting to pull stuff out of hiding from beneath the tree – all the various elements of his disguise, right down to his sunglasses – and putting them on.

'I told you I had,' I replied; we'd had a conversation a while back that obviously he hadn't been listening to as usual.

'Lile don't like me going out. It's easier this way. You can get over the wall,' he said, informing me of what I already knew.

'You don't say,' I muttered, watching him ineptly scramble and slip his way up the tree, finally reaching the apex and then kinda falling out of sight. I followed after him, not with that much grace, and certainly not with the sort of finesse that would've impressed Hanna, but in quarter of the time it had taken Jimmy.

Even before my feet touched the ground, he was already scuttling away.

'Where we going?' I asked, hurrying after him.

'To see something unbelievably cool!' he told me.

There was no point in asking again. He was obviously in one of those moods: the magician moving to the climax of his trick, and actually, it was quite nice to see it, no matter what the reason.

He led me across to the other side of the stonemason's yard, through the gate, then pegged off down the street at a surprising pace.

'Jimmy!' I called, again having to hurry to catch up.

We came to one of those weird borders, night and day, black and white, between our burned-out and demolished area and a relatively intact one – there was even a public garden, with a few old, established trees.

Jimmy entered, taking his time, peering around, checking no one was watching. 'Take a look,' he eventually said, pointing at the largest of the trees.

I paused, not really understanding what I was s'posed to be looking at, wondering how senile dementia first manifested itself.

'It's a tree,' I eventually commented.

'No!' he said impatiently. 'Look! Up there!'

I got a bit closer to the trunk and peered up through the lattice of branches, finally spotting something caught almost at the top. It looked like some kind of battered metal container.

'What is it?'

'What d'ya think it is?'

'I don't know!' I cried, starting to get a little irritated as usual.

'You should. It kept us prisoners long enough.'

I stared at it again, and though it took me a while, finally I realised. 'Satellite?' I asked.

'Cool, huh?'

'Why wasn't it destroyed?'

'I dunno. Obviously it got hit, but for some reason its fire went out on the way down. I guess it's been lodged up there ever since.'

I looked again, realising in that moment that Jimmy had finally found the thing he thought would redeem him in our eyes.

'So?' he said, indicating the tree.

'What?'

'Get it down!'

'*What?*'

'It ain't no use up there.'

'Are you kidding me?'

'You can do it.'

'Oh, can I?' I said sarcastically.

'Sure you can!'

It was useless to argue, and anyway, tell the truth, I was that bit intrigued. 'Okay,' I sighed.

I might've been able to climb a fallen tree, that was more or less horizontal, but that was a bit different from one reaching thirty feet into the air. You've never seen such clumsy ineptitude. Every branch I put my weight on broke. I went up, down, up, down – then spent several embarrassing moments just hanging there, twirling around like something on a Christmas tree. In the end, and only Mother Nature knows how, I finally worked myself up into a position where, by stretching up as high as I could, I could just manage to dislodge the satellite and send it crashing down to the ground.

Jimmy made this loud shushing sound and started checking all round to see if I'd attracted anyone's attention then, the moment he was sure it was safe, eagerly set to work poking, prodding, even sniffing at it. Meanwhile, as many others had learned before me, I discovered that climbing *down* a tree is a damn sight harder than climbing *up*.

'Come on, Big Guy,' Jimmy urged, pulling out a large plastic bag he'd obviously brought to wrap up the satellite, 'we gotta get this back before anyone sees it.'

'Yeah, thanks, Jimmy, I'll just fall down, shall I?'

'Whatever!'

It took me a while, and I cursed him repeatedly and colourfully, but finally I slid down the last few feet of the trunk to the ground.

'Let's go,' he said, even before I was done checking myself for cuts and bruises.

It might not have been a whole satellite but it was surprisingly heavy, not to mention damned awkward to carry. Thank God we didn't have that far to go – the last thing we needed was anyone challenging us, maybe thinking a couple of ageing looters had something interesting hidden away. A group of young guys did check us out as we passed by, probably prompted by Jimmy's overly elaborate disguise, but they changed their minds when I gave them the look.

The worst part was getting it over the fallen tree – we dropped it several times after the bag ripped to uselessness – but eventually we toppled it over the wall into the churchyard and it crashed to the ground

Jimmy followed on behind, then me, finding him already busily scrutinising his trophy. I don't know how much of it remained – a little more than half, I'd've guessed. A lot of the innards had been shot out, bits trailing off – including a kind of broken arm, which, I guess, was its source of solar power. According to Jimmy, it would've had two originally, so presumably one got dislodged somehow.

'Jesus!' the little guy muttered, shaking his head.

'What?'

'If I'd known this was what was terrorising us, I wouldn't have bothered. It's out of the Stone Age.'

'Really?'

'I thought it'd be something real sophisticated. "The Final Solution".' He stopped for a moment, getting down on his hands and knees, sniffing it again. 'Can you smell something?'

I knelt down next to him, also sniffing round, the pair of us like a couple of old bloodhounds. 'Maybe . . . Not nice,' I said, though I wasn't really sure. 'Lena was always on about a bad smell.'

'That's the trouble with getting old,' Jimmy grumbled. 'Nothing works the way it did. I know that smell,' he told me, though he obviously couldn't remember what it was.

'Maybe something took up refuge in it? A squirrel or a bird or something?'

Jimmy never bothered to answer, just took out some tools he'd hidden under the tree with his disguise. I realised my time was up, I'd served my usefulness and could go.

I don't know whether he'd bothered with breakfast or not, but the following morning Jimmy was gone before I was awake. I knew he'd confessed all to Delilah 'cuz I heard their argument in the night: that familiar story of her threatening to leave him if he was going to fill her world with junk yet again.

I went down to see him but he didn't say much, only that the construction of the satellite was so outdated, he didn't even have the right tools to work on it. I stayed for a little while, watching him try to improvise, getting that obsessed look about him. When it became apparent he wasn't going to say any more, that any suggestions I might have wouldn't be welcome, I left him to it.

I mean, as pleased as I was to see him burning with a little passion again, I really couldn't see the point – it wasn't as if the laser was still intact and we could build some kind of cannon or something. All he really had was an oversized squashed tin can with a few odd wires and broken circuits inside, which I wouldn't have thought much use to anyone. Mind you, we weren't talking about 'anyone', we were talking about Jimmy.

I was helping Delilah again, this time by taking the garbage out, which meant walking it up the street a ways and maybe throwing it on a fire, rather than have it stack up and create suspicion. As I headed back I saw Gigi coming out of the smoke from the opposite direction.

I thought she'd probably come to see Gordie. The rivalry between her and Hanna for our little matinee idol was now pretty much out in the open. Not that I understood it – I'd've thought Gigi far too cool and Hanna altogether too serene and sensible. But there you go: love makes fools of us all. Plainly we were in for another day of fighting over who was going to do what for the invalid, and as is the way of these things, the more they tried to please him, the less he appeared to appreciate it. In fact, I had an idea the little shit was beginning to really enjoy himself.

As it turned out, Gigi hadn't only come to see Gordie, she also had something for me. She paused as we entered the churchyard and handed me a note.

It was only folded in two, but I almost tore it, how fast I straightened it out.

My love,

Things are starting to change in here. I don't feel as safe as I did. I think something's going to happen.

No matter what, I want you to know that you made me happier than anyone has a right to be.

I will love you for ever.

Lena

I read it through twice, the kick in my stomach even harder the second time.

'What's going on?' I asked Gigi.

She shrugged in that way she and Gordie have, like she's indicating indifference, but actually she's about to give you bad news. 'She tried to escape . . . A Special got hurt.'

'Is she okay?'

'Yeah, yeah. She's fine.'

I started envisaging it in my mind and my impotence erupted into anger. '*Shit!*'

'It wasn't the first time,' Gigi added. 'More like the fifth or sixth.'

It was funny, no matter how concerned I was, I still couldn't help but feel that bit proud. 'Really?'

'The night you tried to get in there.'

'She tried to escape?'

'She knew it was you – she made it to an outside door, but they caught her and dragged her back.'

I tell ya, that almost reduced me to tears: the thought that while I'd been trying to get to her, she'd been trying to get to me, that we'd been that close. 'Can you get a message to her?'

'Not any more,' Gigi admitted after a moment. 'They got her drugged and secured to the bed. Orders of the bitch.'

'Nora Jagger?'

'There must be a God,' she said grimly, '"cuz sure as hell, she's the devil.'

I cursed several times, kicking at some nearby rubble. Not only was I making no progress, with every day the task was becoming that much more difficult.

Gigi started to walk towards the shelter, expecting me to follow, but I spun around and headed back to the street. I couldn't go in there: sitting around and talking, going over it yet again – what was the damn point?

'Catch you later,' I called.

Gigi looked a little surprised, but I was gone before she could reply.

For some reason that had upset me as much as anything. It'd never occurred to me that Lena might try to escape. In fact, she'd probably be that bit angry with me – of course she'd try to escape! That was her all over, the way she was . . . but now they had her secured to the bed, attending only to her basic needs, like she was some queen bee.

It was more habit than anything that sent me in the direction of Infinity, but somewhere along the line I acknowledged that there was no point, that I'd seen all there was to see. I continued walking, though, so lost in my frustration I didn't give a thought as to where, on and on until eventually I found myself at the ocean, not far from where we came ashore the night we escaped.

I went down the beach and sat on the sand, gazing out across the murky sea to a point where the smoke and water merged to form nothing. I couldn't actually see the Island; for all intents and purposes it no longer existed.

That place had been the most oppressive hell I ever could've imagined. The years I spent wanting to get off it, pretending it didn't matter, 'til in the end it didn't, 'cuz all hope had gone.

I gazed up and down, despair lapping at me in the same way the waves were the sand. I hadn't noticed them when I first sat down, but now I saw there were a few zombie-sick about: little groups who barely had the strength to sit upright, just like on the night of our escape. What was this illness, for Chrissake? Were we likely to get it? Did anyone recover? It looked a bit like a one-way ticket. Okay, if they were lucky, they got replacement organs, but that was only a part of the story – 'ccording to Gigi there was a list of other symptoms as long your arm that someone else's organs just couldn't cure.

Really, I can't tell you what the thought process was – maybe it had something to do with the Island and remembering that once I'd thought there was no way we could ever beat that place. Or maybe it was an old head like mine just needing to be left ticking over for a while, to make sense of stuff in its own sweet time: the zombie-sick, the fires, what happened at Dr Simon's, that damn enticer, and even the convoy of white trucks that turned up at Infinity most afternoons . . .

Whatever it was that caused me to put everything together, to fit isolated facts into an understandable picture, it was like a flash of lightning picking me out on the beach. All my thoughts, conscious and otherwise, suddenly clicked into perfect alignment.

Jesus! There it was: I had an idea!

That night, when everyone was asleep, I slipped from my sleeping bag and made my way down the wall toward the fallen tree, keeping as quiet as I could.

After I'd left the beach, I'd returned via Infinity, just to check I was right, that it was the same routine every afternoon. It was the final piece in a very complicated jigsaw.

When I got back to the shelter I insisted on cooking, even though it was Delilah's turn – which gave me the opportunity to pocket the knife we'd picked up at the camping store. I also took some organi-plasters and bandages, and rummaging through the garbage, found an appropriate screw-top plastic container.

I didn't go all the way down to Jimmy's 'workshop', just far enough that if I did make any noise the others wouldn't hear me.

There wasn't a lot of moonlight filtering down through the smoke, but enough for me to see what I was doing. I'd scrubbed the knife spotless earlier, sterilising it as best I could in boiling water, and now I placed it on a low branch along with the plastic container. Tugging my shirt up to my armpits, easing my pants down a little, exposing my bare skin to the cool of the night. Jesus, was I really going to do this?

Pain's a funny thing. You can never really appreciate how bad it is until you're actually suffering it. I guess 'cuz Nature wants you to learn, but then forget – otherwise you're just gonna live your life in fear.

I placed the blade flat against my bare hip, feeling its shrill coldness, then took a deep breath, and another, all the while telling myself that if I thought about this for too long I'd never go through with it.

The problem was, it had to be precise. I couldn't just make a quick slash and leave it at that: it had to be deep enough that it looked authentic, but not so deep it would do me serious harm. I stood there for another agonising moment, gripping the knife as tightly as I could, the blade poised over my flesh while every fibre of my body screamed at me not to do it.

Jesus! *Oh God—!*

I managed to stifle it to some degree, but I still gave out a cry of pain, knowing I couldn't stop there, that I had to keep going: push the knife down, slide it through my flesh, cut a long, deep incision.

Even before I gave it a proper look, I knew it wasn't long or deep enough, that I'd have to do it again.

'*Oh no,*' I kept moaning, '*no, no, no—*'

I stuck the knife in again, probing at the cut I'd already made, digging deeper, slicing further, feeling my flesh tearing apart. It was probably the worst pain I've ever known – partly, I guess, 'cuz it was self-inflicted. I raised my head and let out this long silent scream to the night, the agony pulsing through me in waves, yet finally managed to pull myself together enough to remember the plastic container and placed it under the wound to catch as much of my blood as I could.

I stayed in that same contorted posture for a good fifteen

minutes, letting the blood slowly drain down, surprised at how little there was.

Finally, when I was sure there was no more, I pressed the two edges of the wound together and stuck a large organi-plaster on it, instantly reigniting the pain and causing me to cry out once more.

I felt faint, nauseous, as if a growler had chomped on my side, but I still managed to wrap the bandage around me, cover the plasters and after picking up the knife and container, returned to my sleeping bag.

Not that I slept much, not with that pain, particularly when I tried turning over. Mind you, with what I was planning, I knew all too well that I had a whole lot worse to come.

CHAPTER NINETEEN

It took a couple of uncomfortable days for the cut to start to heal, for the organi-plasters to really get to work. If I made the wrong move and the others saw me wince in pain, I just told them my ass was still giving me the occasional twinge, which was a conversation I knew no one was gonna be that eager to pursue.

I didn't see the point of making some grand announcement about what I was planning, not then anyway – there wasn't a lot they could contribute, and if I was really honest about it, I was also worried that they'd be so negative about the idea, I'd lose all faith in it.

One person I did need to talk to was Gigi. She'd made herself pretty clear on the subject, but I still wanted to ask her if there was any chance of a little inside assistance. And, of course, though it hardly needs saying, I also needed Jimmy's help – I mean, didn't I always?

I went down to his 'workshop' to find him giving a rather bored-looking Gordie and Hanna a lecture on the development of punishment satellites, pointing out various components and explaining what they once would've done. The moment they saw me, they seized the opportunity to escape.

'Where ya going?' Jimmy called after them.

'We're in the middle of a game,' Gordie called back.

'What about—?' he started to say, but they were already gone. 'Huh,' he grunted. 'I could beat them both blindfolded.'

I smiled agreement, then hesitated for a moment, wondering how to go about this, fearing I was in for a difficult time. In fact, I got so damned irritated with the situation, I just lost all patience and dived in, telling him exactly why I was there and what I needed.

Jimmy stared at me as if he couldn't believe what I was saying. '*Why?*' he said at last.

It was a fair question, and if there was any chance of him helping me, I needed to answer it as best I could. I took a deep breath, propped myself against an accommodating branch and told him exactly what I had in mind. With each new revelation his mouth gaped ever wider until soon he was staring at me as if I was metamorphosing from human to alien.

'Jesus!' he gasped when I finished.

'What?'

'You're not serious?'

'Why not?'

'It's suicide!'

'Jimmy,' I protested, 'you're the one said I had to *think* my way in there.'

'Yeah, but . . . think on.'

The odd thing was, despite the fact that I could see he was genuinely shocked by my plan, I also sensed something else: that maybe, just maybe, somewhere amongst all that mumbled and jumbled disclosure, I'd earned a little of his respect.

'There's an awful lot of assumptions there, Big Guy,' he said.

'I can't just leave her there.'

'What if you're wrong?' he asked.

'What about?'

He made this face, like he was spoiled for choice. 'Everything!'

'Jimmy, listen, don't do this,' I begged. 'I'm scared enough as it is, I know it's not the greatest plan in the world, but it's all I got. Now' – and I was ready to go down on my knees if I had to – 'can you do it?'

He gave me the old market trader's shrug, and then, to my enormous relief, followed it up with the familiar long intake of breath, as if it was absolutely impossible, quite out of the question, but maybe I'd picked the one person in the world who might be able to handle it.

'I could give it a shot,' he said, plainly already running through the idea in his head. 'And maybe, you know, if you did get in there, I could try jamming things up a little from the outside.'

'Just get me what I need,' I told him. 'I can do the rest.'

He made this face like he wasn't so sure about that. 'You're not gonna tell the others?'

'Nope.'

'They'll wanna be involved.'

'Nothing they can do.'

He grunted, like that was my first big mistake. 'Oh, I'm sure we can think of something.'

Okay, so as plans go, this one was frothing at the mouth, and Jimmy was absolutely right, there were so many places it could go awry. Maybe I had the whole thing ass-about-face? I mean, I've already told you, thinking is not my strength; I'd been forced into it 'cuz no one else'd come up with anything – not even Jimmy. Mr Meltoni used to say, 'Know your place and things won't get complicated.' The very last words he wanted to hear from any of his boys was, 'Boss, I been thinking' – he'd fire them on the spot. In fact, if he'd caught me doing what I was about to, I'd've been on my way out the door, too.

Eventually, I did tell the others – what I had in mind was so damn dangerous I didn't think it was right to just slip away without saying a word. Or to put it another way, who knew if I'd ever see them again? We had a long discussion, as I anticipated, a lotta stuff was said I could've well done without, but in the end, no matter how great their doubts, they insisted on participating. Which was just as well, 'cuz Jimmy had come up with a few ideas, 'A little bit of frosting on the cake', as he insisted on calling it.

He reckoned triggering the growlers was down to movement rather than pressure. That day I threw rocks over the fence it had just been single impacts – it had taken Hanna's footsteps to actually mobilise them. What we needed was to give an impression of movement, to have several people throwing rocks one after the other. Jimmy was convinced that would bring them out, and having growlers on the loose would not only be a distraction, but severely restrict the movement of the Specials. Which sounded kind of frightening but feasible. Meanwhile, he was gonna see what else he could do to cause a little extra chaos.

It sounded great, but as far as I was concerned, kinda nibbling at the edges, trying to distract Infinity from what was really going on, which was me getting in there. The thing was, though, *was* I gonna get in there? And if I did, what state would I be in? I needed to talk to Gigi – and soon.

I went to the usual places – or what was left of them – spraying message after message. This time I kept it really simple:

HELP!

It was enough, she'd know it was me, and sure enough, I woke the next morning to find her fast asleep in Arturo's old sleeping bag again.

Actually, it was quite disturbing that she could enter the shelter at night, bed down and make herself comfortable, and not one of us ever heard her. I always thought my old ears were still pretty well tuned to that kind of thing, but I guess I was wrong. It was a good job she didn't wish us any harm.

I'd kinda got used to the reactions when I told someone what I was planning on doing, but no one was more dismissive or more openly hostile to the idea than Gigi and it really threw me. She acted like it was personal, that my recklessness was infringing on her in some way. If it hadn't been for the others sticking up for me, I don't think she'd even have discussed the subject. Delilah and Jimmy got a little short with her, telling her she could at least try to help, and when Gordie and Hanna formed an alliance in my defence, well, she was pretty much forced to change her mind. In the end she said she'd speak to someone, find out what they thought and get back to me as soon as possible.

That afternoon, despite having to drag him away from tinkering with the satellite, Jimmy and me went out to search for all the things he'd need. We went down to the industrial area, finding a lot of places broken into and occupied, mainly by the zombie-sick. I guess they'd gone there to search for something that might ease their condition and just never had the strength to leave. There were hundreds of them, all wailing and pawing at you as usual. Thank God we were able to just push them aside, that their weakness meant their attempts to trash the place hadn't amounted to much and everything Jimmy needed was still there.

We bagged everything up, he gave me a heavy box to carry, and we were out of that place in less than fifteen minutes, waving to those who came to the door to moan and howl after us. I mean, it was a terrible thing, and I did feel sorry for them, but again it went through my head that if it was that contagious – and bearing in mind the amount of contact we'd had with the sick – why hadn't any of us caught it?

Despite how much he knew it meant to me, how lucky we were to find everything on his list, on the way back to the churchyard it became obvious that Jimmy's thoughts weren't on the plan but elsewhere.

'You know, they say smell is the most nostalgic of the senses,' he said as we paused for a few moments to take a rest.

'What?' I asked, my thoughts as far away from his as his were mine.

'I smelled something on that satellite the first day we brought it back.'

'Jimmy!' I groaned, thinking we had more than enough to worry about.

'It might be relevant.'

'Let's just deal with one thing at a time, huh?' I told him, not unreasonably.

'It's cool. You got my full attention,' he reassured me, then got that look about him that meant I had anything but.

'How long's it going to take you?' I asked, trying to concentrate his mind.

'If I had the right tools, I could take it apart in a few hours.'

'Not the satellite! *This!*' I said, gesturing at the bags and box we were carrying.

'Oh . . . Dunno,' he replied. 'I need to do a bit more research.'

'Jimmy!' I cried, frustrated by how casual he was being. 'You said it yourself: it's gotta be one hundred and ten per cent accurate. There's no margin for error.'

'Yeah, *I said it myself*,' he repeated impatiently, '"cuz *I know*.'

I picked up the heavy box again, reminding myself it was fragile and that I shouldn't throw it at anyone, however aggravating they might be, then stomped on. I mean, I didn't like losing my temper with the little guy, especially not with the pressure we were under, but I hoped it might help him focus a little. But I should've known better.

We were almost back to the churchyard and he'd barely said a word the whole way when suddenly he turned to me as if rousing himself from a coma.

'Maybe it's got something to do with the fuel?' he said.

Despite all my doubts, the fact that he kept reminding me he 'wasn't any kind of a chemist and never had been', Jimmy still came up with the goods – at least as far as I could tell without putting them to the test. As much as it pains me to say it yet again, the way he adapts and makes do, how resourceful he is – the guy's invaluable, a genius by anyone's description – certainly his own.

On the other hand, Gigi didn't bring anything like such good news. She hadn't been able to get a message to Lena and wasn't optimistic about any kind of inside help. In fact, she was so luke-warm about the whole thing, to be honest, I wasn't even sure she'd tried. It slightly threw me – somewhere inside I felt an old rusty antenna give a slight twitch. It wasn't just that she was being dis-missive, I had the feeling there was something else. Not that it made any difference; as soon as the time was right, I was going, come what may.

The only problem was – and, shit, that was an irony – I had to wait for Infinity to make the first move. A couple of days passed with torturous slowness; the others not saying much and me kinda grateful for it. I was forced to take off the organi-plasters 'cuz my wounds were healing too quickly: like everyone else, they had to bide their time.

With everything else that was going on, I hadn't been paying too much attention to the kids. I was aware that Gordie and Hanna were spending more time together – not that they seemed to enjoy it that much; they barely said a word to each other – and that more and more of the things they did involved the other. What I wasn't prepared for was Gordie asking me for advice.

I'd got into the habit of sitting out in the churchyard after dark and keeping an eye on things, gauging the City's mood and waiting for my moment, and one night he came out to join me. He took a while to speak, and when he did, it was all about me and my plan. To listen to him, you'd think Infinity were in for the hiding of their lives, that I'd reduce that place to rubble, along with anyone who happened to be inside.

'It ain't gonna be easy,' I told him, noting someone running down the far side of the street and wondering if it meant anything.

'You'll pulverise 'em,' he sneered.

I guess it was his idea of a pep talk, but it was making me feel even more uncomfortable, as if my madness was contagious.

For a while he went silent and I thought he'd said all he wanted to, but he hadn't even started. 'D'you like Hanna?' he asked.

''course I do,' I replied, now knowing where we were going with this. 'She's special.'

He sat there for a moment, slowly nodding his head. 'What about Gigi?'

'Yep, she's special, too. But in a different way.'

Again he nodded. 'Which one d'you like most?'

'Gordie!' I protested, 'I like them both.'

'Huh,' he said, like I was being a big fat disappointment to him.

'Which one *d'you* like most?' I asked, 'cuz that was really the point.

'I dunno . . . Hanna's nicer, but maybe Gigi's more fun.'

I chuckled and he instantly scowled. 'Why you laughing?'

'No old guy would have a problem with that dilemma.'

'So what's the answer?' he asked hopefully.

'Whoa! I can't decide for you – no one can.'

'Ohhh,' he groaned in frustration.

'Anyways, you don't have to decide now,' I told him, getting up. 'But whatever you do, you treat them both with respect – d'you hear?'

He nodded, and as we walked back to the shelter I managed to put my arm round his shoulders without it getting shrugged off. Hey, maybe this being-a-father business wasn't gonna be as hard as I thought.

Another couple of days ground slowly by. It was starting to drive me crazy, and to make matters worse, just as I feared, the others accidentally came out with stuff that made me wonder just how much faith they had in me and my plan. Delilah went on about how Lena wouldn't blame me if I couldn't get into Infinity; Hanna put her arms around me and started to cry, saying it was for no reason, but it didn't exactly put my mind at ease. In fact, Jimmy and his satellite became a bit of a haven from all their well-intentioned comforting, and as soon as I got the idea that was where the conversation was going, I would head off down to see him, grateful for the fact that he almost always ignored me.

The little guy was still utterly obsessed with that satellite in the way that only Jimmy could be: trying to make sense of the bit he had and constantly speculating on the bit he didn't. The only times we saw him were at meals and bedtime. Which was why, helping

Delilah re-bag the food where the rats had got in, I was surprised to see him bustling up towards us.

Gordie and Hanna were playing games on the mini-screen as usual, but he snatched it from them.

'Hey!' Gordie protested.

'What's going on?' I asked.

Jimmy didn't answer, just started punching in information, his fingers moving at astonishing speed for an old guy. Mind you, I was a little surprised at what he eventually came out with.

'I been peeing down there.'

'Sorry?'

'I been peeing down there!' he repeated.

'Oh,' I said. I mean, okay, it wasn't such a big deal; maybe I had dug the new latrines a little too far away.

'How could I be so stupid?' Jimmy cried, returning his attention to the mini-screen, and I glanced at the others, wondering if anyone was making any more sense of this than I was.

'*Urine!*' Jimmy cried, as if it should mean something. 'Ammonia!'

I didn't say anything then but actually, it did remind me that Lena had said something similar.

'They really did put those things up there on the cheap,' he added.

'D'you understand any of this?' Delilah asked, turning to me.

'Not a word.'

'The satellites were solar-powered, but they always had a backup, an alternative source of fuel,' Jimmy told us. 'D'you know what hydrazine is?'

All four of us looked from one to the other, but Jimmy didn't bother waiting for a reply.

'Had a lot of uses: first as a rocket fuel last century, during the Second World War, later for space exploration. It's highly toxic; caused a lot of problems. On more than one occasion, craft falling back to Earth had to be blown out of the sky rather than risk contamination. When all those other countries, tinpot and otherwise, joined in the arms race by building their own long-range ballistic missiles, a lot of them used cheap hydrazine derivatives – I mean, who cares if their missiles are polluting the atmosphere when their job is to cause as much damage as they can?'

'Is that what the punishment satellites used?' I asked.

'Something similar . . . This one,' he said, gesturing towards his workshop, 'probably lost the majority of its solar-power capacity at launch and had to switch over to alternative fuel almost immediately. Which is why it didn't catch fire – or not for long.'

There was a pause and Gordie turned to Hanna, his expression about as interested as when Jimmy gave them that lecture about the satellites before – but I knew there was more to come.

'Thing is,' he continued, 'the way those satellites were put together, the systems they used, most of the backup would've slowly leaked out over the years.'

For several moments we sat there wishing he'd just come out and say it and not tease it out of us as usual, hoping someone might put us out of our misery. I should've known who it'd be.

'So those people on the beach, the ones we keep running into – the "zombies",' Hanna said. 'They're not sick, they're poisoned?'

Jimmy made this face. 'Maybe.'

'Oh my God!' Delilah croaked.

'I don't know what they mixed that stuff with, but not only is it toxic as hell, it's got some kind of aggressive binding agent, so instead of evaporating the way it should, it ends up bonding with everything – concrete, stone, steel, *everything* – which is why this whole damn City is burning, and why the fires go on for so long and keep exploding.'

Again there was a pause as possibilities reared up before us like growlers outta the ground.

'Have we been poisoned?' Gordie asked, suddenly looking a lot more attentive.

Jimmy shrugged. 'Maybe. To some degree. But I reckon there's a kind of micro-climate out on the Island – we always got more extremes of weather, and the wind off the ocean – hopefully that protected us from the worst of it.'

'I never felt well over there,' Delilah grumbled.

She was right: illness had been a way of life. We used to blame the garbage, and probably most of it was – but not all, apparently. Still my mind raced on, careering through this new information, trying to link it with the old: was that why they kidnapped Lena, 'cuz she'd spent all those years underground, in a completely unpolluted environment? I guess that would make her pretty special, but for what purpose exactly?

'So the satellites weren't *protecting* people,' Hanna commented, 'they were killing them.'

But Jimmy's thoughts were already elsewhere and, without another word he turned and hurried back towards his work area, feeding information into the screen as he went.

For several moments there was silence, then Delilah sighed. 'That man never brings good news.'

In a way, she was right, but the little guy could only bring what was available. I also realised something else, that I should've had some idea about before: that was why Infinity were so intent on killing him, they were scared of what information he'd picked up when he broke into their system and what he might add it to now he was back on the Mainland. That he'd tell everyone the satellites hadn't been 'judgement from on high', but a plague, and that, ironically, the person being constantly described as 'the biggest ever threat to society' was, in fact, its saviour.

For the rest of that day my mind was in turmoil. I had no idea if what Jimmy'd said affected my plans to rescue Lena in any way, but for sure I was left with this uneasy feeling that the situation had erupted out of control yet again.

I didn't bother to sit out and watch the street that night. All my confidence had been ripped right out of me. In fact, as embarrassed as I am to admit it, I felt so beaten, so pessimistic about what I was trying to do, that just for a moment it went through my head that maybe it'd be best for everyone if I didn't wake up in the morning.

Which, as it turned out, was a whole lot closer to the truth than I ever could've imagined.

'Clancy! *Clancy!*'

Someone was calling to me from out of the darkness. Took me a while to realise it was Gordie.

'Yeah?' I said, struggling up onto one elbow, but he didn't need to say any more. I could hear it, too: the sound of distant beating and shouting, the slight thrum of a Dragonfly over the City – it was another Clean-up.

I didn't hesitate for one second, jumping to my feet so quickly I had a bit of a dizzy spell and had to stand still for a moment. No sooner had it subsided than I was ready to go.

'Are we still doing it?' Delilah asked.

'I am,' I said, and there was a brief pause, as if everyone was taking that in.

'Got everything?' Jimmy asked.

'Yep,' I said, checking my pockets, feeling the extra bulk.

'Good luck.'

'Thanks.'

'We'll be at the fence.'

I went round and thanked everyone, hugging them, then made my way out into the dark and smoky night.

CHAPTER TWENTY

Once I emerged from the dense vegetation of the shelter I could really feel the atmosphere, as if something tangible was rising up over the City, hanging there like a perfect storm about to break. I clambered across the rubble to the street, trying to work out which direction to take: sound can move in odd ways around a city, particularly with so much smoke. At first I started to walk up towards the Square, but then changed my mind, taking the next turning, heading over in the general direction of the ocean.

Immediately that sound became more specific, more frightening, as it echoed along the street towards me in onrushing shock waves. Over and over that familiar *thump-thump-thump! thump-thump-thump!* was getting louder with every step, more threatening.

I picked up my pace. I needed to work out exactly how I was going to do this before they arrived, and by the sound of it, they weren't that far away – and yet the street wasn't as busy as I'd've expected. I checked the other side, and glancing up an alleyway saw the crowds and panic I'd been anticipating – I'd turned too soon.

I crossed over and headed up the alleyway, at that precise

moment a running mob coming bursting round the corner. I tried to dodge and weave my way through them, but there were far too many and slowly they pushed me back until I was pinned up against a wall. I fought my way out, getting jolted and shoved, punched and screamed at, but in the end I somehow managed to get through.

As I got to the junction, I saw a large group of Specials marching towards me, intent on blocking off the alleyways so no one else could escape. I slipped around the corner just in time, finding the nearest doorway, keeping as far back in the shadows as I could until they'd passed and I could merge into the crowds unchallenged.

I got a real shock when I took my first look down that smoky, chaotic street. Those nights they swept down our way, demolishing the church and everything else, I don't reckon they'd rounded up more than a couple of hundred people – here there were more like thousands: old people, desperately trying to run, to force their stiff old arthritic joints to function; kids darting from side to side like mice looking for a hole to escape; even some of the zombie-sick were getting swept along with it, as if their feet weren't touching the ground, that they simply didn't have the strength to resist. All of them had been flushed out of their hiding places: abandoned buildings, lean-tos, storm drains, anywhere they'd mistakenly thought they were safe. And behind them, like some huge cacophonous wall rearing up towards us, came the now-familiar shouting and beating, the clanking of heavy machinery, the piercing spotlights of the Dragonflies.

Now that I'd joined the flow and knew which way it was being driven, I had to somehow get to the front of it. The only trouble was, the amount of panic, the surging and swirling hysteria, it was damn near impossible. I tried to speed up, to even run a little, but within moments there'd be some kind of obstruction and people would lose it, screaming at each other, not out of anger but just pure, blind terror. All possible exits were closed off, side streets, lanes and alleyways, doors into functioning buildings, anywhere where they thought we might be able to escape.

Yet somehow I managed to slip and slide my way through, using a minimum of force, trying to ensure my progress was as uneventful as possible, acutely aware of the package I was carrying, that if it got broken, this whole thing would be off.

I got shouted at a couple of times by people taking exception to me pushing past, but I just apologised as best I could and kept going. Behind me I could hear the growing thunder: the roar of the engines, the screaming chorus of the hunters, even the occasional loosed gunshot.

I'd known it would be an ordeal, a further vent for madness, but there was something else, too. I couldn't exactly say how, but in some way it felt different. Maybe it was the sheer scale of it, the unpredictable nature of such a huge crowd, or perhaps it had something to do with the uncertainty, that no one had the faintest idea where we were being driven. For sure I couldn't think of a square or park in the vicinity big enough to hold so many people, and if it wasn't going to be that, what the hell was it?

I've never been the greatest sports fan in the world. I used to watch a little on the screen, but the only sporting event I ever actually attended was the track with Mr Meltoni. For sure, I had no idea where any of the City's major sporting venues were. If I had, maybe I would've had second thoughts about what I was planning on doing.

I kept checking the signs to see if there was any indication of an upcoming open area, but it still took me a while to realise that the only destination being regularly signposted was the stadium. Even then I didn't get it, not until it came into view, all brightly lit and glowing, and I heard the muttering of those around me. They started to cry out in protest, trying to turn around and push back the other way, knowing it could only mean something unforgivable. For a few moments they held their ground, refusing to go any further, but the Specials pushed up hard behind us, using their weapons – clubs, electro-shields, shock-gloves – and after a bit of a struggle and several people getting zapped and writhing on the ground, the protest disintegrated and we were herded forward again, into the heart of the stadium through a long, cold tunnel.

We stumbled out onto the floodlit grass, taking a few dazed and blinded steps forward, then stopped and gaped all around, realising we weren't alone. The upper stands were filled with hundreds, maybe even thousands of shooters, all sitting there surrounded by the remains of their fast food and beer – or maybe sushi and champagne – weapons in their hands, eagerly peering down on us.

The Specials stopped their beating and a line of them quickly took up position around the periphery of the field while others blocked the exits. Two Dragonflies hovered overhead, their spotlights shining down like finely stretched luminous webs. I was so shocked for a moment all I could do was stare. This wasn't what I'd imagined, not what I'd had in mind at all. I'd anticipated a square or park, somewhere where there would be nooks and crannies, bushes, places where I could hide if necessary. That would've been dangerous enough – but out there, brightly lit and totally exposed, with nowhere to hide? It was like some huge mass firing squad – which, I guess, was exactly what it was.

All around me I could see others coming to the same conclusion, the disbelief on their faces being replaced by terror. There were cries of helplessness as they frantically looked left and right for a way to escape.

I don't know what set me running – there was nowhere to go. I could see shooters studying prospective targets through their sights, going from person to person, wondering who to take down first. One young woman in particular was smirking at me from the front row as if to say, 'I'm gonna get that big old bastard before anyone else does' and I just turned and fled, dodging around those also running, pushing aside those too scared to move.

From what I'd seen of Clean-ups, no one was that much of a shot. I figured if I ran to the centre of the field, maybe – and I do mean *maybe* – given how inept they were, I just might manage to stay alive.

Some really hap-hap-happy announcer welcomed everyone to the 'main event of the evening' and started geeing them up, saying it was time to, 'Take out the trash!' Someone started shooting even before he finished – 'course, he remonstrated with them, told them to wait for his say-so, but only in a jokey way. And finally, with his voice rising to a deranged pitch, those around me screaming in terror, the shooters baying in excitement, he called out to everyone to, '*Clean up this City!*'

It was like the whole world exploded. Gunshots, laser burns, jeering and howling, insanity on a scale you simply couldn't imagine. I saw the old, the young, the sick, person after person, tumbling to the ground, bodies mounting up, falling on top of each other. Many were so badly wounded they were no longer recognisable as human, but just slashed and punctured weeping chunks of meat and bone. How long it went on, I dunno – I guess it wasn't any more than a minute or two, but it felt like the most godless of infinities.

It wasn't until the shooters stopped – to reload maybe, or to take another gulp of their drinks – that I heard the screaming. It was the most chilling sound that's ever entered my head – a grating collision of terror and pain, and in that moment, realising that everyone here was gonna be cut down, I knew my time had come: that it was now or never.

I pretended to panic, to run blindly, dodging people, leaping over bodies, then suddenly toppled over as if I'd been hit and hadn't immediately appreciated it. Colliding with the grass face-first, smelling the moistness of the watered soil, hoping I'd died a convincing death.

I didn't make the slightest movement, just in case someone had zoomed in to make sure. I was just another lifeless corpse – no more, no less. However, after a few moments, my hand began to stir and slowly inch its way down inside my parka until I eventually located the thick plastic bag I'd dug out of the garbage, its precious contents slopping around inside. I slowly tugged it out and placed it under my forehead, then began to push down with all my might, straining my neck muscles, for a tense moment fearing the plastic might be too strong. Yet finally it broke, exploding all over me, drenching me in a mixture of water and my own blood that I'd drained from my self-inflicted wound.

It covered my face, my hair, my neck and chest, and I hoped the fact that it was real blood, that it was verifiably mine, meant there'd be no suspicion of my 'fatal' wound.

But that wasn't it, of course. That was the easy bit. I slowly raised my head, just the merest fraction, taking in the view around me, knowing it might well be my last glimpse of this Earth.

If it was, then it sure wasn't the one I would've chosen. You've never seen such carnage, nor heard such a terrible noise. The smoke was so thick now I couldn't see most of the people in the stands – which, I guessed, was the reason why a lot of them had stopped shooting. Nevertheless, there was still more than enough going on for anyone to worry about who was dead and who wasn't. Again I kept my movements slow and easy as I reached down into my other inside pocket and located my second precious package, thanking God when I drew it out and saw it hadn't been broken. With all the jostling and fighting, the heavy fall I took pretending to be shot, it wouldn't've surprised me.

I carefully unwrapped it, slightly rolled to one side, priming the syringe as I did so, then stuck it into my stomach and injected myself. I had just enough time to remember to throw it clear of my body before its contents went to work, and then everything around me – the floodlit stadium, the shooters, the screaming of victims, and finally my consciousness itself – faded into nothing.

I once took a bullet for Mr Meltoni's wife. I mean, you don't think about these things, you don't have time. Either you do or you don't, and I did. At the time, the business was going through a bit of an unsettled period, loyalties had got a little blurred and Mr Meltoni must've been concerned, 'cuz he insisted on me accompanying his wife wherever she went. Which, in her case, was pretty much always shopping.

It was a duty I hated every bit as much as walking that damn dog of hers, Mitzi, though what I hated the most was when she insisted on taking it with us, so I had to put up with a double helping of humiliation. She used to make us wait outside – I mean, talk about embarrassing: standing there with this buttoned and bowed ball of expensively coiffeured fluff sitting on my shoes. And I swear that stupid pooch knew how uncomfortable I was, 'cuz she always added to it by pooping in the doorway of Valentino or Chanel or wherever it was. Or maybe she was just making a state-ment. Maybe she hated shopping as much as I did and wanted everyone to know. Either way, for a big guy to have to clear up after that little thing whilst all those fur-coated ladies pushed by with their noses in the air was well up on the shaming scale.

I remember, we were just starting to suffer winter and the first fall of snow was thick on the ground. The sidewalks hadn't been properly cleared and people were slipping and sliding all over. These two guys must've been watching us for a while 'cuz they obviously knew her routine pretty well. Thursday was Gucci day and they were waiting for her just down the street. As it happened, Mrs Meltoni had just called Mitzi and me in to give our opinion on a dress, which was another of my duties I hated. What could I say? 'It's nice? It's okay?' And as for what I thought the dog's opinion was – how the hell did I know? I mean, she was a beautiful young woman. Mr Meltoni took good care of her. It was up to him to pass the compliments.

Not that it mattered what I said, in fact, I reckon she only asked my opinion so she could ignore it. Anyways, thank the Lord, when we left that shop my arms were empty for once – well, apart from Mitzi.

I saw these two guys approaching as we made our way towards the limo. They were both carrying packages, but it was the way they were carrying them – straight out in front of them – that made me suspicious. I got this really bad feeling, a whole tidal wave of it, and suddenly had one of those moments where you become a spectator of your own actions.

I just let Mitzi fall to the ground and leaped to shield Mrs Meltoni. At that precise moment, both guys' parcels were blown away by the guns they had inside them.

I took one in the shoulder – well, more to the back really – as the two guys immediately turned to run back to their vehicle, but one of them slipped, and grabbing his companion, took them both down.

They were just lying there, floundering around, trying to get up, with me slumped a few feet away bleeding heavily and Mrs Meltoni screaming out at the top of her voice. God knows what would've happened next; I guess they'd've got to their feet eventually. But to my astonishment – maybe 'cuz she was so indignant at being so unceremoniously dropped – Mitzi went on the attack, yapping furiously and leaping at the gunmen, getting her teeth into one guy's ear. It was mayhem, old-time variety, though thankfully, a patrol car just happened to be passing by.

Mr Meltoni was really grateful; he even insisted I took a spell off. For some reason, though, his wife was never the same with me again. Even worse, from then on she took to calling her mutt 'Mitzi the Minder' – she even had it inscribed on its damn diamanté collar. Forget the fact that it was me who took the bullet, that I put my body between her and two gunmen.

But the point is, either you do or you don't, and despite what you might think now, you won't know until it happens. And I guess it's just as well that most of us go through our lives without ever having to finding out. It really depends on who you are and what it is you want to protect. Doubtless Jimmy was right: what I was doing was suicide. Someone was probably loading a bullet or firing up a laser that had my name on it even as I passed out. But I was doing what I could to protect the woman I loved, not to mention the child we'd created together, and when it comes down to it, we'd all do that, wouldn't we?

In a way, it was that convoy of white trucks that'd really set me thinking. The fact that they went into Infinity at more or less the same time on set afternoons. It didn't make any sense. They were 'clean-up' vehicles for transporting the dead (leaving them in dumpsters, apparently), so why did they need to go to Infinity?

Of course, anyone with half a brain would've got it straight away. When I told Jimmy, he didn't so much as bat an eyelid, as if I was doing no more than stating the all too damn obvious. If there was one thing Gordie falling victim to an enticer had taught us, it was that the transplant business was *way* out of control. And thanks to Jimmy, we also knew that satellite poisoning meant there was an endless queue of people clamouring for replacement organs. Nothing was coming over from the Island any more and the price had obviously gone through the roof, so I guess it made perfect sense for Specials to go through the bodies after a Clean-up, checking for any that might have something worth taking. Young people mostly, but others, too – like some old dude who looked like he must've recently stumped up the cash for a new young kidney? Who had the typical scar of a back-street transplant surgeon? He'd be taken to Infinity's hospital wing to be investigated . . . wouldn't he?

Okay, and if you're thinking that's a fair example of taking a bullet for someone, then you still gotta little ways to go. See, even if I stayed more still than the dead themselves on that grass, getting dragged off and heaped up along with other possible donors, there'd still be no chance of me getting into Infinity, 'cuz the moment they scanned the truck at the gate and checked life forms against Infinity personnel, it'd be all over. I wouldn't have to *play* dead, I would be.

For a while that was where I got stuck, there just didn't seem to be any way, then I remembered what Dr Simon had done with Lena, how he was able to transport her without risk of being discovered. And that was why I went to see Jimmy, to get him to look up his analysis of what was in that syringe and make up some more.

So now I hope it makes sense? I was actually standing in front of the bullet. It was on its way towards me. Jimmy had warned me a thousand times I was relying too much on conjecture, that if I had one detail wrong, made one incorrect assumption, my whole plan would come tumbling down like a troupe of weak-kneed acrobats. He could've also added that it would probably cost me my life.

Whatever happened, the little guy'd been determined I'd come to no harm 'cuz of him. His role in this was absolutely crucial, his calculations had to be spot-on. I don't know how big the window was between me being scanned at the gate and when the bodies started getting cut up, but for comfort I reckoned I needed to start coming round almost the moment I was inside the compound.

At first he'd said it was impossible, that there were far too many variables – the strength of the mixture, my body weight, what I'd eaten – any number of things. And he kept punctuating his sentences with that same warning, over and over: that he wasn't 'any kind of chemist!'

I hoped he was setting himself up as usual, trying to make a task look even more difficult than it was, but there was an uncertainty about him I didn't recognise. Maybe this was too much even for Jimmy?

Anyways, I'm sure you can fill in the rest. After weeks of intense thought, walking the City, not sleeping at night, that was what I'd come up with – a shot so long it was gonna have to follow the curvature of the Earth. But what did you expect? People don't change: I'm just a dumb old big guy, and to tell ya the truth, it wouldn't've surprised me if I'd never woken from that long cold darkness.

CHAPTER TWENTY-ONE

I don't know when, but at some point I realised my eyes were open, and they'd been that way for a little while. There was no thought there, though, in fact, no connection between them and any other part of my body. I guess I'm dead. I have to be. I don't have any kind of physical presence at all, *nothing* to indicate I'm still part of this world. Finally it's happened . . . I stood in front of one too many bullets.

An automatic door opens somewhere, shushing wide, vibrating when fully extended, then shushing back closed again. Someone must've come in. But come in where? Maybe I'm not dead? Maybe I'm in a coma?

I hear muttering voices, but I don't understand what they're saying. It could be a foreign language, but I don't think so. It's my language; I just don't understand it. And where the hell's my body? Do I have one? Has someone taken it away? Only my eyes remain, sitting in a cold dish of some unspecified solution, with just my bloodshot old pupils staring out.

I feel it. Only dully at first, but slowly it becomes that bit more acute. Someone's taken hold of my dish and is moving it around,

318

slopping the solution over the sides, my eyeballs almost going with it. *Be careful, will ya! That's my only remaining contact with life.* Yet eventually the dish is set down, but along with something else, that I'm pressed hard up against and don't like. I think it's a body – right next to my dish – and at last I realise I'm not a dish at all, I'm still a bag-a-bones old big guy.

The body started rocking back and forth, as if something was causing it to vibrate. There was a saw working near me, buzzing away, eagerly going about its work. I didn't like that sound, not just the buzzing, but the material it was slicing through. It was soft, vulnerable, not at all right for the sharp whirling blade of a circular saw. And finally my mind clicked into gear enough for me to recognise what was going on: the body was being cut up. I could actually hear them going inside it, the slurping, squelching sound of them searching for anything worth taking.

Now I knew where I was. I was at the butcher's and he was going to slaughter me, cut me up into pieces and display me in his window: sell me in portions to be taken away and cooked, roasted or barbecued – Jeez, I had to get outta there. I had to cram myself back into my body, fill it from head to toe, and make it whisk me away.

I tried to move, but they must've secured me somehow; I couldn't budge, not even lift a finger. All I could manage was to open and shut my eyes. I tried again, my brain sending out the necessary signals, but still my body remained dormant, dead.

I heard more movement, the sounds of people lifting a substantial weight: another body, maybe. The one next to me, the one they'd cut up and ransacked, was dragged away. I heard it thump heavily down onto the floor. *Jesus! Was it my turn?* Someone ran something down my scar – maybe his finger? – and made some comment about what a botched job it was . . .

Hey! Wait a moment! I felt that! My body was beginning to respond, to regain some sensation. And at that precise moment, the circular saw was turned on again, whirring back into life, and I could hear it coming towards me.

I wanted to jump up, to get away from there as fast as I could, but I still couldn't move. Time and time again I sent the message out, begging my body to do what I was asking, 'til finally, I tried so hard that body and mind collided and I sort of convulsed.

'Shit!' a male voice near me cried – I guess the guy who'd been holding the circular saw.

'What's the matter?' asked another male from the other side of the room.

'He moved!'

'Dylan!'

'He fucking moved!'

'He's just settling! It's rigor mortis – he's been dead for a day.'

The guy with the circular saw never replied but I could feel him standing there watching me. I dug down as deeply as I could, searching for the places where I was re-forming, where my mind and body were spluttering back into life, and finally I managed to turn and look him in the face.

'Jesus!' he gasped, dropping the circular saw and jumping back.

Despite my head feeling as if it weighed substantially more than my entire body, I still managed to raise it up a few inches. I hadn't been so wrong about it being a butcher's: that was exactly what it looked like, with bodies, parts of bodies, limbs and innards strewn everywhere.

'Kill him!' came the voice from across the other side of the room.

'Fuck! . . . *Fuck!*' his stunned companion kept repeating as he backed further away, and finally realising I wasn't secured at all, I struggled up on one elbow.

I was on a long bench, one of maybe twenty or thirty bodies, most of them, it pains me to say, children. I tell ya, I've never seen anything so repulsive, so utterly inhuman, in all my life.

The guy on the other side of the room despaired of his companion and came at me with a large knife. I didn't know if I had the strength, the coordination, anything at all, to fight him, but grabbed this stool next to the bench and started swinging. The only problem was, I was lurching and swaying around like I'd been on a bender for the last two weeks.

He started jabbing the knife at me, partly posturing, partly hoping to do me some damage. I waited 'til I thought he was in range then swung the stool at him as hard as I could, almost swinging myself off my feet and missing him by the proverbial country mile. But the effort, the need to make myself function, *was* starting to accelerate my recovery. I swung again, this time only missing by half a country mile. One further attempt and – I gotta admit, more by accident than anything – I managed to knock the knife out of his hand. He immediately tried to run but hit the bench and I was able to get in a good shot to the head and down he went. I turned, lurching towards the door, trying to cut the other guy off, managing to nail him just as he was frantically punching the door-open button.

But ya know, my body might've been swinging back into operation, but my mind was still fumbling around for the 'on' switch. For several seconds I just stood there, frowning at the guys on the floor, wondering who the hell they were . . . Where was I? What was I doing there?

I went to the door, opened it a crack and peered out into a long shiny corridor smelling of antiseptic: a hospital, for sure, which explained the bodies, but not what was going on. Why were they being cut up? And where'd they come from?

And then slowly, I started to get a feeling, not remembering exactly, but a sense that something terrible had happened. Something was skulking in a corner of my mind; something I knew I'd regret remembering . . . People being killed . . . carnage . . . *slaughter*. And just like I was in the dark of that stadium and they'd turned on the lights, it all came back to me.

Jesus! This must be Infinity! The plan worked! God bless ya, Jimmy, I knew I could count on you . . . And that meant – oh my God! – *I was somewhere near Lena!*

I went to the door and checked the corridor again. I needed two things: one, to know her exact location, and two – 'cuz it would've been picked up by the scanner if I'd tried to smuggle one in – some kind of firearm.

I had to wait a while, but finally saw a Special approaching. I ducked back in 'til he was just about level with me, then leapt out and grabbed him, yanking him into the room. I hit him in the stomach, winding him, and as he collapsed to the floor, grabbed his laser. He started to struggle, but stopped when he felt his own weapon jammed up against his temple.

'Where's Lena?' I asked.

'Who?'

'Where's the woman they're holding? Where's Dr Simon?' I demanded, pressing the laser harder, making an indentation on his forehead.

He hesitated just long enough for me to be sure he knew what I was talking about. 'I don't know!'

I didn't have time to play games. I flicked the laser to 'stun' and shot him in the leg and he doubled up in agony. 'I'd try harder if I were you.'

He just lay there, moaning with pain, but I went to shoot the other leg. 'No! *No—!*' he begged.

'Five seconds,' I told him, but he didn't need them.

'Top floor,' he cried, 'Everything's up there.'

I upped the laser a little more and shot both him and the two butchers laying comatose on the floor in the head. By the time they came round, I'd either be far away or back lying on that table.

As I made way down the corridor an alarm went off. I didn't know if it was something I'd done, or what Jimmy was up to over by the fence, but as I searched for the elevator, several people who should've challenged me were too busy looking out the window, giving out with these little gasps and cries, the occasional stunned expletive, which I guessed meant the growlers were out.

I found the stairs and decided to take them, glancing out the window on my way up and sure enough, seeing a pack of growlers over by the fence. It took me a couple of moments to appreciate that they had someone down on the ground, that they were jostling each other to get in on the kill. I briefly panicked, thinking it might be Jimmy or one of the kids, but I could just about make out a Special's uniform.

What the hell'd happened, I didn't know. Maybe there was some kind of misunderstanding or malfunction? Surely the growlers could be turned off if necessary? Or maybe Jimmy'd done something? Whatever, the guy was paying dearly; even from where I was, I could hear his screams.

It wasn't hard to work out why he'd gone over there. Someone– and though I couldn't see them clearly, with all that grace and poise, it just had to be Hanna – had climbed the fence and was now surfing the cameras; riding one, doing a couple of little ballet steps, pirouetting round, kicking out the lens, then stepping off and waiting for the next. That was probably what'd set off the sirens. The guy must've gone over there to stop her, maybe shoot her down, but with the aid of the growlers, Hanna's dance of destruction was carrying on unimpeded.

Knowing how competitive Gigi was, I would've expected to see her over there riding cameras too, but there was no sign, and it went through my head that maybe that was just the slightest cause for hope. If she wasn't with them, maybe she was overseeing a little inside help – for sure, it was beginning to look like I'd need it.

When I got to the top floor, it was the same story as below: more and more people were clustering around the windows.

'It left the lawn!' a woman squealed, obviously talking about a growler. 'Look!'

'Some kinda malfunction,' an older Special told her, trying to sound reassuring. 'They'll fix it.'

'How am I going to get home?'

I hadn't really appreciated just how much of a distraction the growlers would be. I saw this corridor leading off the reception area with a private sign over it and had almost sneaked down there without anyone noticing. However, at the last moment the older Special glanced back and caught me.

'Hold it!' he shouted, drawing his weapon.

I ran as laser blasts started instantly scoring the walls and floor around me. Turning, firing back, I managed to drop this young guy coming after me and made it to the end of the corridor and round the corner. There were several doors in front of me, but only one with a couple of guards posted on it. The nearest guy just about got his weapon up and pointed in my direction, but I got my shots away first, leaping over both bodies before they'd even settled. I tried the door, to my relief finding it unlocked.

Nothing mattered to me in that moment other than the person I was desperately hoping to see inside, in whose eyes I prayed I was about to live. However, when I got in there, I was met by an empty

INTO THE FIRE

room, large, expensively furnished – they really were taking good care of her – and yet, the moment that thought entered my head that this was where she'd normally be, I knew something was wrong. Even if it was an unfamiliar place, I should still get a sense of her.

I heard a commotion out in the corridor and punched the button to deadlock the door, then, just to make sure, melted it with my laser, grateful to see that the whole thing was heavily reinforced. No one would be coming through there for a while.

I was tempted to just call out her name, to shout it in the way I'd wanted to for so long, but caution urged me to go quietly. I went through the door at the end of the room into a short hallway and was confronted by two other doors, one slightly ajar. A man's voice came from inside – Jesus, it was only a few words, but I knew who it was immediately. Dr Simon!

I pushed the door open as slowly as I could, inch by inch, breath by breath, dearly hoping to see Lena. However, she wasn't there. It was someone else, and I gotta say, one of the most disturbing sights I've ever seen in my life.

Dr Simon stood there in all his usual finery – immaculately tailored suit, pristine white shirt, shiny silk tie; hair that had never spent more than two weeks away from a hairdresser's scissors or two minutes from a comb – but this time, however, he was jacketless, and his sleeves were rolled up as he massaged someone on the table. I say 'someone', but it couldn't've been more obvious who it was.

Nora Jagger was stretched out on her front, utterly naked, though that wasn't the first thing to strike me about her. The doc was working on her legs, or what little there was of them. See, Gigi had been right: she really had had all her limbs removed, and I tell ya, it really shook me. It wasn't what she looked like, it was what she'd *done*. How could she? What sorta person would have their arms and legs cut off so they could attach stronger – more *lethal*– artificial ones?

I must've made a noise, let out a groan or something, 'cuz suddenly they both turned towards me. Nora Jagger's reaction was instantaneous – she was off that table and scrambling across the room with surprising agility. The reason was all too obvious: her artificial legs and arms were lined up and plugged into the top of this machine, hands and feet in the air, maybe recharging in some way. Just for a moment the sight of her, naked and limbless, squirming across that floor, left me at a loss, not knowing how to react, but I recovered sufficiently to squeeze a laser-blast between her and her prosthetics. She lost balance and toppled to the floor, lying there without a stitch.

'You,' I growled, turning to Dr Simon. His face was white as his shirt. 'I should kill you here and now.'

'I had no choice!' he told me, as if he'd been waiting all this time to explain. 'As soon as they knew about Lena, they wouldn't leave me alone—'

'And how did they find out?'

'You've got to! It's the law!' he started to babble, but Nora Jagger shut him down at once.

'How the fuck did you get in here?' she demanded.

I gotta say, in real life that face was even harder and meaner than it looked on the screen. Her eyes stabbed into mine and I swear I could almost physically feel their invasion – I never seen such ugliness of character, of *spirit*. I've spent my life mixing with the callous, the crazy, the psychotic and the damned, but almost every one of them had something, a redeeming feature, no matter how small. With her you just knew there was nothing. She was evil jam-packed into a truncated body that she herself had brutally abused, lopping off pieces to make herself more fearsome, more able to perform the sick acts conjured up by her toxic imagination.

'How the fuck d'you think I got in here?' I spat back.

She was simmering so violently I almost expected her to explode; not just at me for getting in there, but also at the Specials who should've prevented it. Though what I think she was most angry about was the fact that I'd managed to catch her at such a vulnerable moment, without her limbs attached

'Where is she?' I demanded.

'Who?' she asked, every word spat at me like it was tipped with poison.

'Lena,' Dr Simon informed her.

'Ohhh!' she cried, breaking into the cruellest of smiles, shifting position so she could prop her body up against a chair, apparently not in the least bit concerned by her nakedness. 'Clancy! Come for the little woman.'

'Where is she?' I repeated, snarling the question directly into Dr Simon's face.

He looked frightened enough to tell me, but I couldn't put the fear of God into him the way she could.

'You tell him, I'll rip you apart,' she threatened, 'starting with your insides and working out.'

She meant it. I actually saw him buckle at the knees, his suave, confident demeanour gone in an instant, and it wouldn't have surprised me if he'd peed those perfect pants of his.

I looked at her, then back at him, neither seeming of a mind to say anything and I thought the time had come to take matters into my own hands. Without another word, I shot the glass outta the window and as smoke crept into the room, walked over to the line of artificial limbs in the machine, selected an arm and gave it a tug.

I thought they'd be plugged in somehow, but when I drew it out I saw it was actually just resting in a container of grey cellulose-like sludge that now dripped heavily onto the floor. Even worse, the arm-socket that had been in the liquid was pulsing slightly, almost as if it was alive. I didn't care for that at all, and instead of threatening her with what I might do with it, I thought about just throwing it out the window as an example of what I'd do with the others.

'*No!*' Nora Jagger screamed, seeing my intention. 'Don't you fucking *dare!*'

'Where is she?' I repeated, and she glared at me as if she'd never been so angry with anyone in her life.

'You'd better kill me!' she hissed, 'while you've got the chance!'

'Tell me!' I shouted, leaning out the window, hanging onto her artificial hand like there was a body attached, threatening to let go.

She paused for a moment, thinking it through, trying to find an angle, but too distracted by me holding her arm like that. 'I'll show you,' she eventually conceded.

'He shows me,' I told her. 'You stay here.'

Finally she gave way. 'I hope she's fucking worth it,' she said, those chillingly pale, goat-like eyes promising how brutal her revenge would be.

'I presume there's another way outta here?' I asked the doc.

He turned to Nora Jagger. She glared daggers at me one last time, then reluctantly nodded, giving her assent.

'Tie her up,' I told him.

You could see how scared he was – the whole time he was doing it he was visibly shaking. I got him to help her up and sit her in a chair, then secure her with bandages from his bag, covering him with my laser to make sure he did a good job. She cursed evilly and endlessly, most of it directed at me, but also at the doc and the Specials outside, leaving no doubt what she'd do to all of us if she ever got the chance. I gotta say, the range and venom of it, it was pretty hard to ignore. She got herself into a real mad frothing frenzy, cursing and spitting, until eventually I decided I'd had enough and stuck a couple of plasters over her mouth.

I didn't want to hear that, and I didn't think the doc did either. She should've been locked away long ago, or maybe put to sleep; anything other than having someone like her at large in the community.

I wouldn't've admitted it, but I gotta say, her ranting did rattle me a bit, so much so, in fact, that I decided to hang onto that arm of hers, ignoring the fact that it was still dripping grey sludge, figuring that in terms of trying to escape, it would put her at one helluva disadvantage.

'Let's go,' I said to Dr Simon. 'And you try anything, I'm really gonna enjoy blowing your brains out all over that expensive shirt.'

He led me to this door hidden behind a screen. It was only as I was about to follow him through that I glanced back and noticed a further door in the corner. I hesitated for a moment, then went to take a quick look, just in case. It was a games room, with full-wall screens, but there was no one in there and I left without giving it another thought.

The doc took me down what I guessed was a VIP emergency escape route, constantly turning round and glancing back like he expected to see Nora Jagger coming after us at any moment.

'She's not gonna find her way outta that any time soon,' I reassured him.

'I hope not,' he muttered, unable to stop himself taking yet another glance back. 'I've never seen her that angry. You caught her the one time she has her prosthetics off. That's why there were guards on the door. Normally she wouldn't remove them for any reason.'

I don't know if it was 'cuz I was distracted or what, but we turned a blind corner and suddenly came face to face with a couple of Specials – someone had obviously remembered the escape route and sent them in the other way.

I didn't give them time to draw their weapons – nor me mine – I just swung at them with the only thing available, which was Nora Jagger's arm. Jeez, I didn't know what that thing was made of, but it sure packed a punch; both of them ended up on the ground, laid out cold by the arm of a woman who was tied up a couple of corridors back.

I turned around, half-expecting to see Dr Simon making a run for it, but he was cowering in the corner, his main concern apparently whether he'd messed up his fancy clothes or not.

'Come on,' I ordered.

For a while we kinda half-walked, half-jogged, in silence; he was still occasionally glancing back, but I could also sense him turning things over, weighing up the situation.

'Lena's fine,' he told me, plainly trying to ingratiate himself. 'You don't have to worry about that.'

'Pardon me if I don't believe a word you say.'

'Listen! For God's sake—! You saw her!' he cried, obviously referring to Nora Jagger. 'She frightens the hell out of me!'

I was tempted to concede the point, but however much I agreed about how scary that woman was, I sure as hell wasn't gonna let him off that easily. 'A pregnant woman?' I sneered, like he should be ashamed of himself, being a doctor and all.

He went quiet for a moment and I thought maybe he was feeling guilty, reciting that Hippocratic Oath to himself, but I was wrong; he had a much bigger surprise for me.

'It's not just that, is it?' he said.

'What d'ya mean?'

He paused mid-stride and stared into my face. 'You do know, don't you?' he asked.

'I know everything,' I told him, dragging him on. 'I know about the satellites, people being poisoned, Infinity trying to hush it up. And probably, 'cuz Lena lived in the tunnels all those years, that her and the baby's organs are worth a fortune.'

He never commented, just looked as if he was waiting for me to say more, and I began to feel uneasy. 'What?'

'And?'

'What d'ya mean, "and"?'

'You don't know, do you?' he asked.

Jeez, why were people always saying stuff like that to me? I couldn't help being a dumb old big guy. Did I ever pretend to be anything else? I turned and gave him a real hostile flash of the look.

'Living underground hasn't just kept her healthy, Clancy, it's kept her uncompromised.'

'I know that!' I replied impatiently. He still wasn't telling me anything new.

'She's a *healthy, young, pregnant* woman,' he said, emphasising each and every word.

'Thank God for that,' I commented.

' . . . The *only* one.'

Now it was my turn to pause mid-stride. 'What d'you mean?'

'There are no others.'

I stared into his face, searching for an angle, a way he was trying to trick me. 'You're lying.'

'No! I promise you, as far as we know – in the City anyway – there hasn't been a successful pregnancy for several years.'

331

I dragged him on again, resuming our hurried progress, trying to pretend I was unimpressed when in fact I was utterly overwhelmed. *Jesus!* Gigi had mentioned something about seeing no babies – that was the reason: there *were* none.

'So what were you planning on doing?' I asked.

He shrugged, like there was only one rational course of action. 'Deliver the baby – all those healthy genes, stem cells – and *sperm!* Think of all that wonderful fertile sperm—'

'Jesus Christ!' I protested.

'It's a boy,' he told me.

'I guessed that,' I said, knowing that at some point that might be a cause for celebration.

'You can't take her, Clancy! You owe it to humankind—'

'Go fuck yourself,' I said, not believing I'd once had so much respect for that man.

'Please!' he begged, but I just shoved him on.

He lapsed into silence, leading me down yet another corridor, plainly still deep in thought. I was just starting to get that bit impatient, to wonder if he was up to something, when he stopped at a door much like the one that had led off Nora Jagger's quarters. And ya wanna know something? This time I could actually feel Lena, I could *smell* her, the second the door slid open.

I started to shake, telling myself I had to be careful, that it was everything I maintained my concentration: now would be the worst time of my life to make a mistake. I entered as cautiously as I could, checking the room for any suspicion of an ambush, completely ignoring the figure I could feel lying on the bed 'til finally I simply couldn't do it any more.

She was just lying there, unquestionably tranquillised, staring at me as if she was unable to take it in, her wrists electronically clamped at her side.

'Clancy?' she whispered, like she couldn't believe it, that it was just another dream.

I switched off the locks, allowing myself to give her just the briefest of hugs. As much as I wanted to live that moment, to kiss her, hold her, even cry a tear or two, I knew it was everything that we got away.

'Come on,' I said, helping her out of bed, relieved to find her dressed.

'What's that?' she asked dazedly, frowning at Nora Jagger's arm.

I just shook my head; explanations would have to wait for later. 'Let's go.'

'Where?'

I turned and glared at Dr Simon. 'He'll show us.'

The doc took us out a different door, down another of those interminable long corridors and through some heavy double-doors into a ward I instantly had a bad reaction to. My first thought, with the line of beds in front of me, was that it was a recovery room, but then I noticed other things: bars on the windows, equipment and apparatus that looked in no way beneficial to anyone's health. People had been tortured there – in fact, if I listened real closely, I swear I could hear them still screaming.

'What the hell is this place?' I asked, but the doc ignored me, heading towards the door at the far end of the room.

I don't know if it was the place that distracted me, or maybe 'cuz Lena was still a little groggy and leaning her warm body against mine, but I must've had a momentary lapse of concentration, 'cuz the doc saw his opportunity and suddenly, instead of being a couple of paces in front of us, was a dozen or more.

At first it didn't seem like a disaster, just a pathetic attempt to escape, but I'd underestimated the guy. The reason he'd been so deep in thought was 'cuz he'd been planning how to lure us into a trap.

He started shouting at the top of his voice, so excited that at first I couldn't understand what he was saying, and nor could the voice recognition system either, not until he slowed down and his words became that bit clearer.

'Lockdown! *Lockdown!*' he screamed, and heavy bars descended from the ceiling, creating various different compartments in the room, with us in the central one and him in the one with the door.

I dropped Nora Jagger's prosthetic arm, fumbling for my laser, intending to force him to free us, but he was out of that room surprisingly quickly.

'I'm sorry!' he called back, once he was outside. 'You can't take her! You don't have the right!'

'Come back here!' I shouted, but already I could hear his running footsteps fading up the corridor.

'Shit!' I cursed.

'No!' Lena wailed, 'I should've remembered this wasn't the way out!'

'You been here before?'

'They brought me here after I tried escaping. Don't worry,' she said, seeing the reaction on my face, 'they didn't do much. Too scared of harming the baby.'

I paused for a moment. 'You know?'

'Yeah . . . Sorry,' she said, as if even amongst all that was happening, it should've been acknowledged.

And there, trapped in a torture chamber in the Infinity building, with God knows who on their way, we actually took a moment to briefly unite in celebration over what we'd created. I know that might sound a little crazy when we had far more pressing problems to deal with, but that was what we did.

'How do we get out of here?' I asked, as we reluctantly broke away from each other.

Lena just sighed and shook her head: it was hopeless, and I guess I'd known before I'd asked the question. Out of sheer frustration I picked up Nora Jagger's artificial arm and swung it at the bars, and was amazed to see one buckle slightly. *Jesus, what is that thing made of?* I swung again, this time bending the bar substantially. I was about to try once more, to give it everything I had, when a group of Specials came running down the corridor and into the room.

I had no choice. Even though I'd drawn my laser, I knew there was no way I could get involved in a fire-fight, not with Lena and the baby right next to me.

'Let it go,' one of the Specials told me. 'Nice and easy.'

With a sigh I dropped it, the laser clattering to the floor.

'Kick it under the bars.'

I kicked it with such frustration that it shot across the room and kinda lodged under an air-conditioning unit. Dr Simon peered round the frame of the doorway, making sure it was safe before re-entering. To be fair to the guy, he didn't look that pleased with himself.

'This is much bigger than you two,' he muttered, seemingly more to himself than anyone.

I was about to tell that slimy bastard exactly what I thought of him, what I'd do if I ever got the chance, when I heard another sound approaching down the corridor. At first I couldn't believe it – it couldn't be, not here. And yet those familiar clanking pneumatic footsteps, the slurp-slurp of every stride, it couldn't be anything else. *There was a growler approaching.*

I turned to Lena, noticing as I put my arm around her that her eyes were almost clear of whatever she'd been given. Or maybe it was just fear shining through . . .

And yet, as the footsteps drew closer, it occurred to me that there was something different about them – no less frightening, and in fact, when I looked around I could see the Specials were every bit as intimidated as we were. They sounded less busy, less repetitive somehow, and it soon struck me why; whatever it was wasn't moving on four legs but two. It wasn't a growler at all – but I reckon I might've preferred it if it had been.

I guess it's a similar technology, maybe it was even where she got the idea: the way those things can instantly rend flesh and bone into nothing is probably something she admires. Nora Jagger came striding into the room and I gotta say, if she'd been unnerving before, naked and without prosthetics, she was utterly terrifying now. Those eyes damn near bored through me with their white heat, and her scowl would've sent the sun screaming back to the horizon.

She never said a word, just glared at me as she gestured to one of the Specials to release the lockdown. The bars rose and she walked over, snatching her artificial arm away.

I tell ya, it was the weirdest thing. She just pushed it up the empty sleeve of her coat, with no ceremony at all, and as it got close to the stump of her arm it almost seemed to come to life, like some kind of animal wriggling up there, going into its hole.

'You must be the biggest fool ever,' she told me. 'Did you really think you were just going to come waltzing in here and take your little maid?'

'I'm the father of the child!' I blurted out, like it gave me the right to do whatever I wanted.

'Yeah, well, let's hope it doesn't inherit your brain,' she said, checking her arm, that it felt right. Apparently satisfied, she whirled around, scanning the room, as if, now that she was whole again, she had a little business to attend to. 'Who was in charge of guarding my quarters?' she asked.

For the first time I noticed the older Special, the one I'd sneaked past while he'd been looking out the window. He wasn't gonna answer her, you could see that. He was one of five lined up a little like they were on parade, that she began to circle around, glaring into their faces, waiting for one of them to crack.

When it happened, it was so swift, so brutal, it took your breath away. She suddenly lurched forward, grabbed the older guy and spun him around, getting him in a full nelson. The others panicked, scrambling outta the way, presumably 'cuz they'd seen similar scenes before. But I hadn't.

Jesus! I'll never forget it as long as I live. She just squeezed and squeezed, with those incredibly powerful arms of hers, and at first the guy was bewilderingly silent, almost compliant – then he began to scream, to squeal like a pig being butchered. You could hear the crack as both his arms came out of their sockets, as his body began to break apart, but she hadn't finished with him yet. She just kept on applying pressure, those prosthetic arms locked at the back of his neck, pushing him down, doubling him over, 'til eventually – and God help me, I'll never get the image outta my mind – the flesh and bone simply gave way. His head detached from his shoulders and plopped on down onto the floor, rolling a little ways then stopping, briefly rocking back and forth.

There were muffled cries and gasps and one of the Specials looked away, retching repeatedly, and Lena and me took refuge in each other's arms.

'Clear it away!' Nora Jagger barked, then turned back to me, her sudden smile making her even more repulsive. 'Get the picture?' she asked.

I never replied but I discreetly shuffled away from Lena. I was the one under threat and I didn't want to put her at risk. Anyways, what could I say? All the things I've seen in my life, the bad old days, even the very worst atrocities, were as nothing compared to this. This was violence of an order I could never have even imagined. And yet no matter how shocked I was, how concerned I'd be next, it still hadn't distracted me from the question that had reared up in my mind the moment Nora Jagger had entered the room: how the hell had she got free so quickly? I'd checked those bandages myself; there was no way she was going anywhere, and the door to the outer corridor had been jammed shut. We should've been well away before anyone was able to release her. I just didn't get it – and being the witch she was, she read it in my eyes.

'Yeah, like I said, none too bright,' she sneered. 'You should've searched my quarters properly . . . I had a guest.'

I cursed to myself as my thoughts immediately went to that games room.

'A friend of mine,' she told me, '. . . and yours.' She waited for me to say something, but I didn't have a clue what she was talking about. 'Come on in, my little stool pigeon!' she called to someone obviously out in the corridor, breaking into yet another wickedly self-satisfied smile. 'Or should that be . . . "seagull"?'

It was one of those moments when you're so shocked your brain simply refuses to handle it. I just gaped at the door, staring at who was standing there, desperate for everything to go on rewind. Gigi came shuffling in, not looking at me but still exuding a certain air of defiance.

'Oh, Jeez!' I groaned, collapsing inside as I instantly recognised that I should've known. She always had that slight air of mystery about her; always knew way too much for someone who'd only been off the Island the same amount of time we had. Her story about being recruited by one of the guys off the garbage boats had sounded plausible, and maybe it was true; the only thing was, at some point she'd obviously been recruited by Infinity as well. No wonder she wouldn't tell us where she lived, and why she was so cagey about the organisation she'd joined. She had friends on the inside, all right – right at the very top.

'Why?' I asked her.

It was the obvious question, but I should've known how she'd answer – with one of her all-too-typical shrugs.

'When times are tough,' Nora Jagger chipped in, 'people'll sell anything. Even their soul.'

'And lay down with the devil?'

'One day maybe,' she smirked, giving Gigi one of the creepiest looks I've ever seen.

'You make me sick, lady,' I told her.

'Oh, I'll make you more than that,' she promised, practically licking her lips in anticipation.

I knew she was gonna take revenge for what I did, especially messing with her prosthetics; I also guessed that, no matter how old, I was still a big guy, and she was gonna enjoy putting on another demonstration of her strength.

I glanced round the room, clocking her various sinister-looking toys, the many methods of torture, wondering what she had in mind.

'Oh, I won't be needing them,' she assured me.

'Just your bare hands,' I sneered.

She must've been at least ten feet away, but I got an immediate illustration of just how powerful those legs were when she kinda bounced at me, made this pneumatic spring and suddenly was right in my face; toppling me backwards, trying to twist me round and grab me from behind the way she had that Special, but somehow I managed to wriggle free.

Lena screamed at her, told her to leave me alone, but you could see she was really in her element.

'If you hurt him, I'll kill this baby!' Lena threatened.

'How?' she asked. 'You're going back into clamps and this time you won't be able to move a muscle, not until it's born.'

'I'll will it dead!' Lena told her. 'I'll starve myself – I'll do everything I can to make it die inside me.'

'Lena!' I said, unable to suppress a protest.

'I don't care, Clancy. You come first.'

'We'll feed you intravenously,' Nora Jagger told her. 'And in any case, if this sad old bastard can make you pregnant, there'll be others from that island who'll serve just as well.'

She turned back to me, again that wet-lipped smile appearing, and even though I'd already had one demonstration of what she could do, she leaped forward so quickly, I barely got out of the way in time. Even so, her outstretched fingers raked a mark across my forehead like I'd just fallen headlong into a shredder.

Whether I wanted to or not, I was getting a lesson in exactly what those limbs were capable of. So far I knew that her legs could jump, spring, and I'd be willing to bet, run further and faster than any animal on this earth, but it was the arms that really worried me. There didn't seem to be any kind of delay between her thinking what she was gonna do and them responding, almost as if they were ahead of her, even adding something of their own. No doubt Jimmy would be able to shine a little light on it, but all I knew was that this lethal hybrid of human and machine was rapidly closing in on me.

It didn't take a genius to work out that if I was gonna stop her, I needed to concentrate my efforts on that soft centre the doc had been massaging. I tried to get blows in at the points where her limbs met her body, hoping I might dislodge them somehow, but she was way too fast for me. I went for the stomach, try to knock the wind outta her, but again she blocked me and I was forced to back off.

I thought I had a pretty good idea what she was capable of, what to expect from her and her limbs, but suddenly she dropped to the floor, balanced on one hand and swept me with her legs. It damn near demolished me. Both my shins and kneecaps felt like they'd been shattered into a thousand tiny pieces and down I went. Before I could recover, she'd leaped on me and grabbed me round the neck . Somewhere I could hear screams, cries of '*No!*', but all I knew was the all-encompassing force of those arms locked around my throat.

I must've passed out for a second or two, but when I came to, Nora Jagger was sprawled out on the floor in front of me. She didn't look that badly hurt, but had been dumped unceremoniously on her face. I turned around, wondering what the hell had happened, and saw a couple of Specials struggling with Lena, doing their best to restrain her. At her feet was this piece of fairly solid-looking machinery, maybe for giving electric shocks – but she'd used it as a far more basic form of weapon.

Nora Jagger pulled herself up, her expression demanding blood, leaping at Lena and hitting her so hard she flew across the room and collided with the wall.

'No!' Dr Simon shouted, '*the baby!*'

I tell ya, I went crazy: throwing punches left and right, swinging and missing, doing everything I could to nail that damn ogress. But it was as if she'd put those arms in defence mode, no matter how many punches I threw, they were always in my way, and it wasn't long before I started to puff and blow and had to back off. Immediately she went on the offensive, swinging those prosthetics like sledgehammers, and with such force, all I could do was to dodge or run. A couple of times I wasn't quick enough – it was like being hit by a speeding truck, battered aside by some almighty force. I tried counter-punching, using moves I remembered from my old boxing days, concentrating on the body, and maybe it did worry her that bit 'cuz she suddenly switched to trying to kick me.

The first time she did it, she damn near took my head off. She could jump almost as high as the ceiling, her legs scything through the air so fast you could barely see them. I leapt out of her way, backing off, dodging from side to side, but it wasn't long before I was seriously out of breath again. Mind you, to my immense relief, I saw I wasn't the only one, that she needed to stop too. I guess the thing was, no matter how powerful those artificial limbs, they still needed lungs, a heart, whatever, to sustain them.

For a moment we both just stood there facing each other, each desperately trying to get air back into our lungs, locked eye to eye, then suddenly she sprang into life again, trying another kick, only this time, I guess 'cuz she was tiring, when she landed, she slipped and almost went over. I didn't waste any energy retaliating, just concentrated on avoiding what else she was throwing, and she got this triumphant look about her, like she thought it was all over. However, she was a bit premature.

I played along with it – the notion that I was utterly spent – puffing and panting, doubling over, and sure enough, she moved in for the kill. She leapt at me again, her foot slicing through the air like a blade, this time managing to catch me on the chest, but again when she hit the floor, she looked a little unsteady. I stumbled back towards the wall with her eagerly chasing after me. I'd noticed this high-pressure hose behind me, presumably another instrument of torture, and as she leapt into the air again, expecting to strike the final blow, I moved faster than I could've imagined myself capable of: grabbing the hose and turning it on, training it on her, and just as I hoped, she lost all balance and sprawled out on the wet floor. Before she could recover, I leaped on her and got the hose around her neck, pulling as tightly as I could, watching the fury in those wasteland eyes glazing over as she fought for breath.

I guess those Specials were under orders that as a last resort they were allowed to intervene, 'cuz two of them ran over and tried to wrestle me off her, and when they couldn't, a third hit me over the head with something really heavy. I fell forward but still somehow managed to scramble over towards the laser lodged in the bottom of the air-conditioning unit; no one had retrieved it. I'd just about got my hand around it when I felt this real hard kick, like my nerve system had been punctured, and I knew someone had stunned me.

I was just lying there convulsing when suddenly I felt this wild force lift me up and throw me across the room. Jeez, I tell ya, I'm not exactly a lightweight, but I flew over there like a tin roof in a hurricane: twisting and turning until I thudded up against the wall. I tried to scramble up, but not only were my nerve ends arcing, the pain of the impact was somehow tangling with them and I slumped back to the floor, helplessly listening to the approach of those slurping footsteps.

Icy-blue eyes stared down at me, inspecting me for damage, and plainly she wasn't satisfied yet 'cuz she kicked me so hard my body skipped across the floor like a pebble over a pond. Again I slammed up against the wall, my shoulder feeling like it might've been dislocated. Jesus, she was going to reduce me to nothing but red slush and sinewy slime.

Lena started screaming out in protest again, struggling, a couple of Specials doing their best to hold her, everyone else was just dodging out of the way whenever I was thrown or kicked in their direction. Gigi and Dr Simon were in the corner; he was kinda cowering, turning his face away as if refusing to watch, whilst her eyes were darting around the room, I guessed looking for a way to escape.

Those terrifying arms kept reaching for me over and over, and everywhere she threw me my blood appeared to be already there, and each time the light inside me dimmed a little more. She grabbed me again, with a power, a finality, that made me think she'd had enough, that she felt the time had come to bring this bloody performance to an end. Lifting me right over her head, she gave out with this cry of victory, ready to toss me across the room, to smash me up against the wall one last time, and I knew that would be it: that my body couldn't take any more.

I was aware of being pulled back as if I was about to be catapulted through the air, then there was a sudden gasp, a groan, like some great tree being felled, and Nora Jagger's body tumbled to the floor with mine on top of it.

I stirred, tried to get up, but heard the hum of a power-pack and realised there was a fire-fight going on. The two Specials who'd been holding Lena were lying on the ground not far from me, apparently shot, whilst she'd somehow managed to slide away behind a bench. It didn't leave me with a great deal of choice; I just stayed where I was, taking cover behind Nora Jagger's body, those limbs that had battered me moments ago now offering me a measure of protection. But I just didn't get. What the hell was going on? Who was firing? And most of all, *who'd killed Nora Jagger?*

There was more shooting, another Special went down and the remaining one decided to make a run for it.

I stayed where I was for a few moments, ensuring it was safe, then slowly peered out from behind the body of Nora Jagger.

I don't know who I expected to see – Jimmy or Gordie maybe? Even Hanna? But the only person in sight was Gigi, hesitantly emerging from behind the air-conditioning unit, my laser in her hand.

'What the hell?' I uttered, trying to struggle up, my pain causing me to helplessly lock halfway.

Gigi gave me a hand, straightened me up, made sure I could stand. 'Never trust a double agent,' she told me, slipping the laser into my pocket, like she wanted to confirm she was on my side.

I still didn't understand, but it obviously wasn't the time for explanations.

'Clancy!' Lena called, emerging from hiding. 'Are you okay?'

Actually, I wasn't: I had a mass of cuts and bruises, I could barely move my arm, and my kneecaps felt like they'd been granulated. Nevertheless, I still nodded. 'You?'

'I'm fine,' she replied, ignoring the fact that she'd just collided heavily with the wall.

'What about the baby?'

She couldn't help herself; even amongst everything that was going on she briefly laughed at my conventionality. 'Let's go,' she said, like we had other, far more immediate, things to worry about. 'Can you walk?'

I had to lean on her a bit, leaving the odd smear of blood on her clothing, but we managed. Gigi retrieved the lasers of the dead Specials, beckoning Dr Simon out from his hiding place under a bed. He emerged looking pale and shaken, staring at the mayhem around him, yet still insisting on tucking in his shirt and straightening his tie.

We didn't have to say anything to him; he knew he was coming with us whether he wanted to or not. As we left the room I took a quick glance back at the body of Nora Jagger still lying on the floor, surrounded by all her instruments of torture, slain in her palace of pain. It was so hard to believe that someone like her, so formidable, so full of evil energy, should die in such simple fashion. And yet, maybe there was a kind of justice in it: shot in the back by a kid she thought she had in her pocket.

I took a few uncomfortable steps along the corridor and then stopped.

'What's the matter?' Lena asked. 'Clancy!' she protested, when I hobbled back to the ward.

'Just a second,' I told her.

I don't know why I did it – something must've provoked me, but I just wanted to take another look, to be absolutely sure that monster was dead. But d'you know something? While I was standing there, staring at that prone body, one of her damn legs started twitching . . . *Jesus!* It frightened the hell out of me! And just to prove I hadn't imagined it, it did it again! However those limbs worked, they apparently hadn't entirely shut down. It gave me the creeps, like they had a life of their own, and I took out my laser and zapped her body a couple more times.

'Clancy!' Lena called impatiently, obviously wondering what the hell I was doing, and I turned and shuffled after her, having to steady myself for a moment on the doorframe, a sharp pain shooting down my leg.

Dr Simon led us to an elevator that took us down to the basement and what turned out to be the executive transport area.

There were a couple of Specials there, but Gigi took them by surprise before they could even draw their weapons. Just in that moment it went through my head how easy it all was again: shooting people – taking lives – and that I still regarded it as wrong.

'There's a side door,' the doc told us, pointing to the far corner.

'Really?' I said, my attention distracted by his limo parked nearby.

'No – *no!*' he started, already guessing what I was thinking. 'Not my car!'

'Sorry, Doc, I can't walk that far,' I told him, directing him towards the limo with my laser, guessing it would need his voice activation to unlock.

No matter how battered my body felt, how painful some of its moves, I had no choice but to drive. The only other driver was the doc and we weren't likely to trust him. Lena sat next to me, ready to help if needed, while Gigi sat in the back, obviously taking a certain amount of pleasure in keeping her laser trained on Doc Simon in case he had another rush of blood and tried to stop us.

What the hell had happened back there? I just didn't know. Had Gigi been working for Nora Jagger all along, setting us up with those messages she left? It even went through my head that it was her to blame for Infinity rolling over the church, and that maybe she'd been responsible for what happened with Ray. Then again, she did try to warn us – and for sure, she couldn't have been any more discouraging about our attempts at getting into Infinity. Maybe her loyalties had been split, and seeing Nora Jagger hit Lena, then on the point of killing me, had finally decided her? Or perhaps it'd always been about assassinating that woman and this was just the culmination of her plan? She did say she was a 'double agent'.

I didn't know, and right at that moment, I didn't care. The main thing was she came good in the end. I'd ask her sometime, when the time was right – that was, if we ever got out of Infinity.

I didn't know what I expected to see when the garage doors slid open, but as we paused at the top of the ramp what we got was mayhem and madness. Jimmy must've really messed with the growlers' programming 'cuz those things were *everywhere*, attacking anyone they saw, running in packs from one place to another the moment they registered any kinda movement.

From where we were it looked like most of the Specials had taken refuge in the main building – waiting for someone to rectify the malfunction, I guessed. But over by the main gate there were people trapped in the office and a real battle was going on. I could see Specials firing out the windows, trying to destroy the growlers, but though they were getting hit over and over, not many were being put out of action. Damaged growlers had started sharing their parts with each other, rebuilding, and even as we watched, three-legged ones were getting going again, picking themselves up and resuming their siege of the office.

I looked up to the roof, expecting to see the Dragonflies, figuring they were the only thing that might contain growlers, but it looked like there'd been some kind of accident – one was actually hanging precariously over the edge, and it was stopping all the others taking off.

Specials on the ground floor of the main building were leaning out of windows, firing at growlers, then dodging back inside when they got too near. In a way it was the defining moment of the whole conflict: all those growlers massing outside, making a hell of a noise, snarling and snapping, unable to get in, while those in the building were unable to neutralise them.

It was a stalemate – or it sure looked like it – but one of the growlers had other ideas. It was almost like he'd reasoned it out: suddenly he ran full-pelt at a window, smashing his way through and bounding in amongst the people inside, creating chaos, dragging screaming Infinity staff to the floor. And the moment that growler succeeded, others did the same. I guess there was some kind of organic programming going on, where they learned from each other, 'cuz within seconds growler after growler was running at the windows and smashing their way in.

'Oh my God!' Lena moaned, her voice jarring me into action. I turned in the direction of the gates, steering mainly with one hand, moving as silently and sedately as I could, hoping the growlers wouldn't notice us, but we hadn't gone more than twenty or thirty yards before there was a thud at the back and I knew we were under attack.

I pulled up the exterior cameras to see a pack of half a dozen or more growlers around us. Several of them were repeatedly running headlong at the vehicle, head-butting it, trying to smash their way in, while others were sinking their jaws into whatever they could, chomping down with those razor-sharp rows of teeth, trying to rip bits off. I thanked God that limo was reinforced, bullet- and laser-proofed, but the truth was, in places it was already starting to look like they were getting the better of it. One of them got a hold of the fender, crunched it in its huge jaws and ripped off a whole section of bodywork.

'*My limo!*' Dr Simon wailed.

'You gotta damn sight more to worry about than that,' I told him as I swerved round a growler, the pain in my shoulder causing me to cry out.

'Clancy?' Lena started.

'It's okay,' I told her, though the truth was, I was feeling just that bit faint.

There was this awful scratching, scraping noise and I looked out to see several of the growlers had got their jaws firmly into the bodywork, their legs locked, and with sparks flying from their metallic feet, were doing their best to drag us to a halt. I had to jam my foot down just to maintain our speed, the pain in my leg lancing down to my toes, seemingly impaling me to the floor.

I glanced across at Lena, checking she was holding up okay, her face like day-old ashes, and in that precise moment there was an explosion in my ear, and a growler came through my side window.

I hit the brakes, screeching to a halt with the damn thing actually wriggling away in my lap, its eyes flashing, those huge jaws snapping at everything – *Jesus, I thought that glass was supposed to be unbreakable!* Somehow I managed to reach through the pain barrier to grab its head with my damaged arm and, hugging it to my laser, shot it at point-blank range – it was taking a risk in such a confined space, but I had no other choice.

The growler went all limp and powered down, in an instant nothing more than a pile of junk on top of me.

'Clancy! You okay?' Lena asked.

I picked up the growler, its weight almost too much for me, and with Lena supporting one of its front legs, just for a moment I scrutinised its face only inches from mine. Jeez, that was a killing machine if I'd ever seen one; those teeth could bite your head off. For sure I never wanted to be that close to one again. I was just about to throw it out of the window, to get it as far away from us I could, when suddenly it powered up again: the eyes lit up, the jaws snapped open and it let out a heart-stopping growl right into my face.

I don't know how I dodged it, but somehow I did, lurching to one side just as those massive jaws snapped shut, taking a huge chunk out of my seat. Around me everyone was screaming. It was bedlam. I dodged this way and that, doing my best to avoid that damn thing's teeth, its feet scrabbling at my lap as it tried to get some kind of purchase. It bit into my parka and ripped it right off me, and somehow, in that moment of confusion, I managed to clamp my good arm around its jaws. The only trouble was, it was so damn strong its mouth kept opening an inch or two, with me straining to snap it shut again. I knew I couldn't keep it up for long: I would've had problems with that thing normally, but the shape I was in, I could feel my grip starting to weaken.

'Clancy – *Clancy!*' Lena shouted, and I glanced her way to see she had her laser pointed at the growler but couldn't get in a shot 'cuz I was so entangled with it.

I just about had the strength left to repel it one last time, and maybe, if she could knock it out for a few seconds, get it outta the limo.

'*Do it!*' I cried, shoving it as far away from me as I could, hard up against the dash.

I don't know – maybe Specials were issued with different types of weapons or something, 'cuz I didn't have to worry about throwing it out. Lena blew its head straight off and out the window. Or maybe it's just she was a better shot than me. Either way, she made a real mess of it and I gratefully heaved what was left out and drove on.

This time I got up a little speed – the last thing we needed was another of those things coming through the window. God knows how fast they could run 'cuz they responded immediately, staying with us all the way, hell-bent on wrenching that limo apart. One of them managed to scrabble up on the trunk and I could see it standing there, on the point of puncturing the back window. I slammed my foot to the floor, hurtling towards the gate as fast as I could, knowing I'd have to smash my way through, then, at the last moment, I swerved violently, flicking the tail round, dislodging the growlers, sending them rolling over and over and smashing up against the office wall.

'Special delivery,' I muttered, and glancing in the rear-view mirror saw we'd only just made it through, that iron barriers were sliding outta the ground and stingers erecting their teeth across the entrance.

Jimmy, Delilah, Gordie and Hanna were hiding on the other side of the road. I pulled over, shouting for them to get in even before I'd stopped, not knowing how long those emergency barriers and the general confusion would delay any pursuit.

There was a lot of noisy jubilation as we sped away, most of it centred round seeing Lena again, a little at the fact that we had a limo, though Delilah was surprised to see its owner with us.

'You still alive?' she asked the doc, knowing immediately who he was.

'Just,' he complained, like he'd been the victim of a poorly organised adventure holiday.

'Wouldn't be if I had my way.'

Dr Simon went quiet at that, shrinking into the corner, appreciating how great the enmity was towards him and probably starting to wonder what his fate was gonna be. I decided to put him out of his misery. We didn't have any reason to keep him any longer, so a little further down the street I pulled over.

'What about my limo?' he protested. 'Do you know how much this cost?'

'I know how much it could cost you now,' I warned him.

He sighed, realising it was hopeless, and waited for me to unlock the doors, but Jimmy wasn't happy.

'You just gonna let him go?' he asked. 'Back to his luxury lifestyle?'

'What else?' I asked.

He turned to Delilah like they had something planned. 'You got it?'

'Yep,' Lile replied, reaching into her pocket and pulling out the hunting knife.

'Do it,' the little guy told her.

I wondered what on earth they had in mind, and Dr Simon began scrabbling at the locked door, pleading with them not to hurt him.

'What the hell you doing?' I asked as Delilah moved towards him, but she ignored me, leaning forward – I thought, about to cut his face – but she just nicked his ear and gave it a squeeze.

'Got it?' Jimmy asked.

'Yep,' Delilah replied proudly.

'You can go now,' Jimmy told the doc.

'But—'

'While you still can . . .'

I unlocked the doors and he got out, scampering off like a frightened rabbit.

'What was that all about?' Lena asked as I pulled away.

'We removed his implant,' Jimmy told her. 'I erased all his records earlier. Dr Evan Simon is now officially a "non-person", just like us. He'll be walking the streets and living outta trash cans until it gets sorted.'

I have to admit I couldn't help but snigger at the thought of the doc rummaging through garbage in all his fraying finery. 'And was it you who messed with the growlers?' I asked.

'Those Infinity people ain't so smart,' he said. 'I also set up a real cool collision with Dragonflies.'

'Damn near got us killed,' I complained.

Hanna and Gordie moved forward, peering over the back of my seat. 'So what happened?' she asked.

I told them the whole story: right from when I'd regained consciousness in the hospital wing 'til the moment we'd crashed out through the main gates. Jimmy was as fascinated by Nora Jagger as horrified; kept saying again and again how much he wished he could've seen those limbs, maybe even analysed how they worked. The only thing I didn't mention – and nor did Lena – was Gigi's possible collusion with Infinity. Ever since we'd thrown Dr Simon outta the limo and she'd had no duty to perform she'd gone noticeably quiet, I guess wondering when it was gonna come out. But like I said, now wasn't the time – and who knew when it would be?

I drove on, no longer feeling faint, relief making my various aches and pains dull into something almost bearable. We were passing through the city centre, negotiating the usual scenes of fire and smoke, running gangs, looting and fighting.

'Thank God,' Delilah said.

'What?' Jimmy asked.

'We're finally getting outta this place.'

Jimmy turned to look out of the window and almost immediately gave this sharp intake of breath. 'Stop!'

'What?' I asked.

'Stop, Big Guy! Here! *Here!*'

I screeched to a halt and he opened his door. 'I'll be five minutes.'

'Jimmy—?'

But it was too late; he was already pegging it across the street, heading up this narrow alleyway – only then did it occur to me that we were on familiar territory.

'*Oh no!*' I groaned.

'What's the matter?' Lena asked.

'It's the place he went gaming,' I told her, and the kids immediately started to snigger.

'What?' Delilah croaked. 'You go and haul his ass outta there!'

I was so surprised he'd do such a thing with Infinity probably already combing the City for us . . . 'I don't believe him sometimes,' I growled, 'I really don't.'

'It's his last chance!' Gordie explained from the back seat.

'For what?'

'To play! He's going out in the country . . . and he's *old*.'

'Oh, thank you,' Delilah commented sarcastically.

We went on like that for some minutes: Delilah and me annoyed, Lena keeping out of it, the kids sticking up for Jimmy so that, by the time we'd stopped, his five minutes was more or less up and we just waited in scornful silence, keeping an eye out for any sign of Specials, until finally Jimmy came pegging back across the street, a huge smile on his face.

'Look how happy he is,' Hanna cooed.

The little guy squeezed in, chortling to himself. 'So cool! So cool!' he kept repeating, but Delilah was having none of it.

'What the hell were you doing?'

'Oh . . . You know,' he teased, knowing all too well we didn't.

'Jimmy!'

'Putting the record straight!' he told her.

'What d'ya mean?'

'We can't go without saying something, Lile.'

He had that look about him – I knew it so damn well – but I never said anything, just accelerated away. We'd find out soon enough.

In fact, it was only a matter of minutes: we were driving through a busy area, mostly intact and functioning, with not that many fires and plenty of shops and screens, when suddenly all the screens went blank and a familiar face appeared.

'*Oh my God!*' Delilah croaked.

'You'd be amazed how much power you can get from linking a lot of computers together, even in a video arcade,' Jimmy said, that smug smile now threatening to crack his face in two.

I pulled over for a few moments, sliding down everyone's window so we could all catch what was being said. He really let them have it: spilling the beans, the can, and everything else too, revealing exactly what Infinity had been up to: how they'd lied about the satellites, that they hadn't been a force for good at all but had been slowly poisoning everyone. How they'd lied about him, that the price on his head had just been an attempt to shut him up. And he'd left it on a loop, so that as we drove on and people were gathering around other screens, it kept playing over and over.

'Can't they shut you down?' Gigi asked.

'Not really. I've set it up from alternating sources – it's bouncing round all over the place. Maybe if they shut off the power – I don't think they'd risk it though. Not tonight.'

In a way, I guess that was it: the sweetest of cherries on the most delicious of cakes. The final evidence that we'd done it: we'd freed Lena and come out best against Infinity. Everyone started congratulating Jimmy, giving him the praise he unquestionably deserved, but really, I think we were all congratulating each other, getting back some of that joy we'd experienced when we were floating across from the Island. Finally we were gonna gorge ourselves on the freedom we'd all got so excited about. Not only were we leaving that hell-hole of a city, but who knew, with a bit of luck, Jimmy might've started some kind of revolution. Not to mention that we'd slain the monster that was Nora Jagger. No wonder Delilah started singing, no wonder we all joined in, even Gordie, though he used a funny voice now and then, just to show he wasn't being serious. Hanna exchanged smiles with him, Gigi looked that bit put out and I wondered if maybe we had a winner at last. For sure it looked like it. And suddenly I let out a long loud yell, frightening the hell out of everyone and giving myself something of a jolt in the shoulder.

'Clancy!' Delilah protested. 'What the hell was that?'

'That was the sound of me appreciating the moment,' I told her, reminding her of the conversation we'd had in the churchyard, ''cuz I swear to God, at this moment, I got everything I could ever possibly wish for.'

And I was right. I did have everything: the woman I loved more than life itself was back at my side, our baby inside her and the three of us were escaping to freedom and a better life – not to mention our dearest friends with us. Yeah, okay, if I was really honest about it, I would've liked Arturo to be there, too, but I guess you need a little sadness to understand the true nature of joy. It was as close to perfection as anyone had a right to be, and how often do any of us get to say that? And for how long?

I drove slowly on, soon beginning the climb up into the hills. The smoke was nowhere near as thick as when we'd tried to leave before, and even with my broken window it was being pretty efficiently handled by the limo's air-conditioning, so that, apart from visibility issues, we were barely aware of it.

I have no idea why it suddenly occurred to me – only that it did. I was going over what'd happened, the way you do after a little excitement – the things that could've gone wrong, the things that thankfully went right – and having this slight pang of guilt about the people I'd killed, the number of Specials' lives I'd ended. I even started to count them, 'til finally I decided that wasn't such a good idea and gave up. At least I'd only stunned those guys in the hospital . . .

And then, slowly, oh so slowly, it began to creep up over me, to get into my head, to burrow down into my mind. Oh no – don't tell me . . . *I couldn't have!*

I never said anything, just fumbled my laser outta my pocket, keeping it down in the gap between my seat and the door, pressing the status button and taking a quick look.

Aw, shit! *Shit!* How could I have been so stupid? That's why Lena's laser blew that growler's head off while mine only stopped it for a few seconds. Jeez, how could I have been so damned forgetful? I never changed the setting after I zapped those guys in the hospital! I hadn't killed anyone that night, just stunned them . . . and oh Jesus . . . oh God . . . Gigi used *my* laser on Nora Jagger! The same one I shot her with again as we left . . . *She ain't dead!*

'Oh no!' I moaned, so desperately trying to keep silent it came out as a kind of tortured whisper.

'What's the matter?' Lena asked.

I shook my head. 'Nothing. Just can't believe we're actually going free.'

Delilah gave a cheer from the back, the kids joined in, but Lena looked at me a little quizzically.

'Finally,' I added, as if to reassure her, but I could see she still wasn't entirely convinced.

When we got to the top of the hills, we found a lookout point and stopped, everyone tumbling out of the limo, anxious to say goodbye to the City. Even in the dark, you could see how much less smoke there was, and fewer fires. We could only spot a couple of really big ones, and the others looked to be dwindling, on their way to dying, all that concrete and construction material impregnated with rogue rocket fuel finally degrading to nothing.

Lena came up behind me, carefully putting her arm around my waist, anxious not to cause me any pain. 'You okay?' she asked.

'Fine.'

'You've gone a little quiet.'

'Too much excitement for an old guy,' I told her.

She smiled, though I still wasn't sure she was convinced. 'I'm so happy, Clancy,' she told me, maybe thinking I needed a little reassurance.

'Me, too,' I said, just about managing a quick squeeze.

I'd already decided I wasn't gonna let it upset me, nor anyone else, come to that. I mean, maybe I was wrong – maybe there was another explanation? In any case, sometimes when people get stunned they end up having a heart attack and dying anyway. As far as I was concerned, Nora Jagger was dead, and that was an end to it – where we were going, it wasn't gonna affect us one way or the other.

'You sure you're okay?' Lena asked. 'You took a bit of a beating.'

'Nah,' I replied, male pride winning out over the simmering fire that was my pain. 'I was more worried about you and the baby. How hard she threw you up against that wall.'

We kissed and I had my first go at gently stroking her stomach. Lena laughed for maybe the first time since I found her in that hospital bed, and I fell in love with her all over again. And again.

Was she really the only woman in the City capable of producing a baby? Surely not; there had to be others – 'cuz if there weren't, they were gonna come after her for sure, and we'd never be safe, no matter where we went.

Thing is, I didn't want any of this, and nor, I was sure, did she. We just wanted normality, to find somewhere nice to raise a family and have a full and happy life. What else would you expect from a simple old big guy? What could possibly bring him greater pleasure? Nothing I know.

'We'd better go,' I said, not wanting to chance staying any longer.

'Take a last look,' Delilah called over, and we all paused for a moment and did exactly as she suggested, gazing down at the smoky, smouldering carpet of a city, wishing that hell-hole the meanest of farewells.

'Think I can see the Square,' Delilah said. 'Over there.'

I nodded, though actually the direction she was pointing seemed all wrong to me.

The kids turned back towards the limo, Jimmy and Delilah tagging on behind, but when I went to follow, Lena suddenly stopped, gripping my hand so tightly her nails were digging into my flesh.

'What's the matter?' I asked, but she never replied, just remained perfectly still. 'Lena?'

'I can't see anything.'

'Yeah, well, I think that's Delilah's fanciful imagination,' I told her. 'The Square's over there.'

'No, Clancy! When I got thrown . . . I've gone blind again.'

ACKNOWLEDGEMENTS

Where to start? Where to finish?

First, of course, I have to thank the seemingly imperturbable Jo Fletcher for giving me the opportunity to finally see my words in print. Also Dorie Simmonds for getting me that opportunity. For their tireless efforts, I have to thank my editors – Jo again, Nicola and Talya. I also have to thank Sam Copeland at RCW for being my unofficial counsellor at the end of the phone and listening to my tales of bemusement regarding the publishing industry – again much appreciated.

The Longest-Running Support Award must surely go to my family – my mother and brother. I also owe a mighty debt of gratitude to Rob for kindly giving me a roof over my head when I first moved to London. And finally, I would be very remiss if I didn't thank Angela Etschmayer for not only her encouragement, but also her invaluable assistance in trying to bring my books to the attention of the book-buying public.

That's not everyone, of course: warmest thanks go to all friends who've supported me in this venture and bought my books. I hope I can repay you one day.

IN CONSTANT FEAR
Peter Liney

Over a year has passed since Clancy and the gang managed to escape from the hell that was the City. Pursued by the ruthless leader of Infinity – the corporation behind the mass murders of thousands of 'lower class' citizens – they've been on the run ever since; constantly looking over their shoulders.

Despite this, they have forged a new life working the land on an abandoned smallholding on the other side of the mountains. Hidden there, they are as close to happy as they can be.

Until strange things start to happen in the valley: too many unlucky coincidences convince them that another power is rising against them, and there are many questions to be answered: what is the shadow maker? And who – or what – has begun to howl in the night?

Jo Fletcher
BOOKS